# of Flame and Fury

A WEIRD GIRLS NOVEL

CECY ROBSON

"I was blown away by the depth of passion, humor, and creativity in this story . . . If you are a fan of powerful, sarcastic heroines and cross-over urban fantasy / paranormal romance stories, I highly recommend *Of Flame and Light.*" – ***Grave Tells Romance***

"I fell deeply in love with Cecy Robson's sharp, funny dialogue, hilarious characters and brilliant world building." – ***Book and Movie Dimension***

"When you begin, reading *Of Flame and Light* the rest of the world will slip away. Action-packed with heart, growth, and supernatural awesomeness." – ***Caffeinated Book Reviewer***

When I started reading the Weird Girls series a few years back, I fell deeply in love with Cecy Robson's sharp, funny dialogue, hilarious characters and brilliant world building . . . I really cannot stress enough how much I loved [Of Flame and Light]. – **Book and Movie Dimension**

The Weird Girls Series
Gone Hunting
A Curse Awakened: A Novella
The Weird Girls: A Novella
Sealed with a Curse
A Cursed Embrace
Of Flame and Promise
A Cursed Moon: A Novella
Cursed by Destiny
A Cursed Bloodline
A Curse Unbroken
Of Flame and Light
Of Flame and Fate
Of Flame and Fury

The Shattered Past Series
Once Perfect
Once Loved
Once Pure

The O'Brien Family Novels
Once Kissed
Let Me
Crave Me
Feel Me
Save Me

The Carolina Beach Novels
Inseverable
Eternal
Infinite

In Too Far Novels
Salvatore

Death Seeker Novels
Unearthed

APPS

Crazy Maple's Chapters: Interactive Stories APP:
Shattered Past, Weird Girls and O'Brien Family Series

Hooked – Chat stories APP:
Cecy Robson is writing as Rosalina San Tiago

Dedication

To Jamie. You deserve this, and more.

ACKNOWLEDGMENTS

These past two years were hard. Dang hard. Through the emotional ups and downs we have and are experiencing within our family, one thing has held true, mine and Jamie's relationship.

For better or worse? I remember that line so well. We've seen worse and it's bonded us closer. It's why I'm blessed and compelled to acknowledge Jamie first. He's my rock. My friend. My hero. And yes, the great bringer of comfort food. Babe, I would be lost without your love and compassion. Let's head toward more of the "better."

As always, I also want to thank my agent Nicole Resciniti. It's not merely everything she does as an agent and how hard she fights to expand my career. Nicole is my best friend. During the darkest times, she listens, offering words of comfort and those hugs I frequently need. And during my brightest and most amazing moments, her hugs are just as fierce.

To Kimberly Costa, my wonderful assistant and publicist. Thank you for beta reading and working so hard, at all hours, even through several bouts of illness. You're not simply driven to help me succeed, you're that kind voice I look forward to hearing. I hope you know, you're family now.

To Kristin Clifton, my sweet friend and beta reader. Thank you for your suggestions and support. I'm so glad our love for Bren has bonded us forever.

To Tera Cuskaden, who had the absolute pleasure of copyediting this manuscript. I appreciate your "LOLs" in the comments and the reminders that I've yet to master English grammar. Super thanks for dropping everything to help me. I'm so glad we're friends.

To my wonderful French publisher MXM and editor Cécile Lederman. Your kindness and support are invaluable. Thank you for everything.

To Sean Kelly and his mad proofreading skills. You know you have a real friend when you can text him, out of the blue, and say, "Hey. Want to proofread?" and he, like, does it.

Finally, to my fans who are more like friends. Thank you for your patience when I postponed the release of *Of Flame and Fury* the first time. And the second. Oh, and I believe a third time, too. When I explained the stress the last few years have brought, you were kind when you didn't need to be and gentle with your words and thoughts. My buddies, the moment has come. I hope you enjoy Taran's last book and are ready for Shayna's and Emme's. After all, everyone needs a time to shine.

Chapter One

Love is bullshit.

Or so I thought.

My parents had love. Two rounds from a shotgun cut that love short and catapulted my childhood into hell. Am I okay now? I suppose you can call it that. I survived a childhood that would make the Brothers Grimm think twice about writing stories of scary beasties. To their credit, they were only human, and like most humans, they didn't realize those famished monsters looking for kids to munch on actually exist.

Yeah, I survived my childhood and the monsters along the way. Then I met Gemini, and I learned how to live.

From the moment I met my werewolf lover, I knew I was done for. Forget his strength and looks. Forget that he possesses the rare ability to split into two wolves. These are mere bonuses on a long list of sexy points. His real gift is calming my temper like no one else can.

Usually.

"I think I may have to kill something," I tell him. I give it some thought. "Any of the slutty vamps here yet?"

His chest rumbles where it's pressed against my back, releasing a smooth, almost subtle laugh. He knows I'm kidding. Mostly. Except those damn vampires, who dress like naughty Catholic schoolgirls, have a gift for prancing on my last nerve with their stilettos.

"Not yet," Gemini replies. "You'll be the first to know when they arrive."

His lips skim along the sweep of my neck. I shudder, the motion only briefly drawing my focus away from the terrace. I can't see past the light bleaching the flat stone covering the small exterior space. I wish I could. Beyond, where the mountains of Lake Tahoe reflect on the water, scary creatures stalk, waiting for a chance to kill my sister and her unborn child.

Not that I'll give them the chance.

It's insanity, really. Anyone with a speck of reason would run screaming from this nightmare or fall into hysterics, pleading to be spared. I huff at the thought. I learned long ago pleading is for pussies, and no matter how fast you are, the monsters are faster.

"Are you all right?" Gemini asks.

"Peachy," I reply, not even trying to mean it. God, I'm angry. No . . . I'm more than angry. I'm *furious*.

Since Celia learned she and Aric were expecting the child destined to save the world, my fury has brewed to a deadly calm, more frightening than a horrific scream cut short or the hot breath of evil trailing over an innocent throat. It's a good thing. This fury that stirs me from sleep and burns down to my soul is useful. Sooner or later, evil will lurk from that darkness and find Celia, targeting the little one growing inside her. When it does, my fury will unleash, and the remains of that evil will lie at my feet.

"Taran," Gemini murmurs against my skin. "Our people are in place. We've planned for every possible scenario to protect Celia."

"I know." We plan all the time. Sometimes, we wake up planning. Except the bad guys plan, too, and tend to tuck cards up their sinister sleeves.

My right arm twitches in agreement. She doesn't like anyone threatening us. Like a supercharged battery, Sparky is ready to blow.

"My love," Gemini whispers against my ear. "It's all right." His hand strokes my agitated arm, his gentle touch soothing her in ways I've never quite managed.

I smile softly, feeling her settle with another pass of Gemini's hand.

My zombie right arm is almost a separate entity. The bleached white skin and sickly blue veins that run the length clash against my olive skin tone, causing the suggestive glances I typically receive to avert quickly away. Can't say I blame anyone. As much as Sparky and I have accepted one another, she doesn't always listen, and her temper rivals my own.

Sparky here will fry you like bacon with a strong bolt of lightning or whither you to ash in a blaze of fire. It won't be pretty or gentle. In fairness, neither was the way my original arm was eaten off.

The skirt of my white gown *swishes* as I turn to face Gemini. He's in a tux he was born to wear, the shape outlining his long, lean muscles and broad chest. The dark whiskers of his goatee lie neatly trimmed over a chiseled jaw, and his dark, almond-shaped eyes shimmer as they take me in. He strokes the strand of hair that escaped my fancy bun, letting it curl around his finger. He's so beautiful, and his heart so grand that sometimes, like now, it hurts to look at him. I look anyway, relishing this small pocket of time that remains between us.

My arms wrap around his waist when he kisses me. It's not a sweet, brief kiss. It's one that promises we'll spend the night making love if everything goes well. *If* it goes well. With everything out there . . . Yeah, I really need this kiss.

Gemini pulls away before I'm ready to let him go. His gaze is sharp.

It takes a moment for my hearing to catch up with his supernatural senses. A floor below, voices ripple as the first of the honored guests make their way to the ballroom.

"It's time," Gemini says. The softness he demonstrated in my presence abandons him, leaving nothing but the devastatingly beautiful features of a predator readying to kill.

My hands slowly slip away, the bite of tension that consumes me finding its way into my throat. "I know," I say.

The last few pureblood *weres* in existence arrived in Tahoe late last night. The vampire clans from Eastern Europe, three nights before. As head witch of the region and hostess, Genevieve has welcomed sister covens from as far as South Africa over the last few weeks.

Working as one, the witches created and reinforced the wards surrounding Le Grand Chateau de Montagne, Genevieve's newly constructed magical fortress where this supernatural summit is to take place. Anyone who's anyone will be here for a chance to mingle among the elite and seek an opportunity to get ahead. But the real reason for this gala is why I'm here. It's one last chance to unite the forces for protecting Celia's baby.

Voices echo along the second floor, the collective power of all these formidable beings chilling my spine and sending a quiver down Sparky's length. The pale, bleached skin glows fluorescent white. She doesn't like the magic scraping along our skin. It challenges us to come out swinging.

Settle down, Sparky, I tell my arm. *There shall be no death and destruction tonight.*

The smile Gemini stirred vanishes as I mull over that thought. *Well, maybe, maybe not. None of us are exactly besties.*

Sparky shudders when someone belts out a laugh. It's not a genuine, fun laugh. It's packed with power and warns those in the vicinity that he's not afraid—and that they should be. Gemini chuckles when I roll my eyes. This idiot is only the first of many who will flex their supernatural muscles tonight.

We're not rounding up the good guys. That's not what we're here for. We're attempting to unify a crowd of bloodthirsty freaks.

"Shhh," Gemini murmurs. He lifts my right hand, brushing his lips across the sickly blue veins and over my knuckles. It's fair to say we had issues accepting my new arm, despite the *were* magic used to create it. But you'd never know it by the way Gemini caresses me now. The glowing recedes, as do the trembles. "Rest easy, Taran. I am with you."

He bends to kiss me. But if he does, I won't want him to stop. I avert my chin. "We should head to the party before I do more naughty things that you'll enjoy."

"Hmm," he says. "Very well. But it seems you enjoy them too."

"I'll give you that," I say. My impish smile vanishes when I realize how worried I really am. "Let's stay alive, okay?"

Gemini's worry for my safety tightens his voice. "We will," he replies.

He straightens slowly, his posture stiff as the voices grow louder and the waves of magic rippling through the room turn more pronounced.

I drop the vulnerability I allow in Gemini's presence and reach out with the magic I was born with. I sense the witches, mingling among the throng of *weres* who've just arrived. The spell-wielders are different beings, but their magic is earthy like the *weres*. It's one of the many reasons *weres* and witches are so tight; their mojo complements each other. But then in a shove, their collective power drifts away, and I receive a virtual slap to the ass.

Oh, goody. The vamps are here, showing off their strength and allure since that's how they roll.

Gemini lifts his head, scowling. Yup. He senses them too.

Tonight, is all about the supernaturals. Clans coming together and old bitter rivals burying hatchets. Unity must occur, so Celia and her unborn child remain safe. That doesn't mean everyone will play nice, nor does it mean they'll agree for the greater good. Most just want to spare their hides and keep their fortunes.

Gemini's frown deepens. "Aric is here," he says.

And cue the sense of wrongness. "Without Celia?" I ask.

Gemini jerks out of his jacket and shirt before I finish asking. Like a vat of pouring ink, his twin black wolf materializes from his back.

Large paws, one as black as the rest of the beast, and one white, strike the hardwood floor almost silently. I shadow Gemini as he crosses the suite to the door leading out.

His twin stalks out. Another wolf prowling by, this one brown and white, stops dead when he sees Gemini's twin. Like the black wolf, he's over four hundred pounds of muscle and damn intimidating. He eases away from Gemini's twin, trailing him as the twin trots down the hall.

"Why is Aric here without Celia?" I ask, not liking this one bit. "His biggest fear is someone hurting her or the baby."

Gemini shoves his dress shirt back into his pants, redressing quickly. "He's worried."

"Exactly," I say, edging closer to the door. "So, why would he leave her alone?"

Gemini sets his jaw. "It's extra security. Aric's magic is strengthening."

I help him with his tie, attempting to relax my nerves as I mull over his words. "I haven't felt anything different."

"He's been holding back," Gemini replies, his voice lowering. "Being one of his Warriors and Second in Command, I've sensed it growing and feeding mine."

"I haven't felt anything," I admit. "And I feel everything . . ."

My words lodge as a scary and vicious presence forces its way into the room. I jump away from the door, my firing arm out. Something primal waits just outside. I'm ready to blast away until I catch a trace of familiarity behind it. This beast isn't at our door—he's everywhere.

"Is that Aric?" I ask, barely recognizing what his *were* power has become.

"Yes." Gemini reaches for my hand and escorts me through the door. "He won't hold back tonight."

All right, now it makes sense. "Anything out to get Celia will presume she's with him," I determine. "He's making himself a target."

I barely shut the door with how fast Gemini stalks forward. "Yes," he responds, keeping his voice quiet. "It will divert attention away from Celia."

I grind to a stop. Gemini could easily keep going with my hand still attached. Thankfully, he's always careful not to hurt me. "How bad is it?" I ask.

His gaze darkens as it meets mine. "Worse than we could have imagined."

Chapter Two

My feet tentatively move forward, stepping lightly over the dark wooden floors. Based on Gemini's tone, I'm waiting for something to break through the ivory-painted walls and attack. Gemini doesn't reach for my hand. He's too busy eyeing Sparky as the magic within us charges. He leads me forward with a gentle press of his hand to the small of my back. My tone isn't so gentle. "What's going on?" I ask.

"We're not entirely sure."

"So not making me feel better, babe," I reply when he doesn't answer right away.

He looks around, taking me into a small alcove and further dropping his voice. "Remember when we spoke about Genevieve feeling a change in Lake Tahoe since the arrival of the other head witches?"

"Yes," I say. Celia felt it too. She's not as sensitive to magic as I am, but since moving here, she's always shared an odd kinship with the lake.

God, I don't like how Gemini quiets. "You told me the power of Lake Tahoe is stronger and purer than it's been in centuries. You said it was a good thing," I remind him. I shake my head when he doesn't reply, knowing things are headed from bad to hell. "The evil ante blew up big time, didn't it?"

The muscles along his shoulders clench as if readying to pounce. "Yes."

Son of a bitch. Can't evil just chill for once? "Babe, just tell me what's up."

Gemini stops, turning to face me. "The shift in the lake's supremacy is too severe and rising unusually fast. Genevieve no longer believes it's the witches' arrival stirring it. She feels it's counterbalancing a presence that's invaded the area."

"Why am I just hearing about this now?" I press.

"I only just learned myself. Genevieve informed me an hour ago."

His admission gives me pause and a touch of attitude. Gemini doesn't mean Vieve hit him up on his phone. Oh, no. Wolves *call* each other by howling. Those *calls* are loud and clear. As the liaison between the *weres* and Tahoe's head witch, Gemini hears Vieve's tender and seductive voice whisper along his ear whenever she sees fit.

"An hour ago?" I ask. He replies with a stiff nod. He knows I'm pissed off. "And you didn't tell me."

He raises his eyebrows. He doesn't like my accusatory tone. Poor, hot, deadly werewolf. "If you recall what we were doing at the time," he begins, doing his best to remain calm, "it wasn't the best time to tell you *or* reply to her."

"Oh, I recall." I reel away from him and stomp down the hall overlooking the massive foyer.

The hem of my gown smacks against the iron balusters when I whip around. We've reached the open walkway that leads from the west wing, where the majority of the guest suites were constructed, to the east side dedicated to students and their learning areas.

From here, I can see the entirety of the foyer and the large archway that opens into the ballroom. I don't waste time admiring all the details put into this opulent structure. Uh-uh. I'm too busy fuming over Genevieve and pointing a lightning-charged finger at Gemini.

"*You* should have told me, and *she* shouldn't speak to you when we're naked in bed." I storm ahead, showering the floors with blue and white sparks as I wave my arms. "Or when you have me up against the wall, or on top of the vanity, and especially *not* when I'm bent over a terrace."

"Taran, *wait*," Gemini snarls.

Of course, I don't. It is kind of cute that he thinks I might listen for once.

My gown ruffles along the stark-white marble steps as I make my way to the first level. I don't have to turn to know Gemini isn't far behind. The strain between us crawls up my back, demanding I turn around. Several vamps halt their elbow-rubbing to grin and flash us some fang. The few I recognize snag the champagne glasses levitating in the air and toast our clearly adoring relationship. "Oh, shut up," I snap.

Gemini's movements can be as subtle as air. Not now. He marches behind me, gaining ground as easily as I blink. "You're doing this now?"

"You're damn right I'm doing this now." More sparks. Followed by a zap of lightning that leaves a nasty mark on Vieve's new floors. Sorry, not sorry.

I cross the foyer. It's lit in candlelight and adorned with expensive artwork and paintings of the most famous witches in history. The foyer is so ridiculously large, it takes a hot minute to reach the ballroom. The moment I step through the archway, I scan the room.

"I take it Aric knows?" I'm not really asking. It explains the self-inflicted target on his back.

"He does." Gemini clears his throat, not that it erases his resonating growl. "Genevieve confirmed. She called him directly."

"Mm," I add. "God forbid she do the same with you."

His gaze shifts from side to side, a warning to all those still looking at us that it's a very unwise idea. "She didn't know," he rumbles.

"Do *not* stick up for her," I fire back. "Not when we were doing what we were doing and how hard we were doing it."

"And how hard were you doing it?" a vamp in a too-expensive tux asks.

"Almost as hard as your mother," I reply merrily. He scowls. His scowl deepens when I steal his champagne out of his hand and chug it. I toss it behind me and flounce away, forcing him to dive for the crystal flute before it crashes to the floor.

As you can guess, I'm not Queen of Couth. I have my reasons. The main one is, I don't have long to live.

I'm not being dramatic, and take a seat if you think I'm whining. Since birth, evil has stalked my family and me. The more years that pass, the harder evil fights to take us. I've attended too many funerals and cried thick ugly tears for those I most love. One mistake. One moment of weakness. That's all it will take for the tears to fall for me.

I'm living on borrowed time. It's something I know, just as I know how it'll all go down. Either I'll die alone, fighting whatever's on top of me, or die protecting Celia.

The latter is most likely. There'll be no hesitation, no regrets. I'm prepared to take that killing shot meant for her; however it comes and whoever has the balls to wield it.

I suppose it explains my anger. Every time. No, every *second* Gemini and I are alone is precious. I won't have the luxury of saying goodbye. So, to have someone interrupt those moments when I'm with him, is wrong.

My heels stomp along the gold marble ballroom where the reception is in full swing. Crystal chandeliers illuminate the levitating champagne flutes, and Lesser witches snake their way through the growing crowd hefting silver platters spilling with fancy hors d'oeuvres. I reach for another flute and take a long sip, my gaze bouncing from witch to vamp to *were*.

Oh, and look who's there by the doors leading out to the garden: Genevieve.

The perpetual prom princess dazzles in a burgundy gown that brings out her sapphire eyes and flawless ivory skin. Some women suffer with decades of unrelenting acne. But no pimple ever dared flaw that perfect canvas. Heaven forbid.

Genevieve stands as regal as the queen her peers revere her as, her ebony hair swept into an updo that's both elegant and great-sex disheveled. Vamps, *weres*, and witches alike swarm her like butterflies desperate for a succulent taste of her delicate nectar. I don't envy flowers. Not ones capable of sprouting thorns and cursing your ass so it rests where your tits should be.

Vieve and I used to hate each other. Like, *hate*. While we'll never be besties, we've earned each other's respect and are usually quite cordial. Except every now and then, the pretty flower needs reminding that fire and lightning can fry her petals.

Vieve laughs, softly and amiably as she speaks to Uri. Uri, the master vampire of all master vampires, makes pleasant conversation while his barely dressed dates for the night flaunt their hot, almost naked bods. You can't help but notice their packages beneath their super tight speedos, or the stupid bow ties that match Uri's even stupider red cape.

Vieve smiles at Gemini when she sees him. Her smile dwindles when she sees *me*.

"Taran. She didn't know," Gemini reminds me with a warning growl.

Vieve offers me a stiff nod. "Sister Taran."

"Don't you *ever* whisper in my mate's ear while we're fucking again." I grin to Gemini. "There. She knows now."

I wave to Uri as I walk away. "How's it going, sunshine?"

Uri chuckles. The little diva has always liked drama.

Gemini cuts in front of me, blocking my path. "Was that necessary?" he demands.

I take another sip of my champagne. Hey, this is some primo stuff. "About as necessary as you knocking-out that werecheetah who winked at me."

"That was different," Gemini snaps. "He didn't just wink, he invited you to his bed to show you how a real man fucks."

I give it some thought after I polish off my drink. "He was an idiot and didn't know we're together."

"I was standing just to your left," he barks.

"Talking to Vieve if I recall," I remind him. "Anyway, he didn't matter, and he didn't know."

"He knows now," Gemini fires back, throwing the words in my face. He gives me a once-over. "Are you done now?"

"Eh." I shrug. "For the moment."

He rolls his eyes. Like I mentioned, we're totally in love.

I release my glass carefully. It floats away and joins the other empty glasses on a round table covered in shimmering gold linens. "It's a respect thing," I say.

"You call how you approached our hostess respectful?" he asks.

"I was talking about respecting us, darling," I drawl. "She should know better than to pull that. Call, text, send a raven, and be polite. That's all I'm saying."

"Taran, enough," Gemini mutters through his teeth. He forces a smile onto a passing *were*. I wouldn't call it a friendly smile. I wouldn't necessarily even rank it as human.

The *were* eases away from him, nodding a little too stiffly and almost mowing over a vampire with long, red hair.

Gemini stiffens. I angle around him and to where his focus locks. Hmph. There's good ol' Misha, Celia's sworn protector, man-slut extraordinaire, and possibly the most powerful master vampire to ever walk the earth.

No real news, but vamps lack souls. They give them up in exchange for eternal beauty, sex appeal, and immortality. Misha gave up his centuries ago only for Celia to accidentally regift it back to him. It's why he's so potent. He simultaneously balances life and death.

I'm not shocked to see him here or that he's with some gorgeous . . . No. Sweet baby Jesus chewing on his fist, not *her*.

Ileana Vodianova is the sole remaining female master vampire in Europe. *She's* powerful for all the wrong reasons. In her day, Ileana didn't just wipe out her rivals. She practically conquered the entire continent. Bedding and feeding from lovers like Attila the Hun, Sargon of Akkad, and Boudica, Ileana is a force reminiscent of an earthquake. An earthquake that swallows buildings whole and spits out the bloody bones of its victims. I met Ileana years ago. Well, sort of. Gemini told me who she was and wouldn't let me anywhere near her.

"She'll see you as a threat," he told me. In other words, she'll try to eat you and pick her fangs with what's left of your pinky.

In a sheer white gown, diamond-encrusted thong and, well, that's about it unless you count the earrings and the dazzling red rubies glued to her nips, Ileana stands like a life-sized sex doll created by horny and lonely Dungeons and Dragons enthusiasts. She's tall, curvy, and scary. Very scary.

"Genevieve didn't want her here," I remind Gemini.

He takes a protective stance in front of me. "I know," he says.

"Then why is she here?" I ask, barely above a whisper. "Vieve is queen around here, and this is her castle."

Ileana's attention drifts from Misha to me. She lowers her lashes, slowly and seductively, drawing my attention to what must be diamond dust coating her eyelids. Her long thin tongue glides along her gleaming white teeth as if she can almost taste me.

Gemini's pause is so severe, the room itself pauses with him. "The vampires refused to attend without her."

"You mean Uri refused," I clarify. I'm no longer whispering, and neither is he. Hell, it's not like she can't catch every damn word we utter.

Gemini shakes his head slowly. "No. It was Misha who insisted."

"What?" I ask. Well now, I thought he was on our side.

Gemini narrows his gaze. "Is this a good time to remind you that you can't trust the leech?"

Misha turns and smirks, his features all sin and no sweet. Ileana throws back her head and laughs. Their humor fades when Aric enters the room like a god.

I feel Aric before I see him. Everyone does. No one speaks. No one breathes. The sense of beast and power worsen in his presence. Except for him and the *weres* prowling with him, time simply stops.

There was always a pronounced lethality to Aric, but it was contained to a degree. Around Celia, it would shift into something more protective and vigilant. Tonight, everything I've known of him, and everything that makes him the most powerful *were* of his kind, magnifies, promising to destroy anyone if it suits him.

The darkness Aric carries swallows me, blinding me to everything but the sense of his beast circling me and baring his fangs. "Gemini," I rasp.

Gemini squeezes my hand. "It's all right, love," he says. "You are not his prey."

His words do nothing to reassure me, not with all the pent-up power spilling from Aric's pores.

Aric stalks forward. Gemini's twin wolf leads the way. Two *weres* flank Aric, except they're no mere *weres*. I recognize them from their paintings in the great Den hall. The one with the peppered silver hair is in line to be the next President of the North American Were Council. The other is the most decorated *were* and Warrior of his time. I expected the big guns here. What I didn't expect is how inferior they'd appear in Aric's presence.

I release the breath I held too long. "Tell me Aric's not going all psycho." My head jerks in Gemini's direction when he doesn't answer me. "Gemini. This isn't funny. He's scaring the absolute tar out of me."

Sparky releases an involuntary jolt. Only then Gemini regards me. "Aric will do whatever he has to, to protect Celia. We all will."

I hug Sparky to me, trying to settle her. If Gemini is trying to make me feel better, it doesn't work. "We're all going to die," I reply. "Awesome."

Genevieve approaches Aric first, bowing slightly and repeating the gesture when Aric introduces the *weres* accompanying him. He and the *were* elite were likely inspecting the grounds prior to their startling entrance.

As the presumption of bloodshed fades, the murmurs resume and the tension lifts. I imagine it mirrors medieval times following a trial; heads roll, or they don't, and the crowd disperses with promises to see one another at the next flogging.

My head tilts in the direction of the kitchen when Sparky gives a twitch. The tightness in my heart eases. Celia is here.

I hurry away, needing to see her and assure that she's safe. "I'll be back," I call to Gemini over my shoulder. His brows knit. He doesn't seem to understand my rush. Odd. His link to Celia as his alpha's mate should alert him of her presence. I open my mouth to tell him, but quickly shut it, knowing my announcement will draw more than Gemini's attention.

A team of Lesser witches hurry ahead of me and into the kitchen where the scents of rosemary, lamb, and simmering pots of shellfish drift into the hall. I almost expect to find Celia in the kitchen with how anxious Sparky appears to lead me there. But then she gives another twitch, and I'm urged away from the sound of banging pans and delectable aromas.

My eyes scan the short hall I'm led to, keeping alert when I pass several small suites and an alcove overlooking the path that leads to the lake. We were given a tour of Genevieve's manor when it was first under construction, again at its completion, and a few days prior to our arrival. I still can't pinpoint where I am. There are several hundred rooms, from luxury suites to places of magical study, offices, and libraries, and two other kitchens.

I turn into another hall, and again onto another, the spells designed to disorient having little effect on Sparky.

The echoes of my tapping feet reverberate loudly as I leave the crowd of guests far behind. It feels like I'm headed back into the direction of the main kitchen when I pass another classroom. I round the corner and find my youngest sister, Emme, and our friend, Bren.

Every *were* present is either patrolling in their beast form or in formal attire. Not Bren. As a former *lone*, Bren couldn't give a damn about rules and appearances. He's dressed in dark pants and his best flannel shirt. I'm guessing his roommate, Danny, had a say since Bren isn't in full-out sweats, and his moppy head of curls is somewhat kempt. Bren likes to dress in clothes that are easy for his wolf to tear through. Fine by me. I don't want anything to hold him back if his beastie wants to come out and play.

Emme, conversely, tends to dress in clothes that reflect her soft and gentle demeanor, making her appear younger than her twenty-four years. Tonight, my little sister appears more mature than I've ever seen her.

The smooth fabric of her lavender gown hugs her small curves, and her wavy blond hair is tied in a tight French twist, revealing her fair and angelic features even as she pegs Bren with one hell of a frown.

Emme crosses her arms and holds her ground, keeping still despite her tendency to shuffle her feet when she's nervous or on edge. My sweet sister possesses the ability to heal and is a powerful telekinetic. She seems readying to use the latter on Bren and send him through the wall.

"You want to talk about this, now?" he asks, growling hard enough to shake his chest.

His growls take me aback. He's always used care with Emme. "When else are we going to talk about it?" she asks. "You're avoiding me, and it's not right."

Bren swipes his large hand down his face, scratching his beard like he does when he's frustrated. His growls cease, and guilt etches across the mask of anger he's trying to hold. "Em, it's not like that," he says. "I'm not trying to hurt you."

"Then, what are you doing?" I ask.

For someone with the best nose in the pack, he didn't notice my presence. He growls, caught off guard, relaxing only when he sees it's just me.

I pegged them for mates a while back. The way they were acting, and that kiss they'd once confessed to, had me convinced. Now, I'm not sure.

"I didn't sense you coming, T," Bren offers. "Whatever spell these witches cast is doing a number on me."

"Sure, it is," I say. Something is doing a number on Bren. I think it's whatever he feels or doesn't feel for Emme.

I look to Emme. She bows her head, trying to hide her deepening blush. I ram my hands on my hips. "I'm tired of finding the two of you this way, barely friends, barely something more. What is up with you two?" Neither answers, which annoys me more.

"For crying out loud," I grumble. "Are you sleeping together?"

Again, silence.

If I were a cat, my back would arch, and every tiny strand of fur would stand on its end. "*Are* you having sex?"

Bren's demeanor shifts from frustrated to furiously defensive. "It's not like that, T."

"You keep saying that," I remind him. "Then what is it exactly?" All right. None of this is good. Mates are drawn to each other with a connection that can't be flicked on and off on a whim. This . . . I don't know what this shit is.

"Just tell me what's going on, already," I urge. "Whatever you're experiencing is taking a toll on both of you."

"You're seeing more than there is," Emme replies quietly. "And now isn't the time to convince you or him." She makes it a point not to look at Bren. "Celia is here. We need to take care of her."

"Celia is here?" Bren asks slowly. He watches Emme walk away, appearing confused and unsure how he arrived here.

Like me, he seemed to forget all about Celia. He shakes his head, trying to clear it. I feel the need to do the same. It dawns on me I left the party specifically to meet Celia and make sure she was okay. As alarming as it was to find Emme and Bren alone, their presence shouldn't have distracted me so profoundly.

"Like I said, T," Bren begins. "The witch mojo is really sinking its teeth into us."

He means the disorientation spell, but there seems more to it than mere magic. There's a familiarity threaded into it, not witch, exactly, but something or someone else I know.

I rub my eyes, feeling tired and too distracted to care how much it smears my makeup. "You may be right," I say. I walk to him, stopping in front of him and jabbing my finger into his chest. "That doesn't mean I'll forget what I saw here."

I shoot him one last glare before I hurry after Emme. Bren follows, his large feet stomping behind me. He's worked up, and so is Emme. I hate it and hate the wedge it's driving between us even more.

Emme used to tell us everything. In her own quiet and shy way, of course, but she never hid things from us. Now, she's so tight-lipped, I couldn't pry her mouth open with a crowbar. I may end up talking to Bren alone. Maybe he'll be the one to crack.

"Emme," I call out. I frown when the hall darkens, and she appears to flutter farther and faster away from us. "Emme, don't go without us."

She takes off, running.

"*Em*," Bren hollers. "God damn it, wait!"

Emme rounds a corner and disappears into yet another hall. I pick up my pace, passing a small meeting room. Emme is moving fast, too fast. What's happening to her?

My steps falter when the light sconces dim further. I turn around, the rooms we passed are gone. There are no doors or windows, only a long corridor with dark paneling remains.

Everything feels off, and I can no longer hear the gentle strut of Emme's feet.

"Bren?" I say.

"She's gone," he says.

"I know, but—"

"She's been gone a while," he interrupts. He takes a long whiff. "That wasn't her."

"Excuse me?" I look back to where I thought I last saw her. "Then, who was that?"

"Not Emme," he says, the muscles along his jaw tensing. He clasps my left arm. "Come on. We have to find her."

I double back and into a wall.

"What the fuck?" Bren snaps.

The hall narrows, and darkness swallows what used to be the way out.

Bren's head jerks up. "Did you hear that?"

"I don't hear anything," I respond.

It's the truth. There is no sound. Just me and Bren and our increasing breaths.

"What do you hear?" I ask, keeping my voice low.

He closes his eyes, listening hard, the rise and fall of his chest growing more pronounced.

A light whisper of wind rustles from the darkness, intensifying into a pained moan as it reaches us.

"Aw, hell," Bren says. "Stay with me, okay?"

"Ah, sure," I say, trying to remain calm and more than failing. I can't see well in here, and I'm not certain Bren can either. I turn around when I feel something stir behind us. "Do you think the spells are just surging now that Celia has arrived? They're meant to keep her safe. Maybe they're reacting to her presence."

I whip around. The wall is gone.

And so is Bren.

Chapter Three

I inch backward, my motions dimming the lights further until they vanish completely. My right arm shoots up, lighting like a torch and sparing me from the blackness encasing me.

The sound of splintering wood has me lowering my arm. I jump when thin rivers of blood trickle toward my feet.

Blood is never a good sign. It leads from bad to deadly every damn time. Most would run at the sight. Me being me, and knowing there's no other recourse, I follow the tiny rivers.

I move carefully, not wanting the thickening fluid to touch me. Dark magic is particularly nasty and usually requires a sacrifice. This blood signifies more than death; it's a trigger to whatever will fire next.

My light strobes in and out, in tune with my accelerating heart rate, and against the tiny rivers that expand into a widening pool. The horrible silence resumes, adding an extra dose of eerie.

Don't be afraid, I tell myself. *It's quiet. That's all.*

I don't manage to convince myself. Not when the moaning resumes with the next step I take. It starts out low, almost imperceptible, swelling in volume until it's loud enough to muffle my rattling teeth.

The temperature drops absurdly low. The chill of death is here, expanding quickly, mingling with spirits and dark magic, and determined to drag me to hell.

Son of a bitch.

I reach another wall, another dead end. I release a breath, cursing when more moans join the first, these much higher pitched and much, much closer.

Frozen fingers drag down my spine. I turn around, ready to blast whatever is touching me only to stop dead. The streaks of blood are moving, swirling in freakish directions to form letters and words.

N-Y-T-E-S . . .

My light shakes from my violent trembles.

A-R-E . . .

The letters darken to black, smearing the wooden floors.

C-O-M-I-N-G

I jolt when something crashes on the level above. I don't wait for more of this twisted spelling bee. I take off in a sprint, shaking my right hand. "Get us to Celia," I tell Sparky. "Get us there now."

I just miss crashing into a wall that materializes in front of me. I shake my arm harder. I don't typically order Sparky around. It's not something I *can* do. As connected as we are, she's practically a separate entity with her own set of rules I've yet to figure out.

"Come on, girl," I insist. "Celia needs us."

More by instinct than anything Sparky does, I spin, startling when a new set of words form along the wall.

NYTES

HAVE

COME

Sparky radiates to life, the brilliant light she emits drying and cracking the blood. With a jerk, she leads me left. I follow, running as fast as I can.

The dimness fades slowly, as do the moans. Sweat beads my brow.

"Gemini!" I scream. "Celia is in trouble."

My mate bond with Gemini frequently helps me out of the messes I face-plant into. Except, never has Gemini felt so blatantly absent. I try again, calling to the one wolf who couldn't live without my sister.

"Aric. *Aric*. Celia needs you."

Nothing. Nothing but the dwindling moans.

"Emme . . . Bren!"

God damn it. No one can hear me. I need someone to hear me.

Sparky cuts us right, then left, then left again. The sizzling sound of grilling meat breaks through the quiet ahead. A *poof* of fire follows several rounds of loud clapping. "*Bravo*, Chef. *Bravo*."

I'm almost to the kitchen and out of this maze. I pick up my already ridiculous pace, yelling as loud as I can. "The mate of Aric Connor is in danger!"

The clang of piling dishes and orders to move faster infuse with the overpowering aroma of freshly diced herbs.

I round another bend, and another, the long hallways shortening and the voices of the guests growing clearer.

I holler, my throat burning. "Protect Celia. Protect the Mate!"

Light, brilliant and blinding, bursts alive. I skid past the kitchen and almost fall. I'm back in the main part of the manor and no longer alone. I grip the molding along the entryway, taking in painful gasps of air through my paper-dry throat.

Several Lesser servers pass me, enthusiastically communicating in French as they heft trays of food onto their shoulders. I reach for one and almost fall, my feet cemented to the floor. I try to slip out of my shoes, but everything below my ankles feels encased in stone.

A heavy-set server grumbles by me, admonishing the others for carrying less than her share.

"Wait," I say. "Don't leave." I clasp my knee and pull, trying to break away from whatever has me. No one stops or even looks in my direction.

"What are you doing?" I demand. "Celia Connor needs help."

My right hand smacks another Lesser witch on the arm. She glares over her shoulder, although Sparky barely appears to graze her. The anger she presents with dwindles into confusion. She doesn't see me either.

"Shit," I yell.

Another Lesser bounds forward, bumping me hard and into the next waiter who follows. His tray rattles and tips to the side, but only slightly. I'm here, yet not here. My efforts and presence a ghost of what I really am.

A voice whispers close to my ear. "Nyte," he says, laughing.

"Bullshit," I whisper back.

My focus travels to the floor, where the source of the magic appears linked. I crouch low and stretch out the fingers of my right hand along the slick wood. I sigh with relief when I realize the magic can't adhere to Sparky's flesh.

"Okay, bitch," I mutter. "Want to play? Sparky, let's show this freak how we play."

I inhale slow and deep, tapping into my magic and willing it to meld with the ancient *were* magic that created my arm. I push it out leisurely, not wanting to release too much too soon. Sparky brims with light, anxious to burn, and more than willing to fight. Except I don't need to set the whole place on fire, I just need enough to crack the spell holding me.

I repeat the motion, exhaling as if time is on my side and not as precious as it is. Gradually, my power slides down the length of my arm, pouring from my fingertips and encircling the area around my feet.

"Release me," I order.

The floor creaks but doesn't give. My feet remain glued.

I bare my teeth, forcing through more power. Blue and white mist corkscrews out through my fingers and ribbons along the floor, the ends petting the heels of a Lesser witch. She jumps as if shocked and barely hangs on to her tray.

As she regains her balance, she circles the area, sensing magic, and more than once passing me.

"Nara," she says. "Something is happening."

"Yes," a woman with scraggly hair and a voice to match admonishes. "It's called a party. Get the food out there before Chef has your head."

I ignore them, knowing I can't count on them or anyone else. It's up to me, and I want out.

"Release me," I command, pressing more magic through. The floorboards creak at my fingertips, splintering the wood down the length, and popping them free of the floor.

"Release me, Nyte," I say, exerting more of my power. I clench my jaw, struggling to keep control over my arm. She wants everything to go *ka-boom*. But I need to save, not kill. Not yet.

Ripples of white and blue shoot down the length of the hall, warping the wood and caving the floor encasing my feet inward.

"Release me, now!"

The spell forcibly pops, jetting me ahead several feet. I land on my knees and scramble into a sprint. I race ahead past several severs. Only a few seem to notice the damage I caused, yet it doesn't last. They shake their heads, adjusting their loads and returning their attention ahead as if I didn't just break the flooring apart.

I push past everyone. I'm almost through the hall. The server with long dreads is the only person between me and the main foyer. I yell as hard as I can, my vocal cords almost tearing with how hard I scream.

"Celia Connor is in danger!"

My foot touches the gold tile, and I crash land in a suite.

Upstairs.

In a totally different part of the manor.

I punch the floor with my fists. "What the hell?" I moan.

The room spins languidly, and the walls shift up and down. I struggle to stand and can't keep my feet. This isn't a room. It's more like a raft on the high seas following a particularly nasty storm.

My hands slap against the plaster walls as I tip to the side. I try to steady while the room continues to deviate. But it's like one of those awful rides at a cheap fair, and damn it, I want to get off.

I look ahead, trying to focus on something and smash down the motion sickness building in my gut.

Somehow, the center of the room remains gloriously stable. I start forward, concentrating on that little spot and not the nauseating twisting motions of the section I'm trapped in.

Without warning, the room abruptly tilts right then left. I stumble sideways in whatever direction it shifts until I collapse back where I first began.

Bile sours my stomach and clambers up my esophagus. I ram my eyes closed, taking a few hard gulps of air. All it does is make things worse. I open my eyes, certain I'll be sick. It's only then I realize I'm not alone

Tye, the son of the current President of the North American Were Council, is spread across a large bed. He pushes up on his elbows and stares in the direction of a set of doors. When I first met Tye, he reminded me of someone who should be slapped on a billboard in Times

Square with a bottle of vodka between his thighs and nothing else. Tonight is no exception.

He runs his hand through his long, white-blond hair. The dimple on his cheek pops out when he grins. "How's it going, baby?" he asks.

My stomach flips as the room aggressively distorts in and out. "Tye, help me," I gasp. "Celia is in trouble."

He laughs, his cheer casting a shimmer along his light eyes. He can't hear me, his full attention on the person behind the double doors.

"Come on, sexy," he says. "They're waiting for us. You ready?"

A light and squeaky voice replies from behind the doors. "Am I ever!"

"*Tye,*" I urge.

The doors crashes open, and out pops Destiny.

Destiny is a freak of nature. I mean that in the nicest way possible. Every hundred years, a little girl is born from the union of two powerful witches. That little girl carries the unique ability to predict the future and manipulate magic in ways that scare the absolute shit out of me. Unique, however, isn't a word I'd use to describe Destiny's taste in fashion. Frightening, yes. Nightmarish? Absolutely. From zebra-prints tops with leopard leggings thrown in for pizzazz, to lime-green eyeshadow and enough highlighter to blind, Destiny pirouettes against the flashing lights of the fashion police and points a middle to the sky, flipping off Halston. She always dresses as if she's insane. And tonight, for this special event, she's really outdone herself.

Destiny is in an octopus gown. I don't mean octopus print, that would be a welcomed comparison. I mean she resembles a freaking octopus. Tentacles stretch out from the hem of the black-and-white disaster, levitating from the floor, so each of the thousands of googly eyes glued to the suction cups rattle as she twirls. Purple and lavender feathers top a bun so tight her scalp may need stitches to stop the subsequent bleed. Oh, and that face.

Destiny is a beautiful young woman, even though she tries *really hard* not to be. Obviously, the feathers poking through her bun are there to accentuate the electric purple lipstick and coal rung eyes. Tye's grin widens, giving me a glimpse of the werelion within and the beast who clearly adores this fashionista.

Destiny stops her twirling, waving dramatically. "What do you think?"

He adjusts the jacket of his tux as he rises and prowls toward her. "You look beautiful," he tells her.

He bends, parting the limbs of the octopus gown and leaning in for one hell of a kiss.

It must be love, 'cause *damn*.

I crawl forward. "Destiny," I call. "Destiny, please."

"Destiny?"

"*Destiny!*"

Son of a bitch.

Several long and awkward seconds later, they come up for air. She giggles against his lips. "Are you saying we shouldn't go down to the party and spend the night here instead?"

Tye tugs on her bottom lip with his teeth, smearing her purple lipstick on his teeth. "Hell yeah?" he mutters.

I reach out a hand when the room rocks from side to side, and they go in for another kiss. I exert my magic, trying my best to focus on my power and not the sway of the room. "Hear me, oh great and magical Destiny," I beg. "I need your help to save the Mate and child."

Their kiss is all they know. There's tongue. Jesus God, lots and lots of tongue.

The audible sounds of their smooching can't be real. It has to be the result of a spell or some other shit. "Destiny," I call out. "Celia Wird Connor, the Mate and Carrier of the Unborn Savior of Good, needs you."

I'm struggling to maintain the formal verbiage needed to magically *call* someone. They don't make it easy.

Tye releases a sucker or whatever the fuck he's holding in his hand and trails his fingers along the bodice of her strapless number.

"Seriously?" I ask. "Hey. *Hey.* I'm standing right here." OMG . . . and there's a nipple.

Tye cups her breast, lowers his mouth, and . . . I groan. "*For fuck's sake!*"

Destiny breaks away from Tye and pulls up her dress. "Taran?"

I almost cry with relief. "Yes, dammit."

Both turn from side to side. "Where are you?" Tye asks.

"In the room," I yell. "I need help—*Celia needs help*. Something is after her."

They peer toward the door, and to the ceiling, and then on the floor in the opposite direction of where I'm barely keeping it together. "Here," I yell. "I'm next to the table."

They turn fast, blinking. Destiny stretches out her hands. "I can't sense her anywhere. Can you, pookie cub?" she asks.

Tye shakes his head. "I can't even smell her." He hurries toward the table, searching blindly with his palms out.

"Here," I say. I wince when he smacks me in the head. "You just hit me in the head."

He scans the room, growling. "Taran, your voice is coming from all directions. It's like you're everywhere and nowhere at once."

"Forget me," I say. "Just get to Celia."

Tye whips off his tuxedo jacket and shirt. "Des, take care of Taran— I'll get the others." He bounds toward the wall and only the wall. The door leading out is gone. All the doors have vanished, as have the windows, and any way out.

"What the fuck?" he yells. His fists pound against the plaster. Instead of cracking the walls and breaking through, the walls reverberate as if he's banging rubber. He roars, *calling* and warning the pack.

"They can't hear you, cubbie," Destiny says quietly. Her eyes close, and her arms raise, level with the floor. The octopi limbs elevate, quivering as Destiny reaches out to the magic cursing the room. The makeup she's wearing gives her a skull-like appearance. She chants in a language I don't recognize, beautiful and deadly, gentle and manic, and oh-so-very Destiny.

Magic seeped with the aroma of licorice spreads and engulfs the suite, hammering the foreign power that's invading the house. An invisible force lifts me, and the tips of my feet skim along the floor. I cover my head, preparing for the worse.

"Yield," she yells, bringing down her fists hard to her side.

The room crashes down, and I with it. I roll to a stop at their feet.

I don't even get my bearings when Tye lifts me by the shoulders in one move. "What's happening?" he demands.

"The house," I stammer, still feeling the effects of the dizzying room. "The spells . . . they're turning them against us."

"Who is?" Tye asks.

I rub my face, trying to shake the nausea. "Nytes. That's all I know. Please. We have to get to Celia."

"*No!*" Destiny says.

At first, I think she's denying me, but then something changes in her features. She backs away, anger and fear bleaching her pallor.

"Des?" Tye asks. He hurries toward us when she doesn't answer. "Baby, what is it?"

Her focus bounces between us. "They're here," she says, her voice splintering with emotion. "They're all here for Celia."

The severity of her tone hollows Tye's voice. "Christ," he says.

She swallows hard as her gaze drinks every bit of Tye in. "I love you," she tells him. "Whatever you do, do *not* leave the house."

Destiny's figure disintegrates into a cloud of black and white. She jets in the direction of where the French doors once stood and vanishes.

"Des!"

Like me, Tye knows she just told us goodbye.

Chapter Four

Tye roars, his anger sinking into the terrifying sound. "*Fuck.*"

"No shit," I say. "But Destiny's not alone. She has us, we just have to get out of here."

The aroma of licorice and spice fills the room, creating a sparkling cloud. It passes along the wall, clearing out the curse veiling our surroundings and outlining the transparent image of the door now several yards behind us. The room alters with each pass, darkening the bed frame and altering the bed linens from stark white to gold. It transforms into an entirely different suite. I ignore the alternating shapes of the chairs table and furniture, fixing on the way out that Destiny revealed.

"What the actual hell is going on here?" Tye asks. "Destiny's magic is everywhere, but so is all this shit."

He curses again when the door shifts to a new spot. I'm not waiting for it to move again. I take off, sprinting past my suite and Emme's.

Ahead of me, a vamp rests his back against the wall, smoking a cigar as his leer locks onto a Lesser witch's throat.

"Celia Connor is in danger," I yell.

The vampire pushes away from the wall. "The Mate, Celia Connor is here," he says. "Shall we continue our talk later in my bed?"

For all I think he heard me, he doesn't react with the urgency I expect.

The Lesser smiles, toying with the long strand of his ebony hair. She thinks she has him where she wants him. I hate to tell her she absolutely doesn't. "Perhaps, perhaps not. I'll be sure to let you know."

"Did you hear what I said?" I don't quite finish speaking when my feet grow heavy and start sticking to the stupid floor. I curse loudly, and no one can blame me. Destiny's counterspell lessens the farther I am from her suite.

A furious roar bellows behind me. My feet are getting heavier, and my steps are slowing, but at least I'm still moving. Tye, now an immense white lion, is glued to the floor. He snarls furiously, ripping a paw free with a barbarous jerk.

Agony leaks into his growls. Chunks of flesh and muscle are left embedded into the floor, and blood spews from his paw.

"Don't place your foot back down," I tell him. My eyes widen when I realize he doesn't immediately start to heal. The magic corrupting the house is affecting the witches and the *weres*.

I'm on my own again, but I won't let it stop me. I slam my right hand on the floor and release several bolts of lightning. Instead of penetrating and singeing the wood, they bounce and zigzag down the hall.

"Tye!"

Tye shoves his body against the wall, narrowly shifting out of the way of my lightning. The bolts continue down the hall, neither fading nor dissipating in strength. If that doesn't suck enough, Tye is now stuck to the side of the wall.

I push forward without him, watching the vampire lead the Lesser away. They can't hear me. Maybe they'll feel me. I shoot a bolt directly at them.

Like the previous strike, it bounces away from them. I duck when it rebounds and I reel around to destroy it when it heads for Tye.

Now in human form, Tye's face and body are red with how badly he's raging. "Taran, Celia is walking into the building. Forget this shit and get to her while you can."

"I'm not sure I can," I admit. I haven't stopped moving. It's just getting harder, as if I'm wading through quickly drying mud.

Sweat drips into my eyes from how hard I'm working my muscles. I wipe my eyes, feeling its salty sting as I exert myself past my physical limit.

Excited murmurs spread along the crowd. Celia is here. I fall forward, my elbows and arms sticking at the top of steps in time for her arrival.

Celia steps from a rear hall closest to the kitchen. *Weres* in their beast form—some wolves, some bears, and two cheetahs—lead the way, forming a protective barrier around her as she's escorted through the crowded foyer. They spread out, creating an arc, keeping the curious and most threatening away with warning growls and vicious glares that would have me bolting.

"Ceel," I call out. "Get out of here. You're in danger."

Like everyone else, Celia doesn't hear me. I watch helplessly as she walks deeper into the grand foyer. Her steps reflect the confidence of her inner tigress, the lethal creature waiting beneath a petite young woman who prefers marathon-length runs along the shores of Lake Tahoe to mingling with supernatural royalty.

Celia's inner kitty does a good job of hiding Celia's shyness. I see it though. For all that my sister is a lethal predator, this isn't the path she chose. It found her anyway. Just as Aric found a way into her heart.

Our younger sister Shayna skips beside Celia. The sword Shayna created to "slice any dude in two" dangles against the side of her ballerina build. She's wearing dress pants and a smooth teal silk shirt. Her long dark hair is in her signature ponytail and, like her, bouncing and all set for a pep rally and not bodyguard duty.

Shayna is our perpetual cheerleader. Koda, her mate, not so much. In dark slacks and shirt, he's undressed for the occasion, but like a dangerous storm, ready to obliterate anything that dares cross his path.

"Celia," I scream as she walks farther away from me. "Celia, run!"

My right arm creates a vicious strobe effect. She's bursting with savage magic, and it wants out. Unlike before, the magic gluing me in place now works on my right arm. These spells are learning my power, *so* not what I need.

Three of my fingers are all that remain free. I point them at Koda, who, although he has advanced several feet, remains my closest ally.

Streams of blue and white mist flow from my fingertips, swerving through the crowd to find my target.

My spell weakens as it weaves through the cluster of bodies who strain just to steal a glance at Celia.

"Miakoda Lightfoot," I say. I add force to my words as my power reaches him "Warrior to the Alpha of the Squaw Valley Den Pack and Mate to the Mistress of Weaponry and Skill, hear me and heed my warning."

My stream reaches Koda and wraps around his wrist. I tug him hard and add more energy. Koda's midnight hair brushes against his waist when he glances in my direction. I think he hears me until his attention bypasses me and continues along the open hall. He's in security mode and conducting a sweep of the surroundings. He nods to the *weres* who take point on either side of me. Everyone is in position to watch the carnage about to take place, and no one will be able to stop it.

I don't stop yelling. I don't stop fighting. I also don't move one damn inch. Tye is back in *were* form. Most of his flesh is missing from his side, and his growls are more rabid and pronounced since Celia's appearance. He can scent her and is restless to save her.

Celia reaches the center of the foyer. Like me, she's five feet three at best with long, lean muscles I'll never develop. Her striking green eyes scan the foyer for Aric, and her long wavy hair skims her shoulder blades as she advances. The crystal chandelier casts light along the golden highlights in her hair. Unlike most females who arrived in elaborate hairstyles and jewelry threaded through their tresses, Celia left her hair down just as Aric likes it. She hates the spotlight currently trained on her and continues to search for Aric. I search for Aric too. He'll protect her. He'll save her. At least, he'll try.

The longer Celia waits for her mate, the more I urge her to hear me, and the more her inner tigress grows wary. Celia's beast doesn't take kindly to predators surrounding her, let alone how they regard her and whisper. It's like we're back in school again. Except, instead of the bullies who target us and call us the "Weird Girls" as a play on our last name, "Wird," the crowd eyes her, waiting for Celia to do something glorious.

The ankle-length black dress Celia wears fit her perfectly just the other day. But her little one grows in crazy, magical spurts. He must have had one tonight given how he's pushing the fabric on her belly to its limits. God, she's so vulnerable, and try as I may, screaming and writhing, there's not a fucking thing I can do to protect her.

A hush falls on the crowd when Koda lifts his hand and orders everyone to stop. Those in attendance crane their necks, anxious for a peek of the supernatural savior growing inside Celia.

Celia swallows down a growl, she and her beast were affronted by the increasing curiosity and mounting intensity. If it was up to Celia, we'd spend the evening watching classic 80s movies in our living room and munching on popcorn like it was our job. If it was up to her tigress, she'd eat everyone here.

I don't initially notice Misha. He materializes with Ileana's arm draped through his. She says something to him, smiling against his ear when she tugs his lobe with her teeth. Misha ignores her and the way she laps the blood that trickles. All he sees is Celia.

Celia glances up, smiling softly when he winks at her. It's only then she appears to breathe. With all the tension her arrival stirred, she's happy to see a familiar face. No. I take it back. She's happy to see her friend.

Tye's roars rattle the hall. He's *calling* a warning. Like me, his efforts go unanswered.

My voice cracks with how battered my vocal cords are when I call to Misha. "Misha, *Misha*. Something's after Celia."

His head jerks in my direction, his gaze shifting from side to side. He doesn't see me, but he does feel. "Yes, I'm here. *Please* save my sister."

Misha frowns and abandons Ileana. He snakes his way toward Celia, the other masters giving him ample space. Being as badass as he is, my presence has affected him, except whatever he feels doesn't stand a chance when someone more potent appears.

Aric enters the foyer with Genevieve beside him. The *were* elite he arrived with flank them. The deadly energy Aric omits obliterates mine and halts Misha in place before he reaches Celia.

"Misha, *Misha*," I plead. "You have to get to Celia. Do you hear me? Something is coming for her and her baby."

Misha glances in my direction yet stays in place, cagy of Aric's approach. He hadn't counted that Aric would become this powerful, and neither did anyone else. I respect Aric's game plan and what it took for him to suppress this new side of him, but damn if it's not scary as hell.

The cluster of supernaturals part as Aric draws closer to Celia; they sense the predator within him bare his fangs and fear a lethal bite. I shimmy and squirm, hoping the potent *were* magic pumping through him squashes the spell holding me in place.

It doesn't give and tightens further. Tears burn my eyes. I'm out of time.

Chapter Five

Aric stalks toward Celia, his rough and scary exterior dissolving when she smiles at his approach. I don't catch him close the space remaining between him; the movement is too fast. As if no one else exists, he gathers her to him, clutching her hips and bending practically in half to kiss her. He smirks at the sight of her blush, slipping an arm around her waist and leading her forward.

The yellow stone on Genevieve's talisman sparkles, the magic within it magnifies her power, amplifying the sound of her voice. "Good evening. May I be the first to greet the Most Precious Mate and Mother to Our Cherished Savior." Genevieve purses her lips to halt her grin when Celia stops smiling. Yeah, Celia likes that title as much as you might think. "Welcome, dear Celia Wird Connor, to Le Grand Chateau de Montagne."

The audience explodes with applause, some genuine, most not, both deepening Celia's blush. "Thank you, Genevieve," Celia replies as the clapping ceases. "It's nice to see you."

Celia doesn't bother raising her voice, or with formalities for that matter. She's not trying to be rude or offend Genevieve, she just hates all the attention and the reasons behind it.

Genevieve doesn't appear bothered. She's respected and admired Celia since their first encounter. Me, not so much. If it wasn't for my tight bond with Celia and the history between Vieve and me, they would be best of friends, I have no doubt.

Aric, sensing Celia's growing discomfort, tucks her against him. "Celia, I'd like you to meet two old friends of my father's. Lando and Braeden."

"Aric!" I yell, losing my ever-loving mind.

Aric's head shoots up.

"Old being the operative word," Lando says, chuckling.

His voice lures Aric's attention away from me. God damn it, no. I scream his name again, my distressed cries competing with Tye's roars.

"This is Celia," Aric says slowly. "My mate and wife."

"Ah, Aric," Braeden says. "Congratulations. There is nothing more beautiful than a pregnant mate."

Jesus, you could fry bacon on Celia's reddening face.

The crowd chuckles at her reaction, except for Misha and the she-vamps dressed in naughty Catholic schoolgirl uniforms who rush to his side. Worry etches their stunning features as they glance between their master and Celia.

Aric, he isn't smiling either. He clutches Celia protectively, his guarded features scanning up the curved staircase and stopping on me. He can sense me, and holy Moses, so can Misha. Like a cobra coiling to strike, his narrowing gaze locks on me.

"They're coming for Celia!" I holler.

Tears glide onto my cheeks with how hard I yell. They still can't hear me. I try again, my words cutting off when dread rakes my spine in one painful strike.

I almost snap my neck with how hard I whip it in the direction of the kitchen. The Lesser witch, the server with the dreads, waits beneath the arch.

In a blink, he vanishes from sight. But . . . he's still here.

I can't see him, only sense him, looping through the dense crowd as the guests are directed toward the ballroom and away from Celia.

My power builds. Sparky trembles out of control. I don't have the best aim. Not when most of my arm is glued to the floor, and my fingers are barely moveable.

Whatever is gaining ground toward Celia has no care for her life or that of her baby. It has a job to do.

Well, so do I.

I aim and fire at blank space and a sense of wrong more than anything corporeal, my frustration and fear taking form in blue and white fire and vengeance. I strike my target. There's screaming, smoke, confusion, and the pungent smell of dark magic.

As the smoke clears, the spell holding me crumbles. Tye breaks free, the blood from his injuries splattering the walls as he runs. I manage to scramble to my feet and clutch his mane as he leaps over the rail. He twists his body, cushioning me as we land in the foyer beside Celia.

Aric stands holding an oddly muscular arm encased in gray fur, its claws mere centimeters from Celia's protruding belly. Gemini holds another similar arm covered with patches of spindly black hair that intermix with gray fur.

The fabric cocooning Celia's baby is torn, exposing her skin. Small drops of blood bead along the length of the scratch. The creature just barely grazed her. That doesn't mean Celia doesn't feel the effects.

Celia is breathing hard. She covers her mouth with one hand and clutches her stomach with the other. Misha clasps her shoulders, pressing her back against his chest as he guards her.

That thing, whatever it was, came close to *gutting Celia*. Fury ties a noose around me, threatening to choke me. I turn, wanting to find the creature, my need to kill it corrupting my senses.

Koda and Gemini's twin wolf each have one of the creature's legs. The face of Celia's attacker is distorted but still recognizable as the waiter with the dreadlocks. Angler fish fangs poke through a disproportionately large maw, and squirming snakes replace his long hair.

The serpents along his head hiss, striking at Shayna and trying to sink their fangs into her flesh. She easily leaps out of the way, landing in a crouch, and then thrusts her weight forward to stab the creature in the heart.

The snakes and their owner spit at Shayna. She frowns, avoiding their venom, and stabs again, twirling her sword and cutting a spiral where the heart should beat.

"Dude," she calls to Aric. "This thing's not dying."

Aric's features darken from where he stands with Celia tucked against him. I didn't notice him gather Celia away from Misha. I almost didn't even see him toss the arm until it tried to crawl away. The claws scratch against the tile, leaving marks and chipping the tile. Gemini stomps on the hand with his foot, breaking the bones so it can't move.

"*What the fuck is that*?" Aric growls. His attention, like every *were*, vamp, and witch who forms a blockade around us, takes in the pummeling me and Tye endured. Everyone knows we're in danger, but like us, they can't pinpoint the cause.

There's no sense of neophytes, those witches close to becoming shifters who, although strong and deadly, remain human. Nor does the feel of *were* or vampire match anything this thing might be.

The attention I initially begged for is finally on me, yet now that I have it, I can't think where to begin. "Something has come for Celia," I say. I point to the creature. "It won't end with him. We have to get Celia out of here."

"No," Tye insists. He swipes at the blood oozing from hand. "Destiny made it clear we can't leave the house."

"I know what she said," I say, practically growling myself. "But you saw for yourself that the house isn't safe." I step toward Celia, thinking twice when Aric's livid presence warns me to keep away. "Look, at the very least, we need to get Celia someplace where we can better guard her."

Aric's guttural tone is barely recognizable. "We can't guard Celia effectively if we don't know what we're facing," he replies. His gaze falls to her belly, to that spot that marks how close he came to losing her and their child.

The scrape is nothing compared to the wounds Celia has suffered in the past, but it speaks to the horror that almost transpired. Using care, Aric trails his hand down Celia's stomach, wiping the blood from her skin.

The rage within Aric builds in frightening waves that ripple across the foyer. He releases Celia, slowly, shaking as if afraid to let go.

"*Aric*," she says.

She doesn't beg him to stay with her or plead with him to hold her. But the words are there, reflecting along her beautiful face as Aric sets her in my arms.

God, she's so scared. I hold her close, quivering from what almost happened and what already has.

Gemini is beyond furious at the sight of me. He won't like what I tell him I lived through, but this isn't about me.

The tension congealing the air escalates as Aric approaches the squirming creature. Shayna flicks her sword with expert flair, beheading the snakes before slamming the tip into the creature's eyes.

"Give him to me," Aric tells her.

The request doesn't suggest that she do so in one piece. Shayna swings her sword like a pendulum. The head rolls clean off the shoulders and toward her feet. With a twist of her wrist, she impales the head and scoops it up, offering it to Aric.

Aric grasps the head and slides it from the end of Shayna's sword. "Who sent you?" he thunders.

The creature hisses and snaps his fangs at Aric. "Something stronger than you, wolf," it says, struggling to speak.

Aric presses his hands together, caving the skull inward. "I asked, who sent you," he repeats.

The creature is neither afraid nor appears to feel pain. It spits, fraught to form words with what remains of its face. "Nyte comes for the tigress. Nyte is here for her."

"Nyte won't have her," Aric snarls. He slams his hands together, crushing the head like a rotting and smelly watermelon.

Aric tosses the head over his shoulder. "Let's go," he says. "Braeden, make the call."

Braeden shakes his head. "The phones aren't working, Aric. We already tried."

Aric's movements walk a fine line between human and animal. He reaches Celia and takes her from my arms. She remains in shock, barely registering more than her baby as she cradles her stomach.

Tye drills forward and blocks their way, earning a deafening growl from every *were* with Aric. Tye ignores them, holding his ground despite the large strips of flesh missing from limbs and side.

"Where are you going?" Tye demands. "Didn't you hear me? Destiny says to stay in the house."

"I heard you," Aric bites out. "But where is Destiny? She should be here with Celia like she promised."

Tye balls his fists. "Aric, Celia and this prophecy surrounding your children mean everything to Destiny. If she could be here, she would."

"Then where is she, Tye?" Aric counters.

"I don't know," Tye shouts. "I . . . I can't feel her anywhere."

It's a big deal for *weres* not to feel their mates. It doesn't look good for Destiny, and it sure as hell doesn't look good for us.

Aric rights his stance. As a mated *were*, he can sympathize with Tye. Bottom line, Destiny is not his priority, Celia is. His granite-hard expression is unreadable as he works through the situation. "Destiny isn't dead, Tye," he tells him. "If she was, you'd know it."

He cuts Tye off and looks to me. "Tell me what you know."

"Not much. I can only tell you what happened to me," I reply. Mouthing-off aside, I generally have more to offer, even when all the crazy rains down like acid. Except, for the magic to turn against us like it did, someone must have allowed the enemy in. I don't want to say more than I need to.

Aric nods slowly, understanding when my attention flickers to Celia. Gemini understands, too, although he doesn't keep it together like Aric does. His dark gaze sweeps over my torn dress and the contusions and scratches littering my skin.

Gemini edges closer, ready to make someone pay. "If Taran is this injured, we're not safe in the manor."

"We're worse off outside," Tye barks. "If the grounds were safe, Destiny would be back by now."

"Maybe. Maybe not," Aric adds. "Either way, we can't just stand here." He motions to Gemini. "Let's go."

At Gemini's order, several *weres* form a blockade in front of Tye. Tye *changes* into his beast form, his chest rumbling.

Aric leads Celia away, but Tye is determined to reach her. Koda shoves Tye before he can get close, sending the white lion sailing.

Shayna rushes forward as Tye rebounds off the wall and uses his powerful legs to barrel through the Warriors who charge. She presses her hands on Koda's arm when he growls a challenge, demanding Tye face him.

"Koda, please don't fight him. He's our friend."

Tye loses his mind the closer Celia is led toward the exit. He means to help, except I can't be certain this is the right way.

Urgent mumblings spread through the crowd. Many of the attendants are gathering their belongings while others argue whether to remain or leave with the *weres*. Genevieve addresses her witches, sending guards to different parts of the manor to check for breaks in the wards and alterations to the spells.

There's disarray from all sides despite the way the leaders work to calm their subordinates and reinforce the strategies and alternative plans each has in place.

Celia disappears within the legion of Warriors guiding her toward a doorway that appears with a power word from Genevieve's second in command. Several witches take places on either side of the doorway, keeping vigilant as the first of the *weres* pass through.

I don't leave my spot, watching as they leave and wishing I could tell her goodbye. There's a brief pause, and then she's suddenly visible, pushing through the bodies who swarm her.

"Taran, come on," she says, slipping from Aric's hold. "We have to get out of here."

"I can't," I reply. I don't have to yell across the room. She can make out my speech through the turmoil.

Gemini's palm presses against my back. "Taran, I'm not asking," he states. "We're leaving."

"I can't." I glance away from Celia and up at him. "Emme and Bren are missing."

Tye morphs back into his human form. His torn flesh is no longer actively bleeding, but it's far from healing. "Gemini, Destiny is gone. She sensed something dangerous and went after it." His voice hardens. "She didn't come back. Do you hear me? You don't realize how powerful she is or what she's become—no one really does. Except as lethal as she is, whatever is out there is stronger."

Celia's state worsens the closer she draws. Destiny is among our most powerful friends. If she's in trouble, Emme and Bren are no better off. "What happened to Emme and Bren? Emme was supposed to arrive with the second wave of Warriors, and Bren was to stay with the others outside the grounds."

Shayna's long black ponytail swishes as she shakes her head. "Emme wanted to stay close in case Celia needed her. Bren . . . he uh, didn't want her here without him."

"It was a last-minute change," Koda says. He glances at Aric. "Both were needed closer to Celia."

Aric curses. "And now both are gone."

I sweep the hair that's fallen from my bun away from my cheek. It's only then I realize I'm bleeding from a scalp wound. "I lost them over an hour ago."

Aric whips away from Koda, where they're forming a plan, to ask me, "What did you say?"

I don't want to say everything I do . . . not when everyone who's supposed to be on our side, isn't. "The protective booby traps turned on me—"

Genevieve rushes forward, cutting me off. "That's not possible, Sister Taran. These spells are meant to harm only those who mean harm."

An army of head witches are gathered around her. Despite the clamor of voices and her lack of supernatural hearing, she heard me just fine. It doesn't surprise me. Vieve didn't become who she is without paying close attention.

She presses her lips together. It's her subtle way of demonstrating insult and a warning that I better watch what I say. I slap my hands to my sides. We really don't have time for this. "Vieve, I'm not accusing you of any wrongdoing," I tell her, my voice harsh and raw. "What I am telling you is I spent over an hour in halls that led nowhere and back, rooms that spin like carousels, my body parts glued to floors, all while getting trampled by beings who don't see me and who aren't affected by my magic."

Gemini edges closer, growling when a witch with stark-white hair and skin to match strokes the talisman around her neck and the ruby sparkles with magic. "Sister girl, you don't know me," I tell her. "Keep your hexes to yourself before that talisman ends up on the ground beside your burnt remains."

Oh, and she stops stroking it then.

"Taran," Gemini says. "You keep insisting you were gone a while."

"That's because I was," I contend. "And I've been separated from Emme and Bren almost as long and exposed to these stupid—no offense, Vieve—spells and bullshit magic."

"That can't be right," he mutters. His gaze flickers to Vieve and her ever-pressing lips.

I'm not a fan of his tone or what he tells me. He can sniff a damn lie, start sniffing away.

"Tomo," I say, using his real name and losing the speck of patience I have left. "I went to greet Celia and ran into Emme and Bren. Together, we left to find Celia and were somehow separated in the corridors leading to the rear entrance."

"Love," he says slowly. "You left my side only moments ago."

Chapter Six

I straighten, an awesome feat seeing how everything hurts down to my toenails.

An old witch scoffs, her dark eyes casting a reprimanding glare at the bleached bitch witch who threatened me. "The spells are indeed against us," she says, her Aussie accent thick. She adjusts her position where she's hunched in a chair. She's several feet away from the other head witches, but the power she emits makes it clear she doesn't need them. She motions around with a staff made from a twisted old branch, a coffee-colored stone at the tip. "We may not feel it, but it must be so if she describes spells we were made none the wiser of."

Celia's tiger eyes replace her own. She was strongly "encouraged" not to *change* into her beast form, the same advice given to pregnant *weres* close to their due dates. Celia isn't *were*. Like our sisters and me, nothing like us has ever existed. But we're not taking any chances. For all we know, that little one she carries will fly out of the birth canal sprouting a beak and wings.

Aric whispers something in her ear. She blinks a few times, her tiger eyes resuming their human form.

Aric's friend, the one he introduced to Celia—Braeden, I think— watches her closely. "Incredible," he says.

Yeah, *weres* can't change their body parts like Celia can. It's either beast or human. He's fascinated by her; all the supernaturals are. It bugs me. I hate all the attention she's getting; she's already a target.

Celia doesn't reply and ignores the escalating panic surrounding us. She meets Aric's gaze, imploring him to listen. "I don't want to leave without Emme or Bren," she tells him.

Aric's glance to her exposed belly is brief. I still catch it, and Celia does too. "We don't have a choice, sweetness."

Koda's rock-steady features solidify further when Shayna squeezes his hand. Like me, they're torn with what to do.

Tye shoves his way through. "Aric," he growls.

Aric's fierceness amplifies when Tye takes a step too close to Celia. "I'm sorry," Tye says, tilting his head in respect. "Look, Destiny was scared when she rushed to fight whatever's out there." He jerks his head toward the entrance. "Something strong is holding her back. Do you understand the shitstorm you could be walking into?"

Aric doesn't blink. "Do you understand the shitstorm in here?" he counters. "This thing, whatever it is, is not only powerful enough to take on Destiny, it's strong enough to alter spells the most powerful head witches across the globe spent weeks building. There're countless curses set in place to injure and plenty more that can kill us. I can't allow Celia to stay."

"I hear you," Tye bites out. "But we can't leave. Taran and I were glued to fucking walls and floors. But we survived. I can't be sure we'll survive if we try to leave."

"Celia can't stay," Aric fires back. He rams his finger in Tye's face. "That thing that attacked her, I didn't see it, I didn't sense it. If Taran hadn't shot it and made it visible—"

Aric's voice cuts off. He can't bring himself to say Celia and their baby would have died in his arms. He doesn't have to. The feeling is there, angering everyone who loves her and warning those in attendance that their hides are also on the line.

"It wouldn't have ended well," Aric finishes gruffly.

"I get it," I say. "Except, Tye has a point." My leg muscles ache from running, and I was seconds from collapsing. Funny how the fear of dying a miserable death can give you a second wind. "There could be more of those things that attacked Celia. There could be thousands, and you saw how hard they are to kill."

Gemini scans the literal army of *weres* at his disposal. "Would you be able to sense them?" he asks. "You did that creature."

I glance at my feet when he motions to the nasty remains. My shoes remain miraculously in place, although they've seen better days. "I don't know. I saw that thing when he was just a waiter. I didn't sense anything different about him and dismissed him as a Lesser witch. It was only when he appeared to vanish and stalk toward Celia that I sensed something wrong about him."

Genevieve huddles close with her witches, speaking low. The *weres* listen in, their sharp minds keeping up with every conversation that unfolds. Vieve leaves her sister clans and eases forward. "Your exposure to this foreign power worked in your favor, Taran," she explains. "The more you experienced the darkness invading our magic, the more it ingrained into your senses."

Not *my* senses. She means Sparky, and me, as a part of her.

Tye glances in the direction of the door, his anguish over Destiny obscuring his harsh features. "I'm with Genevieve on this one," he says, his attention returning to us. "Foreign or not, the longer you're exposed to it, the more familiar it becomes." He frowns, eyeing me closely. "My guess is, you're also growing immune to it."

"I wouldn't go that far," I interject. "It's not like I sensed something there. It's more like I didn't sense it."

"What do you mean?" Gemini asks.

"The crowd was dense, bodies everywhere." I spread my arms. "That thing was invisible, more of an empty section of space than anything physical. As far as me growing immune, it didn't feel that way when I was stuck to the floor. The first time it happened, my right arm wasn't affected. This last time it was, and I could only move a few fingers."

The Aussie witch scoffs. "It's learning her power as she learns its'."

"Fantastic," I mumble.

Tye leans into his good foot. "How did you get farther than I did in the hall? I get that your magic is more potent than mine, but you're not physically stronger. I ripped my skin off trying to break free. You continued ahead. Slowly, yeah, but you still kept going."

"Destiny broke through the magic and gave us a way out of the suite," I remind him. "That magic couldn't have extended much farther into the hall. Maybe you caught the tail end of whatever she cast."

"Maybe," Tye says. His jaw tightens. "We won't know until she returns."

If she returns. Destiny's loss would be tremendous. She's our friend, the strongest being we trust, and a force to be reckoned with on the side of good.

My thoughts dwindle when I notice Aric. He's half a second away from barreling through the escalating number of beings in the foyer. Almost everyone is trying to abandon this house of horrors. "Say I am immune," I begin, trying to keep his attention. "Or that I am developing a sensitivity to this foreign power. It's more a reason to find Emme and Bren. They were exposed to it as much as I was, by now, likely more. There would be more of us to get a fix on these things and better ensure Celia's safety."

It's the last bit I throw out there. The final decision to leave is theirs to make.

Aric grinds his teeth, taking in all the information he has. He's making one of those hard decisions leaders like him are forced to make in situations like this, except this time, it involves everyone I love.

His gaze steels on me. No. Don't even think about it. "Aric, I can't," I say before he asks.

Shayna's hand grips the hilt of her sword. "Can't what?" she asks. She glances between us, tears glistening her eyes. She knows what's coming and already hates the plan.

"He wants me to lead Celia out," I reply. It makes the most sense, but it means choosing between my sisters. "This way, I'll sense an attack before it comes."

Shayna releases her sword to clutch Koda's hand. "Then I'll stay here, Pup," she tells him. "I'll find Emme and Bren."

"No," Koda growls. The brutality he's known for undulates his posture and voice. "I'm not leaving you, and I'm sworn to protect Celia."

"I'm relieving you of your charge," Celia says, speaking fast. Her face reddens. It won't be long before she loses control and her golden tigress demands out.

"Celia, this isn't negotiable," Aric tells her.

"Neither is my family," she replies. Her raspy voice quakes, and the irises of her tigress temporarily replace her own. "What you're asking of Taran gives me a chance at life. I need to give that same chance to Emme and Bren. The only way is by allowing Shayna and Koda to stay."

Misha abandons the masters who demanded an audience and marches forward, ready to break someone in two. "Enough of this. We're wasting time we don't have."

We have a choice to make. But when the walls crack and the ceiling splinters, the choice is made for us.

Chapter Seven

I can't say what happens first or even second. Everything hits us at once.

A witch standing guard at the main entrance halts the fleeing mob with her staff as they attempt to exit the manor. She screams and drops her staff when something hauls her up and out of sight. Her staff clangs against the exterior marble steps, and buckets of blood and broken bone rain down, saturating the gang of witches who rush to help. That's it. That's how the witch goes down. One moment she's calming the anxious crowd and preventing a stampede; the next, only pieces of her remain.

My arm floods with light, and I aim. I never get a look at what killed the witch or have a chance to fire. The ceiling along the foyer breaks, and a large chunk crashes on a table filled with champagne flutes. The wall splinters, and several antique paintings topple along the marble staircase. The movements, the disorder, everything is too fast to track.

I'm hauled backward by Gemini. *Weres* take point in front of us and behind, creating a barrier of hulking bodies to guard Celia.

"Protect the Mate," Gemini commands.

Those who aren't beasts answer Gemini's call, "Mate protected." Those who are reply in a cacophony of roars.

Another scream at the entrance. Another shower of blood and bone. The thing near the door isn't merely fast, it sucks you up and regurgitates the pieces.

Genevieve's anger and vengeance blaze through her yellow stone, scattering light as bright as the sun across her incensed features. "*Proteggerli le, mie sorelle*," she orders. *Protect them, my sisters.*

A rainbow of colors lights up the space as the witches amplify their power with their talismans.

Misha eases closer to Celia and lifts her hand, placing it over his heart. "Celia Wird, as you pledged your friendship to me, I pledge my will and life to you."

She yanks her hand away. "No," she tells him. "Find your way out, Misha—you *and* your family. Don't you dare worry about me."

"You ask the impossible," Misha replies.

Misha gives Aric his back when Aric pulls Celia to him. Aric doesn't growl or warn him. Misha is serious about his promise. And Aric . . . Aric's open to anything that will save his mate.

The vampires hiss and extend their nails to dagger-length.

Weres bare their fangs and claws, puffing out their chests, raring to charge.

The witches chant in their respective tongues, their magical stones casting a wash of rainbow light when the chandeliers and sconces flicker out.

Terror-filled screams announce the death of two more guards. Everyone is angry, scared, or poised to strike.

I jump toward the fray but am hauled back, unable to move.

I don't bother turning around, knowing who's keeping me in place. He's so freaking fast, I didn't even see him move. "Aric," I bite out. "Let me go."

"I don't know where you think you're going, but you need to stay with Celia," he orders. "She needs you."

"And I need what's out there dead, so it doesn't hurt her."

He releases me, speaking through his teeth. "Just follow the plan."

Aric pulls Celia and me to the far left when something large crashes against the wall from the opposite side of the room. Cracks spider from the center, depressing it outward. From the entryway, a British vamp casually passes by with a drink, muttering something about the inability of "yanks" to chill vodka to perfection and how the witches don't make enough to pay the electric bills. Somehow and someway, those who remain in the ballroom are still partying away.

"What the fuck?" Koda barks out.

The next strike splits the beam above the entryway. The Brit looks up, then down, as if stunned it would be raining plaster on such a fine evening.

"Grendal," Misha calls. His patience is about as controlled as mine. "What is happening?"

Grendal tilts his head. "Did you say something, Master Aleksandr?"

The collision that follows is so severe, chunks of the ceiling come down all over the grand staircase, peppering the floor at our feet and coating the air with dust.

"What is happening over there?" Grendal demands. "Is it snowing? Is it part of this ridiculous show?"

Grendal is oblivious to the roars, chants, and the cursing flying out of my mouth. "We're being attacked," I yell. "Attacked."

"We have snacks," the Brit replies, like I'm the stupid one here. "But *we* only know them as hors d'oeuvres."

I break away from the group when a faint and familiar growl reaches me from the ballroom.

Gemini loses his mind, charging after me. "Where are you going?"

"It's Bren," I say. I skitter around the *weres*. They only allow me through because they're in charge of keeping things *away* from Celia, not preventing those making a mad dash.

"Dude," Shayna calls to me. "Are you sure?" Her gaze bounces to Koda and Celia. They shake their heads. "We can't hear him."

Bren's yelp slaps at my ears. He never demonstrates pain or weakness unless there's a damn good reason. "It's him," I insist over the bedlam. "He's on the other side fighting something big, we just can't see him."

"Genevieve," Aric hollers. "Release the spells, all of them. It's the only way to stop them from being used against us."

"We can't," she yells. Frustration and embarrassment battle in her features. "Nothing we're doing is working."

The *weres* roar, snarling at the witches, their inner beasts perceiving them as enemies. A polar bear lurks forward, swatting a staff from a witch's hands when she points it at him.

"Stand down," Gemini orders.

I pivot, walking backward as I speak. "This isn't on the witches. Someone else is in control, and he's stronger than Destiny and all the witches."

Shit. He's stronger than all of us. Something squeezes my chest, and that familiar sense that captivated me earlier returns. He? *It* is a *he.*

"Taran?" Gemini asks.

I barely feel my hand rise as I attempt to stop his questioning. When I was with Bren, there was a sense of magic weaved into the disorientation spell. I didn't think it was witch magic, not in the traditional sense I feel around Vieve and the others, but in a way that's unique and that I knew intimately not too long ago.

My eyes widen, and I all but keel over. "I know who's here," I rasp.

Gemini clasps my shoulders. "Who?"

I practically kick myself for not seeing it sooner. "It's Fate. Fate has come for all of us."

Chapter Eight

Johnny Fate, like my sisters and me, is an oddity in the world. As rare as Destinies are, Fates are almost unheard of.

Before Johnny, there were only ever five documented in history. It should be a good thing, right? Like that spotted zebra, precious and extraordinary? Oh, no, it's not. Destinies and Fates can't coexist. Their powers brutally clash and interfere with Earth's natural balance. There's also that whole belief that their mutual presence triggers the start of unspoken evils, but let's not fuss over that now.

I'm not simply yelling as I push forward, I'm abusing my vocal cords. "Johnny Fate is here. He's the one messing with magic and sending these creatures."

I can't be sure anyone hears me over the growing screams and calls to magic. Anarchy reigns as the body count rises. Two fleeing vampires are sucked up through a ventilation shaft. Blood from the mounting carnage at the entrance pools at our feet. How many witches are dead now? Seven? Ten? They were formidable beings, and they never stood a chance.

Another howl of agony echoes from Bren. "Bren!" I yell. "Where are you? Tell me where you are."

His growls abruptly cut off. At least, I think. It's hard to make out anything through the commotion.

My breath catches when he answers me in his human voice. It's faint, but his words hit me harder than the pieces of ceiling crumbling down. "Help Emme. It has her."

It could be that thing that made bloody puddles out of the witches. *It* could be like that thing with snakes for hair. *It* could be that slithering creature in the ventilation system. *It* could be anything, and I can't see it!

"It has Emme," I yell.

A vampire, this one a master, glances down. "Who is Emme?" he asks. His head jerks when one scream follows a furious roar and pieces of organs spew into the foyer. Another witch down, and now a *were*.

The vampire hisses, his claws and fangs lengthening. "My sister," I stammer, hoping he's still listening. "Tell the *weres*. They have to know."

I don't wait to see if he does what I ask. I forge ahead, cringing when something slams farther away from where I last heard Bren. The foyer is almost as massive as the ballroom, wide as it is long. With all these beings, it's damn near suffocating. I use Sparky like a shield and ram forward, at last falling through the archway and into the ballroom.

The air is different here, cleaner, pure. There's no dust, no cacophony of sound. The tension and confusion linger, but aside from a few hushed mumbles, quiet greets me. The abrupt change is jarring, and it takes me a second to clear my head.

I glance behind me. There must be an invisible wall of sorts muffling the pandemonium in the foyer. By the feel of it, there's also another spell, one that makes those close to the entrance look away. The British vampire stands by a table overflowing with food. He lifts a prawn, studying it closely before he's satisfied enough to have a taste. He forgot all about us, the magic weaving through the room blinding everyone to the danger.

The same spell trickles through my nose when I inhale, making me want to forget the others. I ram my eyes shut, compelling my power to break through it. I'll be damned if I'll let another stupid spell keep me from helping Emme and Bren.

With a pop and a painful sneeze, the spell breaks. I startle at the crowd that gathered at my arrival. They tilt their heads, seemingly confused when they see the other guests in the foyer facing one way and appearing ready to maul.

They inch forward, and a vamp helps me to my feet as I work through how to clear this numbing spell.

"Karen," Uri calls. He's exactly where I left him by the fireplace. Ileana is with him too. I suppose she didn't like Celia's arrival robbing her of Misha's attention.

"Karen," Uri calls again. He snaps his fingers in my direction. I didn't realize he was talking to me, and he seems annoyed I'm not immediately racing to his side. "What is happening out there? Is your sister going to honor us with her presence or not?"

"It's *Taran*, moron, and she's a little busy trying not to die right now."

Indignation spreads across Uri's features. Kind of like when you smack a cat on its nose for trying to claw your face off. I should know better than to insult a vamp of his caliber, but I'll deal with his cape-loving ass later.

"C'mon, Sparky," I mutter. "Let's take this spell down."

I release a breath slowly, an exceptionally hard task given how my heartbeat is trying to rip through my ribcage. Within my cupped hands, a spark appears, crackling and creating the one sole light in the dim surroundings.

A sheer ball of blue and white mist builds from the spark, circling and widening with each pass.

"Show me," I whisper against it.

I grin when it bounces and sparkles in my palms; it's listening. I almost lose my focus when something rams the ceiling and my little sister screams in terror.

My voice shakes, and it costs me effort not to lose my concentration. "Let me see," I say, putting more force into the spell. "Let me know."

My magic obeys, my spinning crystalline globe enlarging and strengthening with each pass. I pull from the magic circling between the werebeasts who edge closer and the spaces amid the vamps who've never experienced magic like this. I pull from the empty pockets of space among the witches who scoff and chastise me for using magic instead of cultivating it.

Well, I'm weird for a reason. I wasn't born a witch. I was born with fire and flame deep within me. This magic I wouldn't have without borrowing it from the earth. And don't I take my lion's share now.

I bite through my words, the raw power within me ready to blow. "Show us. Let us see. Let us know."

The globe I create is pretty at first, appearing gentle. "Oohs and aahs," release, as if I'm putting on a show. But as my magic mixes with Sparky's, and Bren's growls turn more pained, my sweet little incantation becomes something more, scarier, potent, and exactly what I need.

"Karen! What are you doing?" a cheetah I don't know asks me.

"What is happening?" Uri demands.

"It's Karen, Master," a vampire says. "She's turned against us."

Ileana glances at Uri, takes a sip of her champagne, and bats her hand in my direction as if she can't be bothered. "Kill her," she orders. Her accent is thick and lovely despite ugly words. "She's clearly the unstable one of the family."

I'm swarmed by a group of vampires, which is the only reason I don't flip off Ileana. I lift my left arm and point, my fingertip lighting up like E.T.'s crazy cousin Spielberg doesn't like to talk about.

"Uh-uh-uh," I say. "Now is not a good time to piss me off."

They retreat when my fire swirls the length of my arm. In truth, I couldn't take on this many vamps at once. Not without more space and plenty of fire. Except, these pretty faces dolled up in their Sunday best don't know that, and sometimes you have to talk a big game to get your shit done.

"*Bren*," Emme calls.

I mutter a curse. Emme is exhausted and hurt and almost out of time.

My magic feels my distress and feeds the misty globe. The werecheetah sets to pounce. He backs away when my little friend rumbles, and several bolts of lightning crackle within it.

"You're insane, Karen," he hisses. "You'll blow us all to hell."

"I know what I'm doing." *I think.* "Reveal yourself," I command. "Show me where you are."

The ball of mist sizzles with lightning and rumbles like a brewing storm that promises disaster. Gemini breaks through the barrier separating the foyer and ballroom as I race to the center of the ballroom. My original arm didn't have the physical strength I need. But Sparky here is everything and more.

Everyone scatters except for Gemini, who lifts me in the air by my waist. I slam dunk the ball into the floor as he brings me down. It imbeds into the marble, casting streaks of light across the room like a disco ball. Uri barrels forward, stopping short when Gemini releases an unearthly growl, and he gets a good look at the virtual weapon at my feet.

I cover my head and crouch, feeling the weight of Gemini's body shielding mine a breath before my nuclearized globe of magic cracks and explodes in one mighty blow.

The strength it takes to break through the veiling spell is like a collision of trains at all sides. Windows shatter outward, and the ceiling comes crashing down.

Roaring, yelling, and hissing ensues. I glance up when Gemini charges into the fray, *changing* into a giant midnight wolf. Gemini races on all fours, his claws scratching through the floor as he charges. He joins his twin, tackling the creature who has Emme.

The creature—the Nyte, I should say, resembles Tim Burton's Tweedledum, only naked with a row of eyes that circle and spin around his egg-shaped bald head. He releases Emme from the impact of the wolves and rolls several feet away.

Emme lands in a heap, not moving, and her limbs twisted in odd directions.

"Emme." I race toward her, grinding to a halt when Bren in wolf form thrusts the creature he's fighting just in front of me.

This Nyte is covered with mouths riddled with fangs where her eyes, breasts, knuckles, and *everything else* should be. The bite marks littering Bren's body ooze. He's missing chunks of fur and muscle; the exposed bone on his hind leg appears shiny against the dim light.

My breath hitches. *This* is what had him.

I throw my hand forward, sending a long stream of fire spiraling into the Nyte's stomach.

The creature lights up like a torch, the scent of smoking meat filling the room. She shrieks, not in pain, but *rage*. She takes off in a sprint, gunning for me, the multiple mouths suckling as though they can already taste me.

The bolts of lightning that strike from my fingertips are larger and scarier than I'm used to. It fries the creature midair, the entirety of her body shattering in moist portions.

I back away from the remains, hauling ass to where Emme lies. Bren, injured and close to collapsing, trails me, snarling savagely, his eyes darting side to side.

The dwindling fire that remains of my globe casts shadows along the wall. It's then I see them, more creatures attacking or being torn apart by the guests.

Winged creatures, closer to demons than anything that belongs on earth, swoop down, lifting anyone they can get their claws into. Their reptilian bodies are covered with armor, and gold stingers protrude from their lengthy and thin tails. Two work together to capture a vampire. The vamp hisses, flailing her knife-length nails. She cuts one Nyte at the ankles and flips, straddling the other and breaking through its sternum. She manages to tear out the Nyte's heart and kill it. Its friend avenges it, puncturing the stinger through the vampire's back and out through her chest.

The vampire falls with a thud, twitching wildly. She must be old, since she's still alive, and she must be something special. A horde of vampires attack the winged Nyte, bringing it down where it hovers near the remnants of the ceiling. The horde shreds it into large mangled bits. One of the vampires, another female, offers a bloody piece to the injured vamp. She sinks her fangs into it and spits it out. "Not blood," she says.

Whatever these creatures originally were, they weren't human. "Jesus, Johnny. What did you do?"

I hop over more dissected parts, some *weres*, some vamps, some Nytes. The Nytes vary in appearance and ability, and they're everywhere. I'm uncertain if they appeared in response to my magic or if they were present the whole time, hiding and waiting to kill.

A random and roaming hand snags my ankle. I scream, 'cause that's what you do when something like that grabs you. I kick it off me and curse at it. It lands palm up, rights itself, and scuttles back at me. I bring down my heel several times, trying to stomp it. It darts out of the way and tries to grab me again. A sense of satisfaction fills me when I jump and the small bones crunch beneath my weight.

"Ow! *Ka-ren*."

My evil grin vanishes. I whirl around. A vamp with no limbs leans against the wall. "I'm just trying to get your attention." She motions with a flick of her chin. "Something's trying to eat your sister, Emily."

Sure enough, there's a giant rug with more mouth than chest, dragging "Emily" away.

Lightning charges within my grip. I throw a bolt like a javelin. Instead of sizzling the Nyte, it stabs through it, the tip sticking out from its back. The Nyte releases Emme, slapping at its back, trying to reach the bolt.

My breath hitches. These things aren't just odd and creepy, they affect my magic in an unnerving way. I blast and blow things up. Never has my lightning maintained a form like this.

Emme's legs slide down the Nyte's side and fall on a mound of debris. She's really hurt and needs help.

I stomp forward, forgetting about the hand skewered to my heel. It wiggles madly, its owner whining with each step I take.

"Ow. Ow. *Ow. Ow!*"

I grimace and look down. "Gawd. I'm sorry."

My knees bend in a small squat, trying to maintain my balance over the uneven and destroyed room as I generate more power. When my next lightning strike does little more than jolt the Nyte, I attempt to toss a small ball of fire. I miss when the hand attached to my shoe yanks hard and tries to pull off me. My fire catches a curtain, precariously hanging on a broken rod, and lights the damn thing up.

My lover, now in human form and as smart as he is hot, snags the curtain. He spins it like a supersized gym towel and snaps it against a giant toad with spikes on its back. The toad roars, the tips of its spikes catching like candles. It spits out its sickly purple tongue, latching onto Gemini's wrist and dragging him toward its gaping mouth.

Gemini allows it to pull him, securing his feet on either side of its maw to keep it from biting. He twirls the tongue around his wrist and pulls hard, yanking out the tongue along with several rows of intestines.

I gag as I shove my way through the fight to Emme. I gag harder when I realize Tweedledum is still alive, rolling through the damage and knocking over supernaturals like bowling pins while his male parts slap against the floor like tiny, wet mops.

"*Ow.*"

"Sorry," I yell at the she-vamp. I shake my foot some more when I realize her severed hand is still attached to my shoe. I know she's mad, but her hand is not my priority, Emme is. I shoot a stream of fire and light up the rug Nyte when he reaches for Emme.

Blue and white flames eat through the Nyte's hide. It ignores the fire and tries to lift Emme. It's not until my magic burns through its exterior and splits its skin open that it finally reacts in pain.

It bellows with the might of a grieving elephant, swerving, clumsily swatting at its back as if unsure how to move its limbs. I realize too late it doesn't have elbows.

Son of a bitch. These freaks are from Johnny Fate. He only paid attention to details when it came to himself. This mission is to do just enough to get what he needs.

The burning Nyte slams into one winged creature taking flight, and another one on the ground having it out with a werebear. The werebear scrambles out of the way as the burning Nyte sets both creatures aflame.

I pump my arm. "*Yes.*" The fight is far from over, but we're starting to get the upper hand. I push toward Emme.

"Ow!"

For crying out loud. The stupid hand is still stuck. I jerk my foot hard. The hand slides down but sticks to the end.

The she-vamp hisses, baring her fangs. "Just yank it off, Karen."

The hand is making grabby motions, and several nails are bloody or missing. "I'm not touching that nasty thing—no offense," I quickly add. I give it one last kick. It flies off yet doesn't quite land.

A snake creature with iridescent wings snatches it up and gobbles it down. The indentations of the fingers open and close the length of its body until it reaches the tail and sort of just . . . *dies.*

I lift my head to meet the she-vamp's scathing glare. "I am like, *so sorry,*" I say.

"Fuck you, Karen," she tells me.

She can be mad at "Karen" all she wants. I'm getting Emme.

Chapter Nine

I reach Emme and drag her near the overturned piano. It offers little as far as protection from the all-out brawl taking place, but it's all I have. I cradle her in my arms, sweeping her sweat-soaked hair behind her. "Emme. Emme, sweetie. Wake up."

She's burning up. I can't tell if it's from the battle or from some poison she was exposed to. "Sweetie, please. We can't stay here."

The room rattles. I glance where it's all-out war in the foyer. Nytes, big and small, charge the group of supernaturals I left behind. I can't tell who's winning, and I can't see Celia. From what I can determine, we're better off in the ballroom, which isn't saying much.

I give Emme a shake, gently at first, until I sense an immense Nyte materialize. "Emme, wake up. The shit's hit the fan, and now it's on fire."

The Nyte, like the others, is unlike anything that should exist on Earth. I see her shadow before I see her. A voluptuous, naked woman shakes out her hands, clicking her talon-shaped nails. Her lower body is that of a black widow. She scuttles down the wall, her girth comparable to a Smart car and her beady red eyes illuminating at the sight of Uri.

Her very nature is unnerving. My ingrained fear warns me against giving my presence away.

Not Uri. He and his family are covered in entrails and thin black fluid. His vampires hiss, marching forward to protect their master. They halt in place when Uri lifts his hand. Uri watches the arachnid creature, analyzing her closely and spotting for weak points.

I adjust Emme's weight on me and stroke her face. My God, her fever is worsening. "Baby girl," I rasp. "You have to wake up."

Uri and the arachnid are squaring off. Uri barely moves. The Nyte readies to attack. She clicks her nails, and her feet scuttle back and forth, excited and fretting over which side of Uri to eat first.

Something splats against the invisible wall separating the foyer from the ballroom. Another witch has perished. What remains of her face stains the divide as her broken body slides to the floor. I swallow down the lump in my throat when I realize who she is.

Her name was Charan. She was in my Mayhem and Menace class at witch school. Her favorite snack was apples drizzled with honey. She liked to sing when she cooked and was one of few who were kind to me.

"Emme," I say, my voice splintering. "Wake up. We need to fight."

More Nytes go down on our side, and the fight dwindles from an ear-splitting uproar to bar-brawl-level chaos.

Uri, now impatient to start the fight, scoffs at the spider. "You're nothing," he tells her. "Trash beneath pseudo layers of power."

The spider Nyte's speech is garbled, as if she's unsure how to place her tongue. "Nyte has come," she tells Uri. "Nyte will triumph."

It's not exactly the comeback I expected, her words slightly off following Uri's comment.

Uri frowns, offended. He tackles her, his movements a mix of speed and grace. With a turn and a partial flip, he locks his strong legs around the Nyte's waist. Like a temperamental child pulling up weeds, he tears the Nyte's legs from her large lower body.

It only takes an instant for Uri to kill the Nyte, a stark reminder of why he is who he is and why so many fear him.

I almost drop Emme when something with the legs of a man and the head of a crocodile skitters by. These Nytes are everywhere, feeding on those too slow to react or ripped to shreds by the more powerful.

Tweedledum is among the Nytes who remain. Gemini's twin leaps on top of Tweedle, determined to take him down. Tweedle swerves from left to right, his multiple eyes spinning and his male parts flapping away.

"Emme," I plead. "Wake up."

She's so sick, her pallor fading to a horrid shade of green.

Bren, now human, stumbles toward me. Like his wolf counterpart, he's covered in bite marks and not healing. "Here," he says. "Give her to me."

I almost don't, feeling protective and stunned stupid by his state. "You look awful."

"Yeah." It's all he says. He gathers Emme against him, using care as he turns her.

I clasp his arm. None of this makes sense. *Weres* heal at an astronomical speed. Yet here he is, kicking on death's door and demanding to be let in. "Bren, you're *not healing*."

He yanks his arm away. "Neither will Emme if I don't do this."

He hooks the bottom of Emme's bodice with his mangled fingers and tugs the fabric down.

"What the hell are you doing?" I demand. I smack his hands when he exposes her breast. "Stop it. Leave her alone, dammit." He ignores me, his full attention on Emme. I try shoving him away. I might as well be pushing a wall. He exposes the other breast and pulls harder, stretching the fabric until it crumples at her waist. I push and strike him. "God damn it, Bren. Stop. Don't make me kill you."

Bren's head pops up, the look of sorrow he pegs me with freezing me in place. He wipes the blood dribbling from his mouth and onto his skin. "You have to trust me, T."

He curls forward, clutching Emme like a lover. As I watch with my jaw dangling down to my toes, Bren's full lips pass along Emme's sternum. His mouth opens and closes over her flushed skin between her breasts and around the swells of her small breasts. He moves up and down, grimacing as if it pains him to leave her breasts when he works his way to her throat.

I avert my eyes certain I'll have to kill him. Instead, I take out my frustrations on a creature resembling a cross between and creepy doll and a baboon with four tails. The little bastard is flinging flaming green poo at a cluster of vamps, laughing his shiny ass off and enjoying himself. I zap him with a lightning strike, making him jump and distracting him long enough for a werehyena to bite his head off.

I turn back to Bren, my temper surging as he drags his tongue down Emme's now-exposed stomach.

"Jesus Christ, Bren." This shit is worse than what I saw earlier with Tye and Destiny. "You have two seconds before I fry you to *were* bits."

Bren lifts off Emme and turns, spitting thorns the size of fingers and more than his share of blood. He wipes his mouth and tugs her clothes back in place. "Come on, Em," he tells her, giving her a small shake. "The poison is out. Heal for me, baby."

I was right. I didn't want to be right. "How did you know?" I ask. Her greenish skin fades to white, still pale, but no longer that shade of death she developed before. I stroke Emme's forehead, the perspiration gathered cooling, and the pinkish tone returning to her skin. "Bren?" I ask when he doesn't answer.

He sets her back in my arms and perches himself on all fours, spitting out more blood and black fluid. "I could smell the thorns." He spits some more, his stomach muscles clenching. I think he'll puke until he turns into a sitting position. "I found Emme fighting that bald bastard over there," he says, jerking toward Tweedle. "Another guy, thing, whatever the fuck it was came out of nowhere, all covered with thorns. He shot them at us. I tried to shield Emme with my body, but then this other thing with the mouths landed on me, and I think the thorny bastard had another go at Emme." He shakes his head. "T, I didn't sense them. I couldn't smell or hear them. At least, not right away."

"That's because they're hidden by Johnny's magic." He scowls, unsure what I mean until recognition breaks across his features. I nod. "Johnny Fate is here, Bren. He's the one sending these creatures and infecting the spells."

"You're sure?"

I cuddle Emme closer. She'd almost died in my arms. "I recognize the magic and can sense part of him around me."

His gaze shifts to Emme. "Where's Celia?" he asks gruffly. "Tell me she's safe. Tell me that little punk doesn't have her."

I can't tell him anything when I don't know myself. I motion to the foyer. "She's there, I think. Aric and the others are with her." Heaven help us. Celia has protection. Emme had none. Celia may be stronger and tougher, but she heals close to a human's pace.

Bren crouches, trying to stand. "Can't they get through?"

"I don't think so. I did, and Gemini was allowed through keeping close to me, but it was a lot of work and took some time."

"Whatever you did, start doing it, T. Celia needs to get out the back way."

He doesn't mean the rear entrance. He means Plan D. Our last-ditch safety net I'm supposedly in charge of.

"I don't know if I can," I admit. Plan D is our "all hell has broken loose and we need to separate plan." The first part has come true. That doesn't mean I'm prepared to leave those I most love under these circumstances. I swallow down the panic churning my stomach.

"You can, and you have to," Bren replies. He reclaims his hold on Emme when he's sure I'll drop her. He strokes her cheek, attempting to wake her.

"Bren, you don't understand. If I can pull off this spell, we'll end up outside. Destiny told me it's not safe out there. These creatures are swarming the grounds."

"You don't know that for sure," he counters. "Have you been out there?"

"No," I admit. "But anyone who's stepped close to the entrance was reduced to blood and bones."

He motions around. "It has to be better than this shit," he says. "What if that thing at the entrance is the worst of them? It won't know Celia is gone, and it'll give you a chance to escape."

The anarchy in the ballroom begins to dwindle down, unlike the mobocracy in the foyer. "Bren, I don't know."

"T, we're the only ones aware of the escape route. Get Celia in here, and then you girls get out. We'll meet you in a few."

Bren's leg is shredded, and blood and poison ooze from the exposed bone. His inner beast is trying and failing to heal him. For all Bren tells me he'll make it out, I think he knows he won't, not that he'll ever admit it.

My legs tremble as I rise. This escape route is our Hail Mary play. I don't want to take it, but I will. I only hope we're not leaping from the frying pan and directly into the mouths of these creatures.

Pale-yellow light streams along the floor as I stride in the direction of the foyer.

"That's right, baby," Bren tells Emme. "Heal. I know you're tired. I know you want to sleep. But we ain't done fighting yet."

Gemini jogs to me. "What's happening?"

The way Bren holds and speaks to Emme tears me up. "Bren says it's time for the Hail Mary pass."

He glares at the magical partition where bloody corpses lay piled against it. "What if we just bring Celia in here? It's safer than before."

I like this idea better. Yeah, maybe we can just stay in here.

Except when I reach the invisible wall, I can't step through. A timber wolf with three heads appears at the entrance, its predator eyes locking on my pregnant sister.

Chapter Ten

I slam my hands against the partition. "*No.*"

The three-headed Nyte bursts through what remains of the main entrance. As wolves, Aric, Gemini, and Bren tip the scales at over four-hundred pounds. Koda, closer to six hundred. This Nyte, covered in iridescent scales and more serpentine in his movements than lupine, matches their combine weight and size.

Aric could give a damn. He secures Celia between Koda and Shayna, ripping his bloody shirt off and gunning for the Nyte.

The Nyte stomps through the fray, swerving and coiling, ramming bodies through walls and partitions, no care for friend or foe. Without fear or hesitation, Aric leaps over the dense crowd scrambling out of the way or busy fighting other Nytes.

Aric punches the Nyte square in the chest. The sound of breaking bone reverberates the barrier against my hands. Black fluid splatters the rabid crowd. Aric doesn't stop there. He fists the looser scales at the Nyte's throat to hold him in place while his free hand rams him over and over, puncturing a hole through the chest.

Through the muffled barrier of magic, I hear the spurting of more fluid as Aric cracks open the Nyte's chest. The center head collapses, its burnt orange eyes fading to black. Two more heads remain. So does Aric's viciousness.

The brutality my brother-in-law demonstrates is hard to watch. Aric is no longer that leader of *weres* I hated for hurting my sister and the man I'd bleed for for loving her just as hard. He's a predator promising carnage and destruction to anyone who dares threaten his mate.

I press my hand against the barrier and draw my magic, using Aric's rage to feed the magic spreading from my palm. Aric snatches the head on the left by the throat, swinging his legs to avoid the snapping jaws of the other wolf head when it strikes at him like a cobra. Aric's quick and aggressive motions crack the larynx of the wolf with his grip. He rips open the skin, pulling out innards through the tear.

Like the first head, the second collapses. With another few strikes, Aric fractures the snout of the remaining wolf head. The Nyte bleeds out through its indented chest. It was the largest of its kind and imposing. Yet it never stood a chance. Like me, Aric will do what it takes for Celia to live.

I scream, packing my power into the divide. Gemini rams it when it starts to give. When it splits, he shoves his body through, keeping it open. I look away as he kicks at the bodies to make more room. His callousness will bother and haunt him later. I'll help him work through it when the time comes. For now, we have to survive.

"Aric," Gemini calls just loud enough to be heard.

Aric, now with Celia, jerks our way. "Go, go," he urges his small group.

The barrier erupts with power, thrusting Gemini back. He curses and slams his shoulder into the barrier. This time, it doesn't give. "Taran, break this thing open."

I'm already trying except this time, it's different. "This thing knows my power," I admit.

"Then let it know how strong you are," he bites out.

He's damn right I will, throwing more of me into the magic.

The *were* guards assigned to Celia are gone. Dead or spread thin among the melee. Aric tucks Celia against him, Koda takes up the rear, his giant red wolf form snapping at anything that draws close.

Shayna is in the lead, her long black ponytail whipping back and forth as she cuts her way through the crowd. She's exhausted, her features pained yet no less determined. Even as her silk shirt sticks to her thin frame, her strikes remain lethal, graceful, exactly what's needed to get Celia through.

Aric edges around the pile of bodies, to the one spot not completely covered with corpses. Celia covers her mouth, scanning the dead. She thinks they died because of her. I want to scream at her this was never her fault. Evil doesn't care. It simply takes.

Aric pounds against the barrier. "We can't get through, and we can't stand here."

"I know," Gemini shouts through the wall. "Taran is working on it."

I mix my magic up, chanting fast and hard. The blue and white mist permeating from my palms spread, making the barrier visible. "Let them in," I demand through clenched teeth. "See them through safe and whole."

"We still need to find Emme and Bren," Celia yells.

Gemini keeps his voice steady, speaking as if we're not out of time. "We have them. They're safe."

Celia nods, tears welling in her eyes as she scans the dead at her feet. "Okay," she stammers.

She's a wreck. Aric can do little more than hold her. "We're going to make it," he tells her. "I swear it, sweetness."

I cast more power. My right arm lights up and illuminates the area surrounding us. It draws attention in all the wrong ways. Koda brings something down large and wiry when it charges. I can't quite make it out, it's too fast. Not to sound selfish, but I'm glad I didn't see it. Tails, lots of them, with suckling mouths at the tips, flail up as Koda goes to town on it.

Aric and Celia jump away from it, cringing. It's always extra disturbing when a *were* is grossed out. Koda's large foot smashes down on it. Squealing follows before the twisted tail slapping against the barrier falls limp.

A toadish creature leaps at Celia. Shayna rams her sword through its eye. Its gooey tongue whips out, lapping the air near her throat. She shakes her sword, trying to set it free so she can kill it. "Um, dude? I know you're like, totally kicking butt in there, but can you, you know, go faster?"

I press my hands harder against the wall. "I'm trying, Shayna."

Emme's agonized grunt almost makes me lose my focus. She is awake and pissed.

She holds Tweedledum suspended in the air. Gemini's twin and Bren the wolf leap toward it. The twin grabs an arm, Bren gets a leg. They rip Tweedle in half like a pinata and . . . more Tweedles pop out.

The baby Tweedles are tiny, naked, and bloody. They bounce around the room like tennis balls, shrieking and rolling toward the fray.

"Oh, my God," Celia says over Aric's "What the fuck?" remark.

Celia glances up at Aric, no longer certain she wants into the room and likely thinking she'll take her chances with the suckling tails.

"It's Johnny Fate," Gemini tells them.

Aric meets him square in the face. "How do you know? Did you see him?"

Gemini shakes his head. "No. Taran feels him, and that's good enough for me."

"Shit," Aric says. Throw in the fact that Johnny almost killed something as strong as Destiny, and yeah, he knows we're screwed.

Warm liquid splatters me in the back. The guests who remain in the ballroom are done with these freaks. They're stomping them, ripping them in half, beating them with candelabras.

I make the mistake of glancing toward the corner. The limbless vamp whose hand I accidentally fed to the snake has a mini-Tweedle clutched between her fangs. She shakes it like a snarling dog with a squirrel. It screams, screams like something being eaten alive, 'cause it is.

Jesus, I'll never recover from that visual.

Frustrated and overwhelmingly skeeved out, I give one last dose of magic. "Let. Them. In," I command. "Let them in now!"

My hand breaks through, creating an opening. I push it down, widening the slit.

"Time to go, love."

Aric's voice remains steady as he holds my sister. Unlike Celia, who falls apart. "Aric," she says. "I don't want to raise our baby without you."

His lips pass gently over hers. A small war is literally taking place behind them, but for now, only she exists. "Nothing will keep me from you or our child. Get to safety. I'll be with you soon. I swear it."

She sniffs, tears streaming down her face as he kisses her.

Aric breaks away when something smashes against the rear of the manor. I'm almost finished making an opening Celia can fit through.

"I have to go," Gemini says. "I won't be long."

I swallow hard. "Don't you dare make me cry," I tell him. "I'm trying to focus."

Like Aric, he's making promises he may be unable to keep.

"You are my love . . ."

"Baby, stop," I beg.

"My pain in the ass . . ."

I choke out a laugh, my vision blurring as the opening expands farther.

"And the woman I want to carry our children."

I swipe my eyes against my shoulder. Children. He said, "children." As in more of us and more years to come even as the fight and gore amplify. "You had to go there," I say, my voice splintering. "Didn't you?"

He kisses my forehead. It's sweet but no less lovely. I push open the way. "It won't hold long," I admit. I grunt. Already, it's fighting to close.

Aric urges Celia through. I catch Koda snag Shayna in his massive arms. He smashes his mouth against hers. Their kiss is more impassioned and longer. That doesn't mean I envy their goodbye.

Celia slips through and into the ballroom. Shayna follows a breath before I lose my grip.

Shayna presses her hand against the barrier to hover over Koda's. His grief-stricken features are enough to shatter a thousand hearts. He never knew love until he found my sister and now, he may lose her.

He bows his head briefly. When he meets her gaze and says what he does, I almost unravel. "You're the best thing that will ever happen to me," he tells her.

Shayna smiles even as her tears fall. "I love you like the moon does the sun, Miakoda."

She wipes her eyes and quickly helps me lead Celia away.

"Emme," I call. "It's time."

Emme, although fully healed through her own power, walks carefully toward us. Bren snatches her into a tight embrace. "I won't leave you," he tells her. "Not like this. Remember what I said, you and me, we're going to make it."

As he releases her, he grasps her hands, kissing them, the gesture as intimate as our goodbyes with our wolves.

"Emme, honey," I urge. "We have to go."

Although it destroys her to walk away from Bren, her face lights up when she sees Celia. She throws herself into Celia's arms. Celia embraces her, her husky voice falling to a reassuring purr. "I'm all right, and so are you. Stay strong, and I promise, I will too."

I crouch down, calling forth a tiny stream of flame to create my magic circle and our way out of here. Ordinarily, I'd use chalk, or even a marker. The chalk I tucked into my dress earlier was smashed to bits during the first twenty-five ass-kickings I survived. And even though I hate using my fire, I don't fret much over damaging Genevieve's floors. They're already destroyed, and my char marks aren't any worse than the shit staining them.

I work through the words of the spell, punching my magic through each syllable as the last of Tweedle's babies are stomped to bits. "Allow our departure," I say.

Gemini's head snaps up when another hard something strikes above. "Taran," he says. "Work faster. Something else is here."

Chapter Eleven

You know what? Fuck you, Johnny. Fuck you and your stupid Nytes and all the shit you're doing to kill us.

I swear up a storm as I focus on the witch magic Genevieve and her groupies taught me. I'm not fond of it, and not being a witch myself, it doesn't come easy.

Another crash to the ceiling.

Aric pounds on the partition, yelling at Celia to come back. Can I blame him? No. We're the geniuses who thought she was safer in this hell pit versus the hell hole on the opposite side.

"Morrell, Adonis, Keisha, Elaine, take point around the Wird sisters," Gemini orders. "Matthew, David, Amber, collect the injured and group them as one."

"Yes, Gemini," a chorus of *weres* answer.

More *weres* are hurt than are ready to fight and protect. I want to thank them. As the mate to the second in command, I think I'm obliged. But everyone is counting on me to get Celia out. I have to make it right.

More crashing resonates over the sound of splintering glass. Aric is busting through the divide, but it costs him. Shards of mystical glass soar into his skin, slicing through his muscles and coating the partition with his blood. The power he possesses is spilling into the divide and weakening it. It's also weakening Aric. He needs his strength to fight what's coming. And what's coming is plenty big.

Uri is belting words in Russian, his tone hateful. Each word smacks at my back like a warning. I don't speak the language, but the way he's looking at Celia makes me think he believes his life is worth more than hers.

Gemini appears to suspect the same. He orders his *weres* to tighten the circle around us. He snarls, ready to challenge the master of all masters.

My body shakes with fear. I need Celia out before Uri rushes the circle and tries to take our place. He remains whole and strong, and his vampires appear to outnumber the *weres*. Once we leave, the vamps will have no choice but to abandon their fight with the *weres* and turn against the approaching Nyte.

A section of granite from the fireplace cracks and falls with the next powerful strike. The floor at my feet shakes from the beating the roof and the side of the manor are taking. This thing is stronger than that three-headed wolf, and it's closing in fast.

"Aric," Celia calls. "Stay where you are. I'll come to you."

She growls. I don't have to look up to know Shayna has her and is keeping her in place.

Koda's *were* essence has flowed through Shayna's system since the time he tried to *turn* her to save her life. Still, Shayna isn't as strong as Celia, and Celia can wipe the floor with her. Hell, Celia can wipe the floor with all of us. Shayna manages to keep her put only because Celia doesn't want to risk harming her baby.

"Uh, uh, uh, little mama," Shayna tells Celia. She keeps her voice bouncy and light, ignoring Celia's guttural growl. "You and Aric, Jr., need to stay put. Dying is not part of the plan, cutie."

It's really not.

My magic spills into the spell. "Grant us peace," I whisper. "Grant us safe passage. By the power of good that surrounds the Earth, make it be."

I continue with the circle and the chanting, trying to keep the same width around since these things matter in witchcraft and wizardry. I reach the end and take a breath, just as something larger and heavier propels itself against the ceiling.

"We need to go," Emme says. "We need to go now."

"By the power of good, make it be." I slam my foot down, sealing the circle, and . . . nothing happens. I try again. Nothing. What the hell?

"Dude," Shayna calls to me. "That's an oval. It has to be a circle."

Jesus God help me. She's right.

"Karen doesn't know what she's doing," a wereraccoon mutters to a werebuffalo.

Gemini doesn't panic. He never does. Well, except that one time when I pulled something that may or may not have caused an international incident. But it wasn't my fault. Mostly.

While he's not panicking, per se, he's not happy. "Taran, we're running out of time."

Smoke billows from the hearth. I'm worried the manor is on fire. But then a stream of smoke with long stretching fingers latches around a vampire's throat and yanks him up the chimney. He screams once before his shoes and one sock crash back into the hearth.

Oh, and I can't make the damn circle fast enough.

"Grant us peace . . ."

Aric breaks through the partition.

"Grant us safe passage." I shove more magic into the spell.

The crowd backs away from the hearth. Aric and Gemini take point in front of Celia.

More banging. Something rams what remains of the partition. The fight from the foyer spills over into the ballroom.

"Allow us to pass," I scream over the noise.

"Get out of here," Gemini growls.

"Allow us our peace."

Several pummels to the house rattle the floor, knocking down the few plates that remain on the tables.

The circle sparks. It's only just starting to work.

"Allow us safe passage," I demand.

The tendrils of smoke grow longer and in number, snagging those who don't move fast enough.

"Celia, stay in there," Aric tells her.

"Get them out of here, T," Bren barks. "Get them out of here, now."

"Grant us safe passage . . ."

Celia's growls thunder against my back. "Dude," Shayna says to me. "I can't hold her much longer."

"By the power of good that surrounds the Earth, make it be."

I slam my foot down, sealing us in. The hearth explodes, granite and mortar striking the circle as blue and white light fires from the base.

My circle holds, protecting us from the debris, except we don't leave.

A Nyte made of dark coal crawls from the ruins of the hearth. Three head witches lift their staffs and fire curses. The spells combine and strike the Nyte in the center of the chest. Lava spews from the hole, igniting the witches and several vampires.

Bren's hands slap against his sides. "Fuck me," he mumbles.

The smoke clears alarmingly fast, unveiling the vampires reduced to mounds of ash. The witches are now mere statues of coal. They crumble as the lava creature moves forward, his heavy steps shaking the floor.

Celia presses her hands against the ward protecting us. "Aric, get out of here."

He shakes his head, not bothering to turn to look at her. "Not until you're gone."

More lava spills from the hole in the Nyte's chest, sliding along the floor but not penetrating. Whatever this is appears to choose what will burn and what won't.

The lava pools around my circle, poking at my magic and trying to find a weakness.

The action makes me lose my mind. I'm many things. Weak is not one of them.

My right arm flares in challenge, and I feel my irises turn white.

"Oh, shit," Bren mumbles.

He and the wolves back away, and they should. "Fire," I rasp. "Give me fire."

I shove my fist out as a torrent of magic, fire, and lightning releases. It flings the creature out and through the window, it's glowing body landing with a thud near the lake.

The force of my strike pushes me back. I land on concrete, rolling. Emme lands next to me. Shayna is more graceful and settles on her feet.

It doesn't compare to Celia's entrance. She flips, landing in a crouch.

The scent of rosemary and water fills my nose. Thousands of plants spread out around us. Through the glass ceiling, thick clouds pass, shadowing the moon.

"We're in a greenhouse," Celia says. She rises slowly, her tigress eyes scanning for trouble.

I ease up, helping Emme, who likely would have remained on the floor if I let her. I'm livid. "How the hell did we end up here?"

Shayna pulls the sword from its sheath. "Beats me, T," she says. "We were supposed to end up at the boathouse."

"I know," I agree. I dust myself off. It's a ridiculous gesture. God only knows what body fluid I'm not covered with.

"Um. Is it possible you messed up the spell?" Emme asks.

She's trying her best not to accuse me of any wrongdoing. It doesn't bother me either way. I could have screwed this whole gig up, but I didn't.

"No," I reply. I face my sisters. "We were supposed to take a boat and cross the lake to meet Makawee, Martin, Danny, and Heidi if we were in trouble."

My sisters exchange glances, confused as to where I'm headed. "Yes," Celia says slowly. "That was the plan."

"But what if they're the ones in trouble?" I ask.

Doubt further plagues their features. "Hear me out," I say. "I asked for peace and safe passage, you heard me, right?"

Shayna twirls her sword, trying to stay loose. "Between the swears and stuff? Sure, dude."

I ignore the comment. When the smoke started lassoing the guests, a lot of creative words gushed out of my mouth that had zero to do with the spell.

"Genevieve helped me develop the spell so we'd end up at the boathouse," I remind them. "Who knows where we would have landed if it was solely up to me. Spells are hard. There's lots of chanting, getting naked, and . . ." My voice trails when they look at me. "Let's just say witch school scarred me almost as badly as nursing school. I still have nightmares about attending both."

I clear my throat. "Anyway. The boathouse was our go-to spot. Except, when it comes to spell casting, the words used in the spell are always stronger and take precedence. They would override the location if it wasn't safe."

Emme's skin appears pale in the moonlight. My words don't help her pallor. "Does this mean that Danny and the others . . ."

She's asking me if they're dead. I don't have an answer nor the time to think those thoughts through. "I don't know, Em. I hope not," I say. "What I do know is that this place is the farthest we can get from the lake, the manor, and the way out of the compound."

Chapter Twelve

We're in a glass house. Literally. Aside from a few rosemary bushes the size of pines and some tree saplings, there isn't much in the form of cover.

Celia sits on the floor beside me. Our backs rest against a wooden door that will absolutely not be opened on my watch. Behind that door perch rows and rows of snapdragons, waiting rather impatiently for their evening dousing of enchanted water. They flap their leaves and click their little teeth, creating a chorus of sound. As far as level of bitchiness, they rank ten out of ten, unlike the gentler mugwort and witch hazel spread before us.

Shayna volunteered for guard duty. Her senses aren't as keen as Celia, but they work well enough to alert us of danger while Celia tries to rest.

"Are you doing okay, Shayna?" I ask. Partial inner wolf or not, she's tired.

Shayna smiles softly. "Yes, just thinking about Koda."

I smile too. I bet she is. My smile fades as my thoughts turn to Gemini. Our wolves won't come here. Not right away.

The tip of Shayna's sheath scratches the surface of the concrete when she inches closer. She stares out into the night, where screams and roars own the darkness. Occasionally, a ripple of magic drifts into the greenhouse and makes Sparky tremble. It's usually the residual power of a curse. But sometimes, like just before, it's the last bit of magic from a dying witch. I've lost count of the fallen, and I'm ready to lose my mind. I can't sit here and do nothing.

Emme returns from conducting a sweep. She wanted to get a sense of where the exits are in case we need to make a quiet escape. "The greenhouse is shaped like a cross. We're at the center and in the largest section. Each tip of the cross has a door leading out."

I rub my stressed eyes. "Thanks, Emme."

More likely than not, we'll blast our way out of here. That's just how we roll. But as the newly appointed head of the Wird girls, I've learned to analyze matters akin to special forces in order to survive.

I miss those days where Celia took the lead. I mean, I always offered support and my ideas, and never waited for permission to act. But as the oldest and our self-appointed protector, leading always came naturally to her. I'd fall into the role of backup and flame-thrower, and that was fine by me.

Since the start of her pregnancy, Celia stepped down from the role. It wasn't a formal announcement, just one that simply happened. Her baby and his safety understandably became the priority. I just wish there wasn't a need for the protection. This little baby deserves a chance at normal. Except he'll never have it.

"How are you doing?" Emme asks.

I think she's speaking to Celia until she edges closer to me. Her pretty shoes are covered with slime, and her dress is stretched out of shape and splattered with black goop. I'm more of a hot mess. My dress, being white, shows the spoils of combat. No dry cleaner in the world can save our clothes. It's just best to put them out of their misery and set them on fire.

"I'm fine. Just a little tired."

Emme can't sniff lies like the other supernaturals can. But she knows me well enough to determine I'm better left alone.

We look to Shayna when she turns her head. "What is it?" Emme asks.

Shayna's wide grin surprises me. "I can feel Koda. He's far, but I think he's in that direction." Her smile lessens. "Sometimes I feel him stronger than others."

I nod, thinking I know where she's headed. "Like when you're in danger."

"Yup, and when I'm in heat," Shayna admits.

"Ah, what?" I ask.

Shayna laughs. Emme finds somewhere new to look. "It's what Koda calls it. His wolf can tell when I'm ovulating, and lately, I'm like this ravaged, amorous beast."

At least she spared us from saying horny.

Shayna rolls her eyes. "You know, horny."

Never mind.

She holds out a hand. "I think I've mentioned how we like to role play."

"Yeah, yes, um," we all say at once, hoping she'll stop there.

She doesn't.

"One time, we were playing dirty pirate slut and Captain Hotness."

"Shayna," Emme admonishes. "That's so offensive."

"Oh, I'm sorry, Emme. I didn't mean to offend you. If it makes you feel better, we didn't go through with it. My hook kept getting in the way, and Koda's skirt was way too tight on him."

"Please stop speaking," Celia begs her.

Emme's face could set this whole place on fire. "Um, how are you doing, Celia?" she asks.

"I'm all right. I'm just trying to focus on the lake."

Emme smiles. "I know it's always brought you peace. Is it helping?"

Celia shakes her head. "Not as much as I'd like it to. It's restless tonight and calling to me."

I adjust my position. "Calling as in wants you with it?"

"I don't know about that," she says. "During some of our rougher times in the region, Tahoe has been more active, responding to the bad and relishing in the good we've managed. I suppose it's trying to communicate what it's feeling as a result of what's happening. That's what I mean by calling."

Her back straightens when the distant growls and hisses increase in cadence. She sighs when they dwindle slightly.

"You look terribly uncomfortable on the floor, Celia," Emme tells her. "Would you like me to look for something you can sit on or possibly rest against?"

"It's not a good idea, Emme," Celia replies. "If we have to abandon this place in a rush, we can't leave traces of our presence."

Emme nods. "That makes sense."

Shayna turns briefly away from her watch. "Should we make a run for it?" she asks. "Nothing is moving out there, yet. We may lose our chance if we don't act soon."

A shrilled scream cuts through the night. Above us, lavender sparks from a leftover spell hit the glass ceiling and cascade down like glitter. Celia scrunches her eyes closed.

"That was Genevieve's Captain of the Guards," Celia says.

I bite down on my lip. Bad idea since leftover dead things coat it. "This isn't good," I say. "Genevieve was grooming her to lead a sister coven in Oregon."

"Why Oregon?" Shayna asks.

"Genevieve is building covens along the entire Northwest," I explain. "Diana, her captain, was a tough witch and a hell of a strategist."

"What about Genevieve?" Emme asks. She wrings her hands. "Do you think she's still alive?"

"I don't know. I haven't caught traces of her voice in a long time," Celia admits. She shifts her weight, her hands rounding on her belly. "But I think Taran would have felt her death if she was gone."

My brows knit. "Me? Why me? We're not exactly close."

Celia smiles. "You were accepted as a sister of the coven. You'd feel her perish no matter what you felt for each other in life."

"Hey, she started it," I counter. I shrug. "Don't put the moves on my man, and I won't feel the need to smack you around."

Celia laughs. "She's a good person, Taran," she says. "A friend to the *weres*."

"Is she?' I smirk. "So, if you catch her cozying up to Aric and whispering sweet nothings into his ear with her oh-so voluptuous bosom inches from his face, you'd be cool with that?" She stops smiling. I clasp my hands behind my neck and stretch out my legs. "Yeah, kitty, kitty. That's what I thought."

Emme attempts to finger-comb her wild blonde hair. She gives up when she pulls out what may or may not be a piece of eyeball. She grimaces, shaking out her hand. "Taran, may I ask you a question without offending you?"

I chuckle. "Probably not, but shoot anyway."

She smiles. It's the first time I've seen her pretty grin all night. "The spell you cast was meant first and foremost to protect Celia and send her somewhere safe."

I sit up, listening closely. "That's right," I agree.

"Then why was she the last to appear here?" Emme asks. "You arrived first. Shouldn't it have been Celia?"

"And me last?" I offer.

"Yes."

Her question has merit. I give her the most feasible answer I can. "The power I launched at that creature fed the spell. Since I'm the one who cast it, it sent me first."

"Why was I next?" Emme asks.

"I fought it," Celia admits.

"Yes," I agree. "You didn't want to leave Aric."

Celia runs her fingers through her long waves. Unlike the rest of us, her hair isn't coated with eyeballs and bowel juices. "My biggest fear is losing my baby." She glances down. "But losing Aric . . . I don't want her to grow up without a daddy."

Like we did, she means. Shayna eases away from her post and speaks softly. "You said, 'her,'" she points out. "You've been calling the little dude 'him' for the longest time."

Shayna is purposely diverting the conversation away from losing Aric and back to Celia's sweet child, where it belongs. Celia knows as much but allows it anyway. She turns to me. "In Taran's vision, the baby I held looked like Aric." She smiles softly. "I don't know. I guess we assumed we'd have a son. Except every now and then, I start thinking that maybe she's a girl."

"Why, Ceel?" Shayna asks.

Celia's cheeks redden. "I don't know. It's nothing specific. I can just picture myself holding a little girl sometimes."

I almost suggest she's having twins, but keep my mouth shut. My vision seems like so long ago. I only saw one child. That doesn't mean there won't be more. Except given what's happening, there aren't any guarantees. The future remains unclear for all of us.

"I feel Puppy again," Shayna says when Celia grows quiet.

Celia greets her with a gentle smile. "I feel Aric too. He just seems far away."

This mate thing can really be a blessing at times like this. I feel Gemini and his twin. It's the only reason I haven't blown this entire compound into oblivion. It wouldn't be the first time I messed up Genevieve's place. As a matter of fact, she's probably come to expect it.

"Can I ask you another question?" Emme asks. "About the spell you cast to get us here?"

"Sure," I ask, wondering why she appears so worried.

"Why didn't I land here first?" Emme questions. "After spending the last few hours fighting, I was drained."

"The last few hours?" I ask.

A small line forms between her eyebrows. "Yes. Bren and I were gone most of the night." Her brow puckers when she looks up at the moon. "Um. I mean, it's almost dawn, correct?"

"No, honey," I tell her. I explain the passage of time. She takes it as well as I did.

Shock worsens her state. "It's still early?" she asks.

"Oh, yeah. The only real time seems to pass within the house. But I'm not positive." I roll my ankle. Emme was well enough to heal my injuries, but my muscles remain tense. "I wish there was a way to question those Nytes and get some answers."

"Knights?" Celia interrupts.

Her features appear strained. I'm not certain why, but it gives me the barest pause. "Not knights as in from a kingdom," I explain, trying to gauge what's happening. "Or night as in the time of day. N-Y-T-E. It's how Johnny announced his presence. I'm not sure if he was trying to be dramatic or if I presume their names wrong, but it's what I'm calling them."

"I understand," Celia says. Her breath picks up then slows as she finishes. "And you're certain it's Johnny?"

"I am," I reply. Her behavior bothers me. She's struggling to focus. I continue only when she appears to settle. "I can sense him. Maybe because I was the closest to him out of all of us."

"I can sense him a little too, dude," Shayna agrees. Unlike me, she doesn't appear to notice a change in Celia. "I didn't know who he was, not at first. But there was something familiar. Once all the, you know, killing started and the body parts began flying, and you told us it was him, I knew you were right." She wipes her nose irritably as if she can somehow still smell Johnny. "I think it's because he's muffling and meddling with the magic like you said."

"I think so too," Celia agrees. She adjusts her weight against the door. Whatever she was feeling appears to have passed.

I quiet, thinking back to the last time Johnny and I faced-off. We beat the absolute shit out of each other. I had a chance to kill him and should have burnt him to ash. But as hard as I fought, I couldn't cast that final blow. Maybe it was because in the little time we knew each other, I became his closest friend.

Friend. I repeat the word in my head as I think how much we've lived through. What a fool I was to think of him that way.

Guilt ravages me. It's the first time I've allowed it to. The whole "trying not to die thing" squashed it down earlier, but now it's here. Like a corporeal being, it points a nasty finger at me.

"I should have killed him."

The words just come out. Celia angles her chin, scrutinizing me in the same way she does when I've suggested something crazy. "If you think this is your fault, you're wrong, Taran. Johnny is the one sending all these Nytes."

"Only because he's alive to do so," I add. I take a chance and remove my shoes. It's a mistake. My feet swell instantly. No way will I be able to slip them back on.

Shayna changes posts, this one slightly closer to us. "No worries, T," she says quietly.

My brows quirk up to my hairline. "No worries? You're kidding, right? Do you see the mess we're in? Have you calculated the body count? All these powerful beings in one place, I should have just tied a bow around our necks and turned us over to Johnny."

"That's not what I mean, dude," Shayna tells me. She cracks her neck from side to side. "Back then, Johnny wasn't the same Johnny he is now. Yeah, he murdered his fans, cost us our people, and tried to take us out." She shrugs. "But he was a desperate little ol' Fate. Desperate people do desperate things, you feel me? Who knows what we would have done in his place? If things were different, if we didn't have each other? Maybe we'd have chosen different paths."

I smirk, knowing she's trying to make me feel better. "You don't mean that."

Shayna winks. "Nope. But it's not easy to kill someone you called a friend. I'm glad I wasn't in your stilettos, T. I like to see the good in others. Whether you want to admit it, you do too." She smiles, for the first time giving me a glimpse of the wolf residing inside of her. "Except now you know there's no good left. Not after all this. No one will blame you for what comes next." She blows a breath hard enough to flutter her bangs. "He's made his own deathbed. Time for us to tuck him in."

Shayna is granting me permission to kill. It's not something someone as perky and goodhearted as her would typically do. But I need to hear it.

Silence crawls along the area, allowing us to hear the gentle breeze sweep through the pines and Celia's growling stomach.

She groans, her features reflecting that same tension again. "Sorry."

I frown. "You didn't get a chance to eat, did you?"

She rests her head against the door. "I had some snacks before we left and in the car on the way over."

Celia is constantly "snacking" on burgers, epic milkshakes, and slabs of venison. Her inner tigress always gave her the appetite and metabolism of a few linebackers, but since the start of her pregnancy, I've started keeping bacon in my purse. Let's just say Celia gets a tad bit hangry.

The tension darkening Celia's delicate features return. Okay. Now I know what's what.

Emme rises, backing away. "You want me to scrounge up some berries or something?"

I slip away too. Celia is famished. A hungry Celia is a *scary* Celia. "There aren't any fruit trees in the greenhouse," I say. "Just herbs and such."

It sucks to share this not so great news. Especially when Celia meets me with a glare that demands bacon.

"Would you like me to gather some mint, possibly basil, or maybe cilantro?" Emme asks.

It occurs to me Emme has forgotten where we are. "They'll choke you," I mumble.

Emme tilts her head. "What will?" she asks. "The mint?"

"And the basil, and probably the cilantro too if the broom humpers grew it." I recall how badly those little saplings hate being bothered.

Emme glances from me to Celia. "Please tell me you're joking," she says.

"I wish I was," I say, cautiously. Any trace of Celia slowly dissolves in her features. Behind her eyes lurks her beast, and that beast is licking her chops.

I keep talking, hoping to distract her. "Herbs dedicated to potions only allow you to pick them when they reach thirteen inches and beneath a quarter moon. Even then, the rules require you bring backup. They'll choke your ass and bury you if they catch you alone, and it'll be days or weeks before anyone finds you."

Emme breathes a sigh of relief when Celia lowers her head to rest against her knees. "Taran," she says gently. "I apologize, but I was left with the impression Plant Day was the easiest part of witch school."

"Compared to Anti-Possession class and Séance and Sciences, it was." I huff. "And don't get me started on the snapdragons. Bastards."

Celia's stomach growls like a motor.

And then, so does Celia.

She lifts her head, her tigress eyes glowing in the moonlight. "There's a rat, ten yards away, drinking water from a puddle." She swallows hard. "I can hear it. I can smell it."

Emme's eyes widen. Shayna slowly turns her head and gapes at her. I don't move at all, scared I'll draw her attention away from the rat and onto me.

Celia resumes that odd staccato breathing I noticed earlier. Again, her ravaged stomach growls. If that's not bad enough, Junior kicks, demanding to be fed.

"Celia," Emme says, her voice cautious. "Would you like us to get you the rat?"

Celia's gaze turns primal. Slowly, she nods, what's left of her civility dwindling fast.

"To um, eat?" Emme clarifies.

Celia makes a noise. Not quite an affirmative grunt. Not quite a growl. And, oh, *man*, not quite human either.

"Ceel," Shayna says. "Do you really think this is a good idea? Think about what you're saying. I get you're a tad hungry—"

Shayna startles when Celia fixes her deadly gaze on her. Celia *does* think it's a good idea. In fact, at this moment, it's the greatest idea ever.

I veer on Shayna. "She wants the rat. Get her the damn rat."

Shayna gasps. "Me? Why me?"

I wave a hand at her. "You're the one with the weapons, and you have the essence of a freaking werewolf lurking inside of you for hell's sake."

"You have fire, T," Shayna shoots back. "As in, let's fire up the barbie, matey."

I scowl at her. "Are you going for Australian or pirate, here? Either way, both suck."

Shayna's jaw pops open. "*You* can kill the little varmint and cook it in one shot."

I scoff. "Oh, and now we're from Texas."

If it sounds like I'm trying to stall, I am.

Emme crinkles her nose. "I hate to say this, but Shayna has a point. It's like the old saying, two birds with one stone, Taran."

I ram my fists against my hips. "Figures you'd take her side," I accuse.

Emme regards me all offended-like. "What is that supposed to mean?"

I point a rather irate finger at her. "You always back Shayna up. Every time. All the time."

"Ah, T," Shayna says. She motions to Celia.

Celia is smiling, in all the wrong ways possible. She glides her tongue across a row of now pointy fangs.

"Now's not a good time to argue, dude," Shayna insists. "Just get her the rat. We won't watch, and nobody has to know. Oh, except Koda. You know I tell him everything. Oh, and maybe Aric, too, so he knows we took care of her and fed her in his absence. And Gemini, too, since if Aric knows, he'll know and—"

"I'm not killing a rat, and I'm especially not feeding one to Celia," I say. Shit. Hungry or not, I can't be the one to offer my sister rat fricassee. A rabbit, maybe. Probably even a raccoon. Who am I kidding? I'm still not over the toad I ran over when I was learning to drive.

Celia's next growl is more terrifying than the last and promises death. We scramble away, placing ourselves as far as we can get from her in the crowded space.

"It mocks me," Celia thunders.

Shayna sighs. "Does it, Ceel? Does it really?"

Celia's maw protrudes, and she hisses. Shayna's eyelids practically peel back and over her head. She holds out her sword. "T. Just kill it before Celia eats us."

"She's not going to eat us." Yeah, Celia's more than a little feral. But aren't we all when we're hungry and—

I almost scream when she rises and prowls forward.

Celia is no longer my sister. She's an extremely hungry and famished predator.

Chapter Thirteen

I knock over a stand of flowerpots when Celia stalks forward, her keen gaze set at my throat. The pots land in a booming crash that doesn't quite muffle the sound of my pounding heart.

Celia charges, leaping over me and barreling down the path between the plants. The rest of us exchange stunned, yet relieved glances, and take off after her. Shayna easily takes the lead, and even barefoot, I make longer strides than Emme.

We ground to a halt when we find Celia crouched low, her long nails protruding into long, thin claws. I don't initially notice the snapdragons until they click their little mouths open and closed, demanding a sprinkling of magical water. The closest ones stretch out their leaves, tugging at what remains of my dress.

I slap them away. "Knock it off," I bite out.

Their clicking intensifies, drawing too much attention for my comfort. Except right now, they're not my priority. My hangry sister is.

Directly in front of Celia stoops the rat. It swipes at its face, disregarding the growling tigress watching her. I expect Celia to gobble the pathetic-looking thing right up. My sister is just *that* hungry. Instead, Celia tilts her head, examining her meal a little too closely.

I start toward her when a sense of wrongness and death fills the air. The intensity is strong and tries to shove me away. I lift my hands, ready to act. Like with all things tonight, this rat is not what it seems.

"What the hell is that?" I ask.

The rat glides its beady eyes from me to Celia and sneers, a pretty ballsy move given its withering state. Its response alone would give me pause, but it's that extra whiff of sickness and gloom that fires sparks from my fingertips.

"Celia, Taran," Emme warns. "Don't approach it. There's something wrong with it."

"Oh, yeah, there is," Shayna agrees. "The little critter is sick, and I'm guessing a bit evil."

I hold up a hand when Shayna yanks a knife from its sheath and takes aim. "Wait," I say. "Not yet."

"You sure?" Shayna asks. She holds tight to her knife. "Master Splinter it's not, T."

A horrible cracking sound interrupts the nasty hiss building in the rat's throat. Its back bows in the wrong direction, snapping the spine as it crumbles to the ground.

"Oh, this isn't good," I say.

Celia backs away, so do we. She scans our surroundings. "Is something else here?" she asks.

"No," I reply. "It did that to itself."

The rodent lifts its head, its body trembling in pain. The small bones along its back shift and move in odd and grotesque patterns beneath patches of scraggly gray fur. Slowly, its limbs expand. Tendons and joints stretch and pop into place. What remains of its fur dissolves inward into dirty and grossly wide pores.

The rat's form alternates back and forth between animal and subhuman, whimpering in torment. It takes time for the body to stop changing from what we found to what it ultimately becomes.

The whole thing . . . is damn hard to watch. More than once, I look away, the sickening effort churning my insides and making me nauseous. When a *were* changes, the process is almost instantaneous. When Celia alters parts of her body into her tigress counterpart, it's mesmerizing. This, what's happing before us, is disturbing. There's no strong beast resuming its equally strong human counterpart, nor is there beauty like with my sister's unique magic. The animal we found was sick and injured, and the naked woman who reveals herself is even more so.

Large lumps of torn and matted hair droop over emaciated shoulders. Deep cuts are sliced into the skin covering her breasts, stomach, and inner thighs. Whoever had her had fun making her bleed. Some of her injuries are old, others fresh enough to trickle blood.

This woman is a relatively young witch despite the harsh lines wrinkling her face. I recognize the spell she used—Mirror. Either she was close to graduating the program, or strong enough to pull off a spell this advanced.

Her long head of greasy blonde hair is a mix of tangles and bald patches. Her eyes—Jesus—are sunken in the way that happens when the tears run out and that horrible numbness sets in.

She wipes her mouth and rises, exposing several spots where teeth are missing. The lack of bruises to her face suggest the teeth were pulled out. I know she sees us. Instead of explaining her presence and, well, her condition, she staggers to the water pump, her dirty feet stepping through the puddle she drank from.

An old bucket remains perched beneath the pump. The witch doesn't bother pumping fresh water. She cups her hands and dips them into the bucket, relishing the long sip she takes.

"Oh, my goodness," Emme says. "Please don't do that. I-I can help you."

Emme recognizes her lack of strength. She likely can't pump the water.

"No," the witch tells Emme. Her irate tone stops Emme in place. "I'm thirsty."

Her voice is dry. The water is filthy. Neither matter. She knows she's dying.

"I-I can heal you," Emme says. She steps forward, gathering the gentle pale light of her healing powers around her hands.

Emme means well. She always does. Except this witch's injuries are beyond repair. Her residual magic is the only thing keeping her standing. Still, I don't stop Emme. This witch doesn't pose the threat she once did.

The witch shakes her head. "Even if you could, you don't want to heal me. I'm the cause of your pain." She sniffs, her fingertips passing along her defeated features as if she doesn't remember her face. "I let him in. The Fate. It took a great deal from me, but I did it. I walked this compound long before he stepped foot, and I made it so he could take his place among us."

It explains the sense of evil that surrounds her.

"Is that possible?" Shayna asks me. "The witches spent, like, months strengthening the wards."

I don't listen to Shayna as much as I study the witch's words. "You walked the compound long before he stepped foot," I repeat. She doesn't just mean walked. This is a spell. "You created a path for him. With magic."

The witch glares at me, annoyed that I somehow spoiled her big reveal. That's when I'm certain I'm right. Maybe I did learn a thing or two in witch school.

"I don't understand," Emme says.

"You can't weaken the wards," I say. "They're set up in layers. It's what makes them so strong."

Shayna motions to the witch. "Then how did she get little ol' Johnny in, T?"

"She was one of many who helped strengthen the wards. I'm right, aren't I?" She shuts her mouth and stares at me. It's a genius plan, really. If I didn't have the urge to slap her upside the head, I might actually give her some credit. "You knew where they were, so you cut out a path, like a zigzag or something similar that would be hard to detect through all those layers."

"Or more likely a maze," Emme reasons. Her attention turns to Shayna. "Should a different witch securing the ward come across an opening to the path, she would meet a wall, misleading her into thinking the wards remained intact."

"Exactly," I agree. "It provided a false sense of security. The only way to detect the breach was if it were made visible either on the ground or by air." It's brilliant. Then again, we never mistook the bad guys for stupid.

"How did Johnny see it?" Celia asks. Her face is a mask of wary predator and pity as she regards the ragged soul standing before us. Celia feels for the witch's fragile state, not that it will be enough to spare her. Bottom line, she screwed us over.

For all the witch seemed to brag about her brilliance, she turns tight-lipped, taking another gulp of dirty water instead of answering Celia.

"A blood sacrifice would make it visible," I answer for her. I take another long look at her frail condition. It's too easy to feel sorry for her, given how close to death she is. Except, I learned a long time ago how manipulative supernaturals can be. This witch is no exception. Hell, look at who she let into Camp Genevieve. "Did you kill her? Or did someone do it for you?"

"I'm stronger than I look," she spits out.

I've clearly insulted her without trying. Might as well keep going. "Strong or not, you didn't act alone," I tell her.

This is the moment to figure out who else betrayed us, and I'm not letting it go. I won't know for sure if she's lying. But maybe I'll find out enough.

The witch runs her dirty hand along the spout. "We tested the path on the creatures first." She laughs in a way that projects rising hysteria than humor. "You wouldn't believe how many died trying to find the right ways in. But the Fate made them plentiful and beautiful. There was no end to his power or his creativity."

Shayna quirks a brow. "You sound a little impressed there, dudette."

Shayna isn't one to be cruel. Like me, she's stunned by how taken the witch is with Johnny. It says a lot about her character. This is a person who's likely always sought power and prestige.

The witch narrows her eyes at Shayna. "He is everything."

"I don't know about that," I say.

My dismissal earns me the death glare. Wow. She was *tortured*. While Johnny, at least the Johnny I knew, is incapable of harming a woman like this, he had to be aware of what was happening. Yet here she is, bragging and seemingly rapt by his mojo.

I'm not certain if she feels the need to convince me of Johnny's awesomeness, or if she thinks we're her last chance to confess her sins before she keels over. Whatever it is, she spills the details without any prompting.

"Once I created the way in, we were able to hide the creatures inside the manor. That was my idea," she says, the barest hint of pride in her voice. "They dissolved into the shadows, falling into a dream state in the classrooms where the stupid witches whispered their dirty thoughts and where they toyed with their inferior magic." A smile lifts the corner of her dry, cracked lips. "His pets hid in plain sight, beneath their beds, and where they bathed, their bodies naked and gloriously exposed to the Fate."

It's more than I ever needed to know. Thanks for the nightmares there, kid.

"They slept," she repeats, her eyes closing with pleasure. "Helping the Fate learn their magic."

"So, Johnny could ultimately manipulate it," I say. She appears to fall asleep standing. My comment wakes her right up.

"Yes," she replies, another scathing glare aimed my way. She doesn't like me answering for her. Her problem, not mine.

"It was the hardest magic I ever tried," she adds. "I never thought I could perform such a task. But I did, and it worked. I did everything they asked and more." She coughs, spitting bile mixed with blood on the floor. "All that the Fate needed was the key to open the door."

And insert the sacrifice here.

This witch is screwed two ways from Sunday and double-dipped into a vat of crazy every day in between. She might have started off with issues, her toe skimming along the pool of insecurity like the rest of us. Or she could have been unstable from the start. Whatever Johnny and his crew did pushed her to a place she won't return from.

"What's your name?"

Her attention grounds on Celia. She didn't expect Celia to speak again. I imagine she expects a quick death, a slash of claws across her throat, or maybe even a knife to the heart. She won't get off that easy. Not once we hand her over to Genevieve.

"What's your name?" Celia repeats, her voice neither kind nor violent.

"Bridette," the witch says.

"Why did you betray us, Bridette?" Celia asks. Like the rest of us, we're not impressed by Johnny or the magic she used to let him in. They're murderers. All their great feats of magic won't change that.

I walk to Celia's side, the cool concrete at my feet sending painful waves through my calves, instead of offering reprieve. It's not that Celia needs me, but I need her. Bridette isn't a demon to kill or one of those monsters to take out before it tears out our insides. Those, I aim for and fire. It's easy. I don't respect the lives of those beings, not when they're gunning for me. And although she caused so much damage, I can't just shoot and fire.

Bridette is a poor, miserable soul who made all the wrong choices. I'm still not certain, though, that she sees it.

She dips her hands into the water again, her thirst more important to her than us. Several large roaches scurry around the rim. Emme clasps her wrists, trying to stop her. "Please don't do that," Emme tells her. "You're better than this."

No, I don't think she is.

Bridette opens her mouth enough to expose the gaping holes where a pretty smile once lived. "It's cold," she says. "It helps the pain."

"Why did you betray us?" Celia asks, again. Unlike before, there's more force to her tone. Bridette may be incapable of tears, but Celia has plenty for all of us. "What was so important to you that you chose to side with Fate?"

"You love your child," Bridette says. She's not asking. It's a fact she already understands. She takes another long pull of water, swishing it in her mouth before allowing it to spill down her chin and neck. Her weary gaze lowers to Celia's belly. "From the moment you heard he was coming, you loved him."

When Bridette tries to laugh, only a haunting and ragged wisp releases. "It's strange, don't you think, tigress?" she asks. "To become so completely enchanted with something the size of a dot? It has no strength. It has no thoughts or ability to communicate. Yet it still manages to steal your heart even as it leeches from you, taking shape inside you because of you and everything you do for him."

Those tears Bridette lacked find their way into her voice. "You'll do anything for him. Lie, hurt, kill, and betray. Whatever it takes, you'll do. It's that power children have over us."

Bridette slaps at the bucket, knocking it over. The water sprays my exposed shins, chilling my bones and coating the marrow with ice. I want to cover my legs and dry them with what remains of my dress. Instead, I don't move, her words keeping me in place.

"You think you'll love nothing more," she says. "Then the gods gift you with another, expanding your heart to hold so much love you're certain you'll explode."

Bridette sways from side to side, humming what sounds like a nursery song in a language I can't make out.

"Where are your children now?" I get the words out myself. Celia can't. We know Bridette's story doesn't end well.

Bridette looks around as if she can't understand where the voice came from. It happens to those tortured souls like Bridette. Things stop making sense, and clarity abandons you.

Indignation that I don't expect from someone so feeble greets me as cold as the water pooled at my feet. "I never found my mate. Not like those foul mutts do. But I did find a woman who loved me as hard as I needed her to." She raises her hands, her bitterness oddly morphing to excitement. "Together, we found a *were* more than willing to share my bed."

Shayna's gaze shifts to me. Neither of us like the "foul mutts" reference, or all the crazy Bridette is spilling like a busted dam. We keep our mouths shut, anyway, waiting, listening, wanting to gather as much information as we can.

"It didn't take long. He fucked me just once." She smiles. "I liked it." Her smile fades. "I shouldn't have liked it, it made Louisa mad. She didn't see what I saw that he was fertile, and his seed was strong." The weight of her confession appears too affect her. She reaches for the spout to steady herself. "The next mutt wasn't as virile. It took a few times until I was pregnant with my second. They weren't *were* or witches like Louisa and I expected." She shakes her head. "Not like yours is bound to be. But we loved them. They were ours."

Her voice trails off, and agony reflects across her gaunt features. Only death has the gift for scarring a person just so.

"Your partner is dead, isn't she?" I ask.

Grief drenches her form, the burdens she's carried threatening to topple her. She tightens her grasps on the spout, her only lifeline in the dank and dim surroundings.

"Johnny killed Louisa?" Shayna asks. As a wife herself, she can't imagine her life without Koda, let alone allowing someone to manipulate her into hurting him. Except that's exactly what Bridette did. It's as obvious as the scars painting her body. "Why . . . How could you help the man who'd take her from you?"

Bridette's choked sob has her curling forward. Still no tears, no reprieve from her torment. "We wanted our children to live," she says. "Whatever it took, we swore to each other we'd do it."

I have the feeling this isn't what her wife had in mind.

"Are you listening?" Bridette asks. "Do you hear me, tigress?"

Celia isn't the only one standing before her. Bridette isn't so far gone to think as much. But her anger isn't aimed at us. Oh, no. It's aimed at my pregnant sister, and it pisses me off.

"My children don't deserve less than yours," Bridette bites out. Dark-red blood pools in her mouth, dribbling over her dried, splitting lips. "My children weren't loved or cared for any less."

Pity is the only thing that keeps me from smacking Bridette. She won't accept the consequences for her actions and is casting blame where it doesn't belong. Celia is a good person. If Bridette had gone to Celia and Aric, they would have protected her and her family. Instead, she crossed to the dark side, no matter what it cost her.

"You love your children," Celia says. When Bridette nods, Celia swallows hard, tears cutting lines into her cheeks. "So did the *weres* you helped kill tonight." She circles Bridette, her claws retracting and protruding as she attempts to rein in her beast. "As did the witches who thought they'd return home to kiss their daughters and sons good night. You not only took their lives, you robbed their children of their childhoods and those they most loved."

"No," Bridette stammers. "You did. You and your child."

Celia's claws extend to their full, deadly length. "You think this is my baby's fault? You think I killed these people? How dare you. My son is destined to help the world. Not because I deemed him to be, because he was chosen."

"Ceel." Shayna tries to snag Celia's arm when Celia lurches toward Bridette.

Celia breaks away, shoving her face into Bridette's. "Until my son is born. Until he stands strong enough to face the evil that's coming, I stand for him, and so do my sisters. We're the ones keeping evil at bay." Bridette shrinks away. Celia doesn't stop. "You . . . all you did was help the very thing that took your wife."

"They threatened my children!" Bridette yells, as if we somehow missed the point.

Shayna and I glance around. Bridette is being loud. It may be a tactic to lure the Nytes and help kill Celia. Mostly, I think Bridette has unraveled and no longer cares about anything. Shayna unsheathes the dagger at her hip. She'll slit Bridette's throat. She'll make it quick. But neither she nor I have the heart to do it.

Neither does Celia.

"Do you want me to feel sorry for you, Bridette?" Celia asks. Her emotions get the best of her, trembling her voice and body. "I already do. I can't imagine the fear and pain you've endured. But to hurt other babies so yours won't hurt, to kill those innocents trying to come together as one . . . You were wrong to do what you did. Can't you see it cost you everything you sought to protect?"

"You would have done the same," Bridette screams at her. Her weakening state curls her inward. "Don't you stand here and lie."

"She's not lying," I snap. Chosen baby or not, Celia would never harm an innocent. "She— No, *we'd* find a way out.

Bridette laughs. It's phony, with enough bitterness to grate my skin. I suppose she's trying to demonstrate self-righteousness even as she stands naked and dying. I can't tell if she was always like this, or if she was once kind and good. Because of her role in this mess, I'll never have the chance to know.

"It must be nice to have each other," Bridette sneers. She wipes her mouth irritably, coating her dirty skin with more dark fluid. "Aren't you just lucky?"

I look to each of my sisters. "Yes," I reply quietly. "We are."

Celia stops breathing and falls perfectly still, a tigress in the jungle having spotted another predator in her turf.

Shayna follows her lead, raring for a fight. Her eyes dart in every direction as she leans one foot forward and prepares to pounce. They hear something.

"What is it?" Emme whispers. Her hands lift, readying to act.

"*Death*," Bridette answers.

Chapter Fourteen

I don't see the Nytes emerge. But Sparky senses them well enough.

Shadows twist and lift from the darkness, coiling around Emme and Bridette. They take shape from one breath to the next, forming into vampires more akin to Nosferatu than the sinfully beautiful creatures they're known as.

My right hand shoots out, casting a glow and scaring off two Nytes who rush me. The closest Nyte hisses, his long tongue slipping in and out between his crooked fangs. I edge away, the light Sparky emits keeping him at bay. Celia ducks and dodges the pair of shadows who round on her. She leaps backward, landing at my side in a crouch.

Shayna spins, using the momentum to unsheathe her sword, swinging it at the Nyte who targets her.

Sharp steel cuts into the partially shadowed creature. As it takes shape, it glances down at the wound, curious like a child. The Nyte beside him pokes at the slice in the skin, moistening the tips of his claws with dark fluid. The way Shayna struck and swung, she should have cut it in half. The only thing that saved it was that it hadn't solidified.

Sparky's glow intensifies, stretching out into a circle. The Nytes hiss, keeping just outside the edge.

Emme and Bridette couldn't escape. These Nytes are too fast; Emme and Bridette can't do more than stand. Thin, knotted fingers wrap over their mouths and throats. The one holding Emme gives a squeeze. Emme winces, whimpering in pain.

With an expert flick, Shayna tosses her dagger. It spins, jetting through the translucent skull of Emme's captor. The thing giggles, I think. His concave chest pushes in and out, and several high-pitched wheezes escape. His friends join in. I'll give Johnny this, his kids are creepy as fuck.

Shayna's initial attack worked against us. They're learning our weaknesses and building one hell of an offense.

Celia's claws protrude from her hands and bare feet. Luckily, only the side of her foot grazes mine. She waits within the protection of my light, ready to act. Shayna is at my back, flexing and relaxing her grip over the hilt of her sword as the remaining Nytes circle us.

The Nytes giggle and shove each other, trying to force the weaker of their brethren into my light. One of the smaller Nytes falls forward. My light neither burns it nor causes any damage. Still, it scampers away, frightened.

The real vampires of this world aren't affected by light or sun. These fear something that can't harm them. I take a chance and step toward Emme and Bridette, hoping to use their fear in my favor.

They scramble away, taking Emme and Bridette with them. I try again, Celia and Shayna moving with me.

"Let them go," I say, putting every bit of my anger in each syllable. "Right now."

"Or what?"

I angle in the direction of the voice, just enough to catch the owner. Anger stabs each word I say, erasing the shock I would have otherwise demonstrated when I see who it is. "Or I will fucking fry you, bitch."

The vampire, the one I saw flirting with that Lesser witch in the hall earlier, grins. Bridette might have paved the way for Johnny to enter over time, but the Lesser witch, the one this vamp chose to sacrifice, was the final key that allowed Johnny and his army in.

The vamp rakes his gaze down my body and laughs. The Nytes join him since, well, this shit isn't disturbing enough. "My dear," he tells me. "Even you, so wickedly hot, can't burn a shadow."

I can if it takes enough form, asshole. I don't offer him that little tidbit. These freaks don't need to know anything more.

"What do you want?" I ask. It's not like I don't know. I just need time to figure things out and catch him off guard.

His sleazy features lock onto Celia. He licks his lips, taking her in. "You know what I want," he says.

Man, this idiot is so going to fry.

Shayna presses closer to Celia. Me, I keep talking. "What will you give us in exchange?"

"Life," he replies.

I suppose he means to sound tempting. "Is that what you offered Bridette over there?" I shake my head. "I don't know, moron, it doesn't look like it's worked out for her."

Bridette glares at me. I roll my eyes. This witch will go down kicking and screaming that she made the right choice.

"She had her purpose, now it's fulfilled."

"That's some bullshit purpose," I say. I swing my light back and forth, just to freak out the Nosferatu bastards and make like I'm the one in control. The snapdragons click their little mouths and little teeth at them when they draw too close. I grin. Maybe I am in control.

"Careful, boys," I tell the vamps. "You don't want to anger those little plants."

I steal a glance at Emme. She blinks back. Yeah, my girl understands.

"You think me or Master Fate cares?" His lascivious gaze returns to Celia. "She's all we want."

"Master *Fate*?" Shayna clarifies. She looks at me. "Am I the only one who thought he said masturbate?"

"No."

"Nope."

Even Emme shakes her head.

The vamp does not approve of the reference. The Nytes do, cracking up in a way that does nothing to ease the tension in the room.

"Shut up," he tells them.

They continue laughing anyway, so caught up in whatever they're feeling they don't notice Emme's building power. Like the other Nytes, they border on mindless, following orders of their master instead of strategizing.

"Looks to me like you're not even in charge," I say. "These dumbasses don't even respect you." I grin. "Or is it Johnny who's laughing at you?"

"You know nothing of the master." The vamp storms forward, his pride getting in the way of business.

He whips around, sensing Emme's magic a little too late. "What are you doing?" he demands.

In a windstorm of movement, the rear door bursts open, and every snapdragon in the greenhouse comes at us.

The saplings, irritated from lack of water and from being yanked from their posts without permission, elongate their stems and leaves to absurd lengths, wrapping around anything they can reach.

Celia hauls Emme and Bridette away, sparing them from the snap-dragons' wrath. The Nytes who held Emme and Bridette don't stand a chance. The saplings cocoon them, entrapping their shadowy forms long enough for Shayna to behead them. The remaining vamps scatter, van-ishing beneath the rows of stands and cowering in the shadows.

Celia overturns an entire row. It crashes onto a Nyte trying to escape on the other side. Celia launches herself on him, straddling his shoulders and tearing his head off.

Hmm. Yeah. We're supposed to be protecting her.

The snapdragons lose their shit; so do all the remaining plants. Emme holds them off by pushing them away from us and into the swarm of Nytes.

Enchanted rose bushes tear the solidifying Nytes to pieces with their deadly thorns. A thyme bush snags a fleeing Nyte by the ankles and beats him against the concrete, crushing his skull and spilling the contents across the concrete.

I'm zapping every shadow zooming past me attempting to flee or fight. My lightning shocks them, solidifying body parts the plants latch onto and punish.

Shayna is a woman possessed. She pivots from side to side, avoiding the plants reaching for her and swinging her sword with precision. Heads roll, literally, and black fluid sprays across the floor.

We're so busy fighting the vamps and staying clear of the enchanted plants and trees, it takes me a moment to realize the real vampire is gone, and so is Bridette.

I clasp a charging Nyte by the throat and slam him on the concrete. "Where is your master?" I demand.

The thing hisses, his tongue lapping frantically, trying to taste me. The lower part of his body dissolves into a shadowy form. Sparky lights up with power, preventing him from fully vanishing. "Where is your master?" I scream.

A throaty hiss mixed with a sneer shakes through his core, rattling me. It's unsettling, so is the creature's voice. "Nyte has come. Nyte will end you."

I clench my teeth. "You're wrong."

Sparky squeezes without my consent, cracking the multiple bones that make up its throat. The Nyte's eyes bulge, and his tongue lashes in circles. Sparky wants him to suffer. I just want this to end. I take over, averting my gaze as I snap his neck.

The Nyte falls limp, what remains of him soiling the ground.

A rather perturbed snapdragon reaches out and smacks me across the face. I smack it back. "We're on the same side, asshole!" I yell.

Explosive, popping sounds fill the area. Birch, ash, alder, and willow trees break free of their pots, their extending roots dragging them forward in a spastic rage. Mouths form along each knot, and they grow from plantlet to tree pretty damn quick.

Shayna is aghast and urges me back. "Dude!"

I bolt, dragging Shayna toward the closest exit. "Time to go, girls," I say, moving faster.

Celia tosses the Nyte in her grasp in two separate pieces, her eyes widening when she sees a forest chasing us. Emme buys us time by throwing a Nyte with her *force* directly at the encroaching trees.

What these trees do to the Nyte . . . Let's just say I've seen my share of alarming shit. This easily makes the top five.

Branches *ram every orifice* in the Nyte's body, pushing through and back out. They knock out the eyes, slide out of the ears to wrap around his throat, and protrude through the stomach to wave bloody intestines at us. Oh, and it just gets rosier from there.

We haul ass. In all the battles I've faced throughout the years, I've never run so fast. Celia has Emme by the hand, dragging her so she doesn't get left behind.

"Oh, my goodness. Oh, my goodness," Emme says. "I didn't know they were going to do that!"

The shrieks of the other Nytes the trees encounter cut through the air. "Oh, *goodness*," Emme says again.

Shayna pats Emme on the arm. "It's okay, Emme. They're in the light now."

I know she's trying to make Emme feel better, but no way are those Nytes having tea with Saint Teresa.

My lungs burn with how hard I'm running and leaping over destroyed crap I have no business leaping over. I'm not a runner, damn it. I do Zumba, for shit's sake.

We break through the exit, the cold air pummeling our chests and the damp lawn chilling our feet.

Celia grounds to halt. Even pregnant, she's not out of breath. Shayna is breathing a little fast but is otherwise okay. Emme and I are doing awesome. And by that, I mean we're not puking yet.

"Taran," Celia says.

The tone in her voice is enough to alert us of danger. My right arm shoots up, lighting our surroundings. Celia's claws are out. Shayna is flicking her wrist and spinning her sword. Her gaze takes in the Nosferatu Nytes that are suddenly there and have us enclosed.

The vampire steps out, holding Bridette by the throat. Her limbs hang loose at her sides. She locks eyes with me. It's the only proof I have that she's still alive.

The vampire is shirtless, allowing him to extend his white angelic wings. FYI, vampires don't have wings.

That little turd Johnny somehow did this to him. Damn, what else has he done? And who else has he altered?

"What's wrong?" he asks me. "Haven't you ever seen a god?"

He flaps his wings, all pretty like, causing a feather to fall to the ground. It dissolves into the earth like a melting snowflake. At once, a plant grows, and a white flower blooms. Cute, but it won't stop me from killing him.

"Honey, those wings don't impress me." I shrug. "It's like sprinkling glitter on shit. You're still shit, only sparkly."

"You *bitch*," he snaps.

I sigh as if bored. "That's my confirmation name. Try something original, freak."

This vamp isn't one for witty comebacks and only smart enough to surround himself with those he thinks will get him far. "Kill them," he orders the Nytes.

"Wait," Bridette says.

The Nytes pause and look to Bridette. They're about as bright as the vamp.

"She is not the one you obey, fools," the vamp yells at them.

They start to advance. Sparky flares, holding them back.

"My children," Bridette says. Spittle leaks from her mouth from the effort it takes her to speak. "What will happen to my children?"

The vampire throws his head back laughing, the viciousness behind it telling me more than I want to know.

Oh, God . . .

"Stupid whore," he tells her. "They've been dead for weeks."

Bridette falls still, and so does the air around us.

The Nytes look high and low, noting something is different. Darkness is approaching, they just don't realize it's coming from Bridette.

Something evil fires deep within her, born of a mother's broken heart.

"*Muerte*," she spits.

My fist comes down against the earth as Celia screams my name. Ripples of power burn through the wet grass and into the ground surrounding us, sending blue and white flames shooting toward the sky.

It's a beacon of beautiful and brilliant light, and our sole protection against Bridette's death curse.

My teeth ache from what it costs me to maintain my flame and shield us against Bridette's final spell. The Nytes are reduced to puddles of black liquid. The god the vamp claimed to be doesn't fare much better. His wings dry and crumble, falling to the moist grass in portions. His stunned face follows, then his body, the remains covering Bridette's naked corpse. One by one, everything dies around us, including the nearby foliage and the enchanted plants in the greenhouse.

In life, Bridette was weak in mind and in spirit. But she wasn't too weak to avenge her family.

Chapter Fifteen

I maintain my shield for several minutes. I'm not sure how long a death curse of this caliber can last. So, I hold it, long after everything stops withering and dying around us.

By the time I finally drop it, we're soaked with sweat, my sisters from my fire and me from the energy it took to hold it.

The salty sting across my eyes worsens when I wipe them. "Sorry," I say. "That just really sucked."

They swipe their faces, doing their best not to look anywhere near Bridette.

Celia's big wavy hair is stuck to her face. "Don't apologize, Taran," she says. "If it wasn't for you, we'd be dead."

"Yeah." I take a step, and man, does it cost me. I've been part of other fights that last for days. This is different. There's no end and no time to rest. That little break on the concrete floor earlier was it. Even then, we didn't exactly relax.

"We have to get out of here," I say. "If the Nytes didn't know where we were, they know now." I motion to the sky. "No one can snag attention like me."

"I hate what she did." Emme's quiet voice draws our attention.

My youngest sister is beyond exhausted. She wraps her arms around her body, protecting her cooling skin against the frigid temperature. She looks slightly beyond Bridette's unmoving body and where her blank stare gazes in our direction.

"I hate it too," I reply. We don't have time to waste being sad, yet here we are. "But I hate what happened to her family more."

Shayna flicks the knives at her waist in the air and juggles them. I can't blame her. She doesn't have to look at Bridette this way, and should another scary monster approach, she's armed and ready to defend us.

"Here's the thing, dudettes," she says. "There's going to be a lot of Bridettes and Johnnies. Whoever is really in charge targets the weaklings all the time; they're the easiest to submit." She catches a knife behind her back and pockets it without losing her stride. "The ones with power are harder. The baddies can't beat them down, but they can threaten their families and all that power they love." She catches each knife, sheathing them one by one without dropping them. "That's what I hate. It was Puppy's biggest gripe about getting the super monsters together. Sure, they can agree to help Ceel, but we can't trust it'll happen. Look at how many of her sisters Bridette took out. And her wife?" Shayna shudders. "This whole war that's coming will be the worst one yet. I say, we hole Ceel away somewhere where nothing can touch her."

"There's no place like that, Shayna," Celia says. "Not if Aric stays with me."

She walks toward the greenhouse, pausing to look at the dead trees, their dry and brittle branches leaning heavily against the glass. "Aric's power makes everyone aware of his presence, even humans blind to our existence." Her hands smooth across her belly. "I don't want him to leave us, but it's an avenue he's exploring."

"You're kidding?" I say. Back when Aric was a butthead and left Celia to report to his pureblood duties, neither held up well. No one could get near Aric without risking their limbs being torn off, and Celia fell into a horrible depression that almost broke her. "Ceel, do you really think either of you can handle the separation right now? Since learning you're knocked up, he won't even let you go to the bathroom by yourself."

"That's not true," Celia says.

"Dude," Shayna interrupts. "We've seen him standing by the door to the loo. He practically spins around in circles, wagging his big ol' tail when you emerge."

"I'm not saying it will be easy, on either of us," Celia replies. "But we're running out of options, and after tonight . . ."

Celia sighs, appearing more tired than I've seen in a long time. "Makawee finished warding the magical stronghold I'm to live in," she adds quietly.

"I guessed as much when Makawee skipped the party and her duties as Omega in favor of assisting with the boathouse escape," I reply.

Sadness marches across Celia's features in a way that breaks my heart. "Aric plans to lead these things away so Bren can take me to the stronghold."

I know Aric well enough to know where this is going. He's going to kill what threatens Celia or die trying.

"Bren is supposed to take you?" Emme asks.

This is news to us. But it doesn't affect me in the same way it affects Emme. Celia nods, appearing close to tears.

"Bren didn't tell me," Emme says.

"And Aric didn't tell us," I point out.

"Aric knows I want you with me," Celia explains.

"Then why is Bren taking you?" Shayna asks. "And why aren't we the ones getting you out of here like we planned?" Shayna asks.

Celia pushes her heavy hair away. "It's a last-ditch effort in case we didn't make it out through the lake." She glances to the demolished greenhouse. "While we were in the foyer and as things started to take a turn, Aric developed this new plan."

"I get it, Ceel. I do," Shayna says. "But since the beginning, we were supposed to stay together, keep you tucked away where you can have Junior in peace, and we can watch over you."

"That remains the ultimate goal," Celia insists. She holds out her hands when we try to interrupt. "You have to understand, when those things started to attack and I was separated from everyone but Shayna, Aric had to develop a new strategy. At first, he was going to have Braeden take me, until he saw Bren."

"Why wait so long to tell us? You had plenty of time for this big reveal in the greenhouse, Ceel," Shayna says, sounding hurt. "I mean, before the Nytes showed up and the plants went all killer psycho on us."

Celia shakes her head. "I couldn't trust what or who could hear me." She motions around the destruction Bridette's death curse caused. "Everything that can listen now is dead except for us."

"All right," I mutter. Like Shayna, I'm hurt to be left out of things. I always want us together, not just because Celia is expecting. I do want to protect her and the baby, but I want us to stay together because the four of us was always the one constant we could depend on throughout our not-so-great lives. "I get we haven't had much downtime. Still, you have to understand where we're coming from. Us, breaking up like this, is a hard pill to swallow, Ceel."

"We're not breaking up," Celia insists. "And I don't want to go anywhere without you."

"Then why leave without us?" Emme asks. "And why have an injured wolf escort you alone?"

Understanding finds a way into Shayna's voice. "The baddies will assume you're with the strongest wolves. With Bren being hurt, he'll be ignored."

"Hurt or not, he'll die before he lets anyone hurt Celia," Emme says. Her gaze drops to her small hands as if they can somehow stop this madness. "I have to be a part of this, Celia. I can heal you if you're hurt, and I can heal him."

"It has to be just me and Bren, Emme," Celia says.

"Are you nuts?" I ask. "You'll both be vulnerable."

"I know," Celia replies. Tears stream down her face.

"Oh, Ceel," Shayna says. She runs toward her and hugs her tight. "Aric isn't the only one trying to lead the super baddies away. You're trying to lead them away from us too."

Aw, hell, Shayna just nailed it.

I thought Celia allowed me to take on the role as protector of the family. But then here she is, pregnant and bordering on defenseless, and she's still protecting us.

"If I make it to the stronghold, we'll be together," Celia assures us, returning Shayna's fierce embrace. "I need you with me. Who will help me give birth, change diapers, tell me it's going to be okay every time I think it won't be?"

Aric, I almost say. I don't only because I hear her heart. As much as it kills her, she's come to terms that Aric may not make it. Even if he does (God, I really hope he does), we're her sisters. We're the ones who laugh and cry with her, just like we do now.

Without looking up, Shayna and Celia lift their dirt-smeared arms and tuck me against them. Emme is already there, like me, doing a hideous job of silencing our blubbering.

"I need you to live," Celia stammers. "If things don't happen like I want them to, I need to know you're safe."

"You suck," I say.

"Yeah, Ceel," Shayna agrees, crying harder. "You kind of do."

Emme sniffs. "It's ru-rude to insult someone who's pregnant," she says.

"Not if they deserve it," I say, bawling louder. "I hate this fucking plan."

"I'm not happy either, Taran," Celia says. She wipes her eyes. "We're just desperate."

I lift my head. "Bridette was desperate too, Ceel, and it cost her everything."

Celia jerks away from me, growling. I think I really did it this time until Shayna leaps in front of her with her sword out. Slowly, she lowers it.

Celia places her hand over her heart. "It's Aric," she rasps. "He's here. He's coming."

Shayna nods, staying alert to our surroundings. "All the wolves are here." She frowns. "And some of the vamps are with them."

She means Misha, but knowing Gemini is also near is what allows me to take that much-needed breath of air.

The ground rumbles at my feet with how fast they're running. Either something is chasing them, or something isn't too far behind.

"Is Bren with them?" Emme asks.

Celia closes her eyes and inhales, her nose wrinkling when she latches onto a scent. "I think so."

Emme bites down on her bottom lip. "You don't know for certain?"

Celia places her arm around Emme. "It's hard to tell for sure. I can't scent them, but I recognize the way they run. It sounds like Bren's stride, and he's favoring his hind leg."

Shayna steals a glance at Emme. "Yeah, I hear it too. He's hurt bad, Em."

"How are the others?" I ask.

Celia takes a long breath. "I can't scent anyone individually, but I do smell blood. Everyone seems pretty beat-up."

"Why aren't they healing?" Emme asks quietly. "If Johnny invaded the magic in the house, it would make sense that their healing powers were suppressed within the manor. But they're out now."

I fall on all fours, grimacing when the squishy and cold mud slides between my fingers and toes. From deep in the soil to the tiny blades of grass, I feel him and his magic.

"T? You okay there?"

I shake my head and swear. "Johnny has his meat hooks in the entire compounds. His magic . . . it's everywhere."

Celia stares hard into the night. "I can feel him." She turns to me. "But I can also feel Destiny. She's fighting his power." She frowns and turns in the opposite direction of where I feel the wolves.

"Is something wrong, Celia?" Emme asks.

Celia turns back to us, appearing stunned. "The lake . . . it's fighting Johnny too."

Shayna does a doubletake. "How can the lake fight Johnny, Ceel?"

"I don't know if it can directly," Celia smiles softly. "But its power and purity are intensifying."

I wipe my hands on my dress. "We'll take anything we can get. Maybe the lake has the goods to help Destiny."

Emme is usually our light. Her kindness filters through in her gentle touch, reminding us there's still good in the world. Tonight, she shares that light with Destiny.

Destiny is out there mixing it up with Johnny. Her magic is fighting his, and now that she's tougher and become something more, I really hope she can gain the upper hand. My worry is, it seems that Johnny is something more too.

Shayna edges closer to me, looking in the direction of the dense trees. Our wolves will be here soon, but it's not soon enough. "Do you think Destiny can beat Johnny, T?"

I huddle closer, seeking her warmth. "I was just wondering that myself. Destiny is stronger than anyone ever gave her credit for. My concern is, she may not be enough. She arrived earlier today. Johnny has had weeks to infiltrate the compound." I make a face. "He's dug his magic deep into the ground and polluted the air with it. This place is no longer Genevieve's. He's claimed it as his.

Celia and Shayna startle when the wolves' heavy paws ground to an abrupt halt. The echo of snapping jaws follows several rounds of hissing whimpers.

"What the hell was that?" I ask.

Shayna looks at Celia. "I don't know. Something with seven, maybe nine dangly boobies."

Celia holds up her hand, stopping her. "They're tails, Shayna."

Shayna makes a face. "You sure, Ceel? They sound all floppy." She makes a bouncy motion with her hands in front of her chest. "You know, kind of like when you or Taran run really fast and forget to wear bras."

"I don't forget to wear a bra," I say over Celia's insistence that they're tails.

Shayna raises her brows and gives me a once-over. I jerk the front of my dress down. "It's a wrap-around," I say, pointing." I tuck my breasts back in the cups and adjust the stupid thing. "It's not practical given my cup size, but it works with the dress."

"If you say so, T."

What sounds like an audible explosion of multiple zits follows. Shayna groans. "It's like, squirting them with milk."

I hold out my hands. "I can do without the visual, Shayna."

Celia is ready to be sick. "They're *tails*, Shayna. *Oh*," she says. She covers her ears at the sound of more squirting. "I think whatever they're fighting is poisonous. It's bursting with venom. I can smell it."

"Are you sure it's not breast milk?" I ask, shooting Shayna a look.

"T, believe it or not, guessing sounds from this distance with so many superbads isn't easy," Shayna replies. "And seeing what we've seen in just the past hour, I wouldn't put it past Johnny to send something with multiple boobs after us."

I shake a finger at her. "All right. I'll give you that one."

"I want to believe Destiny can defeat Johnny," Emme says.

She rises from where she was touching the ground. Emme can't sense magic like Celia and I can. Hell, even Shayna's better at it since Koda gifted her with some of his wolf. But this time, it's different. The longer we're exposed to Johnny's power, the more familiar it becomes.

"I want to believe it too, Em," I tell her. I motion around us. "Maybe with a little help from her friends, she'll be able to."

The abrupt silence announces the creature's defeat. There's a temporary pause before the wolves resume their frantic pace toward us.

We remain vigilant for the next few minutes, my heart leaping to my throat when a giant red blur clears the brush and rushes Shayna.

Chapter Sixteen

Shayna drops her sword and wraps her arms around Koda's massive neck. Blood drenches his fur. Some is his. Some is definitely not.

"We're all right, Puppy," Shayna tells him. He growls softly. "No, cutie. Nothing we couldn't handle."

Gemini's twin wolf follows. I all but cry when he barrels toward me. "Hey, bud," I say. "You had me worried." I cuddle him close, the terror I pushed down finally releasing.

Aric and Gemini rush through the stand of trees in human form, the *weres* with them surround us, forming a blockade. I don't count them, they're too fast and too many. Still, there's far less than when we first began.

I take in the feel of Gemini as he wraps his strong body around me. "You're alive." He says it as if he still needs to believe it.

"You are too," I say, gripping his shoulders. My body shudders. It's freezing. He rubs my back, trying to warm me.

The past few hours were horrific at best, and the end is nowhere near. If we live through this mess, I'll sort through the trauma piece by piece like always. For now, I'll take the momentary reprieve my mate offers.

Celia wipes her eyes, watching Aric as he stands a few feet away taking her in with all the love he feels for her. He seems close to tears, but anger and relief remain the most prevalent in his features.

Aric runs to her, cradling one arm around her shoulders and the other around her baby bump. His nose skims along the top of her head, taking in her scent to tame and settle his beast. "I've torn the compound apart looking for you. I thought you were taken, or hurt or—"

"I'm all right," she whispers. "My sisters took care of me."

He meets her gaze, wiping something I can't see from her cheek. "You were fighting."

She smiles softly. "You were too," she tells him.

"I'm supposed to," he says.

Guilt weighs heavily in his tone. "I lost my mind when we found the boathouse destroyed. I couldn't find any trace of you. Where did you go?"

"We never made it there, love," she tells him. "The spell Genevieve helped Taran design was meant to take us to a safe place. The boathouse wasn't safe anymore, and the spell transported us here."

Aric swallows hard. "Good . . . that's good. What remained of the boathouse was nothing more than burnt splinters."

"It wasn't me," I interject. "Not everything that blows up and burns in my fault."

Aric smirks. "We know, Taran. Your magic carries a very distinct and angry scent." He stops smiling. "This wasn't anything like it."

"It was more akin to Johnny Fate, wasn't it?" I ask.

Darkness shadows his features, and the wolves guarding us snarl with resentment. "Yeah. You were right. The Fate is among us." He grunts, annoyed. "I challenged him to combat more than once, yelling like a fool for him to appear."

I roll my eyes. "He won't appear. He's too much of coward and will let his pets fight for him."

"Pets?" Gemini asks.

"Or Nytes, like he calls them." I catch everyone up on what I saw in the manor and what occurred in the greenhouse. We should probably head someplace safe and talk this madness through. Except, from what the *weres* describe, there is no safe place.

"Where's Tye?" I ask when I finish.

"He left us to search for Destiny," Gemini tells me. His finger trails along my jaw. "We haven't seen him in hours."

"Do you think he's . . ." This is yet another moment where I can't get the words out.

"If he was, she'd be gone, and the entire state would feel her end."

"Good point," I agree. One more reason to hope Destiny makes it. Nature would respond in turn, and the entire West Coast would be affected.

"Where should we go now?" Celia asks.

"Not back to the lake," Aric says.

"Maybe we should," I say. My gaze skips to Celia. I'm not sure I should share what I do, but it's worth a try. "Celia says the lake is calling to her."

"It always calls to her in a way, reminding her it's there to grant her peace," Aric says. "That doesn't mean it actually wants her present."

"That's what I thought at first," Celia admits. "But then, just now, I felt it trying to fight Johnny, love."

The *weres* growl and snap their jaws, responding to what Celia says and eager to rejoin the fight. Aric silences them with a look. "It's not a good idea, sweetness. Me and Gemini swam out there, searching for you. The ward extending into the lake won't come down, and the Elders can't get through it. The lake may be surging in power and fighting what's there, but it isn't enough, not yet."

"There are sea creatures in the water, more of the Fate's creations," Gemini informs us. "Tahoe has begun breaking them apart, but they're still alive and deadly. And like Aric says, the ward is impenetrable."

"Do you think the lake would allow Celia through the ward?" I ask. "I mean, it totally loves her."

Okay. That might be a gross exaggeration. Tahoe was once a booming area filled with supernatural creatures. When the Native American *weres* inhabiting the area were forced out, the magic of Tahoe disappeared with them. But over the last few decades, its magic has surged, making it among the most potent sources of magic on Earth and drawing supernaturals back to the area. I think that's why we ultimately ended up here. The lake was the one place that always brought Celia peace.

"Taran, we can't count on the lake allowing Celia through," Gemini says. "We've been dealing with magic meant to do good only for it to try and kill us. I think that's why the sea creatures weren't immediately destroyed by the lake's purity, and why it won't allow us through the wards. The lake senses the good magic intermixing with the bad."

I press my head against his chest. "It's confusing the lake," I conclude. "It's not sure whether to embrace it or punish."

Gemini nods. "Yes. Johnny is no fool."

Bren emerges from between the *weres*. I noticed him right away. I also noticed him purposely keeping his distance. "T, you were closest to that little bitch. Do you know how he created them?" He didn't take anything he heard well and takes a moment to glare at Bridette's corpse. "These creatures outnumber us and shouldn't exist under our natural law."

Shayna continues to smooth Koda's fur. He's deadlier in his wolf form and wants to stay that way in case Shayna needs him. "The presence of Fates and Destinies disrupt natural law, dude," she reminds him. "Maybe that's all little Johnny needed."

"Maybe," Bren says, his voice rough with pain. "But this is some fucked-up shit he's pulling. Fate or not, you don't mess with the natural order. Not without it coming back to gnaw on his throat."

"Eventually, it will. We just don't have the time to wait," Aric says. He isn't any happier and is only maintaining his composure for Celia's sake. "Fate is playing with us, weakening our defenses. We've had our asses handed to us, and he's not done. That vampire that went after you shouldn't possess wings, period. He called himself a god. Is that what Fate is making now?"

"It's what he claimed, but who knows," I say. "The vamp was cocky as hell. He could have easily been blowing smoke. We didn't get a look at his back. Johnny may have tattooed him and gave those wings life, similar to what he does on himself."

Gemini meets Bren square in the face. "What do you get from the vamp?"

Bren has the best nose in the pack. It doesn't seem to help him this time. He kicks at the pieces of leftover vamp and scratches his scruffy beard. "Can't tell. What's left doesn't give me much. The wings were maybe real, but I don't sense anything godlike about him. Not in this state."

"I've never smelled anything that could be interpreted as godlike," Gemini says, clutching me when the breeze picks up. "Except the events of the evening have taught us we can't dismiss the impossible."

Emme tilts her head. "If Johnny is making gods, they're not as powerful as they should be. I mean, not if Bridette could kill him."

"That's true," Gemini agrees. "But these things are evolving, growing smarter every time they fight us. If they're learning, so is Johnny."

"Which means eventually he could indeed create a god," I say.

The *weres* growl, mimicking the collective feel of the group. Bren is the only one who doesn't join in, staring at the remains of the vampire as if he's missing something important. If possible, he looks worse than before. I ease away from Gemini, worried.

Emme stays near Shayna and Koda. It's the farthest she can be from Bren without joining the *weres* guarding us. "Why haven't you healed him?" I whisper.

Bren freezes. He and everyone can hear me, but it's Emme's reply that causes his muscles to tighten. "He doesn't want me to touch him, Taran."

Gemini shakes his head slowly, making it clear to me that now is not the time to go all "Taran" on him.

Celia looks up. "Misha," she says.

Aric releases her slowly. He doesn't want to, but also doesn't want her upset.

Misha and Ileana emerge, his bodyguards Hank and Tim flanking them, and the naughty Catholic schoolgirls strutting behind them. The schoolgirls still have their damn stilettos on. I've been barefoot for what seems like hours, and here they are, runway walking along the grass save for Edith Anne, who's . . . jumping rope?

Ileana is completely naked. In girlfriend's defense, she didn't have much on to start with. Misha ditched his jacket, and his shirt is filthy and torn. His long blond hair drifts around him in the breeze, and blood and dirt smear his face. Somehow, he still looks good. It must be nice being immortal.

His steady pace slows as Celia reaches him. Aric shadows her. I think it takes everything that wolf has not to snap Misha's wrists and toss them at his feet when he kisses her hands.

"You are well?" he asks.

Celia nods, the smile she greets him with fading "How many did you lose?"

Hank spits what looks like a finger on the ground. "Too many. What've you got?"

Aric and Gemini update the vamps. I keep my eyes on Edith Anne. Out of all the she-vamps in naughty Catholic schoolgirl clothing, Edith is the most . . . Hmm, what's a good word for it? Oh, yes, nuts.

She jumps along in circles, her skin oddly pale for someone who regularly sunbathes naked, and her features are giddy in the most psycho way possible.

Ileana glides her hand down her face, wiping the blood coating her skin. She takes several long, appreciative licks, grinning when several *weres* pause guard duty to watch.

She slides her tongue between her fingers and laughs. "I don't know, mighty wolf," she says, addressing Aric. Amid the chaos and bloodshed, her Russian accent remains delightful and flirty. "These Nytes, as you call them, don't taste like anything I've ever sucked on."

Given all the skilled lickin' she's doing, I agree she must have sucked her share of things in this life.

"We tasted blood, heavy with magic," Aric tells her. "But there's something else."

The *were* closest to us drools when Ileana takes another swipe at her face and resumes her rather enthusiastic licking. Gemini shoots him a warning glare, and he quickly resumes his watch.

"Mm, tasty," Ileana says. It doesn't matter that her hair is doused with body fluids. She tosses it back, her taut nipples pointing north when she moans. "The Fate's power is delicious." She grimaces, somehow maintaining her allure despite her sudden displeasure. "The other component isn't good. It borders on poison."

"Then why aren't you sick?" Shayna asks.

Ileana smiles, regarding Shayna as if she's the most important thing on earth. She has a gift of doing that. It's more than her vampire charm; it's a tactic meant to attract and make others want to please her. She perfected it centuries ago by the looks of it, and works it unfairly well. "My precious mistress of weaponry, what an excellent question you ask," she begins.

Wow, layering the phony adoration with a title. Nice touch.

Ileana winks at me before continuing. She knows that I recognize what she's up to. "Poison doesn't affect me. I'm too old to be taken by such piddly methods. But while the taste reminds me of poison, it's not what it is."

"No," Gemini agrees. "It's different from the scorpion creatures we fought on the way here."

Shayna stops stroking Koda. "Scorpion creatures?"

Bren rolls his eyes. "Yeah, you should have seen them. They were total freaks. One, the female, I'm guessing, had tits all along her underbelly. They dug grooves into the ground every time she moved."

Shayna shoots a rather snarky look our way. Celia doesn't notice, placing her hand on Aric's arm to draw his attention. "There are females and males," she says.

Aric knows where she's headed. "Yeah, and they have all the parts from what we can tell. I don't know if they can use them, or if they're for show. But if they can, they'll be able to breed. It's not enough to get you out of here, love. We have to kill everything here."

Ileana stretches her arms. "Unless they kill us all first, beloved alpha."

I should pay closer attention to the conversation, but Edith Anne is seriously wigging me out. I start for her without thinking only to stop when I realize that's not a rope she's skipping with.

"Edith," I say. "Why the hell are you jumping rope with intestines?"

Ordinarily, I would be met with several eye rolls and more than my share of insults. The remaining Catholic schoolgirls regard me with neither. They exchange looks before Agnes steps forward. "We encountered several winged serpents. Some had claws, others tusks, like boars. All were poisonous. Edith was struck multiple times." She shrugs. "She'll heal. The master said she would."

"Why isn't she sick?" I ask. "Vomiting or something?"

Agnes adjusts her tiny librarian glasses, blinking her almond eyes at me as if I shouldn't ask. Her ponytails are askew, and her full lips pressed tight. She's acting tough, but I can tell she's worried about Edith. "From what I've determined, the poison contains parasites."

Emme stops in place. "Parasites? As in worms?" she stammers. She turns to me. "I can't heal that."

"Nor should you try, sweet Emme," Misha warns. "As a vampire, they won't affect Edith like they will you."

I take a step back. I don't do worms, especially of the supernatural element. "Relax," Agnes tells me. "They'll crawl out of her brain sooner or later."

"Jesus God," I say, holding up my hands. "I'm going to stop your right there."

"Nyte has come . . ." Edith sings.

Okay, she has everyone's attention now.

"Nyte will kill . . . Nyte will open up your gills . . ."

Shayna leans in. "Gills?" she questions.

"I don't want to know," I admit.

"You can't run . . ."

"Edith, stop at once," Misha commands.

"You can't hide . . ."

"*Edith*," Misha hisses. He storms forward.

Tears leak from Edith's eyes. She's lost all control.

"You will beg for all to die."

Misha shakes her hard. "You will not leave me," he orders.

The intestines she carries drop in wet tufts at her feet. She resumes her singing, falling into hysterics. "Nyte has come, Nyte will kill." Her gaze pleads with Misha to save her.

"Heal," Misha commands. "No more of mine will succumb to the Fate."

Hank and Tim rush Misha, trying to haul him away, worried she'll infect him. The Catholic schoolgirls shriek through their tears, begging Edith to fight, to live.

Aric hauls Celia away when she lunges at Edith. "Edith, snap out of it," she yells at her. "Don't give in, you're stronger than this."

I stomp forward, Sparky lighting up like a flare and electrifying. I almost don't remember, everything happens so fast.

Edith whips her face toward me at my approach, hissing in pain. I wrench Sparky back and smack Edith hard. Fangs shoot from her mouth, followed by several long strings of worms from her ears. The parasites land on the ground, writhing and dying in the night air.

Gemini catches me by the waist when I curl forward to vomit.

Edith falls limp in Misha's arms. He grasps her chin and tilts it from side to side. "They're gone," he says. "All of them."

"Well done, precious one," Ileana says. She beams, unlike my sisters, who look as sick as I feel.

I straighten just enough to speak. "We have to get out of here," I manage.

Aric places Celia on top of Koda before she can argue. "We'll head to the perimeter farthest away from the road. They'll expect us to charge the gates leading out, not the wall."

I don't manage a step toward Celia when something else appears.

From the ground a phantom rises, like tar poured in reverse, her liquid body solidifying as quickly as the next breeze passes. An aura of moonlight surrounds the grisly shape she takes, and a blood-red cloak covers the shoulders of her naked and grotesquely thin body. Her deep-set black eyes are too large for her face, despite her disproportionately large head. As she stands, the tips of her midnight hair skim the grass beneath her feet.

I zap the absolute shit out of her.

Gemini grabs me, hauling me away when she slaps at the ground, trying to stand. I zap her again. *Take that, freak.*

Gemini snags my wrists and shoves my hands down. "What did you do?" he asks me.

From her perch on top of Koda, Celia turns slowly my way, her stunned features matching Aric's, my sisters', and everyone who had the absolute pleasure of witnessing my rather impressive ass-kicking.

"What?" I ask.

"You shot Destiny's messenger," Gemini explains through clenched teeth.

"Twice," Shayna points out.

"Her what?" I squeak.

"Dude." Shayna hurries forward. "Witches, powerful ones like Destiny, always send messengers during times of war to speak for them. It preserves their energy."

The "messenger" staggers to her feet, the scathing look she hits me with enough to cut me in two.

"Sorry," I say, to like, *everyone* around me. "Look at the night we've had. When something ugly and creepy"—I hold up a hand—"no offense, girl, rises from the ground, I fire first and ask questions later. Besides, how the hell am I supposed to know what she is?"

"Ah, T," Shayna mutters under her breath. "He's a boy."

Could have fooled me. Poor bastard.

"Taran," Emme says, my humiliation reflecting in her red-hot cheeks. "Messengers are explained in the first chapter of Soothsayers and Mystics."

I blink at her.

"It was one of the first texts you were assigned in witch school," she reminds me.

Emme glances at all the beings continuing to gape at me. Damn. Even the Catholic schoolgirls are rendered speechless. "You did read the book, didn't you, sweetie?" she asks.

Of course, I didn't read the stupid book, or the one after that. Most of it was written in Shakespearenese and boring as hell, not that I can admit it. "He wasn't what I expected," I say. It's the best non-lie I can muster. Damn these supernaturals and their ability to out the truth.

The messenger disappears, but not before flipping me the meanest, nastiest middle finger I've ever seen. I'm serious. That sucker was at least six inches long.

"The compound isn't safe, my friends. You risk your lives the longer you remain among the grounds."

We turn in the direction of Destiny's voice. Her image fades in and out, like the reel of an old movie ready to tear from age. Destiny is hurt.

The bruises covering her arms suggest they were broken, and the cuts lining her face and chest tell us she's fought many, alone.

She lifts her hand and points, her fingers shaking. "The manor," she says. "Each room holds its own danger and connection to Johnny. But once the room is clear of his creations, Fate can't reclaim it, and he will weaken."

"There are hundreds of rooms, Great Destiny," Misha reminds her. "Allow us your true presence so we may protect and heal you."

"I can't, Dear Misha." She shakes her head, the motion causing her pain. "In order to help you fight Fate, I had to become part of the house too. Each room you clear, I'll claim as mine and use its magic to help me heal."

"Will it heal you completely?" Aric asks. He looks to Emme. "Or can Emme help you?"

"Yes," Emme says. She walks toward her with her arms outstretched. "Please let me ease your pain."

Destiny's smile is weak, but there. "The only way to help is to return to the manor. As I reclaim the magic for the side of good, it will improve my state and prevent my death." Her gaze drops. "I wasn't strong enough to defeat him . . . he hurt me badly."

"I'm so sorry, Destiny," Celia says. "I know you're doing this to protect us."

"Don't be sorry, my dear friend," Destiny replies. "Seek solace in the manor. All of you. Help me stop Johnny so I may live to see your children born."

"Are you sure there's nothing else we can do for you, Destiny?" I ask.

"No. Out here, these creatures aren't connected to Johnny as they are in the house. They're too new to the premises."

"Are you saying it doesn't matter how many we kill on the grounds?" Gemini asks.

"No, it does. Their deaths weaken him, too, but not to the degree of the creatures roaming the manor. As his vessels, they grew stronger and more akin to his power as they waited for him." Destiny seems out of breath. "Johnny became one with the magic in the manor when he used his creatures to help infect it. Out here is too spacious even for him."

Bren huffs. "Then let's burn the whole shit down." He looks at me. "Do your thing and get on it, T."

"If you destroy the manor, you'll take me with it," Destiny says. "In order to create a haven for Celia and maintain Johnny's weakness with every blow cast, I created a bond I'm currently too weak to break. For now, you can't stay out here on the compound. The manor is the only place that will keep Celia safe."

Destiny clasps her hand over her heart and falls to her knees. I race to her, stopping when I see the torment raging in her features. "They're coming for you. Run."

Chapter Seventeen

Destiny's image fizzles out, and she's gone.

Aric shouts orders to guard Celia as Koda takes off with her on his back. Aric races beside them in human form, his quick, powerful strides keeping up with Koda's beast. Gemini rallies the most elite of the pack, directing them to surround and form a barrier around Celia.

I glance around, looking to hitch a ride, and almost jump out of my skin when I see what's coming.

Nosferatu must be one of Johnny's favorite films because *damn*. The freaky bastards are back in droves. You know that scene in *Braveheart* when all those dirty, *sexy* Scots run through the field, screaming like the badass warriors they are? It's not like that.

The Nosferatus come at us on all fours like bouncing cockroaches, digging their long, twisted nails into the ground to propel them forward. Instead of bellowing the war cry of their people, they giggle like creepy children out of Rob Zombie's worst nightmare.

I'm only allowed one curse word before Gemini tosses me in the air. I scream—since that is the war cry of *my* people—and crash land on his twin's back, gripping the tuff on his neck while his spine beats the hell out of my ass.

"Son of a *bitch*."

The midnight-black twin swerves through the crowd of *weres:* bears, cheetahs, mountain lions, and wolves until only a few strides remain between Celia and me.

Celia glances behind her like she was born to ride a massive red wolf, her long hair flowing in the wind, her green eyes firing. "Where's Shayna?"

"Coming, dudes!"

No, Shayna's not *just coming*. Very unlike my pathetic entrance into the melee, Shayna runs and twirls like a seasoned ballerina. She lands on the rump of a grizzly, pushes off him, and uses the momentum to leap between the army protecting Celia.

Shayna lands on two graceful feet, riding Koda's haunches, but not, *absolutely not*, before slicing a Nyte in half that scrambles up a tree and leaps from a branch.

The Nyte falls away in two splattering pieces, the part with the head still giggling his ass off. Shayna lowers herself in a split, riding backward to guard Celia's back as Nytes swarm us from all directions.

"Bren has Emme," she calls before we can ask.

The tone she carries as she swings her sword alerts me that they're in trouble.

I fix my position to a less painful one and peer behind me. Bren and Emme remain several yards away from the rest of our group, and the Nosferatus are almost upon them.

A large Nyte assumes his shadow form and jets onto Bren's back. The impact knocks Bren forward. He tucks Emme against him, protecting her as he rolls off to the side.

The only light guiding us is from the partial moon until I take aim and fire. Blue and white lightning cut through the darkness, galvanizing the aerial Nytes and forcing parts of their physical forms to materialize.

The *weres* fall back, tearing into the Nytes I strike. It gives Bren time to adjust Emme against him and stumble to his feet.

Pain scrunches his features, the limp evident in his stride no matter how hard he tries to hide it. Emme clutches his neck, pressing her face against his chest. She tells him something that twists his features. With an angry roar, Bren throws her ahead of him as the Nytes swarm him.

Emme shrieks, soaring into the air. I yell for Gemini to help her, certain she'll fall to her death.

Except my baby sister doesn't need any help.

Emme crosses her arms and whips them out in a "V," tossing the cluster of Nytes fighting Bren with her *force*. The Nytes are thrown like LEGOs, slamming into trees and into the next set of Nytes that appear.

Bren *changes*. His large paws slide along the wet lawn when his injured leg gives. He ignores the pain, bounding forward, and charging toward Emme.

Emme uses her *force* to slow her fall. The landing, while jagged and awkward, gives Bren time to reach her and allow her to smoothly land on his back.

In his beast form, Bren is fast enough to reach the outer perimeter of the group, but not much farther. The manor comes into view, and yet another all-out brawl begins.

Weres collide into the Nytes I zap. If so much as a pinky is made physical, the *weres* rip into them, shaking them hard and forcing them to take shape. The Nytes giggle as they're mutilated. I can't tell if that's the only sound they're capable of, or if Fate is merely laughing at us. The *weres* interpret it as the latter and answer the insult with fangs and claws.

The vampires, *our vampires*, burst through the section of forest closest to Lake Tahoe. Misha and his crew cling to the back of a giant leechy thing, their skin covered in cuts and blood.

"Turn it," Misha orders. He and his vamps hurtle themselves to the side, clutching the multiple legs along the creature's underbelly. They pull hard, using their weight to drive the leech into the fleeing Nosferatus.

A hollow tongue slithers out from deep within the thing's throat. It sucks the Nosferatus down like a vacuum hose and spits them out just as fast until all that remains are piles of black clumps.

This is the Nyte who killed Genevieve's guards, and there's Misha riding it like a hobby horse.

Misha is bold and smart to use the Nyte, and while we've collectively taken out many, the Nosferatus remain plentiful, and their streaming shadow forms are almost impossible to catch. But just as Fate has power, so does Aric. He snatches the shadows that near Celia, solidifying them in his grip. Those he and Gemini don't maim with their bare hands, Shayna beheads, or Koda freaking eats.

It's a fight to reach the manor. I hang on for dear life as Gemini's twin careens over the stone steps leading from the lake and to the building.

The force of power from the water shoves at my back. Waves surge from the lake, each strike along the sand teasing my skin and demanding my focus. I ignore it, focusing on striking the circling Nytes. It's not until we reach the lower terrace and the festering smell from the beach lurches my stomach, that I glance behind me.

The beach is overrun with rotting pieces of sea monsters. There are sections of gutted animals, remnants of large fins and broken teeth and bone. The lake is attacking and destroying Johnny's creations. It's just not fast enough, as the ward remains up. Like a mirror, the celestial blue water of the lake reflects against it and casts a spotlight on the Nytes flying toward us.

Whimpers, screams, yelps, and those damn giggles resonate from all sides. Sweat soaks my skin from my fire and every bit of energy I have left to keep it going.

The first of our group barrels through the rear entrance, trying to fit their massive bodies through a too-narrow space. The next few follow, including Celia and Shayna. Emme and Bren are still farther back. We're almost there, but just like we want in, these Nytes want to keep us out.

I'm knocked away from Gemini's twin when something crashes into me. I barely feel fangs snap near my throat. They're gone as fast as they arrived.

Gemini's twin takes a protective stance in front of me and allows me to use him to get to my feet. A giant lynx with scales protecting its ribs screeches as Gemini beats it do death against a rock. Black fluid splatters his bare chest. "Taran, get inside."

Still winded from the fall and fight, I slip from the twin when I try to climb on. More Nosferatus scramble toward us. Gemini and his twin growl, throwing themselves at them. Damn it, most of us are still out here, and the vampires have only reached the first terrace.

My head spins with exhaustion as my magic builds. I let Sparky guide me, reaching into that deep space that demands fire and destruction. It's not a place I like to go. Not when innocents may die. I warn them the best way I can, yelling even as my throat burns. "Ass kicking in three, two, *one!*"

Weres leap over, and the vampires scramble up anything they cling to, walls, statues, even each other as I slam my hands into the ground. I grunt in torment as ripples of blue and white flames shoot across and in front of me surging in size and length and burning everything in its path.

I can't see through the clouds of smoking bodies, tears singeing my eyes as I pray only Johnny's fucking minions are affected. I choke on the flames, wishing I could cover my ears when they catch and burn the leechy thing. My hands shake, and my spine threatens to crack from the ache of keeping the fire going. It's not until Gemini clasps my elbow that I know to stop.

"Enough, Taran. We need to get into the manor."

I allow him to lead me to my feet and steady me as I swipe at my face. Charcoaled piles of creatures litter a large portion of the lawn closest to the lake, including what's left of the leech, and soot cakes the stone terraces. Several smoldering trees fall over, my dwindling flames barely cast a dim light.

Slowly, the vampires make their way down from their posts, hurrying past and giving me ample space. Misha is the exception. As a master, fire won't kill him. He pauses to wink at me before proceeding up the stairs.

"Is everyone okay?" I ask, finding it hard to speak.

"No," he says. "We lost several on the way here."

"But did I . . . ?" I can't find my words, but I don't need them around Gemini.

"You allowed everyone else through. Now it's our turn to head inside."

Gemini sweeps me up into his arms, moving fast toward the manor. I glance at the destruction, noting how much ass I kicked. There's nothing left really. Another tree topples down, scattering burning acorns like embers along a thick layer of ash that's replaced the back lawn. Down on the beach, remains of the creatures sink into the sand as Tahoe buries its enemies. A harsh splash of waves brings more of Tahoe's victims while the clouds clear, allowing the dull moonlight to poke through.

Gemini reaches the entryway, and still, I stare at the quiet behind us.

"Did I—" I cut myself off when I start coughing. "Did I get them all?"

Gemini shakes his head, his body soaked and his voice rough from battle. "No. There are more out there. I can hear them coming for us."

Chapter Eighteen

Like Destiny said, the rooms where we fought are cleared of Johnny's creations. They're "clean" by supernatural standards, safe to walk through without fear of something skewering you through the heart and roasting you with its breath. Except "clean" doesn't equate to pretty.

Instead of the expensive and treasured artwork, blood and body fluid decorate the demolished walls of the grand foyer. The most prominent stains are thickest at the entrance, where the leechy Nyte first appeared and murdered Genevieve's guards. Gemini nods to the group of *weres* tasked with carrying the giant wolf Aric killed out. The thing lies in limp pieces. It's very much dead after the pounding Aric gave it, but no less disturbing.

"Where are you taking it?" Gemini asks the *weres*.

A she-lion steps forward. Like the others, she's naked, her body littered with cuts and bruises. "To the yard before more of our prey arrive. The alpha demands we clear the space for the injured and for our people to rest."

She refers to the Nytes as our prey. It's easier than the other way around. Except, I'm not positive it's true.

"No," he tells her. "Burn it and any enemy you find in the fireplaces. I don't want these creatures feasting on their dead or reviving them."

The *weres* exchange glances. A smaller male dragging one of the heads frowns. "They are able to revive their dead?"

"We don't know what they're capable of," Gemini says. "But I won't take any chances."

"Yes, sir," the *weres* reply.

"Sir?" a young *were* interrupts.

I remember her. She's a honey badger, small but fierce, and just graduated last year at the top of her class. "Why are there so many?" she asks. "Fate is strong, but this seems too much, even for him."

"We don't know that either, young one," he tells her.

She nods and lowers her gaze. I feel foolish just lying in Gemini's arms as he continues to speak to his pack. "Please put me down, love," I ask.

"Taran, you're in no condition," he mutters.

Probably not. "I need to walk and stretch my legs," I say.

The tension along his features ease when he looks at me, setting me down carefully. I take my place beside him, attempting to appear stronger than I feel.

"Where's Aric?" Gemini asks.

The female who spoke first glances at me. I must look even worse than I thought. "Clearing a suite for the Mate. He doesn't want her among the dead."

"He's clearing a suite by himself?" Gemini asks.

Although he's asking, he's not entirely surprised.

A smaller *were* glances down. "The alpha has a lot of rage he needs to unleash."

I'll bet. "What are you doing with our dead?" I ask.

The she-lion adjusts her hold on the wolf, causing the Nyte's broken ribs to rub together, making a disturbing sound I won't easily forget. "We're piling them in Genevieve's office," she replies.

"Excuse me?" I ask. "Whose genius idea was that?"

I have mentioned I speak my mind, haven't I?

"Uri's," they all mumble.

"Uh-huh," I say. Talk about a petty bitch. It's his, "Fuck you," to Genevieve for ruining his evening.

"I don't like this," Gemini growls.

"Neither do we, sir," the she-lion states. "It had begun before our return, and we must—"

She swallows hard. *Weres* have their beasts to help them through the tough times, but this . . . this is more than simply hard. It's devastating. She clears her throat when her beast gives her another boost of strength. "We must take care of our dead," she finishes.

Gemini nods. "Yes," he says. He looks up toward the devastated stairwell. "I'll see to the alpha."

His twin jets up the steps, taking four at a time and barely making a sound. "Sir," the smallest *were* interrupts. "I . . . Perhaps you shouldn't. The alpha is very angry right now."

I recognize the drop in tone in my lover's voice. It captures every bit of what we're feeling. "So, am I," he says.

The *weres* head in the direction of the fireplace as Gemini jogs up the stairs. "Wait here," he tells me.

"Of course," I reply.

He drops his head and sighs, knowing I won't. I give him the best smile I can muster. It's only then he continues up the stairs.

The grand foyer has transformed into a hospital ward circa World War One. I limp past the group of *weres*, their wounds mending slower than should be possible. Lesser witches, their pilgrim-style uniforms in tatters and covered with muck, carry pitchers of water and trays with food. Some of the food is cooked, most of it isn't. The *weres* don't care. Their beasts demand that the calories burned from stress and battle be replenished.

I pass a large polar bear scarfing down a carton of heavy cream. A Lesser witch waits with a tray stacked with bricks of butter. He's famished, and the food is likely limited. I wonder briefly if Celia will be forced to munch on butter and suck down cream. For a moment, I contemplate making her something decent to eat, except I have other shit to do.

One of the witches I went to school with tends to a *were*. I'm not certain what kind he is. Both of his arms were chewed off, and Merry is doing her best to bandage the limbs.

She offers me a weak smile as I pass. "Ya made it," she tells me.

"You did too," I say.

The part about not all of us making it goes unsaid. I offer a gentle squeeze to her arm as I pass. The deeper I go into the foyer, the more the injuries worsen. It's hard to look at all the suffering, yet watching the dead carried out is much worse. These were parents, siblings, and friends slaughtered by evil.

I shouldn't expect less from Johnny. These Nytes of his weren't engineered to leave survivors. They were meant to ravage and inflict punishment, and didn't they manage their share? Still, there's a part of me that's surprised by it. Johnny isn't evil. That's not the first word I'd use to describe him. He's a giant wimp, so selfish and obsessed with saving his ass that this is what's he's become.

Hundreds attended tonight's event. Lethal creatures that have known bloodshed and pushed through it, emerging victorious. If we're lucky, maybe a third of them will make it through this shitshow. And if we're really lucky, Celia will be among them.

My lips purse as another stab of pain shoots up to my hip. I think I twisted my ankle, and my right knee took a pummeling. I lift my hands, my eyes widening when I realize I'm covered with nasty cuts. I'm more than a little beat-up. Still, I fared far better than the majority.

Shayna skips toward me, a giant bruise taking up the right side of her face. "Hey, T. Ceel is with Koda. She's eating the food Aric found and seems okay, you know, considering."

The spoils of battle stain Shayna's clothes, and a deep gash on her shoulder pokes through her torn shirt, and here she is, still somewhat lively. I inspect her face carefully. "What happened?" I ask.

She shrugs. "There were a lot of baddies, T," she reminds me, her jaw clicking as she speaks. "I jumped off Koda when we neared the door so he could get Ceel inside. Sometimes, the baddies are a lot stronger than me."

And yet she fights them all the same. "Have Emme heal you," I tell her.

"I will. Later. If she's up for it."

Her gaze cuts to the right. I almost jump. Several witches chant, holding down a pregnant *were* whose chest cavity is split open. The witches' magic is the only thing keeping this female down, and alive. I can see the *were's* beating heart, pounding weakly as it struggles to keep the young *were* and her baby alive. Her partner waits by her head, her long hair spilling in messy clumps as she weeps and speaks softly to the mother of her child.

The glow of Emme's healing touch expands, casting excess light onto Bren, where he's leaning against the wall. His arms are crossed, and he appears bored. I know better. Bren is taking everyone in and watching Emme closely. With tension as high as it is, the *were's* partner can easily turn on Emme in her grief. Even as frustrated and injured as Bren is, he stands guard over Emme.

Emme's shoulders tremble with fatigue. Tired and likely hurt herself, tending to the *were* is robbing the small bits of energy she clings to. But where there's darkness, there's Emme's light.

Emme's breathing is ragged, and she's scrunching her face with how hard the intense healing demands her focus. Still, there she is, repairing the *were's* ribs and knitting the skin closed. As she finishes, she meets the *were's* partner and smiles softly, her face bright red and soaked with sweat from her magical efforts.

"Your partner did an incredible job protecting your baby. Your little one is well," Emme assures her. "I can feel it."

The witches and the surrounding *weres* break down. We needed the baby to be okay. We needed hope, and that shining glimmer Emme offers is perfection.

Emme notices me with Shayna. She wipes her face on a towel a witch offers. "Let me heal you, Taran."

I look at the abundance of supernaturals waiting to be seen, creatures and beings who should be in far better shape than they are. Some are being tended by healing witches. Emme's line appears to be the longest. *Damn it, Johnny, you could have used your power for so much better than this.*

"I'm good," I say. Comparatively, I am. There's a *were* holding his severed limbs between his knees, and another older vamp with his head tucked under his arm.

"Are you certain?" she asks.

The glare the vamp's head shoots me assures me there's no cutting in line. "Oh, yeah. Besides, I need to see what's up."

Emme nods, brushing a strand of her dirty hair aside. She crinkles her nose at the smell. I don't take a guess at what it might be. I'll just bet that like everything else, it's nasty.

With my head held semi-high and dress as pretty as Emme's, I limp into the reception hall. Like the grand foyer, it's partially destroyed and littered with wounded.

Uri stands close to the fireplace where that coal creature that bled lava forced its way through. He's looking down at what appears to be a bare foot and not much else. The wretched smell of cooked flesh strikes my nostrils with a punch. I beat back a gag. Shayna isn't so lucky.

She coughs into her hands, trying to muffle it. I can't blame her reaction. The carnage around us suffocates our minds and spirits, embedding deep emotional scars we'll never fully recover from, and with her heightened senses, she's worse off than me.

Uri nudges the foot with the tip of his expensive shoes. The foot is stuck to the floor. He nudges it again, this time more forcibly. The skin strips away from the bone as the foot teeters and falls to the other side. Uri isn't trying to be morbid, he's visibly shaken, a side I never cared to see in this old vamp. His more overt emotion is frightening. Uri is angry, his rage simmering to a boil and warning everyone to mind their distance.

The foot belongs to what's left of one of Uri's dates. Oh, and look, there's his other date, his skull crushed and the bowtie he wore bloody and lying a few feet away. The men were likely his favorites. They must have loved Uri. Humans don't stand a chance against any preternatural. His adoring subjects knew it, and yet when the chaos broke, they likely wrapped their naked bodies around Uri and attempted to shield him.

It makes me sick that Uri allowed them to stay with him instead of ordering them to hide, to run, *something*. He obviously had feelings for them. Then again, Uri has always cared for Uri the most.

Uri's lovers, those he most feeds from, usually come and go. He trades them away depending on his mood, his tastes, his pleasure. These two were something different. He's not walking away from them, and he *is* *furious*.

A shuffle of fabric and a limp that rivals mine has everyone looking up. Genevieve has returned from battle. What's left of her dress hangs in shreds, and blood trickles from the claw marks on her back and throat. The guard to her right is missing part of her hand. The one on her left is covered with burns that limits her movements. They're in pain and working hard not to show it.

As Uri's livid features fix on Genevieve, the guards tighten the holds on their staffs, ready to protect Genevieve. Genevieve doesn't blink, meeting Uri with a rock-steady "fuck you and the bat you flew in on" expression.

"Uri," she says.

Uri kicks the foot away. A Lesser witch shrinks away when it lands near her feet. She survived the attack physically, but emotionally, she's not doing so hot. She shakes violently, gaping at the foot as it might somehow hurt her.

Uri storms forward, baring his fangs at Genevieve. "This is your doing," he hisses.

I launch myself at him. Shayna clutches my waist and drags me back. Uri is milliseconds from tearing out Vieve's throat. Despite our differences, Genevieve is not the enemy, and I'll be damned if I let him harm her.

"Dude," Shayna says. "This isn't our fight. Not yet."

Genevieve returns Uri's anger, the magic building within her curling the tiny hairs on my neck inward. "I am *not* to blame."

"This is your home, your wards, your invitation. You did this to me."

I roll my eyes. "Yes, let's make this all about you, Uri."

Growls erupt from every *were* present when Uri trains his sights on me. Everyone is taking a side and casting fault. This was not the goal of the night.

"Everyone had lost someone this evening," I remind everyone. I ignore the group of vampires edging closer to Uri. "Enough of your bitchiness. We can't leave, and this isn't over."

"You will not keep me here," he hollers. His gaze travels around the room, making a point to stop on every alpha, head witch, and anyone else with an inkling of his power. "None of you will."

"Trust me when I say I'd rather you leave, princess," I bite out. Hisses mix with approving grunts. I dismiss the rather scathing death glare Uri throws my way and focus on Genevieve. "Does he know that the wards are being used against us?"

"*What*?" Uri demands.

Hmm. Guess not. "Oh, yeah, Uri. Instead of keeping things out, they're keeping us in."

Call me nuts, but I don't think Genevieve appreciates the ever-so-gentle way I break the news to Uri. She regards me as if slapped. Uri screams at us, the anger he emits in his magic cracking the walls further. "This is impossible." He sneers at Genevieve. "Only a pathetic and simpleton of a witch would allow this."

"Okay. Now you're just being mean," I say over Genevieve's furious, "*How dare you*?"

Genevieve's magic clashes with Uri's, the sheer power crumbling what remains of the hearth.

I edge in front of Genevieve when Uri takes a step forward, his irises freaking glowing red. I was never subjected to this side of him (thank Christ!). The tumult radiating in his features gives me serious pause and the urge to bolt.

"Knock it off, Uri," I say, feigning a shit-ton more courage than I feel. "Yeah, I get it, wards of this caliber should be impossible to manipulate. But guess what? These creatures aren't supposed to be possible either."

"Then how are they so?" Uri asks through clenched fangs.

"It's Fate," I say.

Uri stiffens, his fangs and that of his family dissolving and resuming their human form. "Johnny Fate," he says.

"Yes," I tell him. "He's invaded the premises and claimed the witch's power."

"He's supposed to be with the shifters or dead by their hands," Uri says.

Shapeshifters are the most frightening supernatural creatures on Earth and carry the power of hell within them. Born witches, they spend their human lives making blood sacrifices to their deity. Once their deity is satisfied and deems them worthy, they sacrifice their souls in exchange for the power to transform into any creature living or dead.

Celia killed one once, with a lot of damn help. I killed the half-form of another. Our actions, while upping our street cred, only made us larger targets.

"Johnny Fate," Uri repeats. He scoffs, thumbing his nose.

Uri doesn't respect weakness. No predator like him should. The way he speaks, he counted on Johnny's lack of spine to work against him with the shifters. In a way, I did too.

I often pondered how Johnny's initial meeting with these ghastly beings would go. They're not nurturing or welcoming. They're ruthless and cruel, and just as selfish as Johnny. More than once, I pictured them eating him and sucking down all his magic right to the marrow.

"Tell me what you know, second of the Wird sisters," Uri orders me.

I did mention I'm not a fan of orders, right? And don't get me started on the stupid title he bequeaths me with.

"Sure," I mutter. "Only 'cause you asked so nicely."

I spill everything I know. The god reference made by the winged vamp sends a wave of alarm and bitterness along the room.

My tone firms. "Destiny has promised to keep us safe here as long she can, and with each room we clear, we will help her and us."

"No," Uri replies.

Sometimes, I just want to zap the shit out of him. "Uri, am I speaking Japanese? Is there something you didn't understand? Until we can figure something out, we're stuck here."

"Exactly," he yells. "Stuck in a manor with bumbling catastrophic spells that disorient and maim while we're tasked with killing malevolent and absurdly strong god-like creatures that hide in the shadows, watching our every move—waiting to strike us down—all due to inadequate peons and a laughable race."

Collective gasps parrot around the room, and magic detonates like mini-bombs. I gather my fire, not to act, but to protect myself against the first magical blow that's thrown at Uri.

Genevieve lifts her chin and shuffles forward. "You dare to insult me, my sisters, and our race?" she asks. She's not yelling. She doesn't have to. The destructive force that licks her words brand her with danger.

Uri smiles, his mounting anger and viciousness taking aim and firing a low blow. "I possess more than insults, you incompetent whore," he tells her.

Genevieve doesn't lose it often. I've only seen it once before when I accidentally blew up her ancestral home (these things happen). She loses it now, all over Uri.

Magic as bright as the sun engulfs her, and her voice reverberates around us. "In my home, you are nothing, vampire. In our world, even less. A tiresome, decrepit creature—a mere leach who deserves a good salting." Her voice drops. "And I'm the so-called peon to stomp her foot on the rancid remains of your carcass."

My jaw hits the floor. I knew Vieve had it in her to challenge a Grandmaster. I just never thought I'd ever see it. Shayna bolts, as in, now you see her, now you don't. She was so quiet, I forgot she was right next to me.

A slight breeze skims my cheek. It's all I feel of Gemini before he and his twin take point between the Grandmaster vamp and the most lethal witch in the Americas.

Chapter Nineteen

"Enough," Gemini snaps. The force of his growls crumble the remainder of the fireplace. "Johnny Fate is our enemy. Do not misplace your anger on each other."

"I know who the enemy is," Uri spits.

"Then shut up," Gemini fires back.

I don't remember moving. I'm just there at Gemini's side, my hands aching with how much magic surges through my core, demanding I protect my mate.

Gemini's and Uri's breathing are so pronounced, their chests heave in and out. No one exists except for them, even those rushing to defend their chosen sides.

"Master," Misha says. "A word, if you will."

Misha doesn't wait for a response. He pushes from the one wall that was somewhat spared from the anarchy. I'm not sure how long he was there. Misha only allows you to see him when and if he wants.

His voice is just above a whisper. No matter, it's sufficient. So is the way he faces off with Uri. "I ask that you stand down."

The potent force Misha issues with his request strikes like a gavel. He's not asking. He's imposing his rule.

To treat his creator as such, especially in front of witnesses and *especially* leaders of the mystical world, Misha is openly demonstrating his dominance over Uri. If Uri didn't know Misha was the superior being, he knows now.

Uri relaxes slowly, fighting to maintain his equanimity. "The more I hear, the more I dismiss these stories as nonsense and lies," he says to Gemini.

He addresses Gemini solely to remind our audience of his position by attempting to demean someone he presumes inferior.

Holy shitballs. Does that ever piss me off.

"Are you calling my mate a liar?" Gemini asks, his voice crisp as frost.

I slam my fists on my hips. "Yeah. You callin' me a liar?"

Uri waves his arms dramatically. "A Fate can't invade such supposed power."

Another jab at Genevieve. Another insult she can't leave unanswered. The yellow stone in her talisman shimmers as she advances. "I grow tired of you, old man."

"I may be old," Uri snarls. "But with age comes wisdom, and I *am* right."

"No, you're very much mistaken, Uri," Destiny replies, her voice calm. "A Fate can do almost anything with the right kind of help."

The supernaturals bent on throwing down mere moments ago ease away as Destiny trails in. The tentacles of her dress sag along the floor, sweeping through the mounds of debris and body fluid. She's no longer using her magic to elevate the limbs of her dress. She's smart enough to preserve her energy for what's to come.

Tye shadows her closely. He's not fully healed, but he is better and ready to act against anyone who edges too close.

Destiny's skin is the color of peach stone. She's better than she was but remains far from well. "Take the time to feel your surroundings, dear Uri," she says. Her standard light voice is heavy with the grief and acridity caging the once majestic room. She smiles sadly, regarding me, and Emme and Shayna, who hurry to stand on either side of me. "You too, my beloved Wird sisters and most cherished Misha. See beyond Fate to what lies beneath."

I'm not certain why she groups us with Misha, and I don't sense what I think she wants me to. Yet something is here, beyond the mourning and rampage, there's a sense of wrongness that jabs my insides and makes me sick.

"No," Misha rasps. Disgust and dread flash across his face.

"No what?" I ask.

Destiny, already weak, smiles softly. "You sense it, Taran," she states. "Allow yourself to know it."

I don't have the heart to tell her than I don't know jack. Magic in so many waves remains a mystery. Still, Destiny is counting on me to know. I dive deep within my soul, searching and asking Sparky for help. It takes a long moment. At first, all I feel is the full attention of the room. Everyone is watching and waiting for me to understand. I start thinking I'll have to meditate or some shit. But when it hits me, all I want to do is scream.

My eyes widen, and my right arm jerks violently. I feel it. Malice, sin, pain—

"*Shapeshifters,*" I say.

I clasp my hands over my mouth, trying to take the word back. Emme and Shayna don't swear like, ever. Celia does on occasion. I make it up for all of them now. Son of a bitch. Of course. Shapeshifters are virtually unstoppable. It's why Johnny chose to side with them instead of the vampires or witches. He fears dying more than anything and wants to live no matter the price. Even if it means his soul.

"Those things weren't shifters," Uri barks out, his voice bordering on hysterical. "There are rules! They can't just take the form of whatever creature they dream up. The creature must have at one point existed."

My voice hollows as I feel the color drain from my face. "Johnny can create anything he wants," I remind him. The entire room gives me more attention than I could ever ask for. "His tattoos come to life, and his singing voice can mesmerize and manipulate—"

"Tell us something we don't know," Uri yells, cutting me off.

The remaining windows splinter when Gemini snarls, "Disrespect my mate one more time, and you need not worry about Fate," he warns Uri.

Uri's eyes morph red with rage. "Master," Misha tells him. "To survive this night, you must listen." Misha is plenty pissed, too, but it's not directed at Gemini. My head pounds from stress. Misha may actually turn on Uri.

I continue, speaking fast yet steady, drawing attention back on me before shit goes down that we're not ready for. "Johnny can cut into his skin and draw whatever he wants. It doesn't have to be anything real, so shifter rules and limits don't apply to him. It's not unreasonable to believe he created every Nyte who attacked us."

Ileana struts in naked and not giving two perky nips about it. "Impossible. Fate does not carry such virtue to produce such numbers." Her Russian accent is lovely in all the ugly. "If these Nytes are markings from his skin, with all we killed, he should be dead or close to it." She tilts her head as if thinking things through. "Yet you claim he not only continues his wrath but that the shifters accompany him as well?"

"The shifters aren't here," I correct. Sparky twitches, agreeing with me.

"I feel them, precious one," Ileana says. She smiles as if pleased with herself. "All of us excellent beings do."

Shayna inches closer, mumbling low. "I feel them too, T."

"I get that you feel them, Shayna, but it's not actually them," I insist. I hold up my hands when Ileana grins. It's a brilliant smile and condescending as all get out. "Their magic is here, or a part of their magic, but they're not. Not yet."

"You're right." Gemini crosses his arms and nods. "Not in the true physical sense."

He senses their essence as I do.

Tye gathers Destiny into his arms, kissing the top of her head. "Tell us what else comes to you, Taran," she says. She covers her mouth, yawning. "You were the closest to him. If anyone will know more of what's happening, it's you." She blinks her heavy lids at Misha. "And your friends."

Destiny closes her eyes, appearing to collapse against Tye. "She's resting," he explains, stopping us when we attempt to reach her. He cuddles her, the knowledge that he almost lost her reflecting heavily in eyes. "Just . . . keep going. She can still hear you, and we need to figure this shit out."

Great. Now everyone is looking at me. I take a moment to wonder how things are getting suckingly worse. But then I continue forward. Onward and upward, I suppose.

The feel of Johnny returns to me, as does the sense of the shifters. I close my eyes as a vision clouds my mind. It's odd. It's not like any vision I've experienced in the past, those where I'm dropped in the middle of a nightmarish scenario that I can't wake from.

From above, as if I'm flying, I see two rivers running parallel. They don't flow in the same direction as I'd expect, but rather, opposite. I try to adjust my position to see where they end and if they ever join farther down. From what I can tell, they continue independently.

"Johnny isn't a shifter," I say, interpreting what I feel. I peer closer when the vision reappears. It's not as clear, yet I see enough. The rivers continue to run opposite each other, but now they're slightly wider than before. It won't be long before they join. I groan when reality smacks me hard on the ass once I figure it out. "But he's close to becoming one."

"How can you possibly know?" Uri asks.

I motion to my arm, not bothering to mention my past experience with visions. "I guess she's showing me."

That's not a lie. My old magic and new magic are still trying to figure it all out. Personally, I like Sparky's visions over the freaky ones I receive that usually involve death and mayhem. I ponder what I saw further, picking apart what I felt. "I think it's why Johnny's magic felt familiar yet, in a way, alien. It's morphing into something preeminent."

The air leaves the room, despite how I tried to relay the information in a casual tone. Yeah . . . Not everyone had figured that little tidbit out.

"If it's alien, as you describe, then he must already be as you fear," Uri states, gnashing his fangs.

"No," Gemini states, backing me up. "If Fate was already a shifter, he would have presented himself just to rub it in our faces."

"And he wouldn't have gone to all this trouble of sending his Nytes ahead of time," I add. I start pacing, needing to move, but think better of it when I see what appears to be a kneecap blocking my path.

"Johnny has spent a lot of time and energy ironing out the details of his plan," I remind everyone. "He wouldn't need these numbers as a shifter. As a Fate and a shifter, he'd only need himself."

"Agreed," Misha says. "He'd also need to demonstrate his worth alone."

"Perhaps," Ileana muses. "But how do you explain such a shifter presence and the Fate's increase in magic?" She wraps her arms around Misha, lowering her lashes. She's asking him for sex, needing to satiate the adrenaline she experienced in battle.

Misha turns from her focus, his brilliant mind contemplating something, not that he appears eager to share.

"What is it, Misha?" Emme asks.

Of all people, it's Gemini and me he focuses on. "My belief is he's drinking the blood of his new masters. That's why we feel their presence. Magic runs thick through their blood."

"Shifter blood?" I clarify. At his nod, I shake my head. "All he's doing is drinking poison."

"It's poison to us, Taran," Gemini adds. He places his arm around me, feeling protective. "Not to someone with magic a Fate possesses."

Ileana cozies up further to Misha, her taut nipple trailing lightly over his muscular arm. C'mon, can't this wait? We're right here.

Again, Misha ignores her, speaking only to us. "Fates are rare entities, a higher and more advanced form of witch. If anyone can tolerate shifter blood, it's a Fate."

I swallow hard. "If that's true, it'll nourish him and maintain his strength and abilities despite the damage we inflict."

Gemini is seconds from raging. Somehow, he keeps it together. "Shifter blood will help nourish him. But while he has the shifters, we have Destiny. It's still possible to harm him."

I glance at Destiny, who still appears well into dreamland. "But can we kill him?" I ask.

"As long as he's tolerating the blood, not yet," Misha states.

Emme looks close to tears. Like the rest of us, she's well past exhaustion. Yet there's no time for rest. Not now.

"Johnny drinking shifter blood is still not as bad as becoming a shifter himself," I stress. "Look at how many people he allowed to die at his concert. If he had already sworn his allegiance to the shifters back then, he could have easily dedicated their deaths to their deity." My focus travels to the carnage permeating through the manor like fresh coats of paint. "Tonight, he added the elite of the mystical world to his body count."

"Mother of all gods," Uri snarls. He kicks the kneecap on the ground. "If he succeeds, he'll be unstoppable."

The impact of what we're facing silences everyone. I don't want to be right about someone I once pitied and called a friend. It's wickedly wrong. It's also genius.

Why wouldn't Johnny gobble down shifter blood if it will help him? Why wouldn't he take the next step into shifterhood? His new buddies likely seduced him with thoughts of immortality and magic unlike the world has ever seen and played on his fears of being harmed. Like Uri deduced, who could take on a Fate with the diadem of a shifter? Not a were. Not a vamp. Not . . . holy shit. Could Johnny be the new evil that's rising? The one Celia's baby is supposed to save the world from?

I jump when Gemini punches his hand. "All right," he says. "We know who and what we're facing. Let's form teams and search the ground for Fate. This ends now."

"No," Destiny says. She yawns and stretches, having woken apparently from one hell of a nap.

We wait for her to say more. She doesn't, returning to her quirky demeanor now that she's had some rest. She bats at a bloodstain on her googly eye dot monstrosity as if it will magically wipe off.

I exchange glances with Gemini and about half of the supernaturals around us.

"Da fuck?" a vampire asks through his still exposed fangs.

His disrespect earns him a slap upside the head from Misha. Shayna steps toward Destiny and over the vamp's unconscious body. "I'm sorry, dude," Shayna says. "Did you just say no?"

"Mm-hmm." Destiny fluffs her hair. As if that's going fix all the lopsided plumage.

We wait for her to say more. We wait some more. When she doesn't, Tye gives his beloved a small nudge. "Hey, Des. Maybe you might want share why we shouldn't hunt and kill Fate."

Destiny drops her hands away, appearing sad. "Fuzzy Toes, I never said Johnny mustn't be obliterated. My brother's time has come. I only mean searching the grounds will do us no good."

"Why?" I ask.

Destiny shrugs. "Because he's in the house."

My jaw drops as uproar ensues. Gemini bends into a crouch, his hands out. Like the rest of us, he scans the area, expecting Johnny to pop on out and kill us all.

That's when Uri loses what remains of his mind. "*He's in the house?*"

Destiny's feathers bounce as she nods. "Oh, yes. I feel him everywhere and with everything."

Emme gasps, her hands shaking as she prepares to strike. "This can't be happening," she says.

I feel her fear and understand what's happening long before Destiny explains. "He must be here in order to use the spells against us."

"Which is another reason he's using the disorientation spell," I add. "We can't kill him if we can't find him."

"And are you prepared to do as much?" Uri asks me. "We would not be here if you did your job last time."

He's right, not that I'm about to admit it. I smile. "I know my job, and I do it well." Mostly. "Unlike you, who only fights when others are watching."

A wave of ire consumes him, despite how low he keeps his voice. "You dare insult me?"

I poke my head around Gemini's back since he jumped in front of me, ready to take on Uri and whatever shit he was ready to do to me. "I do, and I'm not done," I say.

Uri may have helped kill a few beings that attacked, but only because he was challenged, and others were watching. From time to time, the elite have to prove their excellence or risk losing everything. Yes, he's upset about the loss of his dates. Yet under other circumstances, he would have taken his dates and edged away, watching others fight for him and, if it came down to it, used his precious boy toys as human shields if it meant getting away.

I walk around Gemini. "You usually let those you think are lesser than you do the dirty work." I step forward, so does Gemini, so do my sisters, until only feet separate us, and more vamps who appear to defend their Grandmaster. "Are you ready to fight for real, Uri? Or will you hang back and spare your pompous and saggy ass?"

In truth, I could fling a rock against Uri's ass and it would bounce back and knock me out. But Uri is a petty little diva, and that diva doesn't appreciate shade directed at his looks.

Uri smiles with all the sunshine of Great White shark and laughs, that's right, laughs at me and all the awesome insults I flung his way. "My ass will remain as safe as always. Good luck with what will remain of yours."

He walks away. A small army of vamps marches after him without hesitation, except for Misha and his keep. The Catholic schoolgirls wring their hands, scared yet staying put. As the master of their master, Uri can claim them as his and force them to abandon Misha.

Uri stops beneath what remains of the exit. "My son," he tells Misha. "Make a choice and make the right one."

"I do, Master," Misha replies. "It's why I choose to stay with Celia."

What resembles any sense of calm abandons the room. Oh, shit.

I'm not surprised Misha is choosing to stay with Celia. What does shock the hell out of me is his highly public pledge to side with Celia and the *weres*.

A few witches excuse themselves, as do more than a couple of weres who seem to have misplaced their packs. I don't fault them in the least. There's a whole lot of ugly about to go down.

There are all sorts of rules in the supernatural world. Nice ones, that keep those who are part of it from being beheaded without a trial or having their arms ripped off just so the offended can slap you across the face with your own severed limbs. Hierarchy is deeply respected. It goes for *weres* and witches, and especially vampires.

No matter how much money Aric possesses from belonging to a family with generations of pureblood *weres*, or the royal lineage and funds

Genevieve can brag about, they will never match the amount master vampires have accumulated.

Witches can live a couple of centuries. I believe the oldest hag is somewhere around five hundred. *Weres,* if not killed in battle, usually die on the first full moon following their hundredth birthday. The exception is the loss of a mate. The vast majority of mated *weres* die soon after their mate does. The bond they share is so sacred, they die of a broken heart. It's why Celia, and Aric, too, are guarded so fiercely. In losing Celia, Aric will go. There's absolutely no doubt, and everyone here damn well knows it.

Vampires don't die. The young ones can be beheaded or have their hearts destroyed with cursed gold and die, just like, *weres.* You can even set a young vamp on fire and watch the fire eat them up like paper. The older ones, not so much.

Master vampires like Misha, Uri, and Ileana, need both beheading and their hearts destroyed. Good luck with that.

These superbeings of sorts basically live forever, giving them plenty of time to accumulate wealth, buy and sell favors, overtake foreign governments, you know, little things like that.

They also count on each other to maintain their status. Don't get me wrong, friends turn to foes quick. All it takes is the right opportunity or insult.

Uri's voice gathers that timbre mob bosses get right before they stab you in front of your family and force-feed you your liver. "Are you certain of that, my son?"

I almost laugh, except even I'm not that nuts. Misha tends to be Uri's son, especially when it suits him. Uri *made* Misha. The circumstances weren't ideal, yet they allowed Misha to enact a frightening level of revenge against his tormentors and become who he is.

"I am, Master. To guard and protect Celia Wird is to protect our future and that of our legacy."

I don't miss how Misha addresses Celia by her maiden name. Neither does Aric, who stalks in, his arm curled around Celia's waist. As per vamp protocol, Misha should fall to one knee and plead his case. At best, he tilts his head, another no-no according to vamp etiquette, and very much a demonstration of dominance by Misha.

"Misha, don't do this," Celia whispers. "Not for me. You don't owe me anything."

"No," Uri agrees. "His debt to you is paid tenfold."

"There was never a debt to be paid, Uri," Celia hisses.

Celia was never one to kiss ass. But the way she speaks to Uri scares me and spreads a thick coat of tension around the room.

Uri quirks a brow. He's not afraid of Celia or the *weres*. Even the witches can go to hell as far as he's concerned. But regardless of his frigid stance, he is afraid Misha will turn on him.

Uri chuckles. "You show a great deal of strength with your mate so close, Celia," he says.

Celia's stony features make it clear she'd show that and more to him with or without Aric growling beside her. "Keep telling yourself that, Uri," she tells him. "And we'll pretend I didn't help save your dynasty."

Uri stops smiling. We're all afraid of Uri to some extent. Doesn't mean we'll be bullied.

Celia's features soften when she addresses Misha. "I don't want you to stay because of me. You don't owe me anything, Misha. You never have."

"Mm, true," I agree. Sure, we helped save Misha's ass when we first met him. And yeah, yeah, Celia returned his soul and all that. But we steer away from all the manipulative bull and do the right things because it's right, not just to bind someone in blood to return the favor.

Misha meets Celia's gaze. Her heart and loyalty are why Misha fell as hard for her as he did. She's a kind person and likely his first real friend. And regardless of all the wrong Misha is a part of, he recognizes Celia's goodness.

Uri glares at Celia. Celia and Aric meet his glare with equal force. Genevieve eases away, joining the witches and *weres* who take point by Celia.

"No one is keeping you here, Uri," Aric replies in a low growl. "You want to go, get the fuck out."

Gemini edges in front of Aric, his twin at his side snarling. "The point of this reunion was to determine who would stand by us." He trains his lethal gaze on Uri. "And who will choose to save themselves. This is your moment to decide."

Uri turns to leave. Gemini's voice keeps him in place. "The pack will remember this when evil strikes its blow."

Uri motions to the remains of his lovers. "The blow was already struck."

"Maybe," I say.

I don't snap at Uri and am seriously impressed with how well I keep my composure. I motion to the window where another leech Nyte, this one with suckers covering its underbelly, slithers along the wards, testing them out. "Except that blow was just the beginning."

I strut past Uri and give him a pat on the shoulder. "Good luck out there."

Uri leaves, as in, totally disappears. I don't care. He's dead weight, and I trust him as far as I can trust this thing sliming up the wards. Two *weres* in human form (African cheetahs, I think) scale either side of the windows with daggers clutched between their teeth. Runes emanating green light swirl along the hilts. I'm not familiar with magical weapons. I only know they're really good at dicing creepy things. And veggies.

"Hey, there," I say. "Allow me." They look at me and then each other, speaking in clicks. The bigger of the two motions to me with a wave of his hand.

I'm exhausted from battle and from dealing with petty crap like with Uri. But everyone is watching every move Celia makes, and us as her sisters. They want to see if she's worthy of their lives, and I need to remind them they're on the right side.

A thin stream of lightning releases from my fingertip, sharp as a surgeon's blade. Given my tiredness and the preciseness such magic requires, it's tough to maintain. I make like it's easy and force it down. The Nyte screeches, splitting in two and falling away in equal parts.

I didn't expect such an easy kill and avoid allowing it to reflect on my face. I pull it off well enough. The smaller *were* nods at me and says something in a language I don't quite understand.

I nod in return. "Welcome to America," I say. "On behalf of my family, thank you for your willingness to protect the Mate and Child."

See? I can be polite, even as every curse in every language I know bounces in my head.

I meant what I said to Uri. Tonight, is only the beginning.

Chapter Twenty

Gemini and I fearlessly swoop into the—

Scratch that. There was no swooping or fearlessness on my part. The *weres* may have pulverized enough Nytes to claim a few suites for themselves and our allies, but the halls are still screwed up and taking us all over the damn manor. Did I mention, there're creepy critters waiting to tear out your insides and wave them at you in said halls?

"What the fuck?" I say, stumbling into the suite.

Gemini slams the door and growls at it resentfully before turning around to address me. "You are *not* to leave this room without me."

I clutch my heart, trying to see if it's still there and doing my best not to hyperventilate. "Okay."

"Okay?" he questions.

"Yeah. I'm cool with that."

He raises his brows. "You're not going to argue with me?"

"Hell no." I push away from where I'm leaning against the wall. Gemini's wolf pants right with me. "Did you see that thing? It's like *Alien* and that crazy bitch from *The Ring* had a baby, and then it ate them." I cringe and point to his shoulder. "You have a limb draped on your shoulder."

Gemini stiffens when he notices. "It's not a leg."

I bend to pet the twin. He wags his tail. Unlike us, he had fun fighting that thing. "No?"

"No." He wrenches what I mistook for a leg off his shoulder and flings it into the fireplace. "It would seem that thing was male."

I stop my petting.

"We won't mention this ever again," he mutters under his breath.

I hold up my hand. "Fine by me, babe."

He helps me to my wobbly feet and sighs. "Thank you for burning it the way you did."

"Thank you for ripping it off when it tackled me," I say. I bat something gross from his chest. It doesn't come off right away and feels like it has its own pulse. I stop trying and force a smile, even though it's a hell of an effort. "We make a good team, don't we?"

Gemini has no problem returning my smile. "We do, my love." He lifts my hand and kisses it. It's sticky and sweaty from battle, and he could give a damn. If that's not love, I don't think I'll ever find it.

"Come," he says. "Let's find a place to rest and get clean."

"That would be fantastic," I say.

Gemini places his arm around me and leads me forward. We'd stayed behind to care for the injured and the dead while Aric saw to Celia.

Aric didn't just clear a suite for Celia. He cleared *Genevieve's quarters*. Located on the third floor at the center of the house, Shayna reported back that, "It's roughly the size of Kansas and contains enough period furniture to shame the hottest ripped-bodice novels, dude."

The location makes total sense. Here, Genevieve can monitor the magic of her coven and her guests and anticipate a coup or attack. Now, if only bat-shit crazy Bridette had resided in these halls.

I rub at the knot in my neck. The foyer is a room in and of itself, though small by Genevieve's standards. I suppose it's designed for those waiting for an audience with the Tahoe region's head witch. Guests are served champagne and caviar or whatever the fuck or told flat-out she's not to be disturbed. Vieve enjoys her position, and it suits her, as does the former glory of her surroundings.

A plush couch is set in front of the fireplace and stuffy winged chairs placed on either side. A bar takes up most of the right side, its stock of top-shelf alcohol and liquor all but gone.

We nod to the *weres* standing guard by the entrance to Vieve's private residence. "Is the hall clear, sir?" a female asks Gemini.

"For the moment," Gemini responds. "I'm not sure what the next hour will bring." He gives the *weres* the once-over. The female has a nasty scar on her side just below her liver. But the cut closed thanks to Emme. If the magic keeping the *weres* from healing somehow lifts, or we manage to escape the manor, her beast will take over and smooth the scar, leaving no evidence of a hard-fought battle.

"Have the next team take over your positions," Gemini orders. "You need food and rest."

The male bows his head. "We've had our share of food, but we'll take the rest, sir." He lifts his head and addresses me, careful not to look me in the eye directly in front of my mate. "Your sisters are safe."

"Thank you," I say. I was hoping that was the case and wasn't as worried until we met that thing in the hall we just killed.

Relief washes over Emme's and Shayna's faces when they see us walk in. I lift my hand, keeping them in place, along with Koda and Bren, where they're eating at a crowded table full of *weres*.

There's not a lot of food. Mostly meat plates with cheeses. I think about how the *were* said he had his "share" of food, not his fill. It won't be long until we run out of food. Any game on the grounds has likely escaped or was killed. I don't think Johnny's creations necessarily need food, but if I were him, I'd starve my enemies if it meant gaining the upper hand.

Aric brought Celia here as soon as he could manage it, leaving Gemini in charge. Misha and his family accompanied them, as did a few witches who volunteered to "feed" the vampires.

Misha insisted he and his family stay in Vieve's dwelling to help protect Celia. Aric allowed it. He and Misha will never be bros, but he recognizes Misha's loyalty to Celia and the stance he took against Uri.

I look in the direction of what might be the master bedroom. Several witches stumble out, their skin flushed pink and their formal hairstyles spilling against their shoulders and faces from the multiple orgasms feeding the vampires must have aroused. The witch with waist-length silver hair is walking with her legs parted like she's straddling a horse. My guess is she either fed and had sex with Misha, Ileana, or both.

Gemini approaches Koda, whispering low. Koda has resumed his human form and is wearing what would be an extra-long pair of basketball shorts on anyone else. Scars in varying lengths crisscross his torso and back, and his long silky hair lies in a braid against a rather mangled shoulder. Like most of the *weres* at the table, the pains of battle are written all over his skin. He needs more than what's in front of him, yet there he is, giving the lion's share of the block of cheese he was provided to Shayna.

"Where's Celia?" I ask.

Shayna finishes swallowing the piece of cheese she's munching on. "Closet, dude," she replies.

Her response gives me the barest pause. Aric wouldn't just shove Celia in a closet, if she's there, it's likely the safest place in the whole place. "All right," I say. "Which way?"

She motions to the door opposite from where the witches stumbled through. Before I can move, she clasps my arm. "If you can, give her a little while, T. Ceel didn't want to leave us downstairs and continued to fight sleep even though the little momma was plenty spent. It took Aric holding her and his wolf to settle her beast."

"All right."

Shayna motions to her plate. "Want some food?"

I take a small bowl of cheese, prosciutto, and grapes she offers. "Thank you," I say, forcing down a few bites. I'm not hungry. Blood and gore have a way of robbing me of my appetite. I eat just enough to replenish some calories, more because I think I should, and pass the remainder to Gemini. He glances down at it and frowns, not liking how little I ate. "We may not get more later," he warns.

"I know," I say.

Bren pushes away from the table with a hard shove. I don't think he could have sat farther away from Emme. I expect him to play like she's not here and ignore her, but I'm wrong.

Bren lifts his plate marches away from the kitchen, dropping his plate of sliced sausage in front of Emme. She looks up at him. He doesn't look back, limping toward the back of the residence.

Emme rises, ramming a few pieces of the sausage into her mouth. The rest of the meal she drops onto Gemini's plate.

Emme never eats without utensils or shoves food into her mouth. As a preemie who spent time in the NICU, Emme had many physical and occupational delays. Our mother helped Emme through her issues and worked on her skills by teaching her to use a knife and fork and to write at a young age. The skills stayed with Emme, as well as her manners. Yet here she is, chasing after Bren, her cheeks full of food.

I stalk after them. Emme may have healed the worst of my injuries, but my bare feet continue to throb. I welcome the cool feel of the wooden floors as I round the corner into a small bedroom.

The mattress has been pulled, and the bed dismantled, its remains piled against a corner. Shams and blankets cover the floors. Several will sleep in the small space, the security of the sheer number of allies allowing for at least a few hours of solid sleep.

"Emme, stop. Stop," Bren growls.

I stomp toward the bathroom, unable to take what's happening between them. There's so much pain and hurt, and neither will do a damn thing about it. Yeah, yeah, I went through the same thing with Gemini. But that was different. We were lovers, and Emme and Bren are not. I think. God, at least I hope not.

My determined steps falter when I throw open the door. Bren sits on the edge of a jacuzzi tub large enough for a cozy foursome. Emme's face is pink with frustration.

I huff. "What's the problem this time?" I ask.

Bren mutters a few curses. I roll my eyes. "Really, Bren? You'll have to give me more than that."

Emme glances down at her hand, spreading her fingers. It's then I see how raw they appear. Emme is raw from healing? What the absolute hell? Light fills her palms and spreads across her digits when she notices me, notice her hands.

"I'm fine, Taran," she says.

My gaze bounces from her to Bren. "Not completely, are you?"

She swallows hard. No wonder she ate as much as she did. We're sapped from battle. Emme is worn out by every soul she touched and saved.

"Just tell me what's going on," I press when both fall silent.

"It's Bren," Emme says. "He doesn't want me to heal him."

I cross my arms when Bren clenches his jaw and all but cracks three molars. "He doesn't want you healing him, or he doesn't want you touching him?" Bren narrows his eyes, warning me I'm about to cross a line. I run my mouth anyway. It takes more than dirty looks and lines crossed in the sand to stop me. "Which is it this time? And what has you so worked up?"

"I'm not worked up," he growls.

"It totally shows," I quip. I gather my hair around me, allowing the coolness in the bathroom to reach the back of my neck. I could sleep for days, except Johnny Dearest won't give us that option.

"I'm trying to help," Bren says. He swipes at his scruffy beard and swears. "She's bad off. She doesn't need me making it worse."

"Okay, now you're just grasping at straws," I mutter. "She's eaten, she's recovering. Let her help you."

"No," he snaps.

"Quit acting like a damn martyr," I snap back. "Seriously, what's the big deal about Emme healing you, touching you, or otherwise?"

I frown when I see blood oozing down his leg. I ease forward and lift the edge of his long shorts. "Holy shit," I say gasping.

I smack his hand away when he tries to shove the fabric back down. "You have a crater in your thigh."

"I know," Bren replies.

"No, you don't. I can practically stick my head through it!"

Emme's jaw is on the ground. She wasn't aware of that injury. Like me, I was fixated on the seeping wound just above his knee and the hamburger his calf and ankle have become. Bren swipes at the wound, splattering the white tile with green fluid and tearing the skin that had closed open.

"Jesus Christ, Bren," I say.

Emme is rendered speechless, her hands clasping her mouth tight.

Regret and a lot more than that splays across Bren's features, lessening his anger if only for a moment. "Emme needs to keep her strength, in case Celia or anyone else needs her. You saw all the shit we suffered. Not all of us made it, T, and more still might not."

"I saw," Emme says. "And it was terrible."

Something about her soft voice overpowers my yelling and telling Bren how much we need him and everyone else still willing to fight to save Celia.

"I've replenished my strength," Emme insists. "Don't be afraid to hurt me."

Bren swallows hard. "Too late for that, kid," he tells her.

Tears well in Emme's eyes. My lips part. She blinks several times, allowing them to spill. Bren bows his head, burying his face in his hands. God help me, I can't take this.

He jerks when more of the knitting muscle tears open with an audible pop. I sigh and wipe a few tears of my own. "Just let her help you, Bren," I beg. "If nothing else, do it for Celia and her baby."

Bren lifts his head. "Fine," he mumbles, pointing. "But I better be that kid's godfather."

I don't bother telling him Aric's already asked Gemini. I prop myself up on the cold counter and yawn. This bathroom has a modern flair. Square, elevated teal glass sinks sit atop a large cool slab of white quartz. Dark cabinetry line each side. Seafoam gel, soap, lotion, I don't know, seafoam *something* penetrates through my nose permitting me to relax just a little. I start to lift the dispenser beside me to take a good whiff when I catch Emme's state.

For all she insisted on healing Bren, her hands quiver, and she stays firmly in place. Roles have reversed, and now she's the one afraid to touch him.

I slip away from the sink, wincing when my heels smack against the tile and throb. "Hey," I say. "Are you okay?" I clasp her hands and turn them, examining her palms. They don't carry that same redness displayed earlier, and while clearly tired, she appears well enough. Except Johnny's magic has screwed with mine, it could have very well affected Emme's.

"Taran, I'm all right."

She's speaking to me, but again her attention is on Bren.

"Is it hurting you to heal others?" I ask.

"Not exactly," she admits. "The tainted magic within the manor is affecting me, and I'm feeling every injury I touch—it doesn't hurt," she insists when Bren's head snaps up. "I just feel more of the person I touch."

Emme rushes to Bren when he tries to stand, her small hands smoothing over his shoulders and keeping him in place. Bren grunts, his face twisting in agony the moment their skin connects.

I whirl around, yanking open drawers and searching for something that may help his pain. *God damn it. Is it too much for the broom humpers to keep some ibuprofen up in this bitch?*

Emme gasps, her eyes closing and her head falling back. I hurl myself on her, certain she's passing out only to stop short.

Emme's body trembles with the impact of their connection. Light spreads through her hands, cocooning him in her pale light. The light amplifies, swirling back to her and through her body, joining them both in brilliant light.

Emme is not simply healing Bren. Oh, hell to the no. She's doing a lot more than that.

Their shoulders rise and fall in sync, their breathing tortured and increasing in speed. Emme moans, her head lolling from side to side.

Her lips part, and another quiver rocks her body. "I'm almost there," she says.

Oh, shit, and so is Bren.

I drop the damn bottle of basil, peppermint, and lavender oil I managed to find for headaches, and my chin becomes one with the floor. Bren is pitching a massive tent. Massive! I almost expect people to come running out.

Emme cries out, her moans increasing, and her small brows knitting tight. Bren growls, low, deep, pained.

Emme's head tips forward, and she presses her forehead against his. Bren grasps her wrists, holding her in place and keeping her close.

Bren's skin seals closed, what remains of his wolf's healing powers pushing out the infection he developed onto the floor. I toss a few towels on top of the mess because what the fuck else I'm going to do? That's my sister, damn it.

As the last drop of tainted blood trickles down his leg, Bren wrenches away from Emme and grips the side of the sink. I catch Emme when she teeters back. She wipes the perspiration from her brow, her eyes glassy and her lashes fluttering madly.

She tries to speak. Her agonized breathing makes it hard. "I think I got all of it."

Bren nods and blasts the cold water from the sink, splashing his face as hard as he can.

Emme straightens and edges toward him. "Are you all right?" she asks him. "Bren?" she says. "What's wrong? Did I hurt you."

I'm ready to blast his balls into oblivion, but when he turns and looks at her, I can't. There's no erection. No evidence of pleasure. Only sadness plagues his features. His blue eyes shift from side to side as he takes Emme in. He nods once and leaves, his limp is gone, but misery weighs him down in a way I've never seen.

Emme watches him as if he will somehow return. When he doesn't, she leaves without a word, passing Gemini as he enters with a stack of fresh towels.

"Hi," he says, shutting the door.

I glance at the closed door briefly. "Hi," I say.

The sadness Emme and Bren left me with isn't an emotion I want to feel. It's draining, and I need all the bite remaining within me. I turn on the water to the shower and strip out of my clothes. Gemini is already erect when he pulls me into the shower.

We play, lathering our bodies in slow seductive strokes. My breasts remain covered with suds as he thrusts into me from behind. My nipples slide against the glass enclosure as he pounds, the tips straining, and my body begging for more of him. We don't bother being quiet, neither do any of the *weres* and witches and vampires in the surrounding rooms. We need to feel good, if only for a small section of time.

Gemini leads me back to the bedroom where Celia and Aric wait. A twin mattress was placed inside the confines of a walk-in closet. Aric curls against Celia where she lays with her back pressed against his chest, still wearing that torn black dress she had appeared so elegant in.

I'm wearing a long T-shirt Gemini found for me. Celia stirs awake and tries to lift her head. "You all right?" she asks, struggling to open her eyelids.

"Yes," I assure her. "Go back to sleep."

Celia's head bops up and down. She's trying to tell me more. Aric murmurs a sound closer to an animal than man. It soothes her, allowing her to return to sleep. Aric nods in my direction. He's wide awake. The intensity behind his demeanor is telling, he'll guard Celia and what remains of his allies. Others will sleep; he won't be one of them.

Koda sits up at our approach. He and Shayna share a larger mattress. He motions to the opposite side. "Found you a bed," he says.

"Thanks," we tell him.

I look to the mattress beneath the window Shayna likely set up for us. It's a queen, which is nice, but it could have been a pile of straw, and I would have welcomed it. Gemini smirks when Shayna snores softly.

Koda grins, too, gathering her close and kissing her shoulder. Emme lies in the corner of the room wide awake, staring at the ceiling. Bren is nowhere to be found. Maybe it's better.

"How long do we have?" Koda says, losing his smile.

"An hour to sleep," Gemini tells him. "Then we continue the hunt."

An hour, I repeat in my head. An hour to rest. An hour to heal. An hour before the nightmare continues and blood spills once more.

Chapter Twenty-One

One of the many screwed-up things about the manor is the lack of sense these damn halls make. You don't know what you'll encounter or where you'll end up. The she-vamps were headed to Genevieve's office to clear it and ended up in the kitchen with mutant Ewoks wielding knives.

"The fucking brown furball bit my tit," Edith Anne gripes. She holds out her hand. "Don't get me wrong, it felt kinda good. It's the stab to my throat I took offense to."

"I take offense to all of it," I admit, watching them strut their way back to their bedroom. Seriously, I'm ready to beg Shayna to make me the chastity belt equivalent for boobs. These stupid Nytes don't stop at anything.

My eyes are on fire from lack of sleep. I glance at the window and glare at the moon. It remains in the same position despite that it's daytime and close to noon by now. Time is not on our side, and it's become another enemy to fight.

I roll my neck and shift my attention to the door. Our wolves and Misha, along with Misha's bodyguards, left to start the hunt what feels like hours ago. It probably wasn't, though, based on this screwed-up time warp we're in.

My sisters and I were instructed to rest, recoup, and protect. The witches from various covens and different packs within the confines of Genevieve's quarters are also taking shifts to clean the rooms and scrounge for food. They're having an effect. We're not. We're doing something else.

Shayna dubbed our time as #CeliaDuty, and yes, Celia hates the reference almost as much as she hates "The Mate" title bequeathed to her.

"Do you think they'll find Johnny?" Emme asks. She's sitting beside Celia, trying to teach her to knit. It's not going well, and I think Celia would be more inclined to play with the yarn than make a sweater.

"I don't know," I admit. "Bren has the best nose and can usually find anything. But none of the boys can track here as well as they can outside this mess."

Emme glances down. Maybe I shouldn't have mentioned Bren, but he's a part of our lives. I take another look at Emme. At least, he is for the time being. He was our furry big brother we never had. But Emme's our sister. I'm not sure what he'll be if he continues to hurt her.

I cross my arms over another long T-shirt Gemini found for me. Emme did her best to wash our clothes in the sink, and I did my best to dry them without setting them on fire. They were still crunchy when we tried them on, and at best, we looked ready to grace the cover of *Survivor* Afghanistan, if there was such a thing. So, yeah, here I am in a T-shirt and shorts that hang past my knees.

"You all right, T?" Shayna asks. She looks up from where she's manipulating utensils into killer sharp knives with her gift. A group of *weres* from Liberia watch her, examining her work and nodding their approval.

I shrug. "They're supposed to be back by now."

"Unless they actually found Johnny," Celia says. The room quiets. Celia hasn't spoken much. Aric wants to find Johnny and finish him. I guess if any wolf can, it's Aric. He's become so much more. But Johnny has, too, and it scares the hell out of me.

Something falls against the door. The Liberian *weres* pocket the knives Shayna made them and hurry to investigate.

My sisters and I rise. "Stay with Celia," I tell Shayna. She nods, and I hurry after Emme.

The Liberian *weres* shadow the guards at the door. They open it, and several witches pile in. "We found more food," an older witch says, her

European accent light with excitement. "Little treats for children but better than nothing."

"And beat the jingle balls out of some creepy Santa," another witch says. "It wasn't as hard this time. I think Fate is getting weaker."

Cheers follow their entrance. Another couple of weres and witches march in. Emme starts to close a door when I see a box of cheesy crackers on the floor.

"I'll get it," Emme says.

I barely snag the skirt of her dress when she falls forward, and we slam dunk into another part of the house.

"*Son of a bitch*," I say.

I wrench my head up toward the ceiling, wondering if we just fell several floors or if it just feels that way.

"Oh, crud," Emme says. She uses the wall to help her stand and rubs her ass. "Did you get the crackers?"

"No, I didn't get the crackers. I'm not even sure if the fucking crackers were really there or if they were placed there by that prickles bastard."

Emme sighs and helps me to my feet. "I understand your frustration. It's not a good idea to be on our own."

Emme should have been a therapist. She interprets "Taran speak" well.

"Do you know where we are?" she asks.

"Yeah. First floor."

Emme makes a face. "No. Not again."

"Tell me about it," I say. I shake out my hand. "C'mon, Sparky. Time to get us out of here, girlfriend."

With a jerk, Sparky drags me forward, leading the way. "Oh, she seems to know where she's going," Emme says.

"Yeah, she does." I reach out and hold Emme's hand. No way am I losing her this time. God knows I can't fight the little bitch and his pesky minions alone. "We're getting out of here, damn it."

It's what I think, except every time I think we're heading in the right direction, Sparky guides us somewhere new.

We stop short in front of what looks like a meeting room.

"This isn't anywhere close to Genevieve's quarters," Emme points out.

"No kidding," I say. I examine the ornate door and the frame. Protection runes are etched into the door and what I make out as protection spells. "Shit."

"What's wrong?" Emme asks.

I point upward. "These runes and spells are designed to bind things within the space."

Emme pauses. "Like ghosts?"

I curse again. "And phantoms and demons and anything else the witches conjure. If I'm right, it's a classroom. Similar to Anti-Possession Class but not quite."

"Um. Pardon?"

I grimace, remembering. "Anti-Possession class is usually held in the basement where brass protection circles can be secured to the stone floor, and shackles can be fixed to the stone walls."

Emme's hand goes limp. "Shackles?"

I huff. "Oh, yeah. You want something in place in case you fail the practicum and are actually possessed."

"I suppose that makes sense," Emme agrees, slowly. "Um. So, are we going in?"

She's begging me to say no.

"It is where Sparky wants us to be."

Emme gasps. "Oh, my goodness, Taran."

I whip around, thinking she sees something. "What?"

"Maybe Johnny is in there," she whispers.

"How do you figure?"

"Why else would your hand lead us here, to a place where the bad things need to stay in. It's a good place for him to hide since it's not a place we'd choose first to look."

"Maybe," I say. "There's one way to find out." I didn't want to face Johnny like this. But if Emme's right, we can't give up an opportunity to fight him.

Emme's light shines in my hands. She's ready. I'm ready. I nod to her. "Let's do it."

I open the door and step inside the ladies' bathroom. The door, which looks nothing like the door I opened, closes gently shut behind us.

"This isn't a classroom," Emme whispers in my ear.

"I know," I mutter. "Johnny is really getting on my last nerve." With a resolved sigh and another curse, I lead her forward. "We might as well check it out."

As quiet as I try to be, the squeak of my borrowed sneakers echoes along the pink monstrosity. Pink bathrooms, in my experience, are gaudy and overdone. I'll give it to Genevieve, that witch has taste.

The sandstone floors alternate in shades of light to dark pink. Gold veins branch through each tile, and illuminated scented candles float along the open space casting a subtle glow that creates a blissful ambiance. More spa than restroom, bubbling fountains replace sinks, where pink and lavender rose petals spin as they float along each tier.

Emme steals a peek into the sinks. "Is this sanitary?" she asks.

"They are," I say. "The flowers are cultivated with magic and dusted with silver from seedlings. They sanitize the water and possess healing properties. During witch school, I was in charge of them for like, a day."

Emme pauses. "You set them on fire, didn't you?"

My spine stiffens with my tone. "It was an accident, and they started it."

Shayna would just laugh at me and probably point. Emme makes a small face. "Did they really, Taran?"

"*Yes, Emme.* The little bastards would lengthen when they saw me and stab me in the ankles with their thorns. So, yeah, I torched one or eight of them to show them who was boss. Can you believe that innocent act of self-defense cost me four demerits?"

She crinkles her small nose. "Only four?"

"Whose side are you on, anyway?"

She holds out her hands. "I'm just saying the witches tend to be strict. I'm surprised the incident didn't earn you time on the torture rack."

"It's the modern world, Emme," I remind her. "The rack is only used for witches who accidentally sprout hooves." I frown. "And antlers, if memory serves. Damn, no wonder I was kicked out."

The candles flutter as we pass, casting shadows of us against the wall. "What are those?" Emme asks. She motions to the row of stands whose walls curve inward.

"Toilet stalls."

I watch my shadow as we continue forward. If someone were to snap a picture and show me at a later time, I'd know who is who. Gemini has described me as voluptuous more than once. I'm thin, but I inherited the Latina ass and boobs from my mother's side.

Emme's figure is more of a young woman fresh out of her teens. Her figure walks that fine line between youth and womanhood, feminine with still more change to come. She's petite, more so than me. While I know she's a force to be reckoned with, her smaller figure keeps us from accepting how strong she is. Celia is pregnant, yet something about the way Emme carries herself makes her appear more vulnerable.

Emme pokes her head into one of the stalls. "What is that? A bidet."

"No. A Japanese toilet," I explain.

She glides back to me. "Aren't they more technologically advanced? There aren't any buttons or knobs."

"It's more of an enchanted Japanese toilet. It senses your needs and rinses you accordingly. It's what the witches like to call classy."

Emme laughs a little. "I'm not certain classy is a term Genevieve would use."

It's good to see Emme's sweet smile. "No, but it works here," I say.

The bathroom seems bigger than it should. I use Sparky to push back the gossamer curtain that I think marks the end of the room, only to realize it leads to another larger room.

Several glass saunas line the far wall, and massage tables covered with thick bedding poke through a small room just beyond.

"Hmph. I guess this is a spa," I say. "Vieve went all out redoing her new digs. So, what's up with you and Bren?"

"Pardon?" she asks.

Emme's demeanor shifts at the mention of his name. "Emme, I know you heard me," I say. "Have you kissed him?"

Bren admitted as much, except Emme didn't, and I need to hear it from her. The pause that follows tells me more than she needs to.

"We have."

"Emme, Bren has been more family than a friend. He's the last wolf you should kiss."

"He was never just family, not to me."

My gaze falls briefly to the ground. "How long has this been going on?"

"It hasn't." She wipes her hands on her dress. "I always thought he was cute and was attracted to him right away. But I was twenty then, and he was older."

I'm almost afraid to ask. "Did something happen back then between you?" Please say no. Please. I don't want to kill Bren.

"I asked him out on a date," Emme admits. "That night when we cooked our first holiday dinner at the house. He and Danny came over and celebrated with us. Do you remember?" At my gaze, her irises cloud over as time takes her back. "After dinner, Bren played his guitar and sang a song just for me."

That night appears so clear to me then. We'd prepared all our favorite dishes and invited Danny. He asked if he could bring his buddy and roommate, Bren.

I remember the song, "Make You Feel My Love." Emme requested it, and Bren made it his own, his deep voice falling into a subtle country twang. He did sing the song just for Emme. I don't tell her it was solely because she requested it and because she was our little sister and he was trying to be nice.

"He flirted with all of us, Emme." I glance at the floor. The stone appears darker here. "It's just what he does."

"Maybe," she says. "I just remember it made me feel special."

Emme was so young then for twenty, and innocent despite her years even having just graduated nursing school at the top of her class. "Did you go out together?" I kick at the tile, wishing it was Bren's face. I know where this is going.

"No," she admits. She stops in the room and faces me. "He laughed hard enough to spit out his beer."

"Wow." I know what that must have done to her.

"You're just a kid, he told me." She laughs without humor. "And I was. But I'm not a kid anymore." Her lips press together. "And now he knows it."

I just about hurl. "Good Gawd. You *have* slept with him, haven't you?" My voice is no longer soft. It's stern as it gets when worry tarnishes it.

In the flickering candlelight, I see the flood of tears gathering in her eyes. "Some things are better left unsaid," she tells me. "Even to your sisters."

I'm sad to hear her say this. We've always told each other everything. Granted, Ceel and I were always a little closer, having to raise our sisters and take on more responsibility. Except Shayna and Emme were tighter too. They could stay young a little longer. Ceel and I were forced to grow up early to keep our family together. Still, through heartbreak and laughter, we always stood as one.

Or so I thought.

I hug her tight, forcing myself to let go. "You don't have to tell me what happened, Emme. I just wish you'd tell someone."

"It's not that easy, Taran. Not when I don't know what happened myself."

This really isn't the time to talk. She made it more than clear. I only hope, sometime soon, it will be.

I sigh, frustrated, and maybe a little scared too. Someone with a heart as big as Emme's will always hurt more.

"Let's get back into the hall," I say. "There's nothing here."

But then there is, 'cause this is my life.

A giggle, like that of a possessed little girl except not as cute, sweeps through the gossamer curtains, causing them to flutter. The feel of it shoves into Emme and me, lifting our hair before bouncing along the room.

Mother effer. I hate being wrong. And damn it all, is it too much to ask to get back to Celia in one piece?

I sense Emme's gape on me when the girl, woman, spirit, whatever the hell, laughs again. If I turned my head, maybe I'd exchanged freaked-out glances with her. Except the goose bumps making my spinal cord their bitch won't allow it.

"We're going to have to fight our way out of here, aren't we?" Emme asks.

"Yup," I say. I cringe when *Creep Show* girl laughs again.

Emme rolls up the sleeves of her borrowed sweater. "I really hate fighting our way out."

"Beats dying," I remind her, taking the lead.

Emme releases a rather defeated sigh. "Yes, it does."

Although I'm the first one to the curtains, I don't exactly leap through and into action. Not when another creepier, giddier giggle drifts through.

"G-goodness," Emme says. "She's really excited to tear us apart."

"Uh-huh," I agree. Goose bumps spread along Sparky's length. Well, isn't this encouraging? "It's like she can't wait to dig her claws into us."

I lift my head high. I will not be intimidated by a laugh, no matter how disturbing . . . oh, *man*, there she goes again. The giggles turn manic and, if possible, eager.

"Maybe we don't have to fight our way out," Emme stammers. "I mean, every evil entity can't be beyond reason, can they?"

"Sure," I agree. I don't mean it, of course. Neither does Emme despite what she says.

"Screw it," I snap. "This freak is going down."

I charge through the curtains. Emme follows, slamming into me when I stop short. There, past the fountains, the toilets, bare wall is . . . nothing.

I'm not certain whether to be relieved or more frightened. Nothing, peeps, is ever this easy for us.

"Where is she?" Emme whispers. She eases forward to stand beside me, keeping a small space between us. It's the fighting stance we developed over the years. We're close enough to guard each other's backs, but far enough away to avoid friendly fire.

"Taran?" she asks.

I don't answer when I realize something is very different. "We're facing our shadows," I say.

"*We have to fight our own shadows?*" Emme all but shrieks.

"No." Well, crap, at least I hope not. "I mean when we walked in, our shadows faced the wall behind us. Now, they're lined along the exit."

"The candles don't follow light patterns the way the sun does," she reasons. "And they move and . . . stuff."

She's trying to make sense of it all. Deep down inside, my little sister knows we're fucked.

And don't I prove my point when another shadow appears between ours? The shadow rises, flinging her long hair back as she arches and glides her hands down her gi-hugic breasts. Her fingers dance along her body, sweeping lower, reaching her lady parts, and going deep. That's when her laugh turns naughty, gleeful, and taunting.

I groan. *Really?*

We turn around slowly. Emme jumps when she sees what's up. I don't jump. My jaw is too busy crashing to the floor with how messed up this situation is.

The curtains are gone, replaced with a concrete gray wall and bathtub you might find in Rome back when Julius Caesar was your bath buddy. A woman, very naked and very wet splashes about, having the time of her life in that tub.

She winks at us, her blue eyes blazing, and goes to town on the largest and roundest set of breasts I've ever seen in real life. Dark hair gathers around her shoulders and curves.

"Oh, my," Emme gasps. "It's you."

"It is not," I fire back rather defensively. "My boobs aren't that big or round." I wave in giggly girl's direction. "And look at her nipples."

"They're a tad exaggerated," Emme agrees. "And her nipples very much point north not south—"

"Mine don't point south."

"*Taran.*"

"They point straight, damn it."

Creepy gal giggles, splashing more water and very entertained by our bickering.

"Taran," Emme says, again, evidently trying to get me to focus. "Look at her. She has your hair and eyes and . . . It's you. Johnny recreated you with his twisted taste."

"All right. I get it," I say.

"You do see it?" she presses.

"No, Emme. And I don't want to. This situation is messed up enough without the little perv making versions of me he probably whacks off to."

"Oh." Emme grimaces. "Did you have to take it there?"

Creepy gal shoots me an impish grin and a rather seductive smile, very much reinforcing I'm very right to take it there. "Gawd," I groan.

Emme clasps my elbow, her touch soothing me. "Come on," she whispers. "Let's get out of here."

"We're leaving?" I question.

"Well, yes," Emme says. "She's not doing anything. All she did was laugh and take a bath."

It must be a beautiful place in Emme's head. In my twisted mind, the bitch blows up, and demon children crawl from what's left of her boobs. "She hasn't done anything *yet*. That doesn't mean she won't or that her death won't weaken Johnny significantly." I point out. "Let's just kill her and get it over with."

As I always, I said the wrong thing. Creepy gal abruptly stops laughing, and the candles burn out one by one, leaving us in darkness.

Chapter Twenty-Two

I lift my right arm, firing up Sparky. Her light is our sole beacon in the room, casting a sphere that stretches to the foot of the tub.

Droplets pour down the concrete, forming tiny rivers that part at our feet. A *splat*, like the sound of a wet towel striking something hard, has us edging back. Sparky illuminates, spreading her light and showing us how deeply screwed we really are.

Webbed fingers glide down the tub's cement surface, the claws at the tips scraping lines into the tile.

Splat.

Another webbed hand follows.

Splat. Splat.

Oh, joy, here come feet.

Soaking wet hair drapes over sickly yellow skin, veiling what used to be a woman's face. Like falling dominoes, vertebrae push out from the spine in a series of pops, stretching her flesh and exposing deep-red muscle and puncturing fins.

The Nyte lifts her gaunt face, her forearm length mouth baring fangs.

"We should have just let her finish her bath," I admit.

"Um, yes," Emme agrees.

The Nyte smiles.

And I fire.

Blue and white lightning charges in a zigzag motion, widening as it reaches the Nyte. She leaps onto the ceiling, avoiding the strike.

Splat . . . Splat. Splat, splat, splat, splat.

My hand whips up, casting light above our heads. Flipper marks track the ceiling and thick wet goo drops in chunks.

Emme hops away as the muck falls to her right. "I think it's webbing."

"Oh, come on," I say. "Johnny isn't even trying to make sense with these things."

Something crashes behind us, then to the left. A toilet flushes, and more water rushes from the tub. "Where is she?" Emme asks, her hands out.

"I don't know." I feel my irises bleach. "But she's loaded with magic and damn fast."

"Why couldn't we have gotten the Ewoks?" she asks. "I could have just rounded them up and locked them in the freezer."

I shake my head when more gunk falls. "I don't know. Nipple biting is sounding really good right about now."

More wet and sticky globs drop into the toilets. Emme gasps. "Oh, my. I think she's laying eggs."

"Tell me you're joking," I say. She doesn't. "*Emme!*"

"She's a fish, Taran. Remember the Nyte that split in two? It birthed babies all over the place."

"Good point," I say. The sticky plopping effects intensify. "On that lovely note, let's get the hell out of here. There's not enough light."

I clasp Emme's arm.

But it's not Emme.

The candles surge with flames too large for the votives, illuminating yet another show-stopping smile from the Nyte. I jerk away from her, stopping dead when I spot Emme pressed against the wall.

Long webbed fingers cover Emme's mouth, she writhes, her eyes wild and her arms bound to the wall.

I duck when the Nyte takes a swing at me. I don't quite get my bearings before she snatches me by the leg and throws me across the room.

My right arm shoots out, sparing my skull and taking the brunt of the impact when I collide into the wall. Pain rattles me as I bounce and roll across the cold, wet floor. Emme screams my name. I'm disoriented and winded but force myself to move when Emme screams again.

The room abruptly tilts as I push up on my elbows. It's dark, my eyes barely adjusting past Sparky's light.

Emme twists free of the webbing. She lifts the Nyte with her *force*, slamming her into the ceiling. The floor shakes as the Nyte falls, and I struggle to rise.

The creature spits globs at Emme's face, blinding her. Emme struggles to maintain her grip and tosses the Nyte toward the stalls. Emme misses the stone enclosure, pushing the Nyte through the opening and losing her grip.

I build my fire, ready for the Nyte when it leaps from behind the stall. Blue and white flames funnel out, exploding against the stone wall and reducing it to minute particles. I keep firing, striking harder and missing each time.

The candles ignite, blinding me and blowing out just as quickly. I still have Sparky's glow to guide us, but my vision fades in and out.

Splat . . . splat, spat . . . splat.

Damn it. This thing is everywhere.

Claws dig into my shoulders, hauling me up. I punch erratically, managing to nail the Nyte in the throat. As I start to fall, she snags me by my right arm.

I scream when the Nyte bites down. Her needle-thin fangs pierce to the bone and pull at the flesh. Sparky is stronger and tougher than I am. I'll be long dead before she goes, and she proves exactly why. The glow intensifies, lessening the pain. It still freaking hurts, and my swearing proclaims as much, but we're not done fighting Fucked-up Ariel yet.

The Nyte spits out the fangs that don't survive Sparky's tough hide, not that it discourages her. She chomps away, determined to reach Sparky's gooey insides. The way my arm is pointing, all I'll do is hit the ceiling if I fire. It's a long way down, and I'm not certain I'll survive the fall should I strike.

Emme spins wildly, pulling at the webbing stuck to her face. "Taran, where are you? What's happening?"

"She's gnawing on me like fried chicken."

"She's calling you fried chicken?"

"*No*. She's trying to eat me. *Eat me*," I repeat.

"Eat you?"

It's only then I realize the amount of goop stuck to her ear. Screw it. I'll take my chance with the fall. I take a breath and focus, trying to gather my power. *Come on, Sparky. Let's light her shit up.*

The Nyte clamps down with both sets of fangs, her maw trembling violently as the force of my magic builds. Sparky is ready to explode. This does not discourage my freaky friend. Like a famished hillbilly getting his first bite of corn on the cob, the Nyte chomps up and down on my arm.

Flames spiral along my arm, burning her. Instead of screaming in pain, or heaven forbid letting me go, the Nyte tilts its head back and forth, curious, examining my arm like a rare treasure. Whatever. The treasure box is ready to blow.

Heat casts a stream of perspiration across my forehead just a breath before ripples of fire consume the Nyte and the entire ceiling. I'm dropped like a stone, barely managing to stagger to my knees when she charges.

Flames cover her from head to toe, eating at her skin. My right arm isn't enough to shield me from the Nyte's strength. She rams me into the cement tub and submerges me, the quick and rough movements she uses throwing my legs up.

Her hideous laughter is muffled beneath the water, and her gruesome features distort from the waves caused by my writhing. She pins my arm to my chest, holding me down. I panic, losing focus and preventing my power from building.

Drowning is among my biggest fears. Death by rabid and scary creature is up there too. I never counted on this delightful combination. Except here am, losing consciousness fast.

Her laughter and image fade replaced by white light. No. Not light. *Mist.*

My head pokes through the water and above the mist. I'm somewhere else in the manor. The familiar sense of Vieve's spells pokes at me, as do the aroma of lavender, thyme, rosemary, and belladonna (her favorite).

Grunts of pleasure and pain mix in conjunction with hands passing quickly over skin. I turn in the direction of the sounds, my hands covering my mouth when I see Johnny.

He's crouched on the floor with his back to me, naked, his hand moving fast. The colorful tats along his skin crawl up and down his spine and across his shoulders, agitated and aroused. I don't have time to act. The leopard prowling through a section of his inked jungle immediately spots me. It roars, leaping off his back and alerting Johnny.

Paws press into my shoulders, and I slam back into the water.

I break through the surface, gasping and gulping for air.

It takes me a moment to realize I'm back in the bathroom, gripping the edge of the tub. My weakened state has me sliding back into the water. Emme's *force* jerks me back up.

"Taran," she yells. "Get out. I can't hold her much longer."

Emme has the Nyte pressed against the wall beside me with her power, her face reddening with the energy it's costing her. I startle when a severed webbed hand brushes against my back and drags my soggy ass from the tub.

The Nyte should be in agony, chunks of her flesh were burned by my flame, and she's missing a hand. Except here she is, laughing in that girlish and frenzied giggle, what remains of her limbs shaking as if tickled.

I shove my right hand in the water, letting my fury overtake my magic. A bubble forms, then several more, the temperature rising fast and into an atomic boil.

"Drop her," I tell Emme.

Emme doesn't hesitate, collapsing beside me.

The creature falls, laughing at the water stripping the skin from her legs when she tries to rise. I punch her in the boob so hard, I'm almost shocked Sparky doesn't fly out of her back and wave.

I snag her by the hair and shove her down, adding more heat to the furious boil. She splashes, her webbed hand slapping at my arm.

Claws graze the side of my face. I hold tight, knowing it's going to take more power to kill her. I throw out more heat, mashing my teeth from the savagery I release through my magic.

"Come on, Taran," Emme says, struggling to catch her breath. "You can beat this thing."

Steam canopies the ceiling, dripping down like rain. The water in the tub evaporates almost halfway when the creature explodes in a mini and *very swampy* tsunami.

We're hurtled across the bathroom and into the door, gagging and hacking on the chunky water. I wipe my face, spitting out more fishy nastiness and what resembles a tiny webbed foot.

I leap up when I spot more tiny webbed limbs floating along the water. "What the hell are those?"

Emme drags herself to her feet, gripping the door to keep from falling. "I told you she laid eggs."

Chapter Twenty-Three

Emme and I don't exactly walk out of the bathroom; we stagger and limp down the hall.

"Do you know where we're going?" she stammers.

I spit out what might be another limb. "No."

"Does your arm?"

"Probably not," I admit.

The light from my right arm strobes in and out, reflecting Sparky's annoyance. "Oh, like I'm the asshole?" I ask. "Who led us into that disaster?" The strobing lessens in severity, and the light dulls. "Yeah. That's what I thought."

She guides Emme and me a few more feet and turns me where another door just suddenly materializes.

Emme shudders with how cold she is. "This is it?" she asks. She glances up and down. "Aren't we still on the bottom floor?"

My shoulders droop. "Yeah, but this is where she wants us."

Emme takes several steps back and holds out her arms, ready to strike. I grip the knob with my left hand and fire up Sparky. I breathe in, hoping this is the right door to somewhere good.

I push it open and . . . we stumble into Genevieve's quarters.

"God, you stink," Catholic schoolgirl Liz informs me. She stops filing her nails just to give me the once over. "Did you get the crackers?"

"No, I didn't get the fucking crackers," I snap. "Haven't you noticed we've been gone forever."

"Bitch, please, it was a few seconds at best." She tosses back her white-blonde hair and struts into the next room. I suppose I'm boring her. How will I ever get over it?

Shayna stands with her sword at the entrance to the main part of the residence. She appears disturbed by our state. "You dudes okay?" she asks slowly.

She doesn't quite finish asking when the *weres* at her back cringe, covering their noses and racing to their perspective rooms.

"We've had better experiences," Emme answers truthfully.

Shayna nods and swallows hard, the reek we've returned with evidently too much for her too. She does her best to remain calm and ignore the swamp goo we're covered in while doing her damndest to get away from us. "Um, how'd it go?"

I *squish, squish, squish* after her and into the living space. "Oh, it went."

Celia slaps her hands over her nose and drops the small bag of nuts she was given on the table. "What . . ." She takes a few breaths through her mouth, working, it seems, to hang tight to what she's eaten. "What happened?"

Emme wipes her hands on the remains of her dress. Like that's going to do anything. "We were locked in the downstairs bathroom where a swamp creature, capable of laying eggs and spawning mini-mes, crawled out of the tub."

"A swamp creature laid eggs on you?" Maria asks, her Brazilian accent positively lovely despite her obvious disgust.

"Not on us, I don't think," I answer. What do I know? I almost drowned. Right now, I'm pleased as punch Maria appears horrified on our behalf and doesn't comment on the smell.

"Hmph. All you had to do was retrieve the damn crackers," she adds. "You smell like a wet rat who pooped on another wet rat and then had baby poopy rats."

So much for the sympathy. The other good Catholics agree with Maria and motion with their hands for us to shoo and keep our distance.

I want to hug them just to spite them, but I don't want to upset Celia with drama. There's not much food. She needs to keep down everything she can.

I glance toward the bathroom, knowing I should shower, except I'm not excited about what might await me. I cross my arms, pausing when something slimy crawls on my arm and realize it's a half-dead leech.

I jerk my arm and pelt Maria in the forehead. She screams, mashing it to bits. "You did that on purpose," she accuses.

No. I really didn't, but hey, she did insult me. "Nah, of course not," I say. "Come on, Emme. Let's get a shower."

She grimaces. "I'm not really certain I'm ready to head back to a bathroom," she admits.

"Same," I admit. "Let's just use the same one. I'll watch your back, you watch mine."

I don't count on being long until I realize there's not enough shampoo in the world to scrub the memory of swamp monster bits from your hair. We do our best, shoving our bodies into our stiff and destroyed dresses and return to the large living room.

Emme bumps into me when I stop dead.

Colorful streamers created from Post-It Notes line the ceiling, and little origami wolves and tigers dangle from string. Celia looks up from the cushioned chair decorated with bows and covered with ribbon, her annoyance at the Catholic schoolgirls coddling her easing when she sees us.

"What's going on?" I ask.

Shayna grins, glancing up from her origami making duties. It's not one of her real grins that light up every room she skips into. It's one that begs me to be nice and not zap someone into tomorrow. "The vamps thought it would be a great idea to throw Celia a baby shower. You know, to lift her spirits."

Liz files her nails as if she can't possibly be bothered. "Oh, and because she might die and shit."

It's only because Emme grabs me that I don't launch myself on Liz and tear her hair out. "I think they're trying to be nice," she says. "Well, nice for them."

Liz flashes her a condescending smile. "Would you expect any less? Celia is our best friend."

Edith agrees whole-heartedly. "Even though she did get knocked up by a wolf." She grins at Celia. "More apple juice, pumpkin?"

"No, thank you, Edith," Celia mutters.

Celia hates apple juice. It's too sweet for her palate, but there she is with a juice box in her hand and a ribbon tied around the bendy straw.

"It's all we could find that wasn't water," Shayna explains, dropping her voice. "I think the witches were planning something for the kids on Halloween."

And with the lack of food, Celia is working hard to keep up her caloric intake.

Agnes adjusts her tiny librarian glasses, pursing her lips as if we're holding up the baby shower of a lifetime. "Are we ready to start?"

"In a moment, darling," Maria says. "The cupcakes are almost done."

At once, a small timer *dings*. Edith leaps to her feet, her large boobs bouncing as merrily as she is. She flounces to a small table, making a show before bending over and flashing more than I ever wanted to see beneath the skirt. Like a chef presenting her greatest creation, she retrieves a minute pan from an Easy-Bake Oven.

"Again, I think they had something planned for the kids," Shayna reminds me.

I'm not sure what my face looks like, but Emme tries to offer support. "They're really trying," she says. "They mean well."

Yeah, those bitches do. And hey, it's more than we were able to give her. I edge forward and swallow my pride, speaking not simply as Taran, the loudmouth sister, but as a representative of the Wird family and mate to one of the most prestigious packs in the world. "On behalf of Celia and our family, and mate to Tomo Gemini Hamamatsu, Second in Command of the Squaw Valley Den Pack, we thank you," I say. "This is a great honor you bestow upon us—"

"Whatever," Liz interrupts. She shrugs and returns to her nail-filing duties.

It doesn't matter what Liz says or how she acts then. Not when I catch her stealing a glance at Celia. Sadness strikes her features. Like the rest of us, she worries Celia is living on borrowed time. And as bitchy as the she-vamps can be, they love Celia in their own way. It's the only reason I don't kill them when Celia started opening her presents.

"Mine first," Edith insists. She stomps her feet, pitching a hissy.

"Back off," Liz snaps. She whips her file out like a weapon and lengthens her already deadly nails.

"Maria!" Edith complains. "Liz is trying to cut in front of me."

"Like I give a shit," Maria fires back. She curses in Portuguese when Edith tackles Liz.

Hissing and scratching ensue, and they go at it, knocking into the *weres* quietly eating their Goldfish crackers and barreling over chairs. Emme barely gets out of the way when they roll toward her and knock over a small table. The Easy-Bake Oven smashes to the ground, as well as the tiny desserts Edith prepared.

Shayna takes point by Celia, her sword out. She regards Celia, who's doing her best to bury her face in her hand. "Dude, should I, you know, break it up?"

Celia drops her hand away. "You can try if you want. Just be careful, they bite."

"Screw this," I say. They screech when I zap them with lightning, but damn well separate.

Liz jumps to her feet, batting out the flames eating away what remains of her plaid skirt. "Bitch," she tells me.

I roll my eyes. "Yeah, like I've never heard that before." I do a double take when I see Edith breathing a little too hard.

"You hit me in the ass," she says.

"Sorry, Edith," I say. "I wasn't aiming for—"

Her gaze turns lustful. "I kind of liked it."

How did Celia not stake these crazies when she lived with them in that nuthouse?

Agnes adjusts her tiny librarian glasses, appearing annoyed. "Can we get on with this? Edith and I have the next patrol. I'd like her to open our gift in case we get eaten."

"Excellent point, Agnes," I agree. I plop down on the couch, smiling at a *were* when she offers me a small bag of pretzels. "Thank you."

Maria passes her a pencil box wrapped in Post-Its. I take a bite of my pretzels. The gift actually looks cute and carefully wrapped. Small flowers were meticulously drawn and colored, and Celia's name was written in calligraphy. "From me and Agnes, darling," she says.

Celia smiles softly. "Thank you."

She stops smiling when she pulls out two pairs of panties. One crotchless, the other sheer and small enough to fit in gum packaging.

"To wear at your next conception," Maria announces proudly.

"Where did you get panties?" I cut myself off when I realize who I'm dealing with.

Maria appears confused. "I told you, they're from me and Edith." She looks around. "You all heard, correct?"

All the *weres* exchange glances, mumbling in their perspective languages and nodding. Celia carefully places the panties back into the box. "Ah, you shouldn't have," she says, grimacing when Edith shoves another juice box in her hand.

Maria bites on her bottom lip and whispers into Celia's ear. "We couldn't give you the ones we ordered. They're back at the master's house. Just think of them as IOUs for when we get out of here."

Edith laughs maniacally, hooking a thumb Maria's way. "Did you hear that? She thinks we're getting out of here alive."

"We are," I insist.

Agnes adjusts her glasses, considering me. Out of every vamp I've ever met, she's insanely smart, as in nuclear engineer and rocket scientist smart. "You might get out of here alive, witch-wannabee," she tells me. "You are too stubborn to die." She motions to Shayna and Emme. "I don't know about these other two."

Yes, insanely smart yet still a pain in the ass.

"Hey," Shayna says defensively.

Emme glances at the door. It's not that she wants out. Scratch that. She does want the hell out of this nutcase suite. But like me, she's noticed how long Gemini and the others have been gone. We were supposedly gone for a few seconds. They're gone now several hours. She wants those she loves to return alive, and I'm certain that means Bren.

Liz watches Celia place the first gift on the floor. "Cheap bitches," she mutters.

"Our hearts are in the right place," Maria fires back.

"You need more than heart on a day like today," Liz snaps. She points to Celia. "Look at her. Look at how fat she's become carrying the savior of the world. Do you think when she prayed for a child, she asked for cankles too?"

Celia growls. "I *do not* have cankles."

Celia's comment cracks me up. The good Catholics have gifted her with used panties, forced apple juice down her throat, and worked hard to drive us mad. But it's the "cankles" comment that causes her tigress eyes to replace her own.

Shayna laughs too. Even Emme tries hard to suppress her giggles.

Celia turns her tigress glare on us. "You think this is funny?"

"No."

"Nope."

"No way, dude."

The *weres* also find somewhere else to look. I let out a sigh of relief when she blinks and her human eyes return. "Sorry," Celia says. "I'm just a little tense."

"It's all those damn fat-making hormones," Maria whispers. Like Celia can't hear her.

Liz bumps Edith's hip with hers and knocks her out of the way. "Our turn, bitches."

As if rehearsed, Liz and Agnes sashay forward, lifting an office envelope over their heads with flare. They set it on top of Celia's small belly, motioning their hands over it dramatically as if it materialized from nowhere.

Liz snaps her fingers. "This is how it's done. Go ahead, Celia."

The good Catholics have money. Loads of it. Misha makes sure of it. I'm thinking it might be a check or perhaps stock in one of Misha's companies for the baby. I almost slap myself when I remember these are the she-vamps I'm talking about, ladies who flounce around all day dressed like naughty schoolgirls begging for a good hard spank on the ass. Oh, and they don't disappoint.

Celia pulls out an index card, a cartoon of a baby scrolled in crayon on the back. Her nails protrude and withdraw in and out a few times, puncturing the corner of the card.

"Ah, what is it, Ceel?" Shayna asks.

Emme shakes her head. "I don't think we want to know."

Celia looks up, her breathing unusually pronounced. She forces an inhuman smile that has Liz taking several steps back.

"What's wrong?" Liz asks. "You don't like it?"

"Oh, *I just love it*," Celia says.

Okay. Now she doesn't even sound human.

Shayna starts to rise, changing her mind when a sound we've never quite heard from Celia sends her back to her seat. Liz is now standing near the entrance out, the *weres* just behind her and the few witches who remained behind them with their staffs visible.

Our *were* buddy from Liberia looks up and asks his friend something I don't quite catch. His friend shakes his head after another glance at Celia, and everyone edges farther back.

Emme looks from the large group gathering near the door, to us, then back at Celia. Rather hesitantly, she stands and walks with her palms out to Celia.

Celia appears close to eating the poofy chair she's sitting in.

"M-may I?" Emme asks.

When Celia doesn't answer, Emme eases the card from Celia's grasp, careful to avoid Celia's claws. Her eyes widen as she reads it. She covers her mouth, appearing to read it again like she can't believe it.

"Just tell us what it says," I say. Really just how bad can this be?

Emme lowers the card and looks at us. "It's a gift certificate for a tummy tuck—"

"And a chin lift," Celia interrupts. She lifts two pointy fingertips. "Two chin lifts."

Without missing a beat, Edith steps into a "ta-da" pose.

Murmurs erupt near the entrance. We scramble as the first of the injured *weres* and vamps are helped in.

Celia rushes to her feet, barely taking two steps before Aric is on her, gathering her in his arms. Emme breathes a sigh of relief when Bren appears, carrying a werebear whose bowels are protruding through the gaping wound at his side. She looks at Bren briefly before lowering herself to help mend the bear. Bren is careful not to meet her gaze, but dear God, he seems ready to sweep her into his arms.

Shayna pushes through the throng. There are more supernaturals present than we originally had, yet some that chose to reside with us didn't return.

"Koda," she cries out. "Koda, where are you?" She releases a sigh of relief intermixed with a sob when Koda emerges from the growing crowd.

"I'm all right, baby," Koda tells her.

Shayna tackle straddles Koda. Like the rest of the group, he's covered in blood. Shayna doesn't care, and neither do I.

I stroke the fur of Gemini's twin when he trots to my side. Thick gashes line his pelt, similar to the ones imbedded in Gemini's chest. I ignore the blood seeping against my cheek when my head falls against his chest.

He's alive. We were lucky. But not everyone was. "How many did we lose?" I ask.

"Fourteen," he replies. "Including Misha."

Chapter Twenty-Four

The Catholic schoolgirls can't stop crying. Tim, Misha's bodyguard, who lost a foot, won't stop pacing.

Hank, Misha's other bodyguard, crouches in front of where Celia sits on the floor. Out of all the vampires, he and Agnes are charged with leading the family in Misha's absence. Agnes because of her high intelligence and Hank because of his muscle and warmonger mentality. The only one above them is Celia. Yeah, it's nuts. Misha entrusted Celia as Mistress to the House of Aleksandr, a position she became aware of at the worst possible time in her life.

Hank shakes, blood caking his dark hair to his features. He tries to focus regardless of the noise and chaos Misha's absence brings. "Celia, do you have anything?"

Celia shakes her head, tiny wrinkles forming along her closed eyelids. She's worked up and just as worried as the vamps are. She hasn't moved in a while, clutching Misha's tuxedo jacket against her. Ileana found it and gave it to Celia, hoping his scent would help Celia locate him.

"Celia, come on," Hank begs her. "You're more connected to the master than anyone here, can you feel anything?"

Ileana remains naked, with the exception of the tuxedo shirt Misha gave her to wear. I don't think she likes the idea of Celia having a stronger connection to Misha than she, and I very much don't care.

Celia opens her eyes, her shoulders sagging as she holds tight to Misha's Jacket. "Sorry, Hank," she says, her voice heavy with grief. "There's nothing. I can't sense him anywhere in the house."

"How would you?" Liz snaps, her worry turning quickly to anger. "The Fate has overtaken a fortress the incompetent fucking witches were too weak to hold."

Said incompetent witches take high offense to the dig. Their amulets glow, casting spheres of light against Misha's family. Gemini, as the liaison between the *weres* and witches, shakes his head tersely. He doesn't lead the witches, but with the majority of them on foreign land and their head witches absent, they heed his request. The light from their amulets fade, sparkling just enough as a warning to the vampires.

Hank doesn't notice, keeping his attention on Celia. "Try again, Celia," he pleads. "It's only been an hour."

Aric narrows his eyes, his hold on Celia turning more shielding. "An hour too long. This is too much for her in her condition," he warns.

"She is all we have," Hank hisses. "Our master needs her."

Celia squeezes Aric's hand when he releases a warning growl. "Aric, I'm not hurt, nor am I in pain. Please, they just want Misha back."

"No, but you're exhausted from trying to reach him, love," Aric tells her. "You need your strength."

She meets Aric square in the face. "What I need is Misha alive. I can't abandon him if there's a chance we can help him. Not after all he's done for me."

Aric bows his head. Like him, hate him, or not, Misha has helped and protected Celia. He stayed true to Celia when even Aric's own kind forbade their relationship and forced Aric to leave her. His focus wanders to me. "Do you think you can form a magical circle around Celia?"

This is a good time to remind Aric that I'm not a witch. Not in the true sense. But even though I was forced to attend witch school and assigned books I never did read, I did learn a thing or two. "I can, but those things are used to protect the one on the inside."

Aric nods. "I know."

Gemini leans back on his heels. "You're thinking about surrounding Celia with the connection she shares with Misha."

Aric kisses Celia's shoulder. "That's right," he says.

I give it some thought. "You're also keeping the magic Johnny is poisoning the house with, out," I determine.

Aric raises his thick dark brows. I dig my nails through my hair. "This sounds great in theory, but Johnny took that theory out, stomped on it, and made it his bitch. I don't know, Aric. Everything we're trying to do against Johnny is only firing back on us."

Celia isn't convinced. She leans forward, her green irises shimmering with hope. "This is your magic, Taran. Your power," she says. "Johnny can't touch it the same way because it's not connected to the covens."

"No, but he can muffle it," I remind her. "My magic hasn't worked as well as it needs to."

"It's worked well enough, Taran," Celia says. "We're all still here, and so are you."

If this was my choice alone to make, it would be a hard pass. I glance at the Catholic schoolgirls, where they sit on the floor, holding each other. Their faces are blotchy and tear-stained, and their fear palpable. The vamps are dangerous and sadistic fighters, but they aren't masters. Another master could claim them and do what he or she wished. Already I see Ileana eyeing them up.

There are masters out there who are cruel. Edith has told me as much. They could order Misha's family to fight to the death, and they would have to do it. Would Ileana? Who knows? She plays the queen, but her majesty once almost took out the entirety of Europe.

I look to Celia. She won't demonstrate her fear and worry like the vamps will. She'll bottle it up until it becomes too much. I know she's terrified. Just as I know she loves Misha and wants me to help.

Edith crawls across the floor, extending her hand and offering me a piece of chalk. It's pink and thick, like those children use to decorate sidewalks and driveways. I play with it in my hand, wishing I knew for sure that one day, I'll see my little nephew color his design, in a safe, loving home that he and his parents deserve.

Celia smiles. She knows I made up my mind. "Thank you, Taran," she says.

I shake my head. "Don't thank me yet." I have my reservations, lots of them. Ultimately, I do it knowing Celia will remain protected within the circle because the magic comes from me and is meant solely for her.

Misha's vampires gather around me, staying close, but far enough away to allow me to work. The *weres* Emme healed gather, too, curious yet guarded. The witches keep their distance all the while observing my every move.

I force my magic into the line as I walk. There must be a specific location spell that could help me, or one of the thousands of chants the witches know by heart. Except even though I technically graduated witch school after saving the coven's ass, I'll never be that true witch, the one who knows how to stir a potion just so and hex her way through an evil army.

"Help Celia find Misha," I whisper. "Let her see the way. Allow her to be the guiding light to his return."

It's not much. It's just a little something.

As I reach the completion, I add one last bite of mojo. "Power," I say, feeling my irises go white. "Give *me* power."

The circle locks.

I lose my balance.

And fall into oblivion.

Chapter Twenty-Five

Something hard strikes my shoulder, forcing me out of the blackness surrounding me. My eyes water as I blink them open.

Standing over me is Johnny, shirtless and barefoot, munching on an apple. "Looks like you found me."

I shove my right hand out and fire. The strike I mean to blast him with dwindles before it can start, sizzling down to minute sparks that cascade onto the mud-streaked ground.

Johnny slaps my hand away when I try again. My limb falls as if carrying a large weight, it can't possibly hold. "That's not going to do shit," he tells me. "You're in my realm now."

My focus darts briefly to where Sparky rests unmoving. I move my fingers to make sure I still can. "That's the last time you'll ever touch me," I say, returning to Johnny.

My voice is surprisingly calm, considering how furious I am.

"Is it?" he asks. He takes another bite of his apple, ignoring the way the tats on his arms crawl along his skin. The cobra hisses at me, baring its fangs and spitting venom. The spew of poison misses my fingers by a fraction, disintegrating the small sprigs of grass poking through the mud. "I'm not sure about that, T."

I sit up, treating the bed of mud I fell on like a grassy knoll and ignoring the way my breath is visible in the cold. "Don't call me T. Only my friends get to call me that."

A boulder punches its way through the ground. Johnny tosses the apple over his shoulder and falls into a sitting position, allowing the rock to form around him like a throne. He stretches out, giving me a good look at his ripped body.

Muscles line his arms and abs tense as if ready to part and reveal more muscle. It gives me pause. Johnny the rockstar followed a strict regimen of diet and exercise. He had to look good for his fans, his manager and handlers insisted on it. But he was different then. This . . . I don't know, seems overkill somehow.

He licks his lips, grinning. "Like what you see?" He laughs. "I thought we were just friends."

I frown. I really don't like how he looks. Something is off. "We were until you turned all evil and everything."

He laughs again and wipes his hands on his jeans. "You think I'm evil?"

I purse my lips, pretending to give it some thought. "Well, you did join up with the shapeshifters to save your whiney and pathetic ass." I rise, ignoring the scowl he pegs me with. "You also killed and sacrificed your fans—humans with no real way to protect themselves. People who loved you."

"And who promised to die for me," Johnny reminds me, hanging tight to his grin.

I rise, wiping off my hands instead of wiping the floor with him. My voice remains calm, bordering only slightly on condescending. "They only told you that because you duped them with your Tinkerbell voice, lyrics, and magic." I shake my head. "That's not real love, Johnny. That's a spell. No one's ever really loved you."

And don't I strike a nerve with that comment?

"Shut up," he fires back.

Now I'm the one laughing. "Is that the best you can do?"

My laughter abruptly cuts off when my anger pokes through. "All you had to do was be real and honest and true. But you couldn't man up. You were a little bitch from the moment I met you, scared stupid that someone would hurt poor you."

Johnny comes to his feet. "I told you to shut up."

"Poor widdle kid. Poor Johnny," I continue. "He never had friends or family who loved him."

Johnny twitches. Not like someone does when they're nervous. But like in the movies when the frame skips too fast ahead. "You don't know what you're talking about," he says. His speech is garbled, and his movements are erratic. "Fate can't have friends. Fate simply is."

He quivers again, just his head at first, then his hands, and once more his entire body. He points to a tree that wasn't there before . . . and where Misha's limp and naked body is bound to the trunk.

"You bash me," Johnny says, suddenly beside him. He lifts what remains of Misha's face with a merciless yank of his hair. "He did too. See what it cost him?"

Johnny vanishes. *Poof*, disappears. I scramble to my feet and run to Misha. I'm moving fast, but he's edging farther away. When I finally reach him, I press my hand against the trunk, trying to steady myself and catch my breath. "What did he do to you, Misha?"

Misha wasn't merely tortured; his face was skinned. I see Johnny's reasoning, his intent to punish a too beautiful man the way he thought would most hurt. And punish he did. All that remains of Misha's face are chunks of meat and bone.

"Oh, shit. Shit. Shit. *Shit*."

It's all I can say. Misha is still alive. If he wasn't, all I'd find is a pile of ash. At least, I think I would. What does happen to a master vampire with a soul? Does he wither away, aging as he should have done all those years ago before disintegrating, his remains spreading into the wind? Or does he just die, as Johnny will when I get my hands on him.

"Shit," I say, my tears forming fast. I wipe my cheeks, smearing mud on my face and not giving a damn. Misha is bound to the old tree with thick vines. His scalp, covered with blond hair and saturated with blood, is left intact, sticking to his mutilated flesh.

"You put up a fight. Didn't you?"

He doesn't reply. I guess it was too much to hope for.

I walk slowly around the tree, trying to figure out how to free him. I try striking a thinner section with lightning. Nothing happens. I try to burn it but only manage a spark.

Misha is dead. I walk around slowly. With all this madness, even a being as omniscient as Misha could meet his fate. Still, I hoped that he, and my family, would make it. His death is a bitter reminder that even the powerful eventually fall.

My bare feet sink into the mud as I return to him. My vision blurs. We were never close. At first, he fell into my "hell yes" category, as in, "hell yes, hot or not, let's stay clear of this vampire."

Once we started to know him, post-supernatural battle royale, it was almost cool to belong to his inner circle. His wealth, prestige, and vow of protection gave us standing in a world we were thrust into. It was leverage against the supernasties and gave them pause before messing with us.

When we fell for our *weres* and fell hard, Misha became our frenemy, a master vampire we could never fully trust . . . except for one Wird sister.

A small cry finds its way to my throat. "Jesus, Misha. What am I going to tell Celia?"

His head bops up and down when he lifts it. I jolt, beating back a scream. "You can tell her I'll always love her."

"You're alive." A few curses follow before I finally move, my hands grip the vine, yanking hard to see if something will give.

"Look to my feet," he gasps. "The vines . . . they're tied below."

What I mistook for a knot in the tree is a knot of vines covered with mud. I glance over my shoulder. I'm in a canyon of sorts, it's a chilly and damp environment scattering goose bumps across my skin. In the distance, fallen trees line the horizon, abandoned like Johnny's past self.

I pause as a thought occurs to me. *This whole place is a lot like Johnny's past.*

Johnny was once this colorful being, very much like the drawings and creatures inked on his skin. He was worshiped by thousands, this attractive young man who held the underground rock world by the balls. Except then we came along, and it was gone.

Instead of reckoning with the hurt he endured and that he caused, and remembering the great moments as something beautiful, he abandoned it as it never was.

This canyon isn't really a canyon. It *is* Johnny's past.

"Taran," Misha gasps. "What are you doing?"

I pretend to tug on the rope. "Nothing," I say. "Just trying to figure out how I'm going to get you out of here. There's no door, you know?"

He laughs. "You may start by freeing me."

I pretend to tug again, easing out of his reach.

"What are you doing?" he asks again.

For someone I found in his condition, he doesn't sound as weak as he should. "This isn't working," I say. I find a piece of wood and back away. "I should try something else."

My magic isn't working, but I'm counting on Sparky's strength to remain intact. I'm going to need it soon. From where I stand, Misha is no longer working as hard to keep his head up. Nope. He has plenty of energy for that and more than enough to kill. Which is exactly what he's trying to do to me.

"Taran," he calls, drawing my name out like a song. "Don't you want to help your old pal?"

I back away, gripping my weapon tight. "My old pal doesn't use words like 'pal,'" I remind him. "He also doesn't cry like a little peon and allow needle dicks like Johnny Fate to tie him to a tree."

He laughs, his shoulders shaking as the vines at the base of the trunk begin to unravel. "You're not as stupid as I thought."

"You mean as Johnny thought," I correct. I motion around. "All this is Johnny. His thoughts, his bitterness—those Nytes? They're not just part of him. They are him."

Oh, and fake Misha doesn't appreciate me calling Johnny out one bit. "You freak—"

"For once in your pathetic life, be original, Johnny. Call me something I haven't heard." I scream at the sky as if he's somehow up there. "Stop being the loser you always were and the weakling everyone laughed at. Show some balls despite your small, mangy dick—"

I barely duck out of the way of a swinging vine. I'll never run as fast as Celia or even Shayna. That doesn't mean I don't haul ass across this stupid canyon.

Sharp rocks stick up through the mud, and broken bits of tree litter the ground. I don't feel them as I trample through the terrain, and I barely sense the cold mud smearing my soles. Whatever magic Johnny fed into this place to make it what it is, is weakening. What remains is going straight into his version of Misha with the sole intent of making me suffer.

My breath is no longer visible, another sign there's nothing much to this place anymore. Johnny is losing power fast. It would be a great time for my family and friends to find that stupid Fate and kill him.

Son of a bitch. My lungs burn as I race up an incline. It would also be a fine time to sign up for a gym membership and get my ass into shape.

The sound of pained grunts fills my ears. Misha is gaining ground fast. He may not possess the same power or strength the real Misha does, that doesn't mean I can kill him on my own. Johnny's magic continues to suppress and screw with mine. This version of Misha may have more than enough to take me out.

I reach the top of the incline. If I were Celia, I'd charge down this hill gracefully without slowing. But I'm me, so I cautiously maneuver down. My care costs me. I'm not a third of the way down when Misha tackles me, and we're sent tumbling.

The rocks and debris aren't real. Misha still somewhat is. The impact of his body colliding with mine hurts like a mother and forces the air brutally from my lungs. I lose the stick I found as we land at the bottom, near a brook, with me on top of him. The impact stuns him. I punch him in the nuts with my right arm as I scramble away.

He hollers, grabbing his crotch. Sparky hits harder than I do, except she needs my help to do it, and I'm barely able to move.

I army crawl through the mud and up the incline, trying to put space between us. Above me, the sky morphs from sunset orange to a furious red. If the pain in my chest and my breath would allow it, I'd laugh into the wind and throw Johnny some major shade. As it is, I can barely force my middle finger up or my legs to keep going.

Misha clasps my ankle. I grab onto an exposed root, hoping it holds. I don't feel the grooves along the twisted shape, I only feel enough to grasp. I kick out when Misha pulls me harder. He loses his hold, but my victory is temporary.

I glance over my shoulder. He's baring his fangs, and his bloody features contort with rage. I curse when he leaps and snags my foot. My curses turn to screams when he digs his fangs into my calf. I lose my grasp on the root. Like an animal dragging his dinner home, Misha crawls backward, taking me with him.

Aching, burning pain shoots from my calf into my hip. Below the bite, my leg is oddly numb. He's doing something to me, but I don't give it much thought. I need to survive. I will *not* be the prey he mistakes me for.

My free leg kicks hard enough to nail him in what remains of his nose. His fangs release me, and he jerks away. I don't even manage an inch between us before he grips my ankles and drags me the rest of the way.

Misha spits out blood. "You know what your problem is, bitch?"

I wipe my mouth enough to speak. "My balls are bigger than yours?"

Hell, if I can't fight him physically, I'll damn well screw with his mind.

An eerie calm enshrouds his naked form, adding scary points to something already seriously hideous. "No," he says. "It's that you don't know when to stop." He smiles. "And that you fail to see you're already dead."

"Okay," I say, breathing hard. "Now you're just saying shit to sound dramatic."

His kick to my side has me curling inward and screaming in agony. He throws himself on top of me, pinning my legs with his knees and pushing down my wrists. In my state, the only fight left in me is in my right arm. I rip it free when he lowers to bite my throat and punch him in the head.

He jolts, and I do it again. It's not as severe as my first strike, but it allows me to break free.

I trip as I stand, catching sight of the stick I lost when I fell down the ravine. I snag it, clamber to my feet, and swing as hard as I can.

The wood collides with Misha's head, forcing him down. I don't bother running away this time. I'm on him, beating him over and over.

The feel of his skull crushing inward rattles through my arms, and still, I don't stop. It takes the stick breaking in half for me to finally stop swinging. Even then, I pick up the sharpest piece and ram it through Misha's chest.

I back away, shaking and trying hard not to look at the chunks of brain soiling the ground, the thing that was supposed to be Misha, or the brutality I never believed I was capable of.

It's one thing to use my lightning and fire to sizzle and burn, it's another to kill something, however unreal, with your bare hands. I keep walking backward until I can't. Then I sit in the mud and cry alone.

The sun sets in Johnny's makeshift world, my tears stopping long after the moon overtakes the sky.

Chapter Twenty-Six

I spend hours drawing circles, chanting like a fiend, and swearing in between. I do everything I can to get out of here. It feels like hours pass. Except in Johnny's world, nothing really makes sense. I could be months ahead of time or gone just a few seconds like I was in that swamp-creature-infested bathroom.

After a very exhausting effort, I tug at the hem of my dress and huddle near the fire I created.

The spark I conjured was barely enough, just as the kindling I gathered was barely enough to be considered wood. Both worked enough to beat back the darkness and the cold I think I should feel.

The quiet is getting to me. Even the fire is absent of sound. There's no crackle and barely any heat. The coldness I initially sensed when I landed in this hell hole is replaced by the cold sensation surrounding Misha's corpse, where it lays just a few yards away.

Oh, sure, I tried to get away from it, but I didn't get far. The incline was difficult to maneuver in the dark. Dirt fell in chunks as if something stirred beneath. It wasn't my imagination. I'm certain there was lots of stirring and plenty of moaning. The moans were the kicker. Me and Sparky here decided it was best to stay put where creepy things didn't move underground.

The quiet, as unnerving as it is, does make it easier to hear something sneak up. It also gives me plenty of time to think. Me killing fake Misha pops into my mind one too many times. I force it away and focus on Johnny. His features were oddly attractive. I don't mean he's not attractive in general. He was just more so in a CGI kind of way than real flesh and bone. It could be related to the magic around here and the amount Destiny is forcing through the manor. Except Johnny seemed so different from the time I caught him in his lair or whatever that was I saw when I was drowning.

I huddle closer to the fire, hugging my knees and allowing my head to fall forward. I want to sleep. Hell, I need it. I fight it anyway. There's not much I know about this crazy world Johnny created. All I know is sleep will likely earn me a gruesome and bloody death.

Sparky's light fades in and out. She appears weak. I'm hoping she's tired or conserving energy, except around here, that may be too much to hope for.

My head jerks up when the silence is replaced by steps in the distance. I shake out Sparky when she lights up and shuts off, creating a strobe effect. Like a lighthouse, she guides whatever is out there closer. The footsteps turn more audible, faster, scarier.

Shit.

I reach for a rock and shake my hand harder. "Knock it off," I order. "Do you want to be used as an incubator when whatever kills me lays eggs? I don't think so."

Like a rebellious teen, she grows brighter and more obnoxious. The footsteps are almost on top of me. Something reaches the edge of the ravine.

I don't see him. I feel him. He's a predator, vicious and angry, and he's . . . hunting.

I back up and away from the fire as he rampages forward, lifting Sparky like a shield.

"Taran!"

Gemini leaps over the fire. From one step to the next, he's on me, cuddling me and wrapping me in his massive body.

My chest heaves in and out. I think I'm crying, but no tears come. I think I'll pass out, but my eyes are alert, taking him in.

"You're alive," Gemini says. "Jesus. I thought I lost you."

I want to scream with joy and fear and everything I feel at seeing my mate. Other than a pained gulp, nothing else comes out. He strokes my hair away from my face laughing. "You're not saying anything."

I laugh, too, while my pent-up tears cause a sting within my eyes. "Trust me when I say, I'm more shocked than you."

My face is covered with dirt and whatever fake-Misha parts hit me. Gemini doesn't care. He kisses my face and lips, keeping me close as if I'll vanish again. I return his embrace and his love, terrified he'll leave me too.

We fall into a perfect silence, not like the one that surrounds us, but one I need just then. His body is strong, warm, and beautifully real. I welcome it, allowing his strength to reenergize me.

"How are you . . . here?"

His large hand slides along my back. "Misha."

"What?" I ask. "What do you mean, Misha? I thought you lost him?"

"That's what we all believed." Gemini releases a long breath. "He arrived into Genevieve's quarters not long after you were sucked into the fucking circle."

"I wasn't sucked." He makes it sound like I didn't put up a fight. "I fell." Never mind, that's not any better.

He throws back his head, laughing. "You have no idea how good it feels to hear you argue with me."

"I am pretty damn good at it." I rub my face against his chest. He's wearing sweatpants and nothing else. The same clothes he returned in when they thought they lost Misha.

"What happened?" I ask.

"After you 'fell' into the hole, Celia continued levitating above it. None of us could get into the circle, and we wouldn't allow her to move, worried she'd get sucked in."

"You mean fall," I correct.

I don't have to see him to know he's smirking. "We *called* Genevieve back. She couldn't do anything. Misha could."

"How is he?" I ask.

Gemini isn't impressed by Misha. He doesn't care how powerful he is, and his friendship with Celia bothers him. It's not admiration I hear in his voice, it's something else. Perhaps the barest trace of respect. "He came in, weak from battle and bordering on bloodlust with hunger. Aric fed him—"

"You lying," I reply in my thickest Jersey accent.

"I assure you, I'm not. Aric gave Misha his blood."

My jaw is opened in the most unattractive way possible. "Tell me they fell into a passionate embrace. That both had screaming orgasms as a result. Tell me it was so good they spooned like lovers afterward and shared a cigar."

Gemini makes a face. "No. And thank you for that visual." He shudders. "Aric cut his veins open and poured his blood into a glass."

"Oh," I mutter. "I think my way was more exciting, thrilling even."

"For you," he quips. "Not for them. It's an honor to have the blood of an alpha as revered as Aric. Yet there was Misha, holding his nose as he drank. His vampires glanced away, disgusted. Except for Edith Anne, who asked for a sip."

I try not to laugh and totally fail. "Did anyone capture that moment?"

He huffs. "Shayna managed a few selfies . . . until Celia slapped the phone out of her hands and told her to get ahold of herself. If we weren't so desperate, I think the remaining pack would have flipped the vampires *and* Shayna off."

"You do have an exceptionally long middle finger, dear," I agree. As absurdly bad as this whole situation is, I would have made it rain Benjamins to catch that action live.

"Between Misha's connection to Celia and Aric's mate bond to Celia."

"Oh, and don't forget my connection to Celia as her sister," I interject.

He rubs his forehead against mine. "Would you like me to finish? Or do you care to tell the story yourself?"

"You're doing an okay job. Keep going." I nuzzle closer. "Besides, I'm just reminding you that I'm really here, babe."

He pauses briefly before passing his lips along my crown. "Yes, you are, my darling."

I've missed you too.

"The feed from Aric's blood and the connection shared between all of us was enough for Misha to break the circle. Aric was able to grab

Celia, and I was able to take her place. Like you, I fell in. My twin tried to follow but wasn't fast enough."

Gemini's twin is slightly faster than Gemini. And Gemini is freaking bionic. "How do you know he's still with the group?"

He closes his eyes briefly. "I can see through his eyes. It's not as clear here in this realm, and the words sound muffled, but I hear enough."

I'm afraid to ask. "And what do you hear?"

"Genevieve reported that the witches have breached the perimeter and are guarding it. They think they can create enough of an opening to break out of the compound."

"They think?" I ask.

Gemini mulls over his words. "The wards were closer to months, instead of weeks, in the making, love," he reminds me. "The witch covens, although many, haven't had long to weaken them. Celia and Aric will likely get through."

"What about everyone else?"

He shakes his head. "They're not sure. But they'll try."

"If they're not slaughtered getting there." My body numbs. I can't imagine how many witches died simply reaching the perimeter. I think back to the witch with the Australian accent. Is she among those breaking through the wards, or is she already dead?"

"They're in danger no matter where they are. If the opportunity for Celia to escape is there, Aric has to take it."

It's what he says, but I hear the worry in his voice.

"We're almost out of food in the manor. None of us will survive if we remain, no matter how many Nytes we kill."

"I get it. But what happens if there are more Nytes waiting outside the compound? Don't you think Johnny and his buddies have factored that into this screwed-up plan? Aric and Celia are lethal. But they are only two beings, and Fate has created an army."

"I know. It's another reason we must find a way out of here. Fate may have an army, but we do, too, however small. We have to get back and assure all of us who remain make it out alive."

I don't want to think about how many more will perish. It's not fair. Neither is the situation Celia is in. She never wanted the responsibility of carrying the savior of the world. She only wanted a baby with the man she loved. I look up at Gemini. Christ, is that so wrong?

Gemini secures me against him. I don't have to speak for him to know what I'm feeling. But I do say what I have to. "I'm not sure I know how to get back to them."

"You can't use your magic in here?"

My fingers dance along his spine. "Sparky seems out of sorts here, except I'm not certain why."

He growls. "We must be close to his hiding spot. I can't *change*, and my senses are dull."

"Then how did you find me?" I ask. I tilt my chin when I notice how thick his goatee is. "And how long have you looked?"

"Three days."

"You have to be kidding me," I step away from him. "I've been gone three days? It's felt like a few hours—long hours, but not days."

He closes his eyes in that way he does when he's reaching out to his wolf. "Hmm." It's all he says when he looks at me.

I wave my arms dramatically, something I've become really great at since this nightmare began. "Care to elaborate? I'm dying here."

"Your time here appears to match the time inside Genevieve's quarters." He scans the area, pausing when he gets a whiff of leftover Misha bits.

"Stay put," he tells me.

"Nope," I reply. I almost bump into him when he stops short.

"Do you want to die in here?" he asks.

"No," I admit. "This is a sucky place to die."

"Then stay put," he growls.

I grin. "You're so cute thinking your growls have any effect on me. Only in the bedroom, big boy. Only in the bedroom."

He growls again, but I catch the smirk.

"Look," I begin. "Maybe only a few hours have passed, but it's already been too long. I'm sticking with you, and that's just how it's going to be from now on."

His smile is soft and there and so what I need. "It sounds like the best idea you've shared in a long time."

I return his smile. "Consider us two rays of sticky sunshine."

My hand clasps his as we ease forward. When I hesitate to approach Misha any closer than a few feet, Gemini crouches and takes a deep breath. The smell of death and rot to the remains is not pungent, it's barely there at all. Given my time in the supernatural world, I recognize festering aromas as well as I do my own arm.

Misha's blond hair is coated with mud and bits of him, and multiple strands appear glued to the ground and debris. I recognize parts of him as the real Misha, the long torso, the muscles that proclaim speed, agility, and wrath, except now that I look closer, he seems slightly off, just as Johnny did.

"It's supposed to be Misha," I say.

"I gathered as much by the ridiculous hair." Gemini quiets, appearing pensive.

"What is it?"

"Not Misha," he says.

"Well, I figured as much."

"It's Johnny," he says. "At least a part of him."

"Yes," I agree. "This whole place is Johnny, as well as everything he's created. Just like the wards that are still holding our Destiny."

I tell him what happened. All of it, including my suspicions on how Johnny isn't really Johnny anymore.

"CGI?" he repeats when I finish.

I cross my arms and edge farther away from the corpse. "It's the best way I can describe him. You know when we used to watch *Game of Thrones*? How good the CGI was?" He nods. "But regardless of the advances in technology, the special effects were always just a little off. Like, you knew it wasn't real, and not just because dragons don't exist."

Again, he nods. "Johnny was the same way," I explain. "His creatures are real, and his mind-screw of the rooms are spot on."

"The rooms are easy compared to everything else," Gemini says, appearing to understand where I'm headed. "He only has to manipulate the magic within it, not create it from scratch."

"Exactly," I agree. "And while he created the Nytes over time, their deaths are costing him. This realm, or whatever we're in, is costing him too. He can't keep it up. There are no sounds. Barely any scents. Hardly anything real. It's like abandoned artwork, only half done."

I cut myself off. "Oh, my God," I say. "I know what's he's doing."

I think back to how I saw him crouched on the floor when the image of me he dreamed up tried to drown me. I thought the little perv was whacking off to our pain, getting his dirty on while we suffered and tried not to die.

"Taran," Gemini says slowly. "What is he doing?"

"He's not masturbating," I rasp.

He grunts. "Good to know."

"He's painting."

His eyebrows lift briefly. "This place is a painting? As are the creatures?"

My body shudders. "Yeah."

"That's not possible," he argues. "Johnny can't do this."

I hold my stomach certain I'll be sick. "He can if he's not only drinking shifter blood but painting with it."

Chapter Twenty-Seven

"Remember that day we found Johnny in his suite at the Den, when he was under pack protection and on lockdown?"

Gemini stops his growling and pacing just to look my way. "Yes."

"Johnny had broken a vase and was using the shards to cut himself. We initially thought it was self-mutilation, but it wasn't. He used the pieces to create that peacock on his abs that came to life. What if it's not Johnny's skin that's the source of his creations? What if it's the blood he releases when he creates the tats that are the link?"

Gemini rubs his jaw, swearing some more. He's still not as creative as me, but he gets an A for trying. "You think the shifter blood is not just making him stronger, but mixing with his blood to make his Nytes as strong and plentiful as they are."

"That's exactly what I'm getting at," I reply.

"Taran, there's only so much blood a being can consume and so much blood within his body. Given the amount of Nytes we've killed, Fate should be dead by now."

It's what he claims, but he can't deny there's something to my theory. "You're forgetting. Destiny almost died. When she came back, she became something more. Maybe Johnny is something more now, too. If so, he doesn't need all his blood to raise and create these freaks. He just needs enough to give them life and allow them to multiply."

"It's still a lot of blood," Gemini insists.

"I know, and it's cost him. I told you how Johnny doesn't quite seem real. The muscles seem too outrageous for him. I'll bet my savings he's only trying to give the appearance of strength. He's getting weaker. Despite all his power and what he's earned kissing shifter ass, he's running out of juice."

Gemini places his hands on his hips, staring hard at the ground. "Or in this case blood," he says. "He's the last sacrifice."

"What?" I question.

"To the shapeshifters." Gemini straightens. "To become a shifter, it's not just how many sacrifices you make for the deity, it's the quality. Children are worth more than a strong, grown man because of their purity and innocence. *Weres*, vamps, witches—any being of magic is that much more due to the magic they possess. Every death that has occurred in the manor, combined with the sacrifices of his former fans, have given Fate the leverage dark witches spend decades earning for the chance to become a shifter."

I wish I could argue, but he's right. "Add his own blood and the sacrifice he's making to his own body." I shake my head. "If he survives his bloodletting, he'll be a shifter for certain." The muscles along my jaw tighten to the point they hurt. "And like Uri said, unstoppable."

"We have to get out of here and tell the others," he says. "Fate knows he's running out of time. He's going to throw everything he has left into the spells and his Nytes."

I clutch his arm. "Can't you make your twin keep everyone in the house?" I ask. "If he's this weak, this close to death, they may be able to outlast him."

"Taran," he says. "From what we've gathered, he's become part of the house. If he dies, the entire manor will collapse with him."

"But if Johnny lives, we won't stand a chance." I motion around. "He's created all this with his Fate power and a few gulps of shifter blood. What's he going to do when shifter blood is the only blood running through his veins?"

The rage that surrounds my mate is only matched by mine. "We have to stop him while he remains weak. Try another circle, another link, something," he urges.

I do, putting everything I have left into each chant and circle I create. I start out large, thinking I could leech some of Johnny's power from the soil beneath. It doesn't work.

When will I be lucky enough to encounter a stupid foe? I debate dropping in my blood or Gemini's to strengthen the circle, except I can't risk our power giving Johnny the boost he needs.

I'm seconds from collapsing when he draws me closer and leads me to the fire.

"This sucks donkey balls," I mutter.

"I'll take your word for it," he says.

He's trying to make me laugh. I'm too tired, managing barely more than a smile. "How's it going with your twin?"

Gemini scoffs. "Not great. Shayna drew out letters, but my brother can't spell worth a damn. He was able to convey urgency and that Johnny is weak. They also know we're alive. I can't explain where we are, not through him. All I know is, if Bren makes one more Lassie and Timmy fell in the well joke, my wolf will rip his throat out."

This time, I do laugh. As I settle against Gemini, the reality we're in hits me hard. My body shivers. It's cold now, for real. I think it has to do with Johnny's growing weakness and not any power he's putting into this realm.

Gemini keeps me close as we lay against the fire. He strokes my back in long, languid motions. I start to fall asleep. But when he stops, I stir awake, certain something is wrong.

I glance up at him. "What is it?" I ask.

He smiles gently, the adoration in his eyes a welcomed beauty in this abysmal place. The fingertips of his hand stroke my jaw slowly, barely tracing the length. "Will you marry me?"

Gemini straightens along with me. I cover my mouth. "Are you serious?"

He nods. "I'm not giving up on our duties or on us. But if we don't survive, I want to die fighting and knowing I married the most beautiful woman in the world."

I swallow the lump threatening to choke me as my tears build. I'm wearing the same white dress I wore since this fiasco began. All its elegance has been ripped off and tainted with evil and body fluids better left to a supernatural hazmat team. Gemini is in sweats, and we're both filthy.

But he's still my love.

I'm still in white.

And I'm the luckiest woman in the mystical world to have found him.

Gemini strokes the tear away that escapes with his thumb. It probably leaves a nasty streak. He doesn't seem to care, his smile widening. He already knows my answer.

"From the time when *weres* first roamed the earth and ran through high grassy fields, they dreamed of their mates. Some searched the world and never found their match. Those who did didn't need a gathering of friends or pack. They didn't need clothing that sparkled, hides of their kill, or objects of prestige. They just needed each other and their promise to love for eternity."

I smile as I laugh, listening closely.

"I need you, Taran. Need to feel your scent when my lips graze your neck, need your heat as we fall asleep, need your heart to help me through the darkness."

This is the point where I say something equally romantic. Except even a mouthy and loud individual like me often needs to listen and hear what some wait a lifetime for.

"You turn my worst times into my best. You are my passion, the one who provokes my growls both good and bad, and the one I will love forever."

"Thank you," I stammer when he stops. "Thank you for all that you say, do, and make me feel."

He lifts me up, laughing. "Is that a yes?"

I cry into his shoulder. "Yes, *yes!*"

"They didn't need much, those *weres*," Destiny says. "But, they did need one thing you failed to mention."

Gemini eases me to the ground, placing me behind him. He's not positive she's here. Not right away. I am.

Destiny's long black hair falls around her paling face. She was always on the petite side, but the energy she's expended to help us has cost her.

For the small amount of time that has supposedly passed, she looks unbearably thin and frail.

Destiny walks forward, the limbs of her octopus dress dragging behind her. She smiles. It's so like her. She's sick and weak, but here she is, giving it her all.

I approach her, hugging her close. Her head falls against my shoulders. She seems to need my embrace as much as I need to give it to her. "You're a smart cookie, Taran," she tells me. "I don't care what they say about you."

I laugh. "I'm sure they say a lot."

She inches away from me, her smile fading. "I told the others what you said about Johnny, and you're right. All this comes from him, his spirit, his magic, and his blood that now mixes with the shifters."

"Did you find him, Destiny?" I ask.

She shakes her head. "No. It took me a long time to find this. But it's like you said, he's close, and only stronger than me because of the side he chose to take."

My heart breaks a little. I know where she's going. "If he lives, I won't make it this time. He'll be too powerful, and there won't be enough left of me to save."

Every part of me starts to rage. I keep my voice soft just for her. "Then how 'bout we make sure the little bitch goes first?"

"It's what we're hoping for." She wrinkles her nose. "Besides, I paid a lot for this dress, and I was hoping to wear it to a christening next week."

I give her a once-over. "Ah, yes, that would be lovely."

Gemini gathers me to him, placing one arm around my shoulder and nodding respectfully. "How are the others?"

"They're planning to fight their way out. It's best. I can't hold the wards much longer."

"Will they make it?" I ask. Damn it, she's Destiny after all. She should know how this shit goes down.

"Fate and destiny have been altered as a result of Johnny's deeds. I can't see anything past the present, and neither can he. It's why he's determined to complete his task."

"So, regardless of that vision I had long ago, the one where Celia and Aric hold their son, they may not survive it?"

"Nope," Destiny replies. "We could all be slaughtered for all I know."

There's the pick me up we all needed.

She brushes herself off as I just gawk at her.

Gemini clears his throat. "You were saying about the *weres*?"

Destiny fluffs her hair. What's left of her colorful plumage fluttering to the ground. "Hmm?"

More throat-clearing. My man is really working hard to keep his patience. "When I told Taran about the *weres*, and how they didn't need much to marry their mates, just a promise, you mentioned they did need something more."

"Oh. Yes. Yes, yes, yes." She spins, the octopus limbs scraping up debris as she does. "They needed me."

I glance at Gemini. "They needed Destiny?"

She laughs. At me. "No. They needed someone of magic and status to marry them under the full moon."

She spins again, this time with more flare. "I'm here for you. To marry you." She stops smiling, appearing just a little sad. "That is, if you'll honor me with the task."

When Celia and Aric were married, she was in a beautiful white gown on the beach. She said her vows as the sun set and those she most loved in the world gathered around her.

I'm standing in dirty Converse All Star sneakers that are too big for me, beside my half-naked lover, and a makeshift Justice of the Peace wearing an octopus gown mere yards away from a vampire corpse. This is my life, how I was meant to get married, and I'm ready to do it.

Gemini and I smile at each other. "It would be our great privilege to have you," he says.

Light shines down on us as a full moon rises over the canyon, illuminating a midnight blue sky. Fake Misha disappears as grass sprouts from the mud, growing until the tips skim my waist.

Destiny steps forward, sighing from the effort this extra boost of magic cost her.

Gemini's sweats are gone, replaced with traditional Japanese wedding attire. My tattered and dirty dress elongates into the now beautiful fabric hugging my curves and erupting with sparkles.

It's not real, any of it. But our love is.

Beneath the rays of the moon, in a valley of long ago, we exchange vows.

"I, Tomo Hamamatsu, take you, my beautiful Taran, to love as long as my wolf calls to the moon and the birds serenade to the first rays of the sun. In life and in death, I will love you forever."

I blink several times and sniff. "You took all the good lines," I tell him.

He laughs, the happiness behind his dark eyes, helping me to find the right words regardless of all the wrong ones I spent a lifetime speaking.

"I, Taran Wird, take you, my beloved Tomo. You've taught me kindness through your compassion, cunning through your strategy, and love with your heart. I am a better person today because you bless me with your presence and honor me with your devotion. I'll only know reason if you're present to gift it and happiness as long as you remain at my side. I love you, Tomo. You are my mate and my world."

Destiny places her hands over ours. "Love has joined two souls as one. From this day forth, and through eternity, the beasts will protect the mates, the light and fire will fortify the union, and *no one* will break them apart."

Gemini bends to kiss me. I welcome him with all my being.

Fate stole many moments. But he couldn't stop this.

Chapter Twenty-Eight

We spend what feels like the remainder of the night making love beneath the full moon and against the soft grass. Gemini wraps his arms around me to keep me warm and safe in the now very cold and eerie quiet.

I'm dreaming of home, how the warm covers gather around us in our bed, and the comfort familiar surroundings bring. But then our bed starts shaking, and I'm reminded we're nowhere near home.

"Taran, wake up," Gemini urges. "Something is happening."

No, "something" is not happening. All hell is breaking loose.

The valley succumbs to what feels like a massive earthquake. That tall, green grass we slept on crumbles into powder, and rocks and pieces of broken trees bounce along the soil, brutalizing our shins and feet.

That familiar magic I've grown to hate gives me a shove. "It's Johnny," I say. "He's losing control of his realm."

The beautiful midnight sky we were married beneath turns a frightening red, its color bleeding across the horizon and into the soil. As Johnny's world falls apart, we pay the price. Giant boulders and overturning trees bombard us as they push down the incline. Gemini lifts me in his arms and races across the valley, avoiding the pieces of Johnny's broken creation.

"Where are we going?" I ask.

"Somewhere else. We can't stay here."

I just about keel over when Destiny's face presses against the image of the moon, her features distorted as up against glass. "It's happening," she says. "Johnny's power is falling apart. We're abandoning the manor. You need to get out of here."

"How?" we ask at the same time.

"Up, and out through the top of the gorge . . . I think," she says.

"You *think*?" I ask.

"My view is distorted. You're all backwards and stuff. Hurry. As soon as you're out, I'm releasing my hold and blowing this popsicle stand."

"Destiny, where are my sisters?" I ask.

"Almost out," Destiny replies. "Aric and the others are trying to get her to the breach the witches created. But they're not going to make it. Fate is throwing everything he has at them."

It's all Gemini needs to hear to amp up his already neck-breaking speed. Destiny's image fades, and she's gone.

Dirt and hunks of broken trees pelt us from every direction. I press into Gemini. He curls his body, sparing me from most of it. He bites back a curse when something hard, followed by a harder something else, nails him in the head and back.

"Are you all right?" I yell over the clamor.

"I'm Fine. Just keep your head down," he says. "I'll keep you safe."

The canvas to this painted realm tears open; the raucousness paining my ears.

"Do you think you're headed the right way?" I ask.

"I don't know. There's no way to tell." Gemini's body quakes as maliciously as the earth. "Destiny told us to head up this side of the gorge, and that's what we need to do."

The ground once full of mud dries to dust. I choke on it and blink several times to clear my vision. My eyes fly open despite it all when I catch sight of the steep hill we have to climb. There aren't just boulders spinning downward but whole uprooted trees sliding in every direction.

Gemini leaps, racing the length of a large birch and using the slapping limbs to catapult him over the next course of tumbling wreckage.

The side of the gorge dismantles the faster the realm decomposes, turning more perpendicular as pieces drop away. I couldn't possibly maneuver this on my own. Thank God my brave and agile lover is carrying me, and I don't have to climb this alone.

"You're going to have to climb this alone," my brave and agile lover tells me. "I can't carry you."

"What the fuck, Fate?" I shout.

"I got you, baby," he tells me. "I just need my hands free to get us out."

I duck when more shit comes flying at us. "Can't I just hang on to your neck or something?"

We're going to die, and Gemini chokes back a laugh. "We all know you can't hang on to me, love."

I cough up the cloud of dirt caking my throat. "I will if the other choice is *death*."

"It's all right," he assures me when I curse some more. "We just got married. You're not getting rid of me yet."

More rubble rains down. More evidence that we're going to die. The good Catholic Agnes told me I'm too stubborn to die. True. And my mate is too loyal to let me.

"Okay, I trust—"

My words turn into screams when Gemini throws me ahead of him. I flail, plummeting to my death when he catches me, *and tosses me again*!

This continues. I suppose it must. This is Johnny's last chance to get Celia. His last opportunity to prove he can reign as a shapeshifter and that he belongs among the most feared beings on Earth. He can't waste time keeping up a realm he doesn't need.

I don't get used to Gemini's technique. I'm losing my voice, shrieking each time I'm thrown and fall. Gemini is working it, avoiding the ruins of Johnny's world and scrambling around the mess to assure he catches me.

My surroundings are a horrible mix of bleeding colors and commotion. Gemini snags my wrist and clutches me when a large section of rocks breaks away, and I almost fall from his reach. I'm sick to my stomach, choking on garbage that has no business in my mouth.

"I don't know how much longer I can keep this up," I admit.

"You don't have to," he promises. "Last one. Try to hang to the edge, and I'll push you through."

I'm launched in another revolting jolt. The sky clears into a brilliant light. I stretch my hands, reaching when I think I see something I can cling to. I feel it, fasten myself to it, and just about hurl when I realize I'm gripping a Nyte by the head.

A gaping maw, with rows of freakishly large human teeth, makes up most of her face. I say "her" because one dangling boob is slapping at my right cheek, and the other is swinging back and forth, caressing my head.

"Taran, it's dead. *Dead,*" Gemini hollers over my screams. "They all are."

I'm not sure what he means until I look down. Poking through what remains of the side of the gorge are body parts. Heads, torsos, and limbs, you name it or think it, it's there. The remains of Johnny's Nytes we killed.

"We're out of time," Gemini says. He grips my ass and shoves me upward. "Climb!"

I wish I can say I didn't cram my foot in the Nyte's mouth to help me up or hook my hand into her lady parts for leverage. But I did, and would do it again, dammit. The manor is coming apart, and my sisters need me.

I stretch my right hand up and into the white light. I feel around, gripping a hard surface slippery with dust. Gemini clasps my foot, levitating me through and into Genevieve's quarters. I drag my body across the floor in the time it takes Gemini to leap up and land in a crouch in front of me.

The residence is abandoned. I rise carefully, trying to catch my balance. Just as in Johnny's realm, the alarming quaking continues, and everything is coming apart. I scan the area, my senses overstimulated from the bedlam.

I jump and bump into Gemini as the chalk circle I crawled through expands and swallows our way out. "How are we going to get out of here?"

My lover lifts the couch and flings it through the window, striking another leech Nyte sliding down the glass. "Come on," he says.

He clasps my hand and guides me onto the roof. Roaches as large as Gemini, with bleached human faces, skitter toward us. I blast the closest one, my pent-up magic unleashing in a furious bolt and almost knocking me off the roof. Gemini holds tight, keeping me in place.

My fire struck a hole in the roach's chest and the section of roof behind it. Empty sockets where eyes should be glance down as my fire eats through its ribs. Its mouth opens. There's no tongue or teeth. There's only blackness to release the gurgling sound from deep within its throat. I think its dying until I realize it's a call to arms. Dozens of roaches crawl from the levels above and below, their bizarrely slender feet moving fast and clicking against the tiles.

Gemini throws back his head and howls, *calling* his twin.

My strikes hit each mark and beyond, further damaging the burning manor and causing it to tilt. Gemini grips my shoulders. "Taran, the manor is coming undone. Your fire is making things worse. We can't risk hurting Destiny if she remains part of the house. Go. I'll take care of these Nytes."

For all he promised he wouldn't throw me again, Gemini does, down another level and onto his twin's back. More out of instinct, I snag the tuft of his neck, hanging on for dear life as he finesses his way down the multi-tiered roof.

From this part of the manor, I can see the lake, rear lawn, and the stone steps leading down to the gardens and beach. The lake is agitated and whirling with magic. Blue, green, and clear sparkles scatter across the water into the air, creating dangerously large waves that pummel the shore.

My cheek presses against the wolf's fur when he dives to the next level, each altitude providing a different view of the madness.

Destiny was right. Celia didn't make it anywhere near the perimeter. No one did. Everyone left is fighting a horde of Nytes along the sand, lawn, and woods in between, including Uri and all his remaining vampires.

The night sky is alight with magic. Witches from across the globe cast their curses and hexes while the roars of battle sound from the most powerful *weres* and vampires of their kind. My pulse beats in rapid bursts, my body trembling with how badly I need to join the fight.

Gemini's twin peels back his fangs in a snarl, barely making a sound as his nails scrape the stone of the topmost terrace. We're off the roof but still far from the battle.

Johnny makes sure it stays that way.

I'm launched across the terrace when an anaconda Nyte slams into Gemini's twin. Stars burst into my vision as my head bangs the rough surface. I tilt my head up, calling to the twin and barely forming my words as the snake coils around him.

The twin squirms, beating the snake against the stone and digging his fangs into its flesh. I swear when my head becomes too heavy to keep elevated. In the sky, a moth with iridescent wings of silver flutters by. I can't be certain the image is real and blink several times to clear my head. I can't just lie here. Not if I want to live.

My head falls to the side in the direction of the lake. I see several injured *weres* drag Celia down the length of the beach, fighting to keep her away from the increasing waves obliterating the shore. She screams to Aric, who falls back. I don't understand what's happening until Fate's latest masterpiece breaks through the water and faces off with Aric.

A sea dragon, several stories high, emerges from the lake, its partially eaten body falling away from his frame and splashing against the tumultuous water. Sharks with human hands (more of Johnny's creations) leap from the lake, gobbling up the bloody wads.

Koda and Bren rush to stand with Aric, as do the *weres* who were close friends with Aric's father. It's only them, but it's all Aric has now.

Johnny is playing for keeps and has our allies surrounded. The *weres* don't get far with Celia; they loop around, leading her away from an advancing group of Nytes. The only way out now is across Lake Tahoe. But, no way can they risk taking Celia through with those monsters roaming the deep.

"Buck dis sheet," I mumble, forcing myself up.

The moth I saw earlier flutters back, circling me. I'm suddenly alert when its asexual body and multiple arms flap excitedly and dive for me. I fire and miss, fire and miss, fire and, *oof*, it's on me.

Its pincher feet secure my ankles. One set of hands press onto my chest, the other wrench my hands over my head. Another arm protrudes through the Nyte's belly just to press a finger to my lips and "shush" me.

"Let me tell you a story," it slurs in its garbled speech. "Where once a pretty little thing and her pretty little sisters thought they could save the world."

Its voice is the thing of nightmares. It racks my heightened nerves and urges me to plead for my life. My chest rises and falls in convulsive motions, the moth's weight threatening to crush my ribs with each small breath I draw.

"How about . . ." I swallow several times, struggling to catch my breath.

Its hand strokes back a strand of my hair. "Yes, my sweet?"

"How about instead of a story . . . you fuck a donkey instead?" I suggest.

The moth laughs. Aside from spreading more of its weight against my chest, it's too captivated by the scene unfolding at the beach to bother with me.

My head falls to the side. I push aside the hurt, using my anger to build my fire. I can't strike with my arms held down. But I can damn well kindle my fire from my core and surround my body with it. All I need is a little more air, and I can help my friends.

The *weres* attack the dragon at once. Aric scales the neck, yanking through the layers of deteriorating muscle, desperate to reach the brain.

The sea dragon shakes its head, swaying from side to side, trying to fling Aric and the wolves at the sharks. Bright orange light ignites from the sea dragon's underbelly, billowing smoke and fire from the holes in its neck.

"*Aric,*" Koda howls.

The wolves leap from the dragon when fire streams through the openings of its skin. They tumble into the water and are immediately swarmed by the sharks.

The dragon blasts a funnel of orange fire in Celia's direction. Celia breaks free from the *weres* protecting her and takes off down the beach, permitting the *weres* to scramble to safety and leading the dragon away.

In her pregnant state, Celia isn't as fast. She hugs her belly, her bare feet beating against the sand as she fights to keep her baby safe.

"No," I rasp.

My fire builds, brewing into a firestorm but failing to unleash.

Aric hangs tight to the dragon's head, punching it through the eye and blinding it. Like a man possessed with rage, Aric digs his hands through the socket and yanks out lumps of brain.

Aric's attack is savage yet has no effect on the dragon. The monster keeps going, barraging Celia with an undulating stream of flame.

I scream. "*No!*"

Aric howls, leaping off the dragon to take the blow for Celia.

He's too late.

Ileana takes it instead.

Naked, her magnificent body brilliant in the light, Ileana stretches her limbs, shrieking in agony as the fire incinerates her flesh. The power of this ancient vampire spills out from her breaking body, amplifying and expanding into a protective sphere.

Aric tackles Celia and races her away.

Ileana remains standing, through the upheaval of battle, the collective shock around us, and the dispersed groups continuing to fight, she does not fall until the last of the sea dragon's flames lick her bones dry.

I writhe, willing my magic to discharge. The first waves of heat gather along my skin, only to be snuffed when the moth slaps me across the face.

"The little tiger still thinks she can fight," the moth slurs. "Poor little thing. Doesn't she know her cub is just as dead as she?"

The Nyte leans in, licking the blood streaming from a cut above my eye. It expects a free feed, not the headbutt to the face I nail it with. The moth arches up, swiping its nose, its antennae twitching as it analyzes the dark fluid closely.

I clench my jaw, working to restart my fire as the discord on the beach reaches its tipping point.

Uri jumps into the fray. He lifts a large boulder and hurtles it at the dragon, giving Celia and Aric time to escape. The boulder partially crushes the dragon's face, yet it barely makes an impact. The dragon shakes what remains of its head, angling its gargantuan body and stalking after Celia.

Uri rushes to Ileana's remains, lengthening his nails and slitting his throat. Like a fountain, blood pours from Uri's neck, saturating Ileana's skeleton.

Aric bolts down the beach, carrying Celia. Every *were* and vampire in the vicinity is tearing into the dragon, trying to take it and the circling sharks apart.

Everything I see becomes too much to bear, and my body reacts, striking the concrete like a jackhammer, the blazes surging within me set to erupt.

The moth strokes my head, satisfied that Celia no longer stands a chance. "Let me eat you," it tells me. "Let me enjoy another taste before you die."

I grin, even though that much hurts. "How about we send the moth to the flame instead?"

My fire washes over the moth and me, singeing its wings and limbs like paper before cooking its long outlandish form. I push its burning remains off me, grimacing as the moth continues to analyze its dying form.

Gemini's twin hobbles to me, his ribs cracked. He licks my face, encouraging me to my feet when I stumble.

"Taran," Gemini falls next to me. "What happened?"

"A moth tried to eat me," I say.

He stretches his arms to lift me. "No. You have to help Celia and Aric. We're losing, Gemini. They need you."

"Go," I insist when he appears torn. "My fire will protect me from anything that comes."

Gemini kisses my face. "Stay alive. You hear me? I'll be back."

Gemini and his twin catapult over the terrace. I take a long, cleansing breath and try to stand. It takes me hugging the stone pillar for me to get my footing, but I manage and stagger across the terrace.

I'm not moving fast, but I am moving, my head clearing from the beatings it took the farther I walk.

An explosion rattles the ground and has me glancing over my shoulder. The manor splits apart, indenting inward. A crash follows, and another after that. I think it's the magic breaking down Vieve's home and Destiny losing her grip until a VW Thing launches out of the house and screeches to a stop in front of me.

"Dude!" Shayna pushes up from the driver's seat and waves.

I blink at her a few times. Shayna is many things, perky, cute, and fiercely loyal. She is not what anyone would call a safe and conscientious driver. She reaches across the old death trap of a vehicle and flings open the door. "Get in, T. Time to save the day."

"It's okay." I hook my thumb in the direction of the steps. "I'll just walk." *And take my chances with the scary entities wanting to play tug of war with my innards.*

Shayna flings a knife over my shoulder, stabbing a frog with far too many legs and tongues. I hadn't noticed it, but nothing ever gets past Shayna.

"Come on, T," she says. She frowns and looks behind her. With a flick of her wrist, she stabs something on the other side of the car with her sword. Whatever she kills makes a squeamish and gurgling sound. Still, she turns around, grinning, her ponytail swinging away in the breeze."

"What are you waiting for?" Shayna asks. "We have to save Celia." She beeps the horn twice as if it will somehow seal the deal. "And this is just the puppy to do it."

She's right. God help me, she's right. I don't quite get the door shut when Shayna stomps on the accelerator like she's squishing a bug.

Instead of heading toward the beach, she careens around toward the side of the house. "Where are you going?" I screech, reaching for my seat belt.

"To save, Ceel," she reminds me. She glances down to unclick the locking mechanism on my seat belt and almost hits the side of the house. "You don't need that, dude. Trust me."

If I had any breath when that moth creature slid on top of me, I would have screamed, yet still not as loud as I do when Shayna crashes over and through every burning and demolished piece of house she can find. She flips on the wipers when something . . . maybe a liver . . . smacks against the windshield and smears blood across the glass.

"*Oof,*" she says. "I hope that wasn't someone on our side."

Shayna takes the next turn on two wheels, racing at high-velocity, parallel to the beach. We pass Aric, Misha, *and Celia.* "Wait. You're going the wrong way."

"I sure am," she agrees.

I almost think this is another Nyte in my sister's place. But even evil doesn't drive this bad. "Aren't we driving Celia to the perimeter?"

"Pfft, gosh no," she says. "We'll never make it there in one piece, T."

She narrows her gaze, mowing down an effed up version of Humpty Dumpty. She slams on the brakes, puts it in reverse, and runs over it again, spilling black gunk all over the lawn as she peels away.

My fingers turn blue with how hard I'm gripping the side of the car. "Do you even know what we're going to do?"

"Totally. Me and Emme have a plan," Shayna replies. Her skin is smeared with her blood and a lot of something else. Several cuts line her arms, and her ponytail is askew.

"Are you going to tell me what it is?" If it sounds like I'm yelling, I am.

"Sure," Shayna says, smiling. "We're going to hit the sea critter with the car."

"This car?" I ask.

"Yup."

I point down. "This one right here."

"Absolutely, dude," she says.

"Then why are we driving to the front of the house?" I screech at her.

Shayna giggles in that ridiculous giddy way she does when she finds the car keys we've carefully hidden. "T, I'm going to need a running start. Oh, and since you're here, don't forget to fire this bad boy up."

We reach the edge of the line. Shayna donuts around and punches it. "Relax," she says when I gape at her. We'll jump, Emme will catch us, it's all good."

I look at the tier below where our supposed savior Emme is running for her life. She's screaming bloody murder as a battalion of two-feet-tall Oompa Loompas chase after her flinging pieces of flaming candy.

Never in my life did I think I'd say these words. "The Oompa Loompas are after Emme!"

"What'd you say, dude?"

"Oompa Loompas," I repeat, because it didn't sound insane enough the first time. "They're chasing Emme and hitting her with flaming Tootsie Rolls."

Shayna crinkles her nose. "Those aren't Tootsie Rolls, T," she tells me.

Johnny really has gone too far. I fling lightning like a woman possessed, frying the little bastards to bits until they're out of my view.

"She's not going to make it," I say, turning back to face the front.

"Sure, she will," Shayna says. "Emme's good like that."

We're almost to the end when the sea dragon pops its head up. Shayna taps my leg. "Ready to get airborne?"

She doesn't expect an answer. She's just prepping me to jump and trying to be polite.

"One," Shayna says, her tone growing serious.

Beneath the light of the moon, Shayna's ability to manipulate metal unleashes, elongating the hood and narrowing the car's steel frame.

"Two," Shayna says, kicking open the door.

"Three" never comes. Shayna's torpedo soars at the dragon. I aim and fire, slamming the giant weapon with every bit flame I can muster before falling. The torpedo strikes the Nyte dead center, killing it and snapping its neck.

Emme's *force* catches us, floating us down.

"Woo-hoo!" Shayna yells, lifting her arms. She was right, Emme was totally there for us.

I look at the sea of bodies below. Aric hands Celia off to another group of *weres*. The sharks are breaking through the waves and leaping onto the beach. They're after Celia, but the *weres*, and the vampires led by Misha, easily destroy them.

Every witch, *were*, and vampire present refuses to give up. They're fighting hard and smart, and it's working. We're doing it. We're going to win.

It's a stupid thought that doesn't last. From the lake, another sea dragon emerges. It strikes at lightning speed, knocking over the *weres* guarding Celia . . . and swallowing her whole.

Chapter Twenty-Nine

"No. Celia!" Aric roars.

As quickly as the Nyte emerges, it's gone, and so is my sister.

Aric dives into the water. Gemini, Koda, and Bren follow, swimming against the rough tide. More disappear underwater—Misha, Hank, and Tim. Uri, too, I think.

I flop onto the sand, where Emme drops me, digging in my nails and screaming, just . . . *screaming*. I was supposed to be there. I was supposed to save her.

Shayna lands beside me, sobbing into her hands. "Ceel," she cries. *"Ceel."*

Emme collapses between us, barely able to speak. "It took Celia," Emme stammers. "I-I-I tried to get here, but that thing . . . *it took her.*" Her whimper of agony punctures my already breaking heart.

My legs quiver as I stand and stare out to the lake. Moonlight washes along the great expanse, magnifying the already brilliant sparkles brewing from Tahoe's magic.

Bren comes up for air, then immediately dives back down. Koda and Gemini break through the surface next. Each head that pokes up is brief, returning quickly to the water.

Aric is the only one who fails to resurface. He stays down, fighting the harsh waves wreaking havoc against the shore.

Tahoe is raging. It's not until that familiar sense of Fate scrapes a line down my spine that I recognize the root of the lake's fury. I edge away, swiping at my face.

My calves strike the stone steps leading back to the manor, the rough surface scratching my skin. "Johnny's still alive," I mumble.

Shayna and Emme don't hear me over their hysteria. It's okay. Let them be. Let them mourn.

I have work to do.

My injuries make maneuvering the steps hard at first. As my head clears, Sparky lights up. Our magic surges, nurturing me, giving me strength, and cocooning me in fire and light.

By the second tier, I'm racing up the demolished steps. My blistering tears make it hard to see. I blink them away. My sister is gone. This isn't the time to cry and share my sorrow with Shayna and Emme. It's time to avenge my family.

Magical smoke drifts into the air, a mix of colors from the fallen and those continuing to fight. There's dark pink from the head witch of Malaysia. She's somewhere in the woods, alive but just barely.

Blood and pain stain the peach and gold magic of the old Australian witch. Still, she stands, a force to be reckoned with.

Clouds of purple flicker into the night. The Priestess of Columbia's magic is poisonous. Like a beast, it stalks above me and expands into a cloud, searching for its enemies and suffocating those in its path.

The orange fire that greets me at the top is conjured by a skilled pyrogenic witch from Istanbul. It challenges the fire consuming my form. I easily snuff hers out and shove the lingering magic away.

"Back off," I bite out. "You are not my enemy, but you can be."

The heat from her magic sweeps past me and onto her prey.

My sister is dead. That beautiful young woman who wanted to be wanted for so long is gone.

A vampire leaps from the trees, a blur of speed too fast to track with human eyes. My senses fix on him before his feet touch the ground. I slash at an angle with my right hand, severing him in two. He belongs to Uri, and he wanted me dead. He either turned on his master or on us. No matter. I step over his severed and flailing form, the white-hot fire surrounding me lighting him like a torch.

The screeching Nytes, growls, and calls of battle deaden the vampire's screams. I pass a tribe of African witches as I reach the final tier. They hold hands and chant, cursing a giant rat with multiple limbs to stone.

The rat falls over. I use him like a bomb when a pack of mutant pit bulls, led by a zombie on horseback, charge. Shrapnel detonates into the faction, punching holes into their chests and setting their skin aflame.

One of the African witches races to me, gasping at the flaming wreckage I leave behind. "Your sister," she says, glancing around. "The Mate. Where is she?"

"She's dead," I say.

My words bring on a fresh start of tears. She covers her mouth, her eyes pooling. "No," she says. "No."

I have no words to comfort her or me. The thought of Celia's smile and kindness coats me with another layer of sadness instead of gifting me with gentle strokes to my broken soul.

My earliest memory of Celia is of her carrying Emme in her arms. I was barely four. She was five.

Celia stroked Emme's hair, speaking softly to her in our bedroom. I remember that tiny apartment so well. We had so little. Daddy worked as a clerk at a law firm. At night he attended school. I didn't know what it all meant. Celia seemed to.

"Our Daddy is going to be a lawyer soon," she'd tell Emme, rocking her when Emme began to fuss. "You're going to have pretty dolls and a real bed."

"What about us?" I asked. I smirked at Celia's grin.

Shayna looked up, pausing on her intense chewing of a cardboard book.

Celia lifted her chin proudly. "We're going to have a house with a big yard and our own beds." She lowered herself between Shayna and me, using care as she adjusted Emme on her lap. "There won't be rats to wake us at night or bullies to make fun of our clothes in the park. You'll have pretty purple unicorn sheets and new toys that come in a box."

I'm tackled by a bear, his snout too long to be real, and his body disproportioned. It's another of Johnny's creations. He knows I'm coming for him.

My flames intensify as I ramp up my heat. His fangs are near my throat but don't quite touch me. My fire encases him, sweeping across his fur and roasting him down to the bone. He collapses on top of me. I keep still, permitting my heat to finish the job as my heart holds tight to that memory.

I had forgotten about the unicorn sheets I desperately wanted and about telling Celia how much those rats in our apartment scared me.

Daddy never became a lawyer. He never bought us that house with the big yard. Mama never had a chance to wrap brand new toys with ribbon or make my bed with those pretty sheets. They were taken from us too soon. Just like Celia.

The bear falls apart on top of me like broken pieces of coal.

"The Mate is dead!" another witch shouts.

"Kill them," a *were* howls. "Kill them all!"

What's left of the bear falls away from me as I rise. I catch sight of Braeden, lifting a massive and writhing Nyte. This creature is like a giant insect, its armor dense but no match against the brutality the old *were* inflicts. He beats the Nyte against the trunk of a fallen oak, killing it in a show of strength and rage.

Celia kissed Emme on the cheek as she fell asleep in her arms. She was a good mama even then, long before she dreamed of having a child of her own.

"Fuck," I spit out, choking on billowing smoke as I step through. As much as I need to focus, I sob as I break into a run.

The Catholic schoolgirls speed ahead of me and toward the burning manor. Liz swings an ax, decapitating a rogue vampire before chopping off his legs. Agnes tackles another, her librarian glasses flying off her face as she punctures her nails through his chest.

Maria holds down a vampire with gargoyle wings as Edith beats him to death with her fists. Blood sprays across her face. She does not stop, beating the pile of ash the vampire becomes.

"Celia," she screams with her strikes. "You took our Celia."

I want to comfort her. But I don't have comfort to give. What courses through my veins isn't benevolence. Benevolence wouldn't surge my power to destroy like this.

We thought Johnny was in the house. As I stand in front of the collapsing structure, it becomes clear he was only part of it through the way he toyed with us and turned the magic against us.

My power turns me toward the right and in the direction of where he's hiding. My feet squish against the blood-soaked grass as I run across the west lawn.

A witch holds up her staff, leading a band of vampires. "For the Mate!" she screams. She fires a spell that turns a Nyte inside out. "For her child!"

I gulp down air, laboring to maintain my momentum and speed. These supernaturals never knew Celia. Not like us. But maybe they believed in what she had to offer and in the child who would save us all.

I let them fight for her and allow her death to fuel their savagery. I let them take every bit of her, they thought they knew, so they may triumph.

The Celia we knew, the fighter and the spirited woman, her love, graciousness, and unrelenting loyalty belongs *to us*; her sisters, her family, her love.

My pace slows. The thirst to kill can only do so much. I'm only human, after all.

I laugh without humor at my ridiculousness. No human can do what I'll do to Johnny. It'll be slow. It'll hurt. He'll beg for mercy, and it won't matter.

As my steps dwindle to a stroll and my lungs rush to get their fill, I ponder how thin my lightning needs to be to skin Fate alive. Should I start at his feet and work my way up? No. It should be his face. His fans lived and died for those beautiful features.

Protocol demands Aric gets to make the kill as Celia's mate. Except if Celia is dead, Aric is too. That wolf won't walk this earth without her.

Next in the vengeance line comes her family. That's me. I knew her first and loved her the longest. This kill belongs to me.

I don't realize my senses are leading me to the stables until I reach the doors.

My chest heaves in and out as I stand in front of them, the pent-up fury roasting my insides and demanding to be let free.

I should blow the doors off this bitch and burn the whole thing down in one strike. Instead, I ingest the magic from the environment, *Johnny's magic*, and part the doors with an extra dose of newfound power.

The aroma of freshly stained wood wanders through the stable. Alternating shades of red and gold pavers line the ground and lead to open and meticulously kept stalls. Beautifully oiled saddles hang on hooks near the entrance beneath rows of black riding helmets. Above, a few sets of boots rest, their polished exterior reflecting the overhead lights. Thoroughbred stallions are meant to occupy this space. It doesn't appear they ever found their way here. Now, they never will.

It only takes a few steps to find the first painting. It comes into view as my magic breaks through the veil concealing the deceptively empty building. The image is of the fire monster that barreled its way through the chimney. It's neat and very detailed, the colors bleeding deep into the heavyweight paper where it was conceptualized.

Dark crimson dots stain the corner and creature's chest. Johnny must have spilled some of his lifeline when he sought to bring the Nyte to life.

The layers of the veil snap apart as I advance. There's the painting of the leech who killed Genevieve's cherished guards, lying close to the Tweedledum character and the Nyte with mouths that covered his skin.

Bridette lied. Fate and his newest monsters didn't storm Genevieve's stronghold in a magnificent show of force. Johnny simply snuck in, clutching his pre-created visions and supplies. It was easier to go unnoticed this way. As soon as he was settled, all he had to do was bleed and set his Nytes loose. That's why there were so many. He likely spent months visualizing and designing them.

Jesus. There are enough paintings to cover most of the path. Some, I remember our allies fighting. Others I don't remember at all. I wonder how many lives they cost, but I can't wonder for long.

I turn the corner, noting how the details of each painting become less complex and the vulnerabilities more apparent. For all the work Johnny put in ahead of time, it wasn't enough. We thinned the herds of his monsters, and he needed to make more quickly.

I shift slowly when I hear a sound at the opposite end. It's then the man I'm looking for finally materializes.

The veil Johnny used to conceal himself wears thins, dimming in and out until it collapses. I stretch my fingers, the energy lighting the tips causing my knuckles to crack and my hands to tremble.

Very little distance separates us. Just enough for Johnny to run, not that he'll make it far.

On either side of him wait two incensed and massive bulls, one a deep orange, the other fire engine red. Smoke drifts from their nostrils and flames burn in their eyes. I don't have to guess what they can do. It's clear enough he means for me to meet my match.

Johnny's bare feet twist along the pavers, rubbing his deep callouses against the stones. Light blue jeans, splattered in paint, cover the lower half of his body. They're not the expensive kind with holes strategically placed by a designer who believes he's the next big thing. Those wardrobe pieces and indication of wealth are a thing of the past. These jeans are like the ones Johnny had no choice to wear growing up, tattered and too big for his gangly frame.

He stands in front of a large canvas, his hands moving fast as he paints a winged stallion covered with armor. This must be his grand escape plan. Except, like I mentioned, he won't get far.

I was right about the muscles he flexed back in the realm. They were as phony as he is. Like a heroin addict, Johnny has survived by feeding on the only drug he craves, power. An empty wine jug lies on the floor beside him, the bits of clotting blood that remain barely skimming the base. Shifter blood, I presume. Too bad even that won't help him now.

I glide forward, not bothering to be quiet. Skin clings to Johnny's bones. That beautiful silky hair women beat each other to run their hands through lies in a greasy mess against his scalp. He no longer knows food or drink. He only knows his mission.

"Shit," he says. He bends when his palette runs out of gray paint, quickly mixing drops of white and black paint from the small bottles lining a table.

"It's hard to get the right color, you know?" He laughs. "Maybe you don't know. I think you once told me even stick figures don't come natural to you," he tells me.

The orange bull scratches at the floor, singeing lines into the pavers. I stroke a strand of hair that falls against my cheek. "You have a good memory," I reply. "Remember that time I called you an asshole?" He stiffens. "That was a hell of an understatement, don't you think?"

He sticks his brush in his mouth and pulls up his jeans when they sag past his hips.

"I didn't want to kill Celia," he says. He lifts the brush and dilutes the blue color with some water from a Styrofoam cup. "Just like you don't want to kill me."

"No . . ." I disagree. "I do very much want to kill you."

I motion around, sort of surprised at myself for not immediately acting on my rather truthful declaration. "Look at all this, Johnny. Look how you took a beautiful gift and fucked it up. Is your life worth all the lives you've cost?"

He glances over his shoulder and narrows his gaze. The hair on top of his head is almost black now, what remains of the blond hangs past his ears. The back has done a shit job growing out. It hangs in tiers, as if belonging on someone else.

"My life is all I have," he says. "*It's all I ever had.*"

"Cry me a river," I tell him.

Hurt and insult war in his features, matching the chaos outside. Johnny stayed in the confines of this place, listening to ever cry, whimper, and tormented scream. He heard death, and he fed it into his art. Still, he makes this moment all about him. There are narcissists, and then there's Johnny Fate.

He jerks to the side when something strikes the stable to his left. The tension tightening his frail shoulders lessens only when his bulls don't react to the threat.

Johnny wipes his right eye with the back of his hand and resumes our conversation, annoyed by the interruption of another insignificant death. "I got sloppy with my work," he says. He sniffs. "You saw the ones on your way in, right? They were nice."

"You mean the ones who tore so many apart?" I shake my head. "I wouldn't call them nice. More like abominations, just like their maker."

The red bull spits on the floor like a llama, the lava it spews burning a hole through several pavers.

"Shut up," I tell it. I don't demonstrate fear. There's none left to show.

It takes a second or two for Johnny to breathe again. "You're not going to kill me."

"Yeah, I am," I correct. "And your latest creations won't stop me. It's over, Johnny."

His eyes widen when his bulls rock back on their hind legs and prepare to attack. It's not because of anything I say and do. They recognize me as a threat.

Snarls erupt as Gemini's twin takes point to my right. His fur is soaking wet. He doesn't bother shaking it out, his gaze keen ahead.

Gemini flanks my opposite side. Water drips from his hair, down his face, streaking lines down his chest.

"Celia's alive," he says.

Johnny doesn't move. Except for the choked sob that slices my throat, neither do I. "How?"

"The lake is protecting her. It ripped the Nyte apart and carried her to safety. Aric is with her. Nothing can harm her."

Gemini's neck cracks as he turns it from side to side. "You ready, love?"

I nod. Celia is alive.

That doesn't mean Johnny gets to live.

Chapter Thirty

Johnny doesn't hesitate. He sets his Nytes loose. He lost his chance at Celia, and now he must answer to us.

The bulls launch forward, each pound of their hooves against the pavers surging their turbulent fire. Gemini dives for me, yanking me out of the way. His twin leaps over the charging bulls, growling as he guns for Johnny.

The bulls are gargantuan in size and unspeakably fast. Both qualities work against them. Their size and weight drive them to the far end of the stables, their hooves raising sparks as they slap them against the stone flooring to attempt to slow down.

The orange bull bumps into the red when it tries to turn. The red retaliates, biting off his brethren's ear and spitting it on the ground. The orange roars at the red, spitting fire at him until they remember us. They scuff at the ground, snorting with rage and assembling to barrage us.

Everything happens at once. The leopard, the one that prowls on and protects Johnny's back, leaps from his skin and slams into Gemini's twin as he reaches Johnny. The beasts tumble away, their powerful jaws snapping and their claws raking the other's skin.

Johnny swipes the jug, grabs tight to the painting, and bolts toward the rear exit. At the sound of snapping bone, he tumbles to the ground, clasping the sweep of his neck and howling in pain from the injury the wolf inflicts to his leopard.

As one of the tats lining his skin, Johnny felt the initial impact. It's not enough to cripple him, but it does slow him down. He crawls ahead, dragging his jug and painting with him.

Panic spreads along Johnny's features when he realizes the bulls haven't killed us yet. I want to take Johnny out, now, but I can't spare the moment. I don't know what these bulls are capable of, and I don't want us to die trying to kill Johnny.

Gemini nudges me aside. "I'll lead the bulls out and away from you."

The bulls take off at high velocity, the temperature that rises from my core forcing Gemini to give me ample space. "You can't fight something with flames without me," I tell him. "And you can't herd them out alone."

As if sprayed by fuel, the blustering flames immersing the bulls shoot upward, hammering the vaulted ceiling and eating through the wood. I lash out, spinning my hands and projecting my swirling white fire into a sphere.

My quick reaction barely saves me. The orange bull tucks his head and rams me, knocking me to the ground, the tip of one fiery horn scraping my protective fire just below my chin.

The bull bellows, orange flames spilling from his mouth. The fire shield I manifest guards me against the bull's flame, but not the entirety of his crushing impact. I'm pinned by his massive size, his nasty breath spreading steam across my face.

Damn it. How many of these things can land on top of me in one night?

My amplifying heat burrows me into the ground, cracking the pavers and disintegrating them to form a nice cushy bed for me and the nine hundred pounds of bovine straddling me.

The bull hammers his head, smashing his horns repeatedly and trying to break through my shield. I push my hands up, screaming from the effort it takes to maintain my protection and manipulate my power to keep some distance between us.

White flames spread farther past my head and feet. The effort of my will augmenting my heat to disastrous levels. In one mighty jolt, I toss the bull up and through the roof. I roll away and into an empty stall, but it's not far enough. The bull crash lands back like a meteor, the collision taking out a wall and the stall I'm hiding in.

The stall and the pieces of wood I'm buried in are ablaze. I curse, groaning from the jolt. Sparky kept our fire going, the lively heat and flames dissolving the chunks of roof raining down. I force myself up on my hands and knees and drag myself from the deathtrap.

A sinister neigh has me moving faster. I poke my head out of the demolished stall. Johnny's armored Pegasus is awake, he lifts his head from the canvas, his demonic horse sounds becoming increasingly agitated.

Johnny sits on the floor, his legs parted, sorting through the shattered jug pieces. The roof is engulfed and the air thick with smoke and unfathomable heat. And there's Johnny, feverishly licking fragments of broken glass.

"Fuck." He whimpers when he cuts his tongue. He stretches, reaching for a larger piece. He's crying, and it's hard to understand him, but I get enough. "I'm coming, baby. It's okay. Daddy will be with you soon."

He stumbles to his feet and to the canvas, hovering over the painting as he opens his mouth wide. Blood from his tongue drips onto the Pegasus. The horse neighs, opening his mouth to take more of Johnny. Johnny smacks the horse in the head, adjusting his chin so no more than necessary falls to the creature.

My head spins from the rush of magic seeping into the air. The Pegasus's eyes turn a sadistic red, greedily gobbling the meal "Daddy" offers him.

The canvas shakes back and forth as the Pegasus rises, his size growing with each lurch to free himself. Johnny falls on his ass, ignoring the stall that catches fire beside him and sucking down on the broken glass stained with blood and dirt like a famished hound would scraps of food.

"More," Johnny rasps. He wipes the mucous dribbling from his mouth. "Please, just a little more."

The orange bull shakes his head, rising from the crater his body made. I grip a section of wall that remains to steady myself and contort my fire into a giant fist. With a triumphant scream, I punch the bull in the head.

I'm starting to learn triumphant screams never work in my favor. All it does is piss the bull off. He flings his front hooves over the side of the hole and starts to climb out.

"He doesn't like you," Johnny tells me. The Pegasus trots toward him, permitting Johnny to yank on his wings to help him rise. "I hope he kills you and that your stupid sister dies when she finds your remains."

I fire at the bull again, knocking him back in the hole. "Fuck you, Johnny."

Johnny ignores me and climbs onto the Pegasus, smacking at the creature when he tries to chew the glass. "*No, you dumb fuck. It's mine.* It's always mine."

My flame funnels out and toward Johnny. The bull bounds out of the hole and takes the hit. The strike sends him soaring into the rear exit, the force breaking the doors wide open.

Johnny kicks at the horse. The Pegasus flaps its powerful wings, increasing the flames. Hellish inferno or not, this Pegasus is ready to fly.

Screw this.

I force my feet to move and race after the horse when it bounds toward the exit. The orange bull rears back, forcing me to retreat.

Gemini's wolf leaps over me and the bull, swerving around a section of ceiling that falls. The wolf smashes into the Pegasus and tips the large Nyte over. Johnny is initially pinned but pushes his foot free of the Pegasus and scrambles to his feet, running away.

The twin gives chase, tackling Johnny.

Johnny screams when the twin clenches his jaw over Johnny's leg, keeping him put. The Pegasus flips to his feet, kicking the twin through a burning wall.

Gemini's twin angles back, latching onto the Pegasus's neck before Johnny can mount him.

Another section of roof falls. This time, it has nothing to do with the hellfire the stable has become. Gemini adjusts the support beam in his grip and smashes the engine red bull across the face when he charges. The strike crushes the creature's mouth, preventing the lava he spews from reaching Gemini.

Burns covers Gemini's shoulders and arms, and blisters the size of quarters run along his hands and wrists. Despite the obvious pain and lack of healing by his wolf, his strength remains. Using the beam again, he bashes the orange bull trailing me.

The jolt snaps the bull's neck, twisting his head so it faces up. Gemini may not possess the ability to conjure fire, but he has heart. Sometimes, that's all you need.

Gemini swings the beam, catching the other bull on the side. "Taran," he snarls. "Are you all right?"

"Always," I reply to my beloved. But not really.

The orange bull bowls me over, hitting the shield I manage to cast. He jumps up and down, using his brute strength to beat against my protective force. I grunt and curse. This shield is smaller and thinner. It limits the bull's imposing weight, but it's still imposing. Each bounce against my body is like a punch in the gut, and I am done taking beatings.

Gemini calls to me, but he can't reach me. Not when he's fighting the blazing red bull. He improvises, catapulting the raging Nyte straight into Johnny.

Johnny grunts. "Get off me. Get the fuck off me," he orders, his voice shrilled.

The bull digs his hooves into the damaged floor and rises, accelerating at full speed to resume his onslaught. Gemini kicks at a spigot with his heel and dodges out of the way. The water that streams free blinds the bull with steam, giving Gemini the opportunity to lay another impressive strike.

My man is kicking ass. Meanwhile, here I lay like a trampoline. Black smoke billows from the bull's nostrils, moistening his snout, as saliva pools around his mouth. The body fluids build, dropping to sizzle over my face.

This is straight-up bullshit right here. I don't remember Wonder Woman having to put up with snot or body fluids belonging to flaming farm animals.

The bull snorts, his frustration with not immediately impaling me and calling it a day elongating his flaming horns into that of a buck. He swerves them from side to side, using them like a pair of scythes.

Gemini brings down the beam harder upon his prey. He's inflicting damage but failing to squelch its fire even with the water from the pipe.

The bull shakes his twisted neck back into place and charges. The end of the beam smokes as Gemini repositions into a batter's stance. The bull is faster this time. Gemini barely has time to swing when the bull collides into him, sending them both through the last remaining stalls.

Shit.

My fire is effective, but so is the fire surrounding these Nytes. I need to think, and I would if this asshole would quit trying to suffocate me.

A long black stripe runs along his underbelly. I hadn't noticed it before. I do now. It draws my attention to the vulnerable spots his raging heat can only mildly protect. Unlike the Pegasus Johnny was hard at work at, this Nyte doesn't have armor to spare it.

I grit my teeth when the weight of the bull grows more severe. This thing is growing, taking up more space along my shield.

Power. Give me power.

Lightning crackles across my skin and beneath my flame. Sparky quivers. *That's right, baby. Let's show Johnny Boy what we're all about.*

"Power," I insist, building on the words as my skin bristles. "Give me power."

Snap.

Crackle.

Boom.

Rows of lightning bolts eject across my body, puncturing through the underbelly of the Nyte. His fire swells in his anger and pain, but it doesn't hold. He falls to his side, writhing as I scramble to my feet.

The deafening clatter behind me obliterates the chaos of splintering wood. I straighten, trying to breathe through the dense and sweltering air. Gemini is in the throes of battle, taking on the other Nyte as his twin dominates the Pegasus.

The winged Nyte may have been swathed in armor, but it wasn't strong enough given Johnny's weakening state. Gemini's twin bites through the thinner layers at the Pegasus's throat. I think our wolf has him until the Nyte kicks free and dashes from the building. The twin flips over, shaking off his injuries and jets after the Pegasus.

Flames eat through the stable, spreading like a hungry monster from one side to the other as the night air forces its way through the mutilated walls. The breeze should be cold, bordering on freezing, but as it pushes through the blistering temperature, it's more irritating than soothing.

My hands are out and on the offense. I hustle toward Johnny, stopping when the orange bull blocks my path. Gemini is at my back. His weapon is gone, and his skin is raw with burns. The bull he fought looks as good as new. My bull isn't far behind. He shakes off the lightning bolts like pine needles and snorts in challenge.

What remains of the building are mere moments from falling apart, and the Nytes aren't letting us go. I can survive the wash of fire. Gemini can't, not in his state. He won't run or try to escape without me, and I can't drop my fire without being burned.

Johnny glares at us from across the way. "I'll kill you," he says. He's shaking and crying, but it's the hatred lining his features that keeps him standing. "I may be dead, but so are you."

I adjust my weight, readying my lightning to jolt these bulls so we can run. But as pain shoots up through my leg and the feel of hot fluid spills from my heel, I realize where I am.

My magic never completely stays with me, it comes from the environment, from the air that passes along green fields and clears the dank city alleys, from the creatures who stalk in the night in search of their next meal, to infants sleeping against their mother who may never know freaks like me exist. Johnny forgot that little tidbit of knowledge. I'm about to remind him.

I slide my finger over my bleeding heel, careful to draw back enough fire to avoid vaporizing this valuable tool.

The circling bulls train their eyes on us. I keep them in my sights, too, even as I speak to Johnny. "What do you know?" I say. "We might not be so dead after all."

I motion to the floor gleaming with broken glass and where traces of Johnny and shifter blood await. Maybe I'm crazy to do this, or maybe I'm more of a genius than I thought. "This yours?" I ask.

Waiting patiently for an answer has never been my superpower. I bend and swirl my blood and Johnny's. His eyes fly open. I wink. "Yeah," I say. "That's what I thought."

I don't expect the contact of our blood to hurt. I should though. His Fate power and the evil streaming in shifter blood have no business touching me, especially when mixed to perform very heinous things. Like a thorn from a dried rose stem, their magic pokes me, severing my fingertip and forcing more of my blood to trickle from my skin.

The fresh magic I release swirls around Johnny's blood yet fails to fully join. My power and Sparky's repel it, wanting no part of something so vile.

"But we need it," I say, my soft voice drifting to just above a whisper. My eyes glaze over when the first droplet takes a lick of Johnny's blood. I blink several times, suppressing a moan.

"Taran, your eyes . . ." Gemini bites out.

My vision sharpens as it does when my irises bleach from blue to white.

"I know," I say. My voice echoes in the distance, no longer a part of me.

"You don't," Gemini says, his tone cutting through the halo forming around my sight. "Taran, they're glowing . . ."

"Are they?" I ask, not really caring.

"Stop it," Gemini mutters under his breath.

"I will. I just need a little bit," I add, my tone oddly erotic. I push past the sting the merging of powers causes. My magic and the ancient *were* magic taking residence within my right arm fight me, warning me we may be in over our heads.

"Since when has that stopped us?" I ask playfully.

"Taran," Gemini growls. "*What the hell are you doing?*"

My silky voice vanishes, turning dark. "Fighting fire with fire."

A wave of flames ripples from my feet and jets out, pushing away the bulls and making them think twice about charging. Johnny startles, jumping back when the crackling flames stop short of his feet, and my magic becomes the weapon I need.

The blue and white firestorm of flames spin and rise, taking shape and growing in rapid bursts of fire. The long, strong legs are visible first, followed by a massive and imposing back that sprouts an elegant tail.

The tail bats about when then neck punches through, and the head grows. My creation shakes its head so the long, pretty mane flutters. The horn, startling and scary, that pokes through her forehead is my favorite part.

That's right. When surrounded by bull, *be a fucking unicorn.*

Johnny's Nytes never really possessed minds of their own. All they knew was their mission: to kill and protect their creator. My baby is no exception. She gallops forward, drops her head, and impales the fiery red bull, lifting him high in the air and detonating him with fire of her own.

She kicks back when the other bull charges, striking the bull in the head and indenting his skull. I help her with a fireball. It blasts the bull's hindquarters and takes out his legs.

My unicorn rears, bringing down her front hooves and beating on the bull.

Be it the power it took to create her or the amount I've expended all through the night, my flames sizzle out in a rush, and I'm immediately struck by the intensity of the foreign fire. Gemini clutches me, lifting me and hurtling us through the crumbling stable.

We land on the cool grass, mere yards away. I can't stop coughing, clutching my chest, as if it will help ease my screaming lungs. Through the red and orange flames devouring the building, I see her. All blue and white and beautiful flames, my unicorn fights, beating the bull remaining to death. She whinnies, her legs continuing to fight long after the Nyte stops moving.

Gemini is in bad shape, curling inward and pressing his hand against his chest. I want to hold him and tell him we won, and that it's over, that he'll heal. Yet, as I watch the gangly shadow of a man I've grown to hate stumble toward the woods, I know I'm wrong, and there's one more kill to make.

My steps falter, and I trip over my feet more than once. I'm not in better shape than Johnny, only good enough to mildly keep up. It takes longer to close the distance between us than it feels it should. I think he's dying. It seems that way when the first traces of light peek through the treetops.

Johnny clears the wooded path and heads up the incline. I press my hands against my knees to keep up and not fall over. He's almost to the top of the small hill when he stops and bounds back.

I'm not certain why until Bren's and Koda's massive wolf heads poke out at the top, snarling as they stalk forward.

They're healing. They're better. But they're still not as whole as they should be.

Johnny stumbles down the hill and heads right, shaking when Misha, Uri, and their families meet him head-on. A skeletal figure with fangs strolls with them. Her muscles, skin, and hair have not fully materialized, but I recognize Ileana right away. No one in her condition should stroll anywhere.

Johnny doesn't give up or beg for mercy. He holds onto his side as he tries to return to the woods. His features reveal his surprise as he sees me, still alive. The dead expression he pegs me with matches those who watched their friends and family die. I don't feel sorry for him, only those he's made suffer. I suppose he knows that.

He swallows hard when I stop in front of him. Gemini walks to my side. His twin takes point next to Genevieve and the remaining head witches accompanying Destiny and Tye.

All these powerful beings, and I'm the one Johnny fixates on. "You would have done the same, Taran," he says. "You—"

I don't bother with what he has to say. He's said and done enough. I release my lightning in one precise swoop. Johnny's body collapses, his head rolling to a stop in front of Ileana. She lifts the head, biting down on the inside of Johnny's neck like a slice of watermelon.

Johnny Fate dies quietly, like the sickly addict he turned into instead of the revered powerhouse he once was.

There's no eruption of magic or deafening blast of sound. The world doesn't split in two. The apocalypse never arrives. And Ileana doesn't become anything scarier than she already is.

What does happen is that the night ends, and the sun rises.

Fate is dead, and Destiny takes his place. She hovers over Johnny, her arms and that of her octopus gown gathering around him and engulfing him. The dress limbs bubble and slurp as Destiny consumes Fate. I suppose she needs to. Still, it's hard to stomach.

I turn away, relieved as the wounds and injuries inflicting Gemini and the others vanish at a faster rate. Whatever spell suppressed their healing abilities and infected the witches' powers died with Johnny.

It's time to celebrate, but it's hard to celebrate living when far too many have died.

Gemini opens his arms. I'm ready to fall into his embrace and beg him to take me home when he turns me carefully.

My body trembles at Celia's approach. Her hair remains damp, and her small body is wrapped in a blanket Aric holds carefully around her. Shayna and Emme shadow her, their faces blotchy from the tears that continue to fall.

Celia wipes her eyes with the edge of the blanket when she sees me. "Hey," she says.

"Hey," I stammer.

I want to throw my arms around her and cry with her. I want to tell her she's my best friend, that I love her, and that she can never die without me.

Instead, I stagger forward and fall at her feet on one knee. She reaches for me, trying to help me stand, as does Aric, who clasps my elbow to steady me.

I stay in place, taking a long shaky breath. Gemini takes a knee beside me. He bows his head as his palm finds the small of my back. My mate knows me well and understands what I'm about to do.

"I, Taran Wird, mate and wife to Tomo Gemini Hamamatsu, swear my loyalty to you. No one will hurt you or your child in my presence. No one will tempt my loyalty. Nothing shall ever steer me away."

My promise doesn't come out as strong as I want, my voice quakes and tears riddle each word. It doesn't matter. The vow I make is real and there.

Gemini joins me in his promise to keep Celia and her baby safe. Misha kneels on my opposite side, Uri to his right, Ileana just behind them. Genevieve and the witches follow, Destiny and Tye, too. The *weres* gather, as does everyone who survives, taking up every inch of space on that hilltop.

One by one, each being pledges their loyalty to Celia and her baby as the sun breaks through the horizon, and a new day begins.

Epilogue

I didn't feel well for a long time. It was more than the way I killed Johnny. Although I'll admit, his end cost me. As angry as I remain at him for all the atrocities he committed and every life he took, I can't help but remember that he, like everyone else, just wanted to live.

Johnny was always a scared little boy who wanted love. I insulted and accused him of being weak. I meant what I said and believe it was right to take his life. He wouldn't have stopped until Celia and Aric's baby were dead. And if he'd achieved his task and become a shapeshifter, Destiny would be gone, and Johnny would be unstoppable.

I think my struggle is with the word weak. It's what he was. Except, all my life, I protected those who were *weak*. It became our unspoken motto, mine and my sisters.

Until it wasn't.

Until I killed Johnny.

He was a Fate. I get it. An entity more powerful than me. But deep down inside, he remained fragile and scared. It was *that* part of him I was supposed to help, and I guess, was supposed to save. I think that's what screwed with me, why I've felt so sick and why I haven't eaten much.

But as I stare at the tiny stick on the bathroom vanity, the one with two lines, I realize I'm sick for a different reason and am reminded that life goes on.

I sniff, smiling through tears. Yes, Johnny was weak, so weak-minded he always hurt more than he helped, killing and destroying families and taking down anyone who stood in his way.

I'm one of the lucky ones who made it home and who . . . I lift the stick . . . gets to start and have a family of her own.

The smell of bacon and eggs waft into my nose as I step into the hall. My stomach gives a little lurch, for all the right reasons that have nothing to do with guilt.

Gemini's voice, as well as Aric's and Koda's, drift from the kitchen. I don't have to guess they're at the table, making plans to keep the world safe.

Celia looks up from where she's perched on Aric's lap and smiles softly. "Good morning, Taran."

I offer her a rather awkward wave. She tilts her head when she sees my face. I look away.

Destiny watches Shayna and Emme closely. They're teaching her how to make pancakes. Step number one should have been to remove the rainbow-feathered crown covering her tight bun. Yellow, blue, green, and hot pink plumage flutter down and into the batter. "Like this?" she asks.

Shayna takes one look at the first rainbow-colored pancake and throws her head back, laughing. "Yes, queen," she says. "You're getting it."

"It was an excellent first try," Emme tells her. She pats her back encouragingly, careful to avert her gaze from Bren, who can no longer keep his eyes off her. Tye doesn't seem to notice, tearing into the biscuits and honey like it's his job.

Gemini leaves the table and kisses my cheek. "Feeling better?"

I nod. "Hmm."

Should I take him aside? Do I make a formal announcement? How exactly do weird girls like me do this thing?

He frowns, knowing there's something I need to say. I point to the map spread out along the table. "What's up?"

Gemini wraps his arm around me. I fall into his embrace. This is love, peeps. This is real. And damn it all, it's fucking amazing.

He leads me closer to the table as Aric points to sections of the map where marks are made in red. "Nytes, or something like them, were spotted here, here, and here."

There's a cluster of red dots near New Mexico. It makes sense. It's not that far away. There are some in Colorado, the home state of the wolves.

What's strange is there's a single red dot in Pennsylvania, where a large Amish population resides. I know, because it's near where our father grew up.

"Koda, I'm entrusting you and Shayna to strategize with the Dens throughout Montana and Colorado.

Koda lifts a piece of bacon from the plate Shayna offers. "On it," he replies.

"Gemini and Taran, I want you to take the New Mexico territory. My gut tells me this is where we'll find the answers to what's happening."

Gemini squeezes my hip and nods. "We'll be there."

"Actually," I say, stumbling over the word. "We won't."

Gemini stiffens. "Why won't we?" he asks slowly.

Deafening quiet overtakes the room. The coffee Emme made finishes brewing, and the oven timer goes off. Still, no one moves, and I can't speak.

"Are you pregnant?" Gemini asks. My silence is answer enough. A smile, so full of devotion, spreads along my husband's wonderfully handsome features. His hand cups my belly. "Are you?"

"Yes."

The sting of happy and frightened tears casts along my eyes. I sort of laugh, sort of cry, and probably screw up a perfectly lovely moment.

Gemini lifts me, kissing me hard. "I love you," he murmurs against my cheek. "God, I love you so much."

My body gives into his, absorbing the strength I'll need for what's to come. I want babies, lots of them with this amazing man I was blessed to find.

Shayna's jaw is down to her toes, and Emme is covering her mouth as if her lips may fall off.

"You're up, girls," I tell them. My voice is a mix of all the emotions I carry. Instead of fighting beside my sisters, it's their time to shine alone.

Celia leaves Aric's lap, the shock on her face reflecting everyone in the room. She stops just in front of me, torn between hugging me and crying. "Taran, you're going to have a baby."

I start to cry with her. Destiny stops me in my tracks. "No . . . she's not," Destiny says.

Her brows draw tight as she walks to my side, her deep knowing gaze fixed on my stomach. More plumage drifts from the peak of her bun before she speaks again, ignoring the tension surging throughout the room.

Everyone expects doom and destruction. Chaos. Anarchy. Crazy shit. It's what we're used to.

Destiny doesn't disappoint. She glances up, beaming. "She's having two. Congratulations, Taran. You're expecting twins."

This book contains an excerpt from *Of Flame and Light,* Taran Wird's first full-length novel in The Weird Girls Urban Fantasy Romance series by Cecy Robson. The excerpt has been set for this edition only and may not reflect the final content of the published novel.

# of Flame and Light

A Weird Girls Novel

Cecy Robson

Chapter One

You know it's going to be a bad day when you wake up in the morning and the first word out of your mouth is "fuck."

My right arm—or should I say my *new* arm generated after my real one was chewed off by a psycho werewolf (no, this isn't a joke)—buzzes me awake. That's right, *buzzes*.

I do my best to hide my limb. Not just because it's as white as alabaster. Or because of the fluorescent blue veins that run its length. But because it's doing things I can't control, like, interfering with my magic, glowing like a light saber, and now, making noise.

I lift my head, half-asleep, wondering how a wasp nest found its way beneath my pillow, but too exhausted to run away screaming, *yet*. If you were familiar with my life and world, you'd understand pissed off wasps in my bed wouldn't be the craziest or scariest thing that's ever happened to me.

My eyes narrow at the quivering pillow as my haze clears. Maybe I'm tired, or maybe it's because I'm bitter as all hell, but I can't help thinking that the arm *and* the pillow are laughing at me. I pull my glowing and buzzing arm from beneath the fluffy white pillow and swear.

"Really? *Really*?" I ask it. "What's next, singing and origami?"

Apparently, my incandescent light saber arm isn't a fan of sarcasm and proceeds to flicker on and off like a twisted strobe light. I shake it hard and smack it against the mattress, for all the good it does. "Knock it off," I tell it.

It's not that I think it listens, or that I manage to control it. There's simply no controlling this thing, but somehow the glowing recedes and so does the noise, and my arm resumes its "normal" death-like tone.

It quiets, no longer casting light. I should be thankful, right? I should be happy, true?

Oh, I wish.

The color is startling and contrasts horrifically against my deep olive skin. But its eerie tone and its unpredictability aren't the only things that trouble me. There's something wrong with this limb. It doesn't belong on me. And in a way, it doesn't belong in this world.

Maybe, like me, it's something that wasn't supposed to be.

I sigh and clutch it against me. It feels like my old arm, the skin soft and smooth. It moves like my old arm. I'm not limited with either fine or gross motor skills. But it's not . . . *human.*

When I lost my real arm, the Squaw Valley Pack Omega, created this new one using ancient werewolf magic. If I were a *were*, I think things would have been fine, peachy-keen, and all that good stuff. But I'm not a *were*, or human, or witch, or vampire, or anything. Not even a little bit.

My sisters and I may look human, but nothing like us have ever existed on earth. And, because of it, Earth's ancient magic seems to really resent helping a weird girl like me.

I used to wield fire and lightning with ease and catch glimpses of the future. I used to be a badass. I'm no longer a badass, and the only things I catch now are odd glances cast my way.

"Are you the punishment for my sins?" I ask my arm.

I don't expect it to answer, but it does. Sputtering light and buzzing before abruptly ceasing its response and sinking into the mattress.

To anyone watching, this whole thing might be funny. To me . . . nothing's been funny in a long time.

For a moment, I simply stare at it. There's a part of me that wants to cry, wondering what it will start doing next. But I've already cried too long and hard for what it has cost me.

Or should I say, *who* it cost me.

I scan the room. Nothing of Gemini remains. Not his clothes, not our pictures together. I even deleted and blocked his number. For all my arm disgusts me, I never expected it to disgust him more. After all, this was the werewolf who claimed me as his mate. The same male who swore he'd love only me forever.

I suppose forever only counts so long as I didn't change, so long as I remained perfect in his eyes. But I never claimed to be perfect, even if many believed I'd looked the part.

My arm flickers and *zings*, the electrified charge is strong enough to startle me and slap any remnants of sleep away. Yeah. No way am I perfect. Not by a long shot, especially with this thing constantly mocking me and reminding me of everything wrong in my life.

A sharp rap to the door has me glancing toward my right. "Taran?" my perky sister Shayna calls. "I heard your alarm clock go off. Want some breakfast?"

I lift the bane of my existence and sigh. Alarm clock? I suppose that's one word for it.

"T?" Shayna presses. "I'm making waffles."

She semi-sings her last few words which is a very "Shayna" thing to do.

"I'll be right out," I answer.

"Cool!" she responds. "I have plenty."

It's not that I want to eat. It's that I know how worried my sisters are about me. So I sit with them when I can, and plaster on a smile when I need to, but even that's burdensome, which sucks. I don't want my time with my sisters to be a chore. I love them. But I've learned some things can't be helped.

My arm fires with its haunting glow. Case in point.

With a groan, I slip out of bed, pulling on a fresh pair of panties and a bra before heading to my bathroom to clean up. After a few swipes of mascara and some lipstick, I yank on a form-fitting red dress and shove my feet into a pair of platform pumps, doing my best to strut and not collapse back in bed. Yet even though I'm almost to the door, there's one more thing I need. Most women won't leave their homes without their cell phones. I can't leave my room without my elbow-length gloves. It helps me hide the ugly appendage and the light show that accompanies it.

But now that my arm's buzzing . . .

I pause with my hand on the doorknob. What am I going to do about this thing?

I take a breath and wrench open the door, tugging on my gloves as I walk down the hall and into our large kitchen. Shayna abandons the waffle iron when she sees me and skips forward, her ponytail bouncing behind her.

She throws her arms around me like it's been months, not hours, since she's seen me. "Hey, T!" she tells me brightly.

I pat her back, wishing I could hug her for real. But real hugs lead to my very real tears, and I can't keep doing this to my family. "Hey, princess. Wow, everything smells great."

It's the truth, yet my comment sounds phony and forced, even to me.

Her arms fall away slowly. Although she keeps her grin, I sense the worry behind it, as well as her fear. "You look hot," she tells me, punching my good arm affectionately.

No. I look acceptable. I used to spend over an hour styling my dark wavy hair and applying my makeup. Now, I do enough so I don't resign myself to sweats, watching made for TV movies, and stuffing my face with potato chips.

"Thanks," I manage with yet another forced grin. I make a show of taking in all the breakfast foods, including the freshly baked muffins. "Yum. Do you need help setting the table or anything?"

"No. It's all good."

She says nothing more which is unusual for Shayna. Either she's waiting for me to speak or she's debating what to say. I can't take another pity party so I lift a pan filled with eggs and plate stacked with waffles and bring them to the table. "Where's your puppy?" I ask. Or in other words, where's your gigantic scary werewolf husband, Koda?

"Oh, he already ate and left. He's doing more at the Den since Celia's been needing more ah, time with Aric."

Okay, now I really grin, and so does she. Time with Aric is a mild way to describe what Celia desires from her husband.

Our youngest sister Emme walks out of the laundry room blushing, which tells me she's heard us discussing Celia. Shayna's grin quickly turns into a laugh. Emme's shyness has that effect on her.

Emme clears her throat, but not her obvious discomfort. Where Shayna has dark straight hair, Emme has soft blonde waves and fair skin that reddens the longer we take her in.

"Emme," I offer. "What's the big deal? So what if Celia's banging Aric like the lead drummer at a Fourth of July parade. They're married. It happens."

Emme holds up her hand. "Taran, please let's keep their private life private."

I reach for a glass of freshly squeezed juice. "I would if they weren't so damn loud. I swear, I thought the walls were going to come down around midnight when they—"

"Taran . . ." Emme whimpers, shaking her hands like she can't stand to hear another word.

Emme's always been so sweet and angelic. Me? Not at all. "Hey, do you suppose Celia's more flexible now, given how Aric knocked her up? As in ankles behind the head kind of flexible—"

Emme lifts a muffin with her *force* and sends it soaring. I catch it just before it rams me in the mouth. "Eat," she insists. "Just eat."

In other words, for once in your life, shut your inappropriate trap.

Shayna takes a seat beside me, laughing her skinny ass off. Emme sits, too, in time for Celia to stagger down the back steps.

Good God. Celia's long curly hair is tousled from lack of sleep and the insane amount of sex she's had. And her eyes are glazed with a hunger that warns me not to get too close. "Is there bacon? Please tell me there's bacon," she growls as if crazed.

Her entire face beams when Emme levitates a plateful of bacon and lowers it in front of an empty seat. Like a woman possessed, Celia sits and rams about four pieces in her mouth at once. The rest of us watch her in stunned silence as she chomps them down and reaches for another few slices. She freezes when she realizes we're all gaping at her. "Sorry. Would you like some?"

Her tigress eyes replace her human ones, making it clear she's only trying to be polite. And that only an idiot would get between her and her breakfast.

"No, nope, uh-uh," the three of us answer at once.

This seems to settle her inner beast enough so Celia's human eyes once more blink back at us. I pour her a glass of juice, while Emme and Shayna carefully place plates stacked with food closer to her reach. What can I say, we don't want to be eaten.

"Are you all right?" Emme asks her quietly.

Celia slows her frantic munching. "I don't know," she admits, her husky voice trickling with concern. She lifts her T-shirt and shows us her tiny belly. "The baby's not growing."

We've noticed that, too. Her pregnancy had been unexpected, given she was incapable of bearing children. But within two weeks of finding out she and Aric had conceived, her baby bump had appeared and was visible through her wedding gown.

That was two months ago. And now, despite how this baby has been prophesized to rid the world of evil, we're all pretty much freaking out that he or she isn't growing.

"But your body's changing," I insist. I don't exactly ooze optimism. In fact, I'm a *the sky is falling and the earth is swallowing us whole* kind of gal. But Celia doesn't need to hear what's wrong. My girl needs hope and that's what I give her. I point to her chest. "If your hooters don't scream 'I'm knocked up', I don't know what does."

She glances at her girls and then back at me, the tension in her shoulders lifting slightly. "They are a lot bigger," she agrees quietly. She gathers her thoughts, appearing to want to say more despite her obvious hesitation. "And my body does feel like it's becoming something more. Maybe not outwardly, but I can feel the difference inside of me."

"What are you feeling, Ceel?" Shayna asks. "Is your magic changing?"

Celia nods. "The magic that helped me get pregnant seems to complement mine. But my hormones are out of control." Her cheeks flush and she lowers her voice. "Poor Aric. I can't stop having sex with him. It's like every time I see him, I pounce."

Aric bounds down the steps as if called, his eyes glassy from lack of sleep and his five o'clock shadow now a full-out beard thanks to his preference to satisfy Celia's needs rather than shave. His face lights up when he sees Celia, kind of like she did at the sight of bacon.

"Yeah, poor bastard," I mutter.

"Hey, beautiful," he says to Celia, bending to kiss her lips.

She smiles against his mouth. "Hey, wolf," she answers, stroking his beard lightly.

Emme inches away when Celia's stare suggests the need for something more than breakfast. Aric, being Aric, returns that look with equal force. I start to laugh, not because of Celia and Aric, but because of Emme's response. She's glancing around at the food like she knows it's going to end up splattered across Celia's and Aric's soon-to-be naked bodies.

My laugh lodges in my throat when my right arm jerks as if shocked. Shayna lowers her fork. "You okay, T?" she asks.

I shove my arm under the table. "Fine," I say. I reach for glass of juice with my opposite hand, trying to stay calm. Celia and Emme didn't notice my twitch, and I don't think Aric did either, but something about me lures his attention away from Celia.

He cocks his head, his nose flaring as if his alpha wolf has latched onto something. "Taran, what's wrong?" he asks.

Celia's and Emme's attention drifts my way. Shayna rises, fear crinkling her brow.

"I'm tired," I say dismissively, feeling my pulse start to race. I push my chair out. "I should head back to bed. I didn't sleep much—"

All at once, and without warning, pain burns its way across my affected limb, curling me forward in agony. My arm whips out, sending the table and all its contents soaring with freakish speed. Plates shatter on the floor as the table imbeds, with a loud bang, *into* the wall, directly above where Celia sat seconds before.

I lift my head as the burn recedes, searching for her, panicked I harmed her. Tears of relief and residual pain slide down my face when I see Aric lower her to floor and far away from me. She and our sisters stare back at me stunned. But Aric? Holy shit, he's *pissed*.

"Taran, what are you doing?" he growls.

I shake my head, knowing he's angry I almost hurt Celia. "I'm not doing anything . . ."

The burn returns and so does its torment. This time, I can't bite back my screams. I stumble forward. Aric races to me. I don't see him. I only feel his body and hear the crunch of bone when my arm flails and connects with his jaw.

He crashes against the granite counter with a grunt as my arm jerks wildly and the burn increases tenfold.

My vision fades in and out and my body thrashes, the erratic movements of my limb throwing me against the wall. I collapse, my arm still beating itself against the floor with enough force to splinter and punch through the wood. I'm not thinking. I can't. Everything hurts.

No. Everything *burns.*

"Cut it off!" I scream.

Shayna reaches for a knife, elongating it with her power and manipulating it into a deadly sword. She lifts the blade above my spastic arm, her expression torn. By now I'm sobbing, and all but clawing at my face.

"*Please,*" I beg her. "Cut it off!"

"I can't," Shayna chokes out. "I can't do this."

"Pin it," Celia yells. "Pin it to the floor!"

With a flick of her wrists Shayna changes the sword's position and brings the point down toward my raging hand. I barely feel the prick before the room erupts in a ghostly light and Shayna goes flying.

Emme screams as Shayna collides into the far wall. Aric and Celia are scrambling forward, but all thoughts are lost in my torture. I'm retching with how hard I'm crying and from the anguish crawling from my arm and into my chest.

Just as the burn reaches my heart and I begin to lose consciousness, a pale yellow light surrounds me. Slowly, very slowly, the heat charring my insides is replaced with a soothing chill I welcome like a draw of fresh air.

My body shudders as the coolness spreads like a cascade of water from a gentle spring. My pain eases and my cries dwindle. It takes a long time for the ache to lessen, and even longer for my vision to clear. But eventually it does.

Not that I like what I see.

Blood cakes the side of Shayna's face. She winces as the bone along her eye socket pops out and the cut above her eyebrow knits close. Bile churns my gut. If Koda hadn't passed her a portion of his werewolf essence, I would have killed her. There's no doubt. based on the amount of blood coating her skin, and what her body had to do to heal her indented skull.

I cover my mouth. "Oh, my God," I gasp.

"It's okay, T," she says, as if I can't see the pain tightening her small pixie face. "It's okay."

No. Not at all, sweetie.

Aric leans forward. Being a werewolf and of pure blood, his inner beast had healed him faster than Shayna. That didn't mean I hadn't made rubble out of his jaw or that I hadn't hurt him.

Or that I won't do it again.

I had no control over my arm. None. Nor do I believe I have it now.

Aric realizes as much. I don't miss how he keeps Celia behind him, appearing to shield her and their child from whatever I'll unleash next.

"What happened?" he asks, his voice riddled with anger, and maybe something more.

"I don't know," I respond, my voice trembling and my body strangely weak. "I felt pain and it-it went wild."

"Your arm?" It's a question, but he's not really asking.

I nod as Emme's healing light recedes and her hands withdraw from my shoulders. Her face is unusually pale. She swallows hard, struggling to speak. "It's her fire," she says, barely above a whisper. She looks at Aric. "It's eating her alive . . .

Cecy Robson is an international and multi-award winning author of over twenty character driven novels. As a registered nurse of eighteen years, Cecy spends her free time creating magical worlds, heart-stopping romance, and young adult adventure. After receiving two RITA® nominations, a National Reader's Choice Award nomination, and winning the Maggie Award of Excellence, you can still find Cecy laughing, crying, and cheering on her characters as she pens her next story.

Connect with Cecy online:

Website
cecyrobson.com

Twitter
twitter.com/cecyrobson

Facebook
facebook.com/Cecy.Robson.Author

Newsletter
cecyrobson.us9.list-manage.com/subscribe?
u=f331c629f3740e88ab4f6e82d&id=744544daec